DUDLEY PUE

The loan of this book may b
readers, by contacting the li

About the Authors

Sharon Kendrick started story-telling at the age of eleven and has never stopped. She likes to write fast-aced, feel-good romances with heroes who are so sexy they'll make your toes curl! She lives in the beautiful ity of Winchester – where she can see the cathedral from her window (when standing on tip-toe!). She has two children, Celia and Patrick and her passions include music, books, cooking and eating – and drifting into aydreams while working out new plots.

Jennie Lucas' parents owned a bookstore and she grew up surrounded by books, dreaming about faraway nds. At twenty-two she met her future husband and after their marriage, she graduated from university with a degree in English. She started writing books a year later. Jennie won the Romance Writers of America's Golden Heart contest in 2005 and hasn't looked back nce. Visit Jennie's website at: www.jennielucas.com

Maisey Yates is a *New York Times* bestselling author f over one hundred romance novels. Whether she's writing strong, hard-working cowboys, dissolute inces or multigenerational family stories, she loves etting lost in fictional worlds. An avid knitter with a angerous wool addiction and an aversion to housework, isey lives with her husband and three kids in rural regon. Check out her website, maiseyyates.com or nd her on Facebook.

Greek Playboys

December 2021
A Price to Pay

January 2022
A League of Their Own

February 2022
Hidden Heirs

March 2022
Unbending Demands

April 2022
The Ultimate Game

May 2022
A Deal in Passion

Greek Playboys:
A Price to Pay

SHARON KENDRICK

JENNIE LUCAS

MAISEY YATES

MILLS & BOON

First Published in Great Britain 2021
By Mills & Boon, an imprint of HarperCollins*Publishers,* Ltd
1 London Bridge Street, London, SE1 9GF

www.harpercollins.co.uk

HarperCollins*Publishers*
1st Floor, Watermarque Building,
Ringsend Road, Dublin 4, Ireland

GREEK PLAYBOYS: A PRICE TO PAY
© 2021 Harlequin Books S.A.

The Greek's Bought Bride © 2018 Sharon Kendrick
The Consequence of His Vengeance © 2017 Jennie Lucas
The Greek's Nine-Month Redemption © 2016 Maisey Yates

ISBN: 978-0-263-30302-5

THE GREEK'S BOUGHT BRIDE

SHARON KENDRICK

This book is dedicated to the greatly loved
Sara Craven (Annie Ashurst),
whose talent, humour and sharp wit
are much missed.

And if you want a masterclass in writing
romance, read Comparative Strangers
(and prepare to tingle...).

CHAPTER ONE

HE RECOGNISED HER straight away, though it took him a moment to remember why. Xan Constantinides gazed at the tiny redhead whose thick curls were tumbling over her shoulders and a flicker of something between desire and anger whispered across his skin. But he welcomed the distraction—however temporary—which allowed him to forget the promise he had made so long ago. Was it the wedding of one of his oldest friends which had pushed the unavoidable into prominence, or just the march of time itself? Because it was easy to believe that nothing would change. You acted as if the fast days weren't spinning into years. And then suddenly there it was—the future—and with it all those expectations...

A marriage he had agreed to.

A destiny he had always been determined to honour.

But there was no point in thinking about it now, not with a packed weekend lying ahead of him. Friendship and a valuable business partnership dictated he must attend the wedding of his friend the Sheikh, even though he usually avoided such events like the plague.

Xan returned his attention to the redhead. She was sitting on her own in the small terminal of the private airfield, waiting to board the luxury flight, the fiery disarray of her hair marking her out from the other women. Her clothes marked her out too and not simply because they were a far cry from the skimpy little cocktail dress she'd been wearing last time he'd seen her—an outfit which had sent his imagination soaring into overdrive, as it had obviously been intended to do.

Xan slanted her an assessing glance. Today there was no tight black satin Basque or skyscraper heels, nor fishnet stockings which had encased the most delicious pair of legs he had ever seen. No. She had taken the word *casual* and elevated it to a whole new level. Along with a pair of tennis shoes, she was wearing cut-off jeans which displayed her pale, freckled ankles and a plain green T-shirt which echoed the cat-like magnificence of her emerald eyes.

It was the eyes he remembered most. And the slender figure which had failed to fill out the curved dimensions of her skimpy uniform, unlike her over-endowed waitress colleagues who had been bursting out of theirs. And the way she had spilt the Old-Fashioned cocktail all over the table as she bent to serve him. The dripping concoction had caught his trouser leg—icy liquid spreading slowly over his thigh. He remembered flinching and the woman he'd been with snatching up her napkin to blot at it with attentive concern, even though he'd been in the middle of telling her that their relationship was over.

Xan's lips flattened. The redheaded waitress had straightened up and mouthed an apology but the defiant glint in her green eyes had suggested the sentiment wasn't genuine. For a moment he had found himself wondering if it had been a gesture of deliberate clumsiness on her part—but surely nobody would be that stupid?

Would they?

And now here she was in the most unexpected of places—waiting to board a luxury flight to the wedding of Sheikh Kulal Al Diya to the unknown Englishwoman, Hannah Wilson. Idly, Xan switched his cellphone to airplane mode as the redhead began to scrabble around inside an oversized bag which looked as if it had seen better days. Was she also a guest at the glittering royal marriage? His lips curved with something like contempt. Hardly. She was much more likely to have been hired to work at what was being described as the most glitzy wedding the desert region had seen for a decade. And in a country which demanded the most modest of dress codes, it was unlikely that she would be showing as much of her body as last time.

Pity.

Sliding the phone into his pocket, he allowed himself the faintest smile as she glanced up to notice him staring at her and a spark of something powerful passed between them. A full-blooded spark of sexual desire which fizzled almost tangibly in the air. Her magnificent eyes widened with disbelief. He saw the automatic thrust of her nipples against the thin T-shirt and his groin tightened in response.

Sometimes, Xan thought, with a frisson of anticipation, sometimes fate handed you something you hadn't even realised you wanted.

It was him.

It was definitely him.

What were the *chances*?

Somehow Tamsyn managed to stop her jaw from dropping—but only just. She'd been expecting the great and the good to be gathered together here at this small airport, ready to board the royal flight which would whisk them to Zahristan, but she hadn't really been paying attention to the other guests as they were all being guided into the small departure lounge. She'd only just got her head around the incredible fact that her sister Hannah was about to marry a desert king and would soon become a real-life queen. And even though Hannah was pregnant with the Sheikh's baby and such an unlikely union made sense on so many levels, Tamsyn hadn't quite managed to contain her disgust at the proposed nuptials. Because in her opinion, the man her sister was marrying was arrogant and domineering—and it seemed he chose his friends on the same basis.

She stole another sneaky look at the Greek billionaire who was lolling against a sofa on the other side of the small terminal, his exquisitely cut suit doing nothing to disguise the magnificence of his muscular body. Xan Constantinides. An unforgettable name for an unforgettable man. But would he remember her?

Tamsyn offered up a silent prayer. *Please don't let him remember her.*

After all, it was months and months ago and only the briefest of encounters. She bit the inside of her lip. Oh, *why* had she decided to send out a message of sisterly solitude to the woman the tycoon had been in the process of dumping in the swish bar where she'd been working? At least until her employment had come to a swift but wholly predictable termination...

She'd noticed Xan Constantinides from the moment

he'd walked into the twinkly cocktail bar. To be fair, everyone had noticed him—he was that kind of man. Charismatic and radiating power, he seemed oblivious to the stir of interest his appearance had created. Ellie, one of the other waitresses and Tamsyn's best friend, had confided that he was a mega-rich property tycoon who had recently been voted Greece's most eligible bachelor.

But Tamsyn hadn't really been listening to the breathless account of his bank balance or his record of bedding beautiful women before callously disposing of them. His physical presence made his wealth seem almost insignificant and she surprised herself by staring at him for longer than was strictly professional, because she wasn't usually the sort of cocktail waitress who ogled the better-looking male customers. And there had never been a customer quite as good looking as *this* one. She remembered blinking as she registered a physique which suggested he could easily go several rounds in the boxing ring and emerge looking as if he'd done nothing more strenuous than get out of bed. When you teamed a body like that with sinfully dark hair, dark-fringed eyes the colour of cobalt and a pair of lips which were both sensual and cruel—you ended up with a man who exuded a particular type of danger. And Tamsyn had always been very sensitive to danger. It was a quality which had hovered in the background during her troubled childhood like an invisible cosh—just waiting to bang you over the head if you weren't careful. Which was why she avoided it like the plague.

She remembered feeling slightly wobbly on her high-heeled shoes as she'd walked over to where the

Greek tycoon had been sitting with the most beautiful blonde Tamsyn had ever seen, when she heard the woman give an unmistakable sniff.

'*Please*, Xan,' she was saying softly, her voice trembling. 'Don't do this. You must know how much I love you.'

'But I don't *do* love. I told you that right from the start,' he'd drawled unequivocally. 'I explained what my terms were. I said I wouldn't change my mind and I haven't. Why do women refuse to accept what is staring them in the face?'

Tamsyn found the interchange infuriating. *Terms*? He was talking as if he was discussing some kind of business deal, rather than a relationship—as if his lovely companion was an object rather than a person. All she could think was that a woman didn't just come out and tell a man they loved them, not without a certain degree of encouragement. Her irritation had intensified while she'd waited for the barman to mix two Old-fashioned cocktails and when she'd returned she had noticed Xan Constantinides watching her. She wasn't sure which had annoyed her more—the fact that he was regarding her with the lazy assessment of someone who'd just been shown a shiny car and was deciding whether or not he'd like to give it a spin—or the fact that her body had responded to that arrogant scrutiny in ways which she didn't like.

She remembered the peculiar melting sensation low in her belly and the distracting tingle of her breasts pushing against the too-skimpy top of her uniform. She remembered being acutely aware of those cobalt eyes being trained on her, uncaring of the woman beside him who was trying very hard not to cry. And

Tamsyn had felt a kick of anger. Men. They were all the same. They took and they took and they never gave back—not unless they were forced into a corner. Even then they usually found some way of getting out of it. No wonder she deliberately kept them at arm's length. With an encouraging smile she'd handed the woman her drink, but as she lifted the Greek's cocktail from the tray, Tamsyn had met a gaze full of sensual mockery.

She told herself afterwards that she hadn't deliberately angled the glass so that it sloshed all over the table and started to seep onto one taut thigh, but she couldn't deny her satisfaction when he recoiled slightly, before the blonde leapt into action with her napkin.

She was sacked soon afterwards. The bar manager told her it was a culmination of things, and spilling a drink over one of their most valued customers had been the final straw. Apparently she wasn't suited to work which required a level of sustained calm, and she reacted in a way which was inappropriate. Secretly she'd wondered whether Xan Constantinides had got her fired. Whether he was yet another powerful man throwing his weight around and getting the world to jump when he ordered it to. Just like she wondered if he would remember her now.

Please don't let him remember her now.

'Would all passengers please begin boarding? The royal aircraft will be departing for Zahristan in approximately thirty minutes.'

Obeying the honeyed instruction sounding over the Tannoy, Tamsyn bent to pick up her rucksack as she rose to her feet. Didn't matter if he remembered her because he was nothing to her. She was on this trip for one reason and that was to support Hannah on her wedding day, no matter how big her misgivings about her choice of groom. Because, despite having tried to persuade her big sister not to go through with such a fundamentally unsuitable marriage—her words had fallen on deaf ears. Either Hannah hadn't wanted to listen, or she hadn't dared—probably because she was carrying the desert King's baby and there was all that stuff about him needing a legitimate heir. Tamsyn sighed as she rose to her feet. She had done everything she could to influence her sister but now she must accept the inevitable. She would pick up the pieces if necessary and be there for her—just as Hannah had always been there for her.

Hooking her bag over her shoulder, she trooped behind the other passengers—many of whom seemed to know each other—thinking this was like no journey she'd ever been on, with none of that pre-flight tension which usually made everyone so uptight. But then she'd always flown budget before—with that feeling of being herded onto the aircraft like wildebeest on the Serengeti, followed by a futile attempt to claim a few inches of space in the overhead locker. Not so on this flight. The glossy attendants looked like models and were unfailingly polite to all the passengers, as they gestured them forward.

And suddenly Tamsyn heard the sound of a deeply accented voice behind her. Rich and resonant, it sounded like grit being stirred into a bowlful of molasses. She felt her throat dry. She'd heard it once when it had cursed aloud in Greek before asking her what the hell she was playing at. It had made her spine tingle then and it was making it tingle now as the powerful Greek tycoon moved to stand beside her.

Tamsyn stared up into a pair of cold blue eyes and wished her heart would stop crashing against her rib-cage. Just like she wished her nipples would cease from hardening so conspicuously against her cheap T-shirt. But her senses were refusing to obey her as Xan Constantinides dominated her field of vision, his presence imprinting itself on her consciousness in a way she could have done without.

She noticed how softly his olive skin gleamed be-neath the pristine cuffs of his snowy shirt. And that he carried with him a faint scent of sandalwood, un-derpinned with the much more potent scent of raw masculinity. Somehow he seemed to suck in all the available oxygen around them, leaving her feeling dis-tinctly short of breath. He was the epitome of vibrancy and life, and yet there was a darkness about him too. Something unsettling and strangely *perceptive* in the depths of those amazing cobalt eyes. Suddenly Tam-syn felt vulnerable as she looked up at him and that scared her. Because she didn't do vulnerability. Just like she didn't react to men—especially men like this. It was her trademark. Her USP. Beneath her fiery ex-terior beat a heart of pure ice, and that was the way she intended to stay.

She told herself not to panic. People were slowly filing forward and in a few minutes she'd be safely on the plane and hopefully sitting as far away from him as possible. If it had been a commercial flight she would have been perfectly entitled to ignore him, but this was not a commercial flight. They were all guests at the same exclusive royal wedding and even

Tamsyn's shaky grasp on protocol warned her that she mustn't be rude.

But she could certainly be cool. She didn't have to gush or be super-friendly. She didn't owe him anything. She was no longer in the subservient role of waitress and could say exactly what she wanted.

'Well, well, well,' he murmured, his English faultless as he pulled his passport from the inside pocket of his suit jacket. 'Fancy seeing you here.'

Tamsyn fixed her face into a mildly questioning expression. 'I'm sorry? Have we met?'

Cobalt eyes narrowed. 'Well, unless you have a doppelganger,' he drawled. 'You're the waitress who hurled a drink into my lap last summer. Surely you can't have forgotten?'

For a moment Tamsyn was tempted to tell him that yes, she had forgotten. She thought about pretending she'd never seen him before, but suspected he would see through her. Because nobody would ever forget crossing paths with a man like Xan Constantinides, would they? Not unless they were devoid of all their senses. She gave him a steady look. 'No,' she said. 'I haven't forgotten.'

His eyes narrowed. 'I was thinking about it afterwards and wondering if you made a habit of throwing drinks all over your customers.'

She shook her head. 'Actually, no. It's never happened before.'

'Just with me?'

'Just with you,' she agreed.

There was a pause. 'So was it deliberate?'

She considered his silky question and answered it as honestly as she could. 'I don't think so.'

'You don't *think* so?' he exploded. 'What kind of an answer is that?'

She heard his incredulity and as Tamsyn met his piercing gaze she suddenly wanted him to know. Because maybe nobody had ever told him before. Maybe nobody had ever pointed out that the opposite sex were not something you could just dispose of, as if you were throwing an unwanted item of clothing into the recycling bin. 'I'm not going to deny that I felt sorry for the woman you were dumping.'

He frowned, as if he couldn't work out which particular woman she was talking about. As if he were running over a whole host of candidates who might have fitted the bill. And then his face cleared. 'Ah, *neh*,' he murmured in his native tongue, before the frown reappeared. 'What do you mean, you felt sorry for her?'

Tamsyn shrugged. 'She was clearly very upset. Anyone could see that. I thought you could have done it in a kinder way. Somewhere more private, perhaps.'

He gave a short and disbelievingly laugh. 'You're saying you made a negative judgement of me based on a few overheard words of conversation?'

'I know what I saw,' said Tamsyn doggedly. 'She seemed very upset.'

'She was.' His eyes narrowed. 'Our relationship was over but she refused to believe it, and this time she needed to believe it. We hadn't seen each other for weeks when she asked to meet me for a drink and I agreed. And I left her in no doubt that I couldn't give her what she wanted.'

Slowly Tamsyn digested all this, her curiosity aroused in spite of herself. 'What was it she wanted that you were unable to give her?'

He smiled at her then—a brief, glittering smile which momentarily made one of the female ground staff turn and look at him in dazed adoration.

'Why marriage, of course,' he said softly. 'I'm afraid it's an inevitable side-effect of dating women—they always seem to want to push things on to the next level.'

It was several seconds before Tamsyn could bring herself to answer. 'Wow,' she breathed. 'That is the most arrogant thing I've ever heard.'

'It may be arrogant, but it's true.'

'Has nobody ever dumped *you*?'

'Nobody,' he echoed sardonically. 'How about you?'

Tamsyn wondered why she was having a conversation like this while waiting in line to get on a plane but, having started it, it would be pathetic to call time on it just because he'd touched on a subject she found difficult. No, she had never been dumped, but then she'd only ever had one relationship which she'd ended as soon as she realised that her body was as frozen as her heart. But she wasn't going to tell Xan Constantinides that. She didn't have to tell him anything, she reminded herself, replacing his question with one of her own.

'Did you complain about me to the management?'

He dragged his gaze away from the pert stewardess, who was ticking off passenger names on her clipboard. 'No. Why?'

'I got the sack soon after.'

'And you think I orchestrated it?'

She shrugged. 'Why not? It happened to my sister. The man she's marrying actually got her fired from her job.'

'Well, for your information, no—I didn't. I have

enough staff of my own to look after without keeping tabs on those employed by other people, no matter how incompetent they are.' There was a pause. 'What happened to your sister?'

It occurred to Tamsyn he didn't have a clue who she was. That he had no idea it was the Sheikh himself who'd got her sister fired, or that after Saturday's glittering ceremony he would be her new brother-in-law. To Xan Constantinides, she was just a judgmental cocktail waitress who couldn't hold a job down and he probably thought it ran in the family. 'Oh, you wouldn't know her,' she said truthfully, because Hannah had confided that she hadn't yet met any of her Sheikh fiancé's friends and was absolutely *terrified*, because they were all so high-powered.

Their conversation was halted by a smiling stewardess with a clipboard and as she was given her seat number, Tamsyn turned back to Xan Constantinides with a forced smile.

'Nice talking to you,' she said sarcastically and saw his navy eyes darken. 'Enjoy the flight.'

Her heart was still pounding as she took her seat on the aircraft and picked up the book she'd so been so looking forward to—a crime thriller set in the Australian outback—which she'd hope would pass away the hours during the long journey to Zahristan's capital city of Ashkhazar. But it was difficult to concentrate on the rather lurid plot, when all she could think about was the powerful Greek who'd managed to have such a potent effect on her. She tried to sleep, and failed. She stared out of the window at the passing clouds which looked like thick fields of cotton wool. She attempted to tuck into the variety of delicious foodstuffs which were placed before her, but her appetite seemed to have deserted her. She was just thinking gloomily about the days of celebration ahead of her, when that gravelled molasses voice broke into her thoughts.

'I suppose you'll be working as soon as we get there?'

Tamsyn looked up to see that Xan Constantinides had stopped in the aisle right beside her seat and was deigning to speak to her. She looked up to meet that distracting cobalt stare. 'Working?' she echoed in confusion.

'I'm assuming that's why you're here,' he murmured.

Suddenly Tamsyn understood. He thought she was here to act as a waitress at the royal wedding!

Well, why wouldn't he think that? She certainly wasn't dressed like the other women on the flight, with their discreet flashes of gold jewellery which probably cost a fortune and their studiedly casual designer outfits. Her sister had tried to insist on buying her some new clothes before the wedding, but Tamsyn had stubbornly refused. Because hadn't Hannah helped her out too many times in the past—and hadn't she vowed she was going to go it alone from now on?

'Just because you're going to marry a rich man, doesn't mean *I* have to accept his charity,' she remembered responding proudly. 'Thanks all the same, but I'll wear what's already in my wardrobe.'

Was that why Xan Constantinides was so certain she was a member of staff rather than a wedding guest? Because she was wearing old sneakers rather than those fancy shoes with the red soles which everyone else seemed to be sporting? Suddenly, Tamsyn thought she could have a bit of fun with this and liven up a wedding she was dreading. Wouldn't it be priceless to have the Greek tycoon patronise her—before he discovered her connection to the royal house of Al Diya?

She met his scrutiny with a bashful shrug. 'Yes,' she said. 'An event like this pays very well and they wanted to have some British serving staff among the Zahirstanians. You know, to make sure the English-speaking guests felt at home.'

He nodded. 'Good of them to fly you out in style.'

Tamsyn bit back an indignant laugh. Any minute now and he would start asking her if she'd ever been on an airplane before! She reached out and gave the plush leather of the armrest a quick squeeze, as if it was the chubby cheek of a particularly attractive little baby. 'I know,' she sighed. 'Let's hope I don't get too used to all this luxury before I go back to my poverty-stricken existence.'

'Let's hope not.' His smile was brief and dismissive—the smiling equivalent of a yawn—as if he had already grown bored with her. His gaze drifted towards the curvy bottom of one of the stewardesses, as if already he was miles away. 'And now, if you don't mind—I have work to do.'

Tamsyn opened her mouth to say that *he* was the one who had started the conversation, but something made her shut it again, as he continued his journey up the aisle of the plane. And she wasn't the only person looking at him—every female on the plane seemed to be following his sexy progress towards the front of the aircraft. Resentfully, Tamsyn found herself noting the powerful set of his shoulders and the way thick, dark tendrils of hair curled around the back of his neck.

She thought she'd never seen a man who was quite so
sure of himself. He seemed to inject the air around him
with a strange and potent energy and she resented the
effect he seemed to have on her without even trying.

An unfamiliar shiver whispered its way down her
spine and she clenched her hands into tense little fists
as the plane soared through the sky on its way to the
desert kingdom.

CHAPTER TWO

TAMSYN STOOD IN the centre of the huge room, her head spinning as she gazed around her in amazement. She'd known that her sister's fiancé owned an actual palace which she was going to be staying for the forthcoming wedding celebrations, but the reality of being here was so far outside her experience that for a moment she felt as if she were dreaming.

Drinking in her surroundings, she craned her neck to look up at the high ceiling which was vaulted and gilded with gold. She didn't think she'd ever seen so much gold! Soft drapes fell from the floor-to-ceiling windows which overlooked surprisingly green and lush gardens—surprising, because this was, after all, a desert country. Her bed was huge and closer to the ground than she was used to and it was covered with rich brocade and velvet cushions. And everywhere she looked she could see flowers. Big, claret-coloured and sunset-hued roses crammed into what looked like solid gold vases. Their heavy scent vied with the incense which was burning softly in one corner, in a container which seemed to be studded with genuine rubies and emeralds. As for the bathroom, Tamsyn swallowed. The bathroom was something else—exceeding the standards of every upmarket hotel she'd ever worked in—and she'd worked in quite a few. She spent several minutes running her fingertips over the fluffy bath-robe and eying up the gleaming glass bottles of bath oil and perfume, wondering if she'd be able to take some of them home with her.

She had sent away the servant who had hovered around after her arrival, because just the thought of *having* a servant had made her feel uncomfortable, since that felt like *her* natural role. She'd thought she would be alone until she was summoned to the pre-wedding dinner, but a knock at the door interrupted her reverie and Tamsyn went to answer it, her eyes narrow-ing as she stared at the woman who was standing there. She was wearing beautiful silk robes of sapphire blue, which flowed to the ground like a waterfall. Her shiny hair was covered in some gauzy veil of silver and the sparkling earrings which dangled from her earlobes echoed the aquamarine brilliance of her eyes. Tamsyn stood in shocked silence, realising that for a few sec-onds she hadn't recognised *her own sister!*

'Hannah,' she breathed. 'Is that really you?'

Hannah came in and closed the door behind her, before enveloping Tamsyn in a crushing bear hug. 'Of course it's me—who did you think it was?'

Tamsyn gave a mystified shake of her head. 'I can't believe it. You look so different. Like…like a real-life queen.'

A wry smile touched her sister's lips. 'Well, that's kind of appropriate, seeing as of Saturday that's ex-actly what I'm going to be.'

Tamsyn stilled. Was she imagining the strained quality in Hannah's voice or the faint shadows around

her eyes? 'You don't have to go through with it, you
know,' she said instantly, but her sister shook her head.

'I'm afraid I do. I can't back out of it now and I don't
want to. I have to do this—for the sake of the baby.'

At the mention of the baby, Tamsyn's gaze swivelled
to her sister's belly. She supposed that most people
might not even have guessed Hannah was pregnant—
she looked more like someone who'd just come back
from holiday having been a bit too liberal with the
hotel buffet. But she knew Hannah better than anyone.
Hannah who had acted more like a mother than a big
sister when they were growing up. They had shared a
mother who had given them up when they'd been very
young—but they each had different fathers.

Just the thought of *fathers* made an acrid taste rise
up in Tamsyn's throat because her own had been a
waster in every which way. She tried her best not to
judge all men by his miserable standards, but sometimes it was difficult. But then, life was difficult,
wasn't it? Everyone knew that. These days she understood why Hannah had kept her in the dark about
her parentage for so long, though she had been bitter
and angry about it for a long time. But now was not
the time to rake up the perceived sins of the past. She
was here, not because she wanted to be—but because
she was determined to support her beloved sister—the
only family she had left in the world.

'So what's it like living with a sheikh? Is Kulal
treating you properly?' she demanded.

Hannah shot a nervous glance in the direction of
the door as if she was afraid someone might be standing outside, listening.

'He is.' The Princess-in-waiting forced a smile. 'How was your flight?'

Tamsyn hesitated, thinking it would probably be unwise to offload onto her pregnant sister on the eve of her wedding. No need to mention that she'd met Xan Constantinides once before and certainly no need to mention that she'd tipped a drink over him. 'Very comfortable,' she said. She saw Hannah frown—as if she hadn't been expecting such polite diplomacy so she injected her next remark with just the right amount of carelessness. 'I bumped into some Greek tycoon in the queue.'

'Xan Constantinides?'

'That's him.' Tamsyn paused and then, despite her best intentions, she couldn't resist her next comment. 'He's pretty full of himself, isn't he?'

Hannah shrugged. 'Why wouldn't he be? He made billions at an early age and is built like a Greek god. Apparently women fall at his feet like ninepins and I guess those kind of things can go to a man's head. And of course, he's never been married—which makes him a bit of a target for predatory women. Never even got close, so Kulal tells me.' She frowned. 'You didn't... you didn't fall for him did you, Tamsyn?'

'Oh, please!' Tamsyn manufactured a disbelieving snort. 'I don't go for men with egos the size of Mars.'

'And you didn't fall *out* with him, I hope?' continued Hannah nervously.

'Oh, come on, Han. As if I could be bothered!' Tamsyn gave an airy shrug. 'Why, I barely exchanged two words with the man.'

'Good. Because Kulal is very fond of him and they're in the middle of some hugely important business deal together.' Hannah smoothed down her silky robes, the movement drawing attention to her massive diamond engagement ring which glittered on her finger like a constellation of stars. 'But that's enough about Xan. I thought we could discuss your wardrobe.'

'My wardrobe?' Tamsyn's eyes narrowed with suspicion. 'What about it?'

There was a pause, during which Hannah seemed to be choosing her words with care. 'Tammy, what are you planning to wear to the rehearsal dinner tonight?'

Tamsyn had been waiting for this. Bad enough that Hannah seemed to have morphed into someone completely different—ever since the arrogant Sheikh had swept into her life and carried her off to his desert kingdom. Why, she barely recognised the elegant creature who stood before her as the same person who had once made beds for a living as a chambermaid at the Granchester Hotel. But that didn't mean *she* had to do the same, did it?

'I've got a very nice dress I bought down the market,' she said. 'I'm going to wear that. And how many times do I have to tell you not to call me Tammy?'

'Tamsyn, you *can't*. You can't wear some dress you've bought down the market to a royal wedding!'

'Why not?'

'Because…because….' Distractedly Hannah began to pace around the vast suite, her silken robes swishing against the floor as she moved. 'Well, the guest list is pretty daunting, if you want the truth. Even to me. Especially to me,' she added, on a whisper.

'I'm not daunted by other people's wealth,' said Tamsyn proudly.

'I know you're not—and there's no reason you should be. It's just...'

'Just what? Come on, Hannah—spit it out.'

Hannah drew to a halt beside Tamsyn's open suitcase, shooting a quick glance inside before sucking in a big breath which failed to hide her instinctive grimace. 'You can't wear any old thing,' she said gently, as she turned to look at her sister. 'Not to a function as important as this. It's my wedding and you're my sister. I'm the bride and the groom just happens to be a desert king. People are going to be looking at you, you know—especially as you're the only family I've got.'

Tamsyn's first instinct was to say she didn't care what other people thought. And if she fancied wearing her canvas sneakers beneath the dress she'd picked up for a bargain price—then that's exactly what she would do. But something about Hannah's anxious face tugged at a conscience she would prefer not to have. Suddenly she recognised that any defiance in the clothes department might reflect badly, not necessarily on her—but on her sister. And hadn't Hannah always done so much for her? Cared for and protected her during those deprived days of their fractured childhood...didn't she owe her for that?

'I don't have any fancy clothes,' she mumbled, feeling once again like the little girl who'd been mocked in the school playground because there was nothing in her lunchbox but a few scraps of bread and jam. *You're poor*, the other children used to taunt—and Tamsyn had been too ashamed to admit that her foster father had spent all his money on gambling and womanising and her foster mother had been too weak to object. Her education had suffered as a consequence and she'd left school without qualifications, which didn't exactly make her a big player in the job stakes. Money remained tight for Tamsyn and what little money she *did* have she certainly wasn't going to waste on an expensive dress she'd only get to wear once. 'I'm not stupid, Hannah,' she said huffily. 'I'm not planning to let you down. I'll make the best of what I have, just like I've always done.'

'I know you will. And when you bother to pull out all the stops you can look amazing. But this is different. I don't want you and I to stick out any more than we already are. So let me give you something to wear, Tamsyn. Something beautiful—the like of which you will never have worn before.' There was a pause. 'Please.'

Tamsyn had vowed she wasn't going to accept any more of Hannah's charity, no matter how scared she was about the future. Her latest job in a café paid only peanuts and in the meantime her overdraft was getting steadily bigger. The latest blow had been the recent rent raise on her crummy little apartment, leaving her wondering how on earth she was going to pay it.

She thought about the glamourous women she had travelled over with on the Sheikh's private plane and wondered what glorious surprises they would be pulling out of their suitcases for the glittering dinner tonight. And then she thought about a pair of cobalt eyes and the way they had trained themselves on her. She'd seen the way the Greek's gaze had focussed in on her scruffy tennis shoes and the disdainful curve of his lips in response. Was it that which made her suddenly decide to take up her sister's offer? To dress up for the party so that she might fit in, for once in her life?

'Okay. You can find me something to wear, if you like,' she said, casting a doubtful glance at Hannah's covered head. 'But I'm definitely not wearing a veil.'

Peering into the silvered surface of the antique mirror, Xan gave his tie a final unwanted tug. Raking his fingers back through the raven disarray of his hair he did his best to stifle a yawn as he deliberated on how he was going to get through the long evening ahead.

He *hated* these affairs with a passion and part of him felt deeply sorry for his royal friend, for being forced to marry some gold-digging little chambermaid from England. Contemptuously, his lips curved into their habitual line of disapproval. How could Kulal—a desert king renowned for an extensive list of sophisticated lovers—have fallen for the oldest trick in the book? There had been no official announcement but you wouldn't need to be a mathematician to work out that a hasty wedding arranged between one of the region's most exalted sheikhs and an unknown commoner—was bound to end up with a baby a few months down the line. Had the chambermaid deliberately trapped him, he mused? And if so, how could his friend bear the thought of that deception for all those long years which lay ahead?

He thought of his own marital destiny and not for the first time, began to see that it could have much to commend it, because Sofia was sweet and undemanding. He couldn't imagine her ever trying to trap him by falling pregnant—probably because he doubted she would ever consent to sex before marriage. His mouth hardened for it was many months since he had seen his unofficial fiancée and he knew he couldn't keep putting it off their arranged marriage indefinitely. Up until now it had been a private and completely confidential agreement between two families, but the longer he stalled, the more likely that the press would get hold of it and have a field day with it. His jaw clenched. He would set in motion the formal courtship when he flew out of here after the weekend, with a wedding pencilled in for the middle of next year.

But for now he was still technically a free man and unwillingly his thoughts turned to lust, for it had been a while since he had enjoyed a woman in his bed.

He was discreet about his relationships—for obvious reasons—and nobody outside their immediate families knew he had been promised to a beautiful young Greek girl. His recent sexual abstinence had certainly not been caused by a lack of opportunity— but because he had become jaded and bored by the attentions of predatory women on the make.

He scowled at his reflection before turning away. The press didn't help his endeavours to maintain a low profile and he cursed the obsession which made certain newspapers speculate about when he intended to tie the knot. Wasn't it such careless speculation which caused women to pursue him, as if they were hunting down some particularly elusive quarry? Didn't they realise that the chase was the thing which fired up a man's blood? Xan's mouth flattened. At least, that was what he had been told—for he had never had to pursue a woman. They came after him in their droves, like dedicated ants flocking to a spoonful of spilled honey. Some he enjoyed and others he discarded—but he made it plain to each and every one that there was no point in wishing for any kind of future with him, though he never explained why. And wasn't the truth that he enjoyed the protective barriers which his long-term engagement placed around him? It kept women at a safe distance and that was the way he liked it.

A servant came to fetch him to take him to the pre-wedding dinner and Xan quickly became aware of the excitement in the air as the wedding grew closer. Tall, burning flames lit the courtyard and in the distance he could hear the low beat of unfamiliar music which only added to the febrile build of atmosphere. Through wide corridors scented with jasmine and gardenia and lit with gold and silver candles, he followed the silent servant—taking his place at last in some inordinately grand ballroom, which he hadn't seen on his last visit.

He had visited Zahristan once before, when Kulal had taken him out to the desert to see the state-of-the-art solar panels which the country's scientists had designed, and in whose manufacture Xan had invested a great deal of money. He had combined the work trip with some serious riding on the most magnificent stallion he'd ever mounted and then he and the Sheikh had camped beneath the blinding brilliance of the stars in an opulent Bedouin tent. Xan remembered thinking that his powerful royal friend had the world at his fingertips—yet now he was being forced into a corner, trapped into a relationship he did not really want.

And wasn't exactly the same thing happening to *him*? Briefly Xan thought about the Greek girl with dark eyes who was everything a man could possibly desire. No. He was walking into his future with his eyes open. Not for him the lottery of chance or ignorance. There would be no skeletons emerging from the closet of Sofia, for she was someone he had known all her life. She was pure and beautiful and... His mouth hardened as he allowed the unwanted thought to flit into his mind.

The chemistry would come later.

Most of the other guests were already assembled in the huge gilded ballroom, which led into a banqueting hall almost as vast. Beneath chandeliers which glittered like shoals of priceless diamonds, women paraded in their finery, the men beside them wearing dark suits, desert robes or uniform. For some reason Xan found himself looking round for the redheaded waitress but couldn't see her anywhere and he wondered if she was somewhere deep in the palace kitchens, loading up her tray. Instead, he accepted a drink from someone else—a sharp-sweet cocktail containing fire-berry juice and drank it silently as they awaited the arrival of the royal couple.

At last, a single musician stepped forward to play a fanfare on the traditional *mizmar*, heralding the arrival of the Sheikh and his bride-to-be and there was a murmur of expectation as the couple paused in the open doorway of the ballroom and all heads turned in their direction.

And then he saw her.

Xan's fingers tightened around his drink so tightly that for a moment he was afraid that the delicate glass might shatter. He expelled a long, low breath as his disbelieving gaze settled on the feisty redhead who was following behind the royal couple as if it was her every right to do so.

His eyes narrowed. No sawn-off jeans and canvas shoes tonight. She was wearing an exquisite dress of emerald silk which matched the brilliance of her eyes and looked as if had been made just for her. The design was simple and in many ways modest, but it accentuated her body in a way which her sexy cocktail waitress uniform had failed to do. In that rather *obvious* black satin ensemble she had looked more like a little girl playing dress-up, while tonight she looked like a woman. Xan swallowed. A very sensual woman. Her lustrous red curls had been caught back, displaying dazzling diamond and emerald earrings which brushed the sides of her long neck. He felt the pooling of blood at his groin and suddenly she turned her head to look directly at him—as if some sixth sense had told her he was staring. A faint flicker of triumph illuminated her extraordinary eyes before, very deliberately, she turned her back on him and began chatting to a tall man in some sort of military uniform who seemed to be devouring her with his hungry gaze.

Xan felt the hard beat of a pulse at his temple. He had imagined her gliding around between the guests with a tray of drinks in her hand and this sudden unexpected elevation of status left him feeling confused. If she wasn't a waitress, then who the hell *was* she? He found himself dipping his head to speak to the blonde woman beside him who had been slowly edging herself closer in a way which was boringly predictable.

'Who is that woman in green?' he questioned silkily. 'The one who entered with the Sheikh and his fiancée.'

The blonde gave a discernible pout of disappointment followed by a slight shrug. 'Her? Her name is Tamsyn,' she said reluctantly. 'Tamsyn Wilson. She's the sister of the bride.'

Xan nodded as suddenly it all made sense. The reason why she had been dressed down and out of place on the flight over. The reason why a cocktail waitress was hobnobbing with one of the most powerful royal families in the world. Wilson. Of course. The bride's sister. The bride who had trapped his friend into marriage by getting pregnant. Xan gave a short laugh. How the redhead must have been laughing to herself when he'd made the—very understandable—assumption that she was here on a working trip. Was she enjoying the fact that he'd made such a fundamental mistake? He watched as she walked straight past him, ignoring him completely, her glorious fiery head held high in the air. And he felt the corresponding roar of his blood in response.

It was a long time since Xan could remember the minutes passing so slowly and never had he been so comprehensively ignored by the person he most wanted to speak to. He'd never had to work to get a woman to join him—usually the briefest of glances would send them scuttling over with an eagerness which was sometimes enough to kill his desire stone-dead. But Tamsyn Wilson wasn't playing ball. He watched her dip her glorious red head to the side as the Sheikh introduced her to a group of people and he saw the automatic light of interest in the men's eyes. He thought about infiltrating the group and commandeering her for himself, but instinct told him such a plan would be foolish. Only a quick glance at the seating plan yielded up the satisfying information that once again, they were seated next to each other. Xan's lips curved into a smile of anticipation. Far better to have her captive at his side and then...

Then what?

He hadn't yet gone that far in his imagination, but the increased pound of blood at his groin gave him a very good idea of how he intended the evening to end. And why not? His formal courtship of Sofia had not yet started. Was it not better to indulge his desires and rid himself of them? To eradicate all restlessness before finally settling down?

The distinctive sound of the trumpet-like *mizmar* broke into the chatter as servants began guiding the guests towards the galleried dining room, where the gleam of the dazzling long table and the perfume of countless roses awaited them. Xan stood beside the vacant chair next to his, watching the redhead approach without any kind of smile on her face, the defiant spark of her eyes the only acknowledgement she had seen him.

In stony silence she came to stand beside him.

'So,' he said softly as the faint drift of her scent washed over his skin and it became clear she wasn't planning to greet him with any kind of rapturous joy. 'We meet again.'

Her expression was cool. 'It would seem so.'

'Would you care to sit down?'

She gave a sarcastic elevation of her eyebrows. 'Since the alternative is eating on the hoof, I suppose the answer must be yes.'

Her insolence was turning him on almost as much as the slender curve of her breasts beneath her exquisite green silk dress. Xan pulled out her chair, her mulish look indicating that such display of chivalry was unnecessary but as she lowered her bottom onto the carved golden seat his blood pressure rocketed once more. As he guided the chair back in, his fingers briefly brushed against her narrow shoulders and he had to resist the urge to let them rest there and to massage away the undeniable tension he could feel.

'You didn't tell me you were the bride's sister,' he said, as he sat down beside her.

'You didn't ask.' She turned to him, her eyes full of an emerald light which tonight seemed almost unworldly. 'You just *assumed* I was here to work, didn't you? To ferry drinks around and wait at table. That someone like me couldn't possibly be one of the guests.'

'Was that such a crazy assumption to make, given the circumstances?' he mused. 'Last time I saw you that's exactly what you were doing. You made no mention of your connection with the bride and you have to admit, you didn't exactly blend in with the other guests on the plane. At least,' he amended softly. 'Not until now.'

'Now that my sister has given me the dress she secretly had made for me?' she demanded hotly. 'Or forced me to wear a necklace I'm terrified is going to fall off and deplete the royal coffers by several million quid, is that what you mean?'

Xan found himself having to bite back a smile. 'You cannot deny that you look very different tonight.'

Tamsyn picked up a jewel-encrusted goblet and sipped at the cold fizzy water it contained. No, she wasn't going to deny she looked different but beneath her fine new trappings—she felt exactly the same. Like someone who never fitted in—not anywhere. And tonight the sensation of being out of place was even more acute than usual. It wasn't just that everyone here was richer than her and seemed happy in their own skins, her disorientation was compounded by the unfamiliar feelings which were ripping through her like a spring tide. Feelings which were hard to define and even harder to understand. She wondered why she was feeling such a powerful *desire* for the man beside her, even though he was the most arrogant person she'd ever met. She wondered why her skin had felt as if it were on fire when his fingertips had brushed against her shoulder blades. Or why, beneath this fancy dress which Hannah had foisted on her—the tips of her breasts were as raw as if someone had been rubbing them with sandpaper.

Remember how he looked down his nose at you when you were boarding the flight. Remember how upset that ravishing blonde had been when he'd been cold-heartedly dumping her in the cocktail bar.

Yet right now it was difficult to think about anything other than the smile which was softening the edges of his lips and making her wonder what it would be like to be kissed by Xan Constantinides. Her gaze twitched to his long olive fingers and once again her throat constricted with an unfamiliar surge of lust. Because she didn't *do* desire. It was yet another side of her character which made it hard for her to fit in. It was her own private and horrible little secret—or rather, it was *one* of them—that despite all the fiery promise of her looks, she was about as responsive as a piece of wood. Hadn't she been told that by men deeply unhappy that she wouldn't 'put out', until she'd stopped going out with men altogether because life was easier that way?

'No, I'm not going to deny I look different tonight,'

she said. 'Which is why I assume you're talking to me, which you clearly didn't want to do when you thought I was nothing but a lowly waitress. Or was it the sight of my canvas tennis shoes which made you decide I wasn't worthy of your time?'

He looked as if he was about to contest the point before seeming to change his mind and subjecting her to a smile of such intensity that Tamsyn's heart felt as if it was going to burst right out of her chest.

'Look, why don't we wipe the slate clean and start again?' he suggested smoothly, extending his hand with practised ease. 'I'm Xan Constantinides. Short for Alexandros, in case you were wondering.'

'I wasn't,' she said moodily.

And you're Tamsyn, aren't you?' he continued, undaunted. 'Tamsyn Wilson.'

Behind her unsmiling lips, Tamsyn gritted her teeth. He hadn't bothered finding out her name before, had he? But now he'd discovered she was related to Hannah, he was behaving *very* differently She glanced up at where the prospective bride and groom were sitting next to one another on some amazing dais. Hannah was smiling but Tamsyn knew her well enough to see the strain of the occasion on her face—*and* she was pregnant. And since Hannah had stressed that Xan was engaged in some important business with the Sheikh, then shouldn't she at least *try* to be polite to him, at least for the duration of the meal itself?

'Yes,' she said, as a delicate mango and walnut salad was placed in front of her. 'That's my name.'

'So why don't you tell me something about yourself, Tamsyn Wilson?'

Picking up a golden fork to half-heartedly push

her food around the plate, Tamsyn wondered what the Greek tycoon would say if she told him the truth. That if her parents had been married, her *real* surname would have been one of the most memorable in the world. But she had never used it. She'd never had the right to use it—not then and certainly not now. She looked into his cobalt eyes and tried to suppress the insane flutter of her heart. 'What would you like to know?'

He gave a shrug of his broad shoulders. 'Why don't we start with the obvious. You say you're no longer working at the Bluebird Club?'

'I told you—I was sacked.'

'So what are you doing instead?'

Perhaps if she hadn't been feeling so out of place then Tamsyn might have engaged in small-talk. She might have skated over her nomadic existence and pretended she was just like every other woman there. But somehow those words wouldn't come. Maybe Xan Constantinides was too unsettling a presence and those cobalt eyes too deeply penetrating. Because the idea of putting a positive spin on a life which had felt like it was spiralling out of control lately, suddenly seemed too big an ask. Why bother trying to impress someone who was only deigning to speak to her because she was soon to be related to the Sheikh?

'Oh, I have a terribly glamorous life—you wouldn't believe,' she said airily. 'I work in a coffee bar by day and stack supermarket shelves by night.'

He frowned. 'Those sound like very long hours.'

'Go straight to the top of the class, Mr Constantinides—they are.'

His eyes narrowed. 'Aren't you qualified to do anything other than waitress work?'

She put the golden fork back down on the plate with a clatter, her starter untasted. 'Actually, no, I'm not. Exams were never really my number one concern when I was at school.'

'So why not retrain to do something else?' he questioned as he lifted up his own goblet, his steady cobalt gaze surveying her over its jewelled rim. 'You seem bright enough.'

Tamsyn nearly laughed out loud and not just because the remark was deeply patronising. That was the trouble with rich people. They had no idea how the world really worked. They'd been cushioned by their wealth and privilege for so long, that they couldn't put themselves in someone else's shoes. 'And who's going to fund me while I do that?' she questioned, trying to keep her voice from shaking. 'When I've just had a rent raise from my landlord? And before you tell me to move to somewhere cheaper, I've lived in London all my life and can't imagine going anywhere else. Some problems don't have easy solutions, I'm afraid. Not unless you're prepared to throw wads of cash at them, which isn't an option for most people. Welcome to the real world, Mr Constantinides.'

Xan wondered if she was aware that her defiant words were causing her chest to heave, making it difficult for him not to stare openly at the silk-covered perfection of her breasts. With an effort he focussed his gaze on his wine glass, twirling the stem between his fingers and watching as the different jewels sparkled in the light from the overhead chandeliers. 'It's true I have made a sizeable amount of money,' he conceded. 'But that certainly doesn't guarantee a trouble-free life.'

'You mean like someone forgetting to peel your grapes for you, or your private jet failing to take off on time?'

'That's a rather predictable response, Tamsyn,' he mused softly. 'You know, I'm almost disappointed. I was hoping for something a little more original.'

'Oh, dear,' she said, pushing out her bottom lip in an exaggerated pout. 'The billionaire is disappointed. We can't have that, can we?'

He met the hectic glitter of her green gaze and the pooling at his groin increased. Xan shifted in his seat. He had tried to be polite but she was having none of it and he suspected he knew why. Because something was flowing between them. Something powerful. The kind of physical attraction he'd been encountering from women ever since he'd reached puberty though it had never felt like this before. Women didn't usually glare at him as if he was the devil incarnate, or try to rub him up the wrong way. He suspected that Tamsyn's supposed dislike of him was masking a much deeper response and that her darkened eyes were telling the real story. A flicker of a smile curved his lips. She wanted him just as much as he wanted her. And why not? Why not enjoy one final taste of freedom before destiny beckoned?

But he didn't intend spending the entire meal fighting with her and not simply because fighting was a bore. Because he understood the psychology of women only too well. They always wanted what they thought they couldn't have. She needed to understand that she was in danger of missing out if she continued to be insolent towards him. He would make her wait and make her squirm, so that by the time she came to him she would be so aroused that…

The pressure at his groin was almost unbearable as, very deliberately, he turned his back on her and began to speak to the Italian heiress to his right.

CHAPTER THREE

IT WAS JUST a wedding. That was all. Just a few more hours to get through before she could go home. That's what Tamsyn kept telling herself as she made her way towards the grand throne room, in yet another outfit which Hannah had insisted she wear. She supposed her sister must have secretly had all these clothes made for her before she arrived, but she couldn't deny that the long, floaty dress suited her. Unlike the dramatic emerald gown she'd worn to the rehearsal dinner last night, this one was a much gentler hue. The soft grey colour of a pigeon's wing, the bodice and silk-chiffon skirt were sprinkled with tiny crystals which sparkled like stars as she moved.

Tonight, the jewels she'd been loaned were diamonds—some more chandelier drop earrings, along with a priceless choker which blazed like ice fire around her neck. And just like last night, when Tamsyn glanced in the mirror before leaving her suite, she didn't recognise the image reflected back at her. To the outside world she looked sleek, expensive and polished but inside she felt….disgruntled. And although she hated the reason for her discontentment, she wasn't deluded enough to deny it. Because wasn't the truth that her irritation had been caused by Xan Constantinides ignoring her throughout most of the pre-wedding dinner? He'd been laughing and joking *in Italian* with that stunning woman on his other side and making out like *she* was invisible. And yes, she *had* been behaving in a particularly waspish manner beforehand, but even so…

She'd made her escape as soon as the food part of the evening was over. She'd gone back to her suite of rooms and run herself a deep and perfumed bath— then spent most of the night tossing and turning as the image of a man with black hair and cobalt eyes kept haunting her thoughts. More than once she'd awoken to find the tips of her breasts all pointy and aching and a molten heat throbbing between her thighs, causing her to writhe frustratedly between the fine cotton sheets. She'd told herself she needed to pull herself together and put the infuriating Greek right out of her mind, but somehow it wasn't turning out to be that easy.

The moment she entered the throne room, Xan Constantinides was the first person she saw, despite the fact that the Sheikh was already at the front of the gilded throne room, waiting for his bride. Tamsyn's heart gave a powerful lurch as she willed her face not to register any emotion.

He looked…

She swallowed against the sudden rawness in her throat. He looked delectable. In a charcoal suit which suited his colouring, he stood taller than any other man there else. Even more disturbing was the fact that he seemed to sense when she entered, because he turned his head and she was caught in that cobalt stare, making her feel as if she was imprisoned there. As if she *wanted* to be imprisoned there. She willed him not to come up and talk to her and then of course, she wished he would, but Tamsyn told herself to concentrate on the ceremony itself and to fix her eyes on the bride, who was just arriving.

Hannah looked gorgeous, her pregnancy bump a subtle swell and well disguised by her unusual wedding gown of beaten gold. She'd apologised for not making Tamsyn her bridesmaid, explaining that it wasn't Zahristanian custom to do so. Not that Tamsyn had minded. Marriage had always seemed such an outdated institution to her and one which rarely lasted. More than once she'd wondered why it couldn't be replaced by something more modern.

Yet she sensed the historical significance of the vows being made, though Hannah's voice was so low she could barely hear them and the Sheikh looked so stern that Tamsyn was certain he felt as trapped as her sister did. But she clapped and cheered along with the other guests once the couple had been pronounced King and Queen, and she toasted their health in spiced fire-berry juice, as was traditional.

The meal which followed was far more formal than the one they'd eaten last night and Tamsyn told herself she was pleased to sit between the Sultan of Marazad and a representative from the desert kingdom of Maraban. Glad to be miles away from Xan Constantinides and relieved she didn't have to endure his unsettling presence.

But that was a lie.

All she could think about was the Greek tycoon, and her body seemed determined to reflect her increasingly distracted thoughts. She felt as if her skin had become too tight for her body. As if her senses had suddenly become sensitised. The sound of her heart seemed amplified, its beat a million times more powerful than usual. And there was no respite from these unsettling feelings which made her feel as if she was fighting something deep inside herself. Nowhere she could escape to, because she couldn't just get up and leave in the middle of a royal wedding. She tried to chat politely to the men on either side and not glance further down the long table to where a Hollywood actress and a female member of the British royal family were giggling like schoolgirls at something Xan was saying.

She wondered how early she could decently leave, especially when a troupe of musicians started playing in the galleried ballroom next door. She knew there would be dancing after dinner because Hannah had told her so, but Tamsyn had no intention of watching couples circling the dance floor and pretending she was fine on her own. Usually, she was—mainly because she had made self-sufficiency into an art form. She never yearned for a partner because that was the only way she knew how to function. If you didn't yearn for something, you wouldn't be disappointed—and anyway, relationships were a waste of time. Experience had taught her that.

Yet tonight she keenly felt the absence of something in her life. Or rather, someone. Maybe it was the inevitable sentimentality conjured up by the wedding vows, or the realisation that Hannah was now married which was making her feel so shockingly alone. Or perhaps it was the just the realisation that there was nothing waiting for her back in England other than a pile of mounting debts.

Dabbing at her lips with a napkin, she decided to slip away, just like last night. Who would notice *her* when there were so many important guests present? She rose from her seat and was just bending to retrieve the Dior bag Hannah had insisted on lending her, when she heard a rich voice from behind.

'You're not leaving?' came the silky question.

She didn't need to turn around to know who was speaking, but prior knowledge offered no protection against her feelings and Tamsyn's heart was hammering as she straightened up to meet that mocking cobalt stare. He didn't want to talk to you last night, she reminded herself—so why not continue with that state of affairs and everyone will be happy. She gave him a tight smile. 'Oh, dear. Nobody was supposed to notice.'

'Where are you going?'

Tamsyn shrugged. *Where did he think she was going?* 'Back to my room. Or should I say—to my vast suite of rooms.'

'But the night is young.'

She opened her eyes very wide. 'I didn't think people actually said that kind of thing any more.'

He raised his brows. 'You're implying it's clichéd?'

'I suspect you're clever enough to work that one out for yourself, Mr Constantinides.'

Their gazes clashed in look which made Tamsyn feel almost *playful* and the desire to flirt was overwhelming. Yet she never flirted—she wasn't sure she even knew how. She'd always been closed up and defensive because she didn't particularly like men and she certainly didn't trust them. So how come she was suddenly playing a game she'd never played before and finding she was comfortable with it? How come she wanted to tease this darkly impressive individual and for him to tease her back? She found herself wanting to stroke her finger over the curving lines of his sensual mouth, and…and…

And she had to stop this.

Because this was dangerous. More than dangerous. Tamsyn's heart clenched with something which felt uncomfortably close to vulnerability, and that scared the hell out of her. 'I have to go,' she said.

'Not yet.' He laid his hand on her arm. 'I get the distinct feeling that I really need to change your impression of me.'

Chin lifting, she offered him a belligerent gaze. 'And why would you want to do that?'

'Call it a peace-making move in honour of your sister's wedding, if you like. Just a little light-hearted fun, that's all. And the dancing has only just started,' he observed. 'You can't possibly leave until you've had at least one dance.'

'I didn't think it was obligatory. I wasn't planning on dancing with anyone.'

An arrogant smile touched the edges of his lips. 'Not even with me?'

'Especially not with you.'

'Oh? And why not, *agape mou*? Don't you like dancing?'

His voice had deepened and the throwaway endearment in his native tongue made him even more irresistible. Tamsyn stared into his dark blue eyes. When she was younger she had thrown herself around a dance floor with the rest of them, swaying beneath the flash of lights, to the DJ's heavy beat. She had shaken her arms in the air and tossed her curls while her skin had glowed and grown hot. But she'd never been asked to dance by a devastatingly handsome man in a fancy ballroom, while wearing a silken dress which pooled around her ankles.

'Because it's a bad idea,' she prevaricated.

'Stop fighting it, Tamsyn. You know you want to dance with me,' he said with silky perception, his hand moving to the small of her back as he propelled her gently towards the dance floor.

Even then she might have stopped him had Tamsyn not glanced up at the dais and seen the newly married Sheikh looking down on them, with what looked like bemusement in his eyes. Was he surprised she was planning to dance with such an honoured guest as his rich pal? She knew Kulal didn't like her, just as she didn't like him. In fact, they'd had an almighty row before the wedding when he'd turned up on her sister's doorstep. But you had to let bygones be bygones, especially now that he was her new brother-in-law.

So why not show the Sheikh she could behave with dignity—and prove to herself that she wasn't a total social misfit? Why *shouldn't* she dance with the best-looking man in the room? With a resolute nod of her head, she allowed Xan to lead her onto the ballroom, pleased there were enough people to ensure they could just blend into the crowd. Just one dance, she told herself. One dance to fulfil her obligations and she could be off.

But life never quite conformed the way you wanted it to. One dance became two, which then somehow morphed into three, and each dance seemed to propel them closer, so that their bodies felt as if they were glued together. And Xan wasn't saying anything. Well, neither was she, come to think of it. Tamsyn blamed the loudness of the lilting music but the truth was that she couldn't think of anything she wanted to say other than something wholly inappropriate.

Like: *I love the way you make me feel when you tighten your arms around my waist like that.* Or, *could you possibly press yourself a little closer?*

Did he realise that, or did she somehow silently communicate her wishes to him? Because surely there must have been a reason—some defining moment—when Xan Constantinides thought it was perfectly acceptable for him to run his fingertips down her back in a way which even to her inexperienced self, spoke of careless intimacy. For several minutes, she let him do just that and she couldn't deny how good it felt. She began to shiver each time he made the tantalisingly slow journey from the top of her neck to the base of her spine. Her heart was hammering and the rush of heat to her face echoed the molten heat which was clenching at her sex. Yet far from being disturbed by the sultry desire she was experiencing Tamsyn was aware of an intense feeling of *relief.* Briefly she closed her eyes as she dipped her forehead to rest on his shoulder as she felt the squirm of excitement. So she wasn't frigid, after all. She could feel the things other women felt. Sweet heaven—could she feel them! It was as if someone had just flicked a switch and brought her body to life, so that every sinew and fibre was thrilling with the potent power of his proximity.

She heard him murmur something in her ear, it's meaning a mystery because it was said in Greek. But then he pushed one thigh hard against hers, as if urging her legs apart and she found her super-susceptible body obeying his silent command. Her knees widened and a sudden thrill of pleasure shot through her as she felt the pressure of his hard thigh pushing against the softness of hers. Her breasts were thrusting insistently at his chest and her knees had become all wobbly and weak. She could feel the rub of her panties over a sudden honeyed slickness and felt an insistent yearning to have him touch her there…to whisper his finger over her most intimate place. To ease that escalating ache which was making her want to squirm with frustration. She swallowed, trying to ignore the heat which was flaring in her cheek—and that was when alarm bells started ringing. What was she *doing*? After years of being purer than the driven snow, was she really planning to make a slutty spectacle of herself on the dance floor—just because some super-smooth man was pressing all the right buttons?

Removing her hands from his shoulders she flattened her palms against his chest, trying not to be distracted by the hard wall of muscle as she stared up into his face. 'What the hell do you think you're doing?' she demanded.

He didn't look the slightest bit bothered by her furious accusation as he lifted his broad shoulders in a careless shrug. 'I should have thought that was perfectly obvious.'

'So suddenly you're all over me, having ignored me all the way through dinner last night?' she accused.

'You were so combative that you deserved to be ignored,' he said softly. 'But I thought we'd agreed on a truce tonight?'

'Does…?' She swallowed, willing the erratic hammering of her pulse to subside. 'Does a truce involve you coming on to me like that, in such a public way?'

'Oh, come on, Tamsyn. Let's not be hypocritical about what just happened. I thought you were enjoying yourself.' He flickered her a slow smile. 'I know I certainly was. And most people are too busy dancing to notice how close we were getting.'

Tamsyn shook her head, aware of the swing of heavy diamond earrings against her neck and nervously she touched the sleepers to check the precious jewels were secure. Which they were—unlike her. She was one seething mass of insecurity. And fear. She mustn't discount the dominant emotion which was making her feel so scared. She felt as if she'd just stepped onto a sturdy wooden floor and it was about to give way beneath her. As if Xan Constantinides had the ability to waken something inside her—something which had been sleeping all these years. Suddenly the defiant persona she had perfected to protect herself from the kind of life her mother had lived, was in danger of crumbling before her eyes. Suddenly she was terrified of just how *exposed* he was making her feel. As if she was nothing but a bunch of sensitised nerve-endings which were jangling with hungry need. She shook her head again.

'Look, I can't do this,' she whispered. 'I'm sorry. Enjoy the rest of the party but I'm going to bed. It's going to be a long flight tomorrow and I have a double shift on Monday. Nice meeting you, Xan,' she said, and without another word she began to walk off the dance floor, aware of people turning to look at her as she hurriedly brushed past them.

Xan watched her go, caught in a rare moment of indecision, his eyes drawn to the bright shimmer of curls which cascaded like flames down her back. The voice of reason was urging him to let her go, because she was trouble. Anyone could see that. All mixed up and not his type. But the hunger of his body was more powerful than reason and he'd never had a woman walk away from him before—not like this. Was this how Hannah had snared the Sheikh—the two very ordinary Wilson sisters possessing a simple but effective strategy which would make powerful men lust after them?

Like a man hypnotised he found himself following her, mesmerised by the slender curve of her glittering bottom as she left the dance floor, surprised when she didn't look back. Not once. There was no furtive side glance to check whether he was on her tail. And *that* was exciting, too. Her steps were determined—as if she really *wanted* to get away from him. This was the chase, he realised—the chase which other men spoke of but which he'd never encountered before. He could feel the tightening of his groin and hear the wild thunder of his heart, when suddenly she disappeared from sight and he was unprepared for the disappointment which flared through him. Purposefully increasing his pace, he rounded the corner and saw her—and perhaps the sound of his footsteps was enough to make her stop and turn around—a look of bewilderment on her face, as if she was genuinely surprised to see him. As if she doubted her ability to make a man follow her.

'Xan?' she said, creasing her forehead in a frown.

'Tamsyn,' he answered, and began to walk towards her, aware of her nipples pushing hard against the crystalline bodice of her dress. As he approached, he could feel the warm rush of blood pumping through his body and in that moment he felt as if he would die if he couldn't have her.

He had reached her now and could see her darkened pupils making her green eyes appear almost black— just as the moist tremble of her lips indicated an unspoken desire to have him to crush them with his own. And he would, he thought hungrily. He would take the wildcat Tamsyn Wilson to his bed and subdue her in the most satisfactory way possible.

CHAPTER FOUR

BENEATH THE FRETWORK of lanterns lighting the palace corridor, Tamsyn's heart was thundering as she watched Xan approach, his powerful body outlined by the dark fabric of his formal suit. His face was dark too and his eyes glittered out a message of intent which started a tug of longing deep inside her. It scared and excited her and she wanted to carry on running, but something was keeping her feet fixed to the spot.

'Nobody has ever walked off and left me standing alone on the dance floor like that,' he observed huskily.

From somewhere she found a remnant of her usual flippancy. 'Oh, dear. Poor Xan. Is your ego suffering?'

'It's not my ego I'm thinking about right now,' he ground out.

Some of her composure began to slip away as Tamsyn became aware of how big and strong he looked and how it had felt to be in his arms. *Hadn't it been the most incredible sensation she'd ever experienced?*

She cleared her throat, trying to dispel her euphoric recall. 'Look, I thought I'd made my feelings clear. I'm tired and on my way to bed. I don't know why you're chasing me through the corridors as if we're a pair of kids playing cops and robbers.'

'Yes, you do. You know exactly why,' he said softly. 'Because I want you and you want me. We've wanted each other from the moment we met, Tamsyn and unless we do something about it, it's going to drive us both crazy.'

It was one of those slow motion moments and Tamsyn felt her heart leap in her chest. Like when you heard something life-changing on the news. Only this wasn't something which was happening to somebody else—it was happening to *her*. She was being propositioned by Xan Constantinides—the arrogant Greek billionaire!

Her throat grew dry as she looked at him, trying not to drink in all his dark beauty, knowing she had plenty of options available. She could call for a servant. Or carrying on walking and even if he followed, she could slam the door in his face, because instinct told her he wouldn't charge at it with a battening ram, even if he looked physically capable of doing so. But even as these thoughts flickered through her mind, she realised none of them were an option. Xan Constantinides might not like her very much—nor she him— but she couldn't deny that something had happened when he'd touched her on the dance floor.

He'd cast a spell on her. Woven some sensual kind of magic which was snaring her with invisible threads. She stared into the rugged beauty of his face, aware that this was a chance to shake off the real Tamsyn—the one who'd become brittle and defiant in order to survive. This was her opportunity to become someone else for a change. Somebody soft and dreamy and different.

'You want to kiss me,' he persisted softly. 'You want that very badly, don't you, Tamsyn?'

She wanted to deny it. To tell him that he was talking rubbish and to take his ego somewhere else. But she couldn't. She found herself lifting her eyes to his, her heart filled with foreboding and longing as she attempted a shrug which didn't quite come off. 'I suppose so,' she mumbled.

He seemed to find this amusing for his lips curved into a mocking smile. 'You suppose so?' he echoed, stepping forward to tilt her chin upwards with his finger. 'I don't think I've ever been damned with so much faint praise.'

This was Tamsyn's cue for a clever retort but right now she didn't have one because he was slowly lowering his mouth on to hers. His lips were brushing over her trembling lips and she was finding it impossible not to respond. Her hands fluttered to his shoulders for support and suddenly he was pulling her closer with effortless mastery as he deepened the kiss.

And Tamsyn just lost it.

She'd been kissed before—of course she had—but never like this. She'd only ever known the thrust of a tongue and the unwanted slick of saliva. She hadn't realised that a kiss could feel like a one-way ticket to heaven. Did her dreamy gasp startle him? Was that why he drew back, before glancing both ways down the corridor and lacing her fingers with his. 'Come with me,' he said, his voice curiously uneven.

'Come where? Where are we going?'

'Where do you think we're going?' His eyes glittered with unmistakable promise. 'I'm taking you to bed.'

His masterful and slightly callous statement should have shocked her, but it didn't. Instead it thrilled her and Tamsyn could feel her cheeks glowing as he led her through endless corridors, the click-clacking of her high heels against the marble floor the only sound she could hear above the deafening thunder of her heart. Afterwards she would try to justify her behaviour by telling herself she'd been disorientated at finding herself in a desert palace, which was only adding to the fantasy-like feel of what was happening. As if the real Tamsyn Wilson was looking down and seeing a breathlessly excited woman who couldn't wait for the powerful Greek tycoon to take her to his bed.

Lit by soft lamps, his suite was just as fancy as hers—only with a much more masculine feel. Strong scarlets and deep golds dominated the high-ceilinged room and on an inlaid desk she noticed a golden pen, studded with diamonds. A collection of horse paintings took up an entire wall and one in particular caught her eye—a black stallion with yellow flowers looped around its glistening neck, as it stood against a sunset backdrop of the stark desert. Xan didn't say anything until the heavy door had closed behind them and as he drew her into the powerful warmth of his body, Tamsyn felt her heart thunder.

'Now,' he said softly, tilting her face upwards. 'Where were we?

For once in her life she had no smart answer. All her usual flippancy drained away from her as Tamsyn stared into the Greek's rugged features and her heart gave a great punch of delight. Yet she didn't have a clue how best to respond to him. Would he be horrified if he knew what a novice she was and should she tell him?

Did it matter?

She swallowed.

Why should it matter—and why *should* she tell

him? She couldn't be the only virgin in the history of the world and there was no shame to it—even though sometimes you were made to feel like a freak just because you'd reached the grand old age of twenty-two without ever having had sex. But then, she'd never responded to a man like this before, because no man had ever made her feel like this. And was it such a crime to want to capitalise on it? To feel like a normal woman for once, instead of someone who was made of ice from the neck down?

She tried to remember what he'd just asked her. Some flirty question about what they had just been doing and that certainly wasn't something she would be forgetting in a hurry. 'You were kissing me,' she reminded him softly.

He gave a slow smile. 'So I was,' he agreed, framing her face between his palms and looking at her for a long moment before lowering his mouth to hers, exploring her lips with a thoroughness which left her reeling.

Against the jewelled bodice of her gown Tamsyn could feel her breasts growing heavy as he reached down to whisper his thumb over her peaking nipple, lazily circling it in a way which made her moan with pleasure. She pressed her lips against his neck, feeling the rapid beat of a pulse there. As his hand began to sweep luxuriously down over her satin-covered belly, she felt another great clench of her sex and she shivered. Did he sense that already she wanted to explode with pleasure? Was that why he moved his head back to survey the rapid rise and fall of her chest.

'I think we need to get on the bed,' he said unevenly. Tamsyn wasn't known for her compliancy and when people 'suggested' something, her natural instinct was to rebel. But she found herself nodding at him like some eager little puppy. 'Okay,' she whispered, tightening her grip around his neck like the clinging tendrils of a vine. 'Let's.'

Xan felt his erection pushing almost violently against his trousers and silently he cursed, because the effect she was having on him was undeniably... *urgent.* She made him feel about fifteen years old instead of thirty-three, and while he was in such a high state of arousal it made more sense to keep movement to a minimum. So why not push her to the floor and do it to her right there, on the silken rug? It would be fast and a little bit dirty but he could rid himself of this fierce hunger which was running through his veins like a fever. His mouth hardened because that might be the perfect solution—a quick coupling to alleviate their mutual frustration and allow them to discreetly go their separate ways soon afterwards?

But something about the way she was responding to him was making such an action seem almost unsavoury. She was holding onto him as trustingly as a tiny kitten—leaving him with little choice other than to carry her across the room in a macho display which wasn't really his style. He was taken aback by how shockingly *primitive* the gesture made him feel as another spear of lust shafted through him.

Bemusement filled him as he set her down beside the brocade-covered divan, because Tamsyn Wilson wasn't turning out to be what he'd expected. In fact, none of this was what he'd expected. She was confounding him with mixed messages. The street-wise minx was behaving in a way which was almost *naïve.*

He'd imagined that someone so sassy and sexy would by now be unzipping him, before taking him boldly in her hand, or her mouth—because that seemed to be the current trend for first time sex. The cynic in him often wondered if this was the moment when women attempted to showcase their sexual skills in as short a time as possible—rather like a job applicant deftly running through their entire resume on a first interview. But not Tamsyn. She seemed more concerned with removing those ostentatious diamond earrings and finding a low table beside the bed on which to safely put them, quickly followed by the glittering diamond choker. And while she was turning round to do that, he moved behind her, lifting the thick curtain of her curls to drift his lips over her neck. He felt her tremble then slump against him and she wondered if she could feel his hardness pressing into her bottom.

'I want you,' he said, very deliberately, as he turned her round to face him.

'D-do you?' she said, her voice barely a whisper.

How did she manage to sound so convincingly *shy*, he wondered? Pulling a couple of clips from her hair, he unzipped her gown so that it slithered to the ground in a pool of glittering silk and net and she was left standing in nothing but her bra and panties. He felt another kick of desire. Her legs were bare and he bent before her to remove one silver shoe, quickly followed by another, but when he stood up again he was taken aback by how tiny she seemed without the towering heels.

Shrugging off his jacket and yanking off his tie, he let them fall to join her discarded dress. 'Unbutton my shirt,' he growled.

Tamsyn's fingers were trembling as she lifted them to Xan's chest, because for all her bravado she'd never seen a man naked and she'd certainly never undressed anyone before. Yet her instinctive fear was banished by that first sweet touch of the skin which sheathed his hard muscle and she heard him groan as the buttons flew open. Now what, she wondered, as she gazed at his bare chest—too daunted to think about attacking the zip of his trousers.

Did he sense her sudden nervousness? Was that why he gave another slow smile and unclipped her front-fastening bra so that her breasts spilled into his waiting palms and suddenly her nerves were all but forgotten? She writhed as his thumbs circled her nipples and her excitement grew as he moved his hand down between her thighs. Pushing aside the damp, stretched panel at her crotch, he found her slick heat, sliding his finger against the engorged bud with practised ease. And this was *heaven*. Her hips were circling of their own accord and she was moaning now and the part of her brain which was urging her to be careful, was abruptly silenced by the most powerful desire she could ever have imagined.

'Xan…' she breathed, looking up to meet the smoky lust which had narrowed his eyes.

'You are just as hot as I thought you'd be,' he declared unevenly.

She should have said something then, but she couldn't even think of the words—let alone form a sentence with them—not when he was laying her down on the bed and pulling off the rest of his clothes with unsteady hands. And then he was naked—his body warm and strong as he lay down beside her. His hungry kiss was fuelling this wild new hunger which was spiralling up inside her and suddenly Tamsyn was on fire. His lips were on her breasts and her belly—tantalising her until she thought she would go out of her mind. And when he guided her hand to his groin, there was no shyness as she encountered the hard ridge of his erection. Instead, she felt nothing but joy as she began to whisper her fingertips against it. But he shook his head as he reached for something on the nightstand and she heard the little tear of foil and realised he must be sheathing himself.

This was it. The moment she'd never thought she'd reach because she had always been unresponsive and afraid. But she wasn't afraid now as he moved over her and spread her legs apart. Not even when she felt that brief burst of pain and momentarily, he stilled. Instinct told her to angle her hips and to propel them forward so that he slid inside her completely—and once her body had grown accustomed to his width—those incredible sensations of pleasure were back. And how. She cried out with it so that he stilled once again and his words came out clipped, like bullets.

'I am hurting you?'

'No. No. Not at all. It's…*oh!* Oh, Xan. It's heaven.'

'Is it now? Then I had just better…. *Do. It. Some. More.*'

With each emphasised word, he thrust deeper and deeper, until her nails were digging into his back. Tamsyn could feel the build-up of something. Something so delicious she didn't believe it could get any better, except that it did. And then better still. It was like being whizzed to the top of a high tower block and being told to jump off, and willingly she did, gasping out his name in an expression of disbelief as she went flying over some sunlight ledge.

As he heard the helpless sound of her cries, Xan knew he couldn't hold back. Not a second longer. And when his orgasm came it left him shaken. His head fell back and it took several breathless minutes before he could distance himself by rolling away from her. Because he needed to do that. He needed to make sense of what had just happened—even though all he could think about was the folly of what he'd just done.

He had seduced the Sheikh's sister-in-law!

And against all the odds, she had been a *virgin*.

He stared down at her, at where her magnificent hair tumbled like fire against the muddled pile of pillows. Her eyes were closed though experience told him she was not asleep, though he suspected she wanted him to think she was. But she was in his room and he wanted answers.

Now.

'That was some…surprise,' he drawled.

She opened her eyes and he steeled himself against their beauty, but somehow they had lost their luminous quality. They looked as flat as pieces of jade as she returned his stare and he could see her dreamy expression being replaced with her more usual look of rebellion.

'What, that the woman you'd clearly slotted into the category of "she'll be up for anything", turned out to be less experienced than you imagined?' she challenged.

He made a growling little sound at the back of his throat. 'Didn't you think it was a big enough deal to tell me I was your first lover?' he demanded. 'Or that it might be the *polite* thing to have done?'

At this, Tamsyn nearly burst out laughing. 'Polite? We haven't exactly been polite to each other up until now, have we?' she retorted. 'At what point *exactly* was I supposed to tell you? You'll forgive me if I don't know the protocol for this kind occasion.'

'Well, neither do I!'

'Are you saying that I'm the first virgin you've ever had sex with?'

'*Neh*… Yes,' he translated.

There was a moment of silence. '*Why*?'

'Why do you think?' he questioned sarcastically. 'If someone your age has waited all this time to have sex, it's usually an indication of her having unrealistic expectations.'

'Such as?'

He shrugged. 'Holding out for a wedding ring is the first thing which springs to mind.'

'You really are the most arrogant man I've ever met.'

'I don't deny it,' he said, unabashed. 'But at least you can't accuse me of being dishonest.'

But wasn't there a part of Tamsyn which wished he had been? A previously unknown side of herself which longed for him to tell her that it had been wonderful and she was wonderful, and from now on she was going to be his girlfriend.

Had she taken *complete* leave of her senses?

She needed to face the facts, like she'd always done. She'd just had sex, that was all. It might not have been the smartest move to chose Xan Constantinides as her first lover but she wasn't going to deny how superb he'd been. And what she was *not* going to do was to regret it. Didn't she have enough regrets already, without adding one more to the list? Couldn't she take pleasure from the most amazing thing which had ever happened to her, without carrying around a whole shedload of guilt?

She shifted her weight again and the slippery golden sheet slithered away to her breast and suddenly he was saying something in thick and urgent Greek before pulling her hungrily into his arms. Maybe Tamsyn should have been daunted by the newly massive erection she felt pressing against her belly but she wasn't—mainly because she was remembering what had just happened. And she wanted it to happen all over again.

Eagerly she raised her face to search for his kiss, feeling a shiver of excitement rippling uncontrollably through her body as the Greek billionaire reached blindly for a second condom.

CHAPTER FIVE

TAMSYN HAD HEARD plenty about the 'walk of shame' but she'd never experienced it before. The furtive walk from a man's bedroom back to your own, wearing last night's clothes and praying that nobody would notice you. But how on earth was she going to manage that when she was wearing *full evening dress*?

Tamsyn quickly realised it was a naïve and futile hope. Not only did she pass countless servants silently scurrying through the sunlit corridors—she even had the misfortune to encounter a large group of wedding guests who were clearly being given an early-morning guided tour by one of the Sheikh's assistants. It would have been almost comical to see their reaction to her sudden appearance, if it had been happening to anyone other than her.

The guide's voice faded away and everyone's mouths fell open as a barefooted Tamsyn rounded the corner, wearing a now crumpled grey evening dress and dangling her silver high-heeled shoes from one hand, while her other tightly grasped a pair of priceless diamond earrings and a matching choker. The guide seemed to recover himself—maybe he recognised her as the Sheikh's new sister-in-law—because he cleared his throat and gave a strangled kind of smile.

'You are lost, mistress?'

Tamsyn gave a thin smile. Yes, she was lost—but only in the emotional sense of the word, and once again wondered what on earth had possessed her to indulge in a long night of sex with a man she instinctively sensed was dangerous.

You know why. Because you couldn't stop yourself. Because the moment he touched you, you went up in flames.

Ignoring the knowing side glances of the men and the hostile glare of the women in the group, Tamsyn gave a determined shake of her head, making her unbrushed curls fly around her shoulders like angry red corkscrews. 'I'm just on my way back to my room,' she said cheerily. 'It seemed a pity not to get up early and watch the sun rise over the desert.'

They obviously didn't believe a word she was saying, but since she would never see them again after today—who cared?

She made it back to her room at last, tearing off her dress, throwing aside the shoes and carefully putting the jewellery down, before escaping into the sanctuary of the luxurious bathroom. At least the steam of the hot shower and the rich lather of perfumed soap made her feel marginally better, but not for long, because flashback images kept coming back to haunt her. Imagines of a hard, muscular body driving down on hers and warm arms enfolding her and holding her tight. *Just concentrate on what you're supposed to be doing*, she told herself fiercely as she dragged a brush through her unruly curls. She had just slithered into her old denim cut-offs and a clean T-shirt, when there was a rap at the door.

She wasn't going to deny the leap of her heart in response, or the determined pep talk she gave herself as she walked across the palatial suite. She told herself to play it cool. If Xan Constantinides wanted her phone number then she would give it to him, but she wasn't going to act like it was a big deal. She might never have had sex before but over the years she'd listened to how friends and colleagues dealt with the thorny issue of The Morning After. And apparently the most stupid thing a woman could ever do, was to come over all eager.

Composing her face into what she hoped wasn't an over-the-top smile, it faded immediately when she opened the door to discover it wasn't Xan standing there but the newly crowned Queen of Zahristan— her sister Hannah! A sister whose face was filled with anger as she walked in without waiting to be invited, pushing the door shut behind her, before assuming a grim expression of accusation which Tamsyn recognised all too well.

'Would you like to tell me what's going on?' she demanded.

'I could ask the same thing of you!' retorted Tamsyn, reframing the accusation and turning it on its head since attack was always the best form of defence. 'It's the first day of your honeymoon—so what are you doing barging into my bedroom at this time in the morning? Won't your new husband be wondering where you are?'

Hannah bit her lip and Tamsyn was shocked to see the despair which briefly darkened her sister's eyes because she was usually cheerful, no matter what life threw at her. And despite her own predicament, Tamsyn felt her heart plummet as her worst fears began to materialise. Was Hannah's marriage already starting to go off the rails, even though she had only been crowned Queen the previous day? She had warned her sister that it was a mistake to marry such a man as arrogant as Kulal. She'd begged her not to go through with the marriage just because she was pregnant, but Hannah hadn't listened. What if the powerful Sheikh was being cruel to his pregnant wife—what then?

'So where's Kulal, Hannah?' Tamsyn probed, as suspicion continued to stab at her heart like a dagger. 'Doesn't he mind you being here, quizzing me, on the first morning of his honeymoon?'

'I'm not here to talk about my relationship!' declared Hannah, but Tamsyn could hear the sorrow in her voice. 'I'm here to ask whether you spent the night with Xan Constantinides.'

And despite all her bravado, Tamsyn felt a shiver whisper over her skin. Was it hearing someone else say the words out loud which drove home the true nature of what she had done? After years of fiercely guarding her innocence she had let the Greek tycoon lead her back to his suite and take her virginity with barely an arrogant snap of his fingers. A man she barely knew. A man she would probably never see again.

And it had been the most amazing thing which had ever happened to her.

They had spent the night having passionate sex— over and over again. He'd said things to her in Greek she hadn't understood and things to her in English which she had, and which made her blush just remembering them.

'You drive me crazy. Your breasts are small but the most perfect I have ever seen,' he had growled at one point, lifting his head from her nipple, where the lick of his tongue and the graze of his teeth had been enough to have her writhing on the bed in ecstasy. 'And do you want to know what else about you is perfect?'

She remembered thinking how delectable he looked with his cheekbones all flushed and his black hair wild as a lion's mane from where she'd been running her fingers through it. She remembered an instinctive feeling of sexual power flooding through her as she met his hectic cobalt gaze. 'Yes,' she whispered. 'Yes, I do.'

But he had answered with the urgent thrust of his seemingly ever-present erection, and Tamsyn had almost passed with pleasure as he brought her hurtling over the edge of fulfilment, again and again and again.

She must have fallen asleep eventually, because when she opened her eyes it had been to discover herself alone in the rumpled bed with bright sunlight on her face and only a scrawled note occupying the space where Xan had lain. She had picked it up with trembling fingers and read it.

Gone riding in the desert. That was the most perfect night.
Thank you.
Xan.

Tamsyn's heart had sunk for it had read like the farewell it was obviously intended to be. There had been no line of kisses. No phone number or email address, or invitation to have dinner with him back in London.

Well, what had she been expecting—everlasting love?

Of course she hadn't, but even facing up to the folly of her actions didn't make it any easier. She'd done some pretty stupid things in her time, but sleeping with Xan Constantinides must rank right up there with some of the worst decisions she'd ever made. Easy come, easy go—that was probably how he saw it. If you slept with a man without even going out on a formal date, then why would he treat you with respect? Tamsyn swallowed. Was she doomed to follow the path laid down by her own mother, despite her determination to live her life in a very different way?

Now she stared into Hannah's aquamarine eyes which were so unlike her own. She guessed they each carried a legacy from their different fathers—both useless in their different ways—and fleetingly she wondered whether that was why they'd both made such bad choices when choosing men. Except that she hadn't chosen Xan—he had chosen her.

And he had done a runner as soon as possible.

She shrugged her shoulders with a familiar gesture of defiance. 'Yes, I spent the night with Xan Constantinides.'

'But Tamsyn, *why?*'

For the first time Tamsyn felt like smiling as she looked at her sister. Her pale-faced sister with dark shadows under her eyes. 'You're honestly asking me that? You might be a married woman now—but surely you're not completely immune to the charms of a man like Xan Constantinides.'

At the mention of marriage, Hannah flinched. 'No, of course I'm not,' she said quietly. 'And that's precisely why he's the wrong kind of man for you, Tamsyn. He might be obscenely good-looking and have the kind of sex appeal which should carry a public health warning, but he's known for his…his…'

'His *what*?' prompted Tamsyn, though her heart was smashing against her rib cage because she guessed what was coming.

'Let's just say he *enjoys* women! He enjoys them very much.'

'I wasn't expecting him to be celibate!'

Hannah sucked in a long breath, her face growing serious. 'It's more than that. He usually dates actresses. Or models. Or heiresses.'

'Not waitresses on short-term contracts who are always getting fired for insubordination, you mean?' offered Tamsyn drily.

'And you…'

Tamsyn watched as Hannah unconsciously rubbed her enormous gold and ruby wedding band, as if reaffirming to herself that she really *was* married. And once again she wondered why her sister was standing *here* on the first morning of her honeymoon, looking like the very opposite of what a glowing newlywed should be. Why wasn't she romping in bed with her husband? 'I what, Hannah?'

The new Queen chewed on her lip. 'I know you were inexperienced with men, Tamsyn,' she breathed. 'And by associating with someone like Xan, you're operating right out of your league.

'Oh, don't worry,' Tamsyn assured her airily. 'I'm

not anticipating any kind of future with him. I'm not *that* stupid.'

'But what…' Hannah sucked in a deep breath. 'What if you're pregnant?'

Tamsyn knew she didn't have to have this conversation, no matter how close the two sisters had been when they were growing up. But in a way she *did* need to have it, because wouldn't voicing her inner fears help put them into perspective? Like when you had a terrible nightmare and the shadows in the room seemed to symbolise all kinds of terrible things—yet when you put a lamp on you soon saw that the imagined monster was a chair, or a dressing table.

'We used protection,' she said quietly.

Hannah's eyes were very big. 'So did we,' she whispered. 'And look what happened.'

And suddenly Tamsyn was made very aware of how easily a woman could be trapped by her own passion. Hannah had accidently become pregnant by the Sheikh which was why she had married him. Who was to say the same thing wouldn't happen to her? She found herself uttering a small, silent prayer. 'We'll just have to hope it doesn't happen to me,' she said quietly.

'And what if it does?'

'Then I'll deal with it. But I'm not going to project like that. I'm just going to carry on as before.'

'Doing what?'

Tamsyn patted the back pocket of her cut-offs to check she had her cellphone. 'Doing what I always do. Adapting. Moving on.'

Distractedly, Hannah began to pace up and down the room, the silken shimmer of her flowing robes seeming to emphasise the growing differences between them. Stopping in front of one of the tall windows which overlooked the palace gardens, the streaming sunlight had turned her pale blonde hair into liquid gold and Tamsyn thought how scarily royal she looked. 'Kulal says we might be able to find a role for you in the London Embassy.'

'As what? The new attaché?' enquired Tamsyn, deadpan.

'I'm serious, Tamsyn. There are always cleaning jobs available—or we thought you might like to help the chef in the Ambassador's private kitchen.' Hannah gave a somewhat helpless shrug. 'Something like that.'

'Well, thanks but no thanks,' said Tamsyn firmly. 'I don't want to be beholden to your husband and I'd prefer to make my own way in life, just like I've always done.'

At this, Hannah walked forward to place her hand on Tamsyn's arm. 'But if anything *happens*,' she said fervently. 'If you find out you *are* pregnant—then you will come to me for help, won't you, Tamsyn?'

'If I were you, I think I'd be concentrating on your life rather than mine,' said Tamsyn sharply. 'I've never seen you looking so pale. What's the matter, Hannah—have you suddenly discovered there are serpents in paradise?'

Was her remark too close to the bone? Was that why Hannah's face crumpled and she looked as if she was about to cry? Tamsyn felt a sudden pang of guilt as her sister turned towards the arched doorway, but any remorse was quickly cancelled out by the enormity of what her sister had just said to her. Because that was something she hadn't even considered. Her stomach performed a sickly somersault as Hannah left the room and Tamsyn stared unseeingly at one of the priceless silken rugs. What if Hannah's fears were true? What if she *was* pregnant?

She tried to put it—and him—out of her mind, though it wasn't easy on the flight back to England. Especially when the stewardess had answered her studiedly casual query about Xan by informing her that Mr Constantinides had summoned his own jet and left Zahristan earlier that morning.

But the anxious wait to discover if she was carrying his baby was even harder when she was back in London and the whole thing seemed like a dream. Tamsyn tried all kinds of coping mechanisms. Just like she'd promised Hannah, she threw herself into her latest job—working in a steam-filled café in one of the tiny back roads near Covent Garden, which was mainly frequented by taxi drivers. It wasn't the best-paid work she'd ever done and it certainly wasn't the most exciting. She suspected it had been called The Greasy Spoon in an ironic sense, though it certainly lived up to is name since no meal was served unless it was swimming in its own pool of oil. But she wasn't going to waste hours hunting for some rewarding position which was never going to materialise. She needed to be *busy*—doing something other than neurotically ticking off the endlessly long days as she waited for her period. She needed to focus on something other than the fact that her first and only lover had not bothered to seek her out—not even to enquire whether she had arrived home safely.

She hated the way she kept glancing at her phone. Even though she hadn't given him her number, hadn't part of her thought—*hoped*—that the Greek tycoon might have somehow tracked her down? It wasn't outside the realms of possibility that he could have asked the Sheikh, was it? But deep down Tamsyn knew she was clutching at straws and it was never going to happen. For a man to go to the trouble of finding you, he had to like you enough to want to see you again. And you certainly didn't have to *like* a woman in order to have sex with her.

But she wasn't going to beat herself up about it. She hadn't planned on being intimate with Xan, but she hadn't planned to be a virgin for ever either. She had been waiting—not for a wedding band, because marriage was something she simply wasn't interested in. No. She had been waiting for someone to make her feel desire—real, bone-melting desire—even though she'd secretly thought it would never happen. Yet it had. Xan Constantinides might not be a keeper, but she wasn't deluded enough to deny that he'd had a profound effect on her.

So she tried to be practical rather than wistful. She would probably see him again at the naming ceremony of Kulal and Hannah's baby, sometime in the not too distant future. And before that happened, she would need to school herself in the art of pretending not to care. If she worked on it hard enough, she might actually have achieved that blissful state by then. Her heart pounded. And if she *was* pregnant, what then? Then the world would look like a very different place.

But then her period arrived and for some inexplicable reason, she cried and cried. But not for long, because she knew tears were a waste of energy. She just carried on getting up every morning and going to work. It was dark when she started and dark when she finished and although spring was just around the corner, the bitter wind was harsh and unremitting.

And then she had one of those days when everything seemed to go wrong. A customer queried his change, causing the sharp-eyed manageress to watch her like a hawk, which made Tamsyn clumsier than usual. Outside, heavy rain was bashing against the window, making the steamed-up café resemble a sauna, and some inane pop quiz was blaring from the radio, the words incomprehensible above the laddish shouts of conversation. She had just muddled up two egg orders and was anticipating the kind of stern lecture which usually preceded being asked to leave a job, when the doorbell tinged and unusually, the whole place became silent.

Tamsyn looked up as a reverential hush fell over the boisterous customers and she had another of those slow motion moments. Because it was Xan. Xan Constantinides was walking into the crowded café and every single eye in the place was fixed on him.

She wasn't surprised. Not just because his costly clothes proclaimed his billionaire status, it was more the sense that he was a super-being—somehow larger than life and more good-looking than anyone had a right to be. His rain-spattered dark overcoat was made of fine cashmere and she doubted whether any other Greasy Spoon customer had ever worn handmade shoes, or moved with such a powerful sense of purpose.

She hated the instinctive ripple of recognition which shivered through her body. Hated the sudden clench of her nipples beneath the manmade fabric of her uniform. He was walking towards her, those cobalt eyes fixed firmly on hers and Tamsyn was doing her best to look at him with the kind of politely questioning smile she would give to any other customer, even though she wanted to spit venom at him. But the manageress was literally elbowing her out of the way, surreptitiously patting the bright red perm which the steam had turned to frizz, her fifty-year-old face filled with the gushing excitement of a schoolgirl as she stepped forward.

'Can I 'elp you, sir?'

Was Xan clued-up enough to realise the power structure which was being acted out in front of him? Was that why he turned the full wattage of his incredible smile on the manageress? Or maybe that's just what came naturally, thought Tamsyn disgustedly. Maybe he used his remarkable charisma as a means to an end, no matter where he was.

'You certainly can,' said Xan, his honeyed Greek accent sounding almost obscenely erotic. 'I was wondering if I might borrow Tamsyn for a little while?'

The woman's smile instantly turned into a grimace. 'She doesn't finish her shift until seven,' she answered unhelpfully.

And that was when Tamsyn piped up—and to hell with the consequences. She stared at Xan, determined not to be affected by the gleam of his gaze as she tried desperately to forget the last time she'd seen that powerful body. Yet how could she forget all that olive-skinned splendour as he'd held her tightly in his arms? Or discount the temporary sanctuary he'd provided as he rocked in and out of her body all night.

And then he had left her. Had walked away as if she didn't exist. Left her open to pain and self-doubt. Was she going to keep coming back for more?

'You can't *borrow* me,' she snapped. 'I'm not a book you take from the library.'

'Tamsyn! I will not have you speaking to a customer like that!' the manageress cut in, revelling in the opportunity to administer a public telling-off.

'Please.' Xan's intervention was smooth. 'It's no problem. I can see you're very busy here and unable to spare her. I'll come back at seven, if that's okay.'

Tamsyn wanted to scream at them to stop talking about her as if she wasn't in the room, because hadn't that been what all those case-workers used to do when they held those interminable meetings to discover why she kept bunking off school? And she wanted her stupid, betraying body to stop reacting to the Greek. She didn't *want* to look at the sensual curve of his lips and be reminded of how it had felt to have him kiss her. 'I'm busy at seven,' she said.

The cobalt eyes narrowed. 'Really?'

'Really.' It was a lie, but Tamsyn didn't care—because surely a small white lie was preferable to doing or saying something you might later regret. And she didn't owe him *anything*.

'Then when are you free?' he persisted.

'I'm not,' Tamsyn answered. 'There's absolutely nothing I want to say to you, Xan. It's over. You made that perfectly clear. So if you'll excuse me—the kitchen has just rung the bell with another order.'

And with that, she marched over to the aluminium serving hatch to pick up the bacon butty which was already growing cold.

CHAPTER SIX

STANDING HUDDLED IN a shop doorway opposite the now dark café, Xan waited for Tamsyn to emerge but it was already ten after seven and still she hadn't shown.

The shop doorway remained defiantly closed and he wondered if perhaps she'd slipped away unseen from the back of the building. He wondered what lengths she would go to in order to avoid him.

He'd imagined...

What?

That she would be deliriously happy to see him, despite him having failed to contact her after their passionate night at the palace? Despite the fact that he'd hired a private jet to get away from Zahristan as quickly as possible the next morning, after leaving her only the briefest of notes, and then had disappeared for the best part of three months?

Yes. That's exactly what he'd imagined because it had happened so often before. Women took whatever crumbs he was prepared to offer them. They were grateful for anything they got and even when they complained it wasn't enough, they still came back for more. He'd meant it when he'd told Tamsyn he wasn't deliberately cruel—despite the tearful accusations sometimes hurled at him in the past. He was just genuinely detached. He'd learnt detachment from the moment he'd left the womb—that was one of the inevitable legacies of having a mother who was so bogged down with self-pity that she barely deigned to notice her child. He never raised hopes unnecessarily, or proceeded with a relationship if the odds were stacked against it. And breaking the heart of his friend's new sister-in-law was never going to be on the cards.

He shouldn't have bedded her in the first place which was why he hadn't hung around the day after the wedding. Why he'd deliberately avoided seeing her and instead gone riding with the Sheikh, who had seemed to have enough problems of his own without Xan adding to them.

He had waited for the dust to settle and his libido to cool and for a short period of time to elapse. Then he had flown out to his beautiful waterfront estate in Argolida on the Peloponnese Peninsula, to begin the future which had been mapped out for him so long ago. There had been several meetings with the young woman he'd once agreed to marry and he had gone through the motions of what was expected of him. It should have been simple, but it had turned out to be anything but. He had stumbled at the first hurdle—he who never stumbled. Failure wasn't a word which featured in his vocabulary and for weeks he had attempted to cajole then scold himself into a state of acceptance—an acceptance which had stubbornly refused to materialise. He'd witnessed Sofia's bewilderment as he struggled to find the right things to say. He had pictured his father's distress when he explained that the marriage was a no-go he should never have agreed to. For the first time in his life he hadn't known which way to turn. If he married Sofia he could not make her happy, but if he walked away—what then? Her pride would be wounded and his family's reputation tarnished.

It had been at the beginning of a conference call with the Sheikh last week that a solution had suddenly occurred to Xan. It wasn't perfect—but then, what in life could be regarded as perfect? But it would suffice. It would have to. And surely it was better than the alternative.

His throat dried as the café door swung open and Tamsyn stepped out into the rainy night and suddenly every thought drained from his mind. Yet why should his heart race like a train when she was dressed so unbecomingly? In her faded jeans and ugly padded jacket, she shouldn't have merited a second glance. But something seemed to happen to his vision whenever Tamsyn Wilson was around and he found himself unable to tear his eyes away from her. It had happened the first time he'd laid eyes on her but it was a whole lot worse now. Was it because, despite her sassiness and outspokenness, she had been an innocent virgin— thus defying all his jaded expectations? He kept replaying that moment when he'd first penetrated her sweet tightness and she'd made that choking little cry, her mouth open and moist as it had sucked helplessly against his shoulder.

Her hair was tied back, her ponytail flowing behind her like a curly red banner, but her face was pale. So pale. From here you couldn't see the freckles which spattered her skin like gold. He found himself remembering the ones which reposed in the soft flesh of her inner thighs. How he had whispered his tongue over them…tantalising and teasing her, before bringing her to yet another jerking orgasm, which had left her shuddering against his mouth.

He began to walk towards her, aided by the red gleam of the traffic lights which was reflecting off the wet road like spilled blood. And then she saw him, her eyes first widening and then narrowing as she put her head down and increased her speed and Xan felt a flicker of excitement as he realised she was trying to get away from him, just like she'd done at the palace. Did she really think she would outpace him? Didn't she realise he'd seen the yearning look of hunger in her eyes when he'd walked into that steamy café, and it had echoed the hunger in him?

'Tamsyn!'

'Can't you take a hint?' she shouted back over her shoulder. 'Just go *away*, Xan!'

She didn't slow down as he followed her along the wet pavement but he caught her up easily enough, his long strides easily outperforming her small, rapid steps. 'We need to talk,' he said, as he caught up with her.

She stopped then. Lifted up her chin to glare at him and the raindrops glistened like diamonds on her freckled skin as she stood beneath the golden flare of the streetlamp.

'But that's where you're wrong!' she contradicted fervently. 'We don't *need* to do anything. Why would we when there's nothing between us? Didn't you make it plain that's what you wanted when you slipped out of bed that morning, taking great care not to wake me?'

'Why?' he parried softly. 'Did you want there to be something between us?'

'In your dreams!' she declared. 'Even if I did want to get involved with a man—which I don't—you're the last person on the planet I'd ever choose! I already told you that.'

A low sigh of relief escaped from his lips and some of the tension left him. 'That's probably the best news I've heard all week,' he said. 'And yet another reason why we need to have a conversation.'

Tamsyn steeled herself against the sexy dip in his voice, brushing the rain away from her cheeks with an impatient fist. 'You just don't get it, do you?' she hissed. 'I'm not interested in what you've got to say, Xan. I've just been sacked and it's all your fault.'

His eyebrows shot up. '*My* fault?'

'Yes! If you hadn't come into the cafe—swaggering around the place as if you owned it and demanding I take a break I wasn't entitled to—then I'd still have a job. Your attitude made me so angry so that I answered you back, giving that witch of a manageress the ideal opportunity to tell me not to bother coming back tomorrow.'

'So that's the only reason you were fired?' he questioned slowly.

Tamsyn told herself she didn't have to answer. That she owed him nothing—and certainly not an explanation. Yet it was difficult to withstand the perceptive gleam in his eyes or not to be affected by the sudden understanding that since Hannah had gone away to live in the desert, she really *was* on her own. That once again she was jobless, with nobody to turn to—with outstanding rent to pay on her overpriced bedsit. Giving a suddenly deflated sigh, she shrugged, all the energy needed to maintain the fiction of her life suddenly draining away. 'Not the only reason, no,' she agreed reluctantly. 'I guess I'm fundamentally unsuited to being a waitress.'

Beneath the streetlight, his eyes gleamed. 'All the more reason for you to have dinner with me, since I have a proposition to put to you which you might find interesting.'

The suggestion was so unexpected that Tamsyn blinked. 'What sort of proposition?'

Tiny droplets of rain flew like diamonds from the tangle of his ebony hair as he shook his head. 'This isn't a conversation to have in the rain. Let's find a restaurant where we can talk.'

Her stomach chose that moment to make an angry little rumble and Tamsyn realised she hadn't eaten since breakfast. She told herself it was hunger which made her consider his suggestion—it definitely wasn't because she was reluctant to see him walk out of her life for a second time. But then she looked at her damp jeans and realised what a mess she looked. 'I can't possibly go out looking like this.'

'You could go home first and get changed.' He gave a small inclination of his head. 'I have a car here.'

Tamsyn stiffened as a black limousine began to drive slowly towards them. Was he out of his mind? Did he really think she'd let someone like him within a mile of her scrubby little bedsit? She could just imagine the shock on his over-privileged face if he caught sight of the damp walls and the electric kettle which was covered in lime-scale. 'I live miles away.'

'Then let's just go to the Granchester.'

Tamsyn nearly choked as he casually mentioned the exclusive hotel where her sister used to work before being fired for sleeping with one of the guests. 'The Granchester is just about the most expensive hotel in London,' she objected. 'We'll never be able to get a table at this short notice, and even if we could there's no way I could go somewhere like that for dinner, wearing this.'

'Oh, we'll a get a table,' he said smoothly, as the limousine drew up beside them. 'And my cousin's wife Emma is staying there at the moment. You look about the same size as her. She'll lend you something to wear.'

Tamsyn shook her head. 'Don't be so ridiculous. I can't possibly borrow a dress from a complete stranger!'

'Of course you can.' He spoke with the confidence of someone unused to being thwarted, as he opened the door of the car and gently pushed her inside. 'Don't worry. I'll fix it.'

Afterwards Tamsyn would put her uncharacteristic compliance down to his distracting presence, or maybe it was just his sheer *certainty*. She'd never experienced the sensation of a man taking control of a situation in such an unflappable way. She wasn't used to someone offering to *fix* things. She was used to drama and chaos. She wondered if there was some biological chink in her armour which made her yield to his superior strength, or whether she'd just had the stuffing knocked out of her by the loss of yet another job? Either way, she found herself climbing into the back of the taxi with Xan sliding next to her as they began to drive at speed through the rain, towards the Granchester.

The rain-blurred lights of the city passed in a streak while Xan made a phone call. She heard him say her name as he began speaking in rapid Greek, before laughing at something the person on the end of the line must have said. And it was the laugh which made Tamsyn's heart clench with unexpected wistfulness. Imagine living the kind of life where you could just jump into the back of a limousine without worrying about the cost, and laugh so uninhibitedly as you chatted on the phone—as if you didn't have a care in the world.

Like a glittering citadel, the Granchester Hotel rose up before them and as the car slid to a halt, a doorman sprang forward to greet Xan like an old friend. The flower-filled foyer was busy as expensively dressed guests milled around, looking as if they had somewhere important to go. A woman was walking purposefully towards them, one of the most beautiful women Tamsyn had ever seen. Slim and smiling, her hair was as pale as moonlight and she was wearing a short blue dress which hugged her hips and a tiny cardigan just a shade darker.

'Xan!' she said fondly, rising up on the toes of her ballet pumps to kiss the Greek tycoon on both cheeks, before turning to Tamsyn with a wide smile. 'And you must be Tamsyn,' she said. 'I'm Emma and I'm married to Xan's cousin. I gather you need something to wear for dinner tonight and time is tight—so why don't you come with me and I can sort you something out?'

It was weird—maybe because Emma was so polite and so...*gracious*—that Tamsyn didn't find herself frozen by her usual air of suspicion. Instead, she smiled back and the three of them walked over to an elevator which nobody else seemed to be using. And of course, the presence of Emma in the enclosed space meant that Tamsyn's conversation with Xan was temporarily interrupted, although she couldn't help but be acutely aware of his presence and the mocking light in his eyes. What on earth have I got myself into? she wondered as the elevator slid to a silent halt and they stepped directly into an enormous room whose wall to ceiling windows gave a stunning view over the glittering skyscrapers of London.

'Xan, why don't you help yourself to a drink?' Emma gave another soft smile. 'Tamsyn, come with me.'

In a dream-like state, Tamsyn followed the elegant blonde down a long corridor and into a dressing room which led off from an huge bedroom. Maybe if she hadn't just lost her job for the umpteenth time and maybe if the image of her tiny bedsit hadn't just flashed into her mind, then she might have told Emma she'd changed her mind, thanked her for her kind offer and just left. Xan might be keen to put some mysterious 'proposition' to her, but despite what she suspected was his tendency to always get his own way—she doubted whether he would actually try to keep her here by force.

But she didn't do any of those things. Perhaps it was the blonde's serene presence or just the fact that Tamsyn was tired. Bone tired. As if she could sleep for a hundred years and then maybe a hundred more. So she nodded politely as Emma ran her perfectly manicured fingernails—a deep shade of blue which matched her cardigan—along a line of colour-co-ordinated clothes hanging in the biggest closet Tamsyn had ever seen.

'I'm not going to stand over you and influence your choice,' she told Tamsyn softly. 'Just wear whatever takes your fancy—and that includes shoes, if they fit. I'll go and entertain your man and see you back in the sitting room.'

Mutely, Tamsyn nodded. She wanted to tell Emma that Xan wasn't her anything but surely that was an over-complicating factor and things were complicated enough already. Her heart was racing as she quickly washed in the en-suite bathroom before slithering into a long-sleeved dress in green cashmere which she cinched in at the waist with a belt. Her tiny feet swam like boats in tall Emma's sleek footwear so she packed the toes of some green suede shoes with wads of tissue paper. Liberating her curls from their elastic band, she raked a comb through them in a vain attempt to tame them and, tucking her own damp clothes under her arm, walked back towards the sitting room.

She was surprised to hear Emma speaking in Greek to Xan, but the conversation died away as she walked into the massive room. She couldn't deny the inordinate amount of pleasure she took from the look of disbelief on Xan's face as slowly he looked her up and down. It reminded her that she really *could* scrub up well—even if she had to rely on the charity of other people in order to do so.

The tycoon was rising to his feet, dominating the room with his powerful presence, a faint smile curving his lips. 'I've told Emma we have a table booked downstairs.'

It seemed almost rude to just *use* the kind blonde's

apartment like some kind of upmarket changing room, but Emma was also getting to her feet, giving Tamsyn another genuine smile which made her feel momentarily disconcerted.

'And Zac is just flying in from Zurich,' she said, her cheeks growing pink with pleasure. 'Where it appears that my husband has bought yet another hotel.'

It was only then that Tamsyn made the connection and she wondered how she could have been so dense. Emma was married to Zac Constantinides—the billionaire owner of the Granchester group of luxury hotels and Zac was Xan's *cousin*? Why hadn't Hannah reminded her of that? As the lift zoomed them back down to the hotel foyer, she wondered why she hadn't made the link herself, when it wasn't exactly the most common surname in the world. Probably because her mind and her body had been so full of new and conflicting emotions. And they still were. Surreptitiously, she touched her tongue to lips which were as dry as washing hung out in the sun, achingly aware that she was far from immune to the statuesque man who walked beside her.

They were shown into Garden Room, which overlooked an outdoor space which was surprisingly big, given its central London location. A discreet notice on the wall informed customers that the gardens had recently won a top horticultural award and although it was dark outside, cleverly placed lighting illuminated the tall shrubs and rare trees. As the maître d' showed them to what was obviously the best table—tucked away in a corner but with a birds-eye view of the floodlit gardens—Tamsyn became aware of people watching them. Or rather, they were watching Xan.

Did he realise that, or was his sense of self-worth so strong that he didn't notice?

'So why have you brought me here?' she questioned as she sat down to face a gleam of silver and crystal, tightening her hands as she laid them down on the snowy linen tablecloth. 'And more importantly, why have I *let* you?'

He paused for a moment while the waiter handed them menus, a wry smile touching the edges of his lips. 'Because we have been lovers and because you're curious.'

She gave a defiant tilt of her chin. 'I don't usually let people move me around like I'm a chip on the gaming table.'

'I get that. Just as I don't usually rush in and mastermind a transformation scene for my dinner dates,' he added drily, flicking her a cool cobalt gaze. 'You look absolutely sensational in that dress, by the way.'

Stupidly, the compliment made her want to squirm with pleasure until Tamsyn reminded herself that she still didn't know why she was here. But he was right. She *was* curious.

'So what do you want to talk about?'

'Why don't we choose what we want to eat first, otherwise the waiter will keep hovering over us.' He glanced at the menu before fixing her with his dark blue gaze. 'Would you like me to order for you?'

Tamsyn glared. Did he think she was so poor and humble that she'd couldn't interpret the French menu? Didn't he realise she'd worked in more fancy restaurants than he'd probably had hot dinners? She was sorely tempted to tell him she'd changed her mind, when she spotted something being lit with blue flames on a nearby table. Something delicious enough to make her mouth water and once again she was reminded that it was ages since she'd eaten.

'I'll have the lobster thermidor and the green salad with vinaigrette on the side,' she said carelessly. 'And no wine—just sparkling water.'

She enjoyed his faint look of surprise as he slapped his own menu shut and handed it to the waiter. 'I'll have the same,' he said, leaning back in his chair to study her.

'So,' she said, when he appeared in no hurry to break the silence. 'I'm still waiting for some sort of explanation. I mean, you've been content to ignore me for weeks and then you just turn up out of the blue and bring me here with the offer of some mystery proposition. What is it, Xan? Do you happen to own a café with an opening for a waitress who urgently needs a job?'

Xan realised that he was going to have to exercise great care in his choice of words because Tamsyn Wilson was both volatile and unpredictable. In a way she was the worst possible candidate for what he had in mind, but ironically it was her very unsuitability which made her the ideal candidate.

'You're in a bit of a fix right now aren't you, Tamsyn?' he questioned softly.

Her emerald eyes narrowed suspiciously. 'How do you know that?'

He shrugged. 'Call it intuition or call it observation. You seem to switch jobs quite frequently and being fired doesn't seem to freak you out as much as it would some people.' His gaze stayed fixed on her face. 'And I noticed you had a hole in your coat.'

She blushed and seemed to hesitate. As if wondering whether or not to brazen things out and keep pretending that, apart from urgently needing a job—everything else was okay. But the strain around her eyes told him that her plight was chronic and maybe she realised that, because some of her defiance seemed to ebb away as she lifted her shoulders in a shrug which didn't quite come off.

'I've known better times,' she admitted.

'But your sister has just married one of the wealthiest men in the world,' he probed. 'Surely she can come to your rescue if you're in need of money.'

For the first time he saw emotion on her face. Real emotion. Was it pride or distress which made her lips tremble like that? 'I'm not going to ask Hannah for help,' she said fiercely. 'She's helped me too often in the past and it's about time I stood on my own two feet.'

Xan nodded, realising that her misplaced pride was playing right into his hands. 'Then I think I can help you,' he said quietly. 'Or rather, I think we can help each other.'

She had recovered from her brief spell of vulnerability and that familiar challenge was back in her eyes. 'Me, help the powerful Xan Constantinides? Gosh. I can't imagine how I would do that.'

Xan paused for a moment because even though they meant nothing, the words he was about to say still had the power to make him tense. He'd had a blueprint for his life and up until now it had all gone according to plan, for he had micro-managed and controlled every part of it. It was how he had won a straight scholarship to Harvard from a humble village school and made a fortune in the property market, soon after graduating. He'd thought of matrimony to Sofia as just another stage in his game plan, but suddenly all that had changed. Suddenly he could understand why they called it wed*lock*. His eyes didn't leave Tamsyn's face.

'By marrying me,' he said.

CHAPTER SEVEN

XAN HAD NEVER seen anyone look so startled. Across the restaurant table, he watched Tamsyn's lips open and the pink tip of her tongue reminded him of the erotic pathways it had traced over his sweat-sheened skin. He shifted his weight a little and swallowed, because Tamsyn Wilson had given him more orgasms in a few short hours than any other woman—so many he'd lost count, and a man never forgot something like that.

The hardness in his groin increased, because didn't his current dilemma provide him with the perfect opportunity to feast on her delectable body once more? He hadn't pursued the affair not just because she was Kulal's new sister-in-law but because she had an inner wildness which made him uneasy—a wildness he had responded to in a way he didn't quite trust. Because something about her fire and her spirit had made him ignore his instinct to take her to bed in the first place. And ignoring his instincts had made him feel as if control was slipping away from him, which he didn't like. He didn't like it at all.

'Did you really just ask me to marry you?' she was saying, her green eyes unnaturally bright in the flicker of the candlelight.

'You want me to repeat it for you?' he drawled.

He was curious to see what her reaction would be, because that would colour his future behaviour towards her. If she looked as if he was about to present her with the moon on a platter and make her every dream come true, then he would have to be wary. But if, as he suspected—she cared as little for him as he did for her—there was no reason why they couldn't both enjoy what he had in mind.

But there was no sign of longing or triumph on her freckled face. Her green eyes were as suspicious as they'd been before. And Xan couldn't deny a brief kick of incredulity, for he was used to women making no secret of their adoration for him.

'Is this some kind of bad joke?' she was demanding. 'Have you had a bet with someone to see how much of a sucker I can be?'

He shook his head. 'I have often been described as difficult, but I am never knowingly cruel.'

There was a trace of uncertainty in her demeanour now. He could see her computing his words and failing to make sense of them.

She waited until the waiter had deposited their food in front of them before raising her eyebrows. 'So, why? I mean, why do you want to marry *me*? Did it take you all this time to realise that you can't possibly live without me and the only way to guarantee having me for the rest of your life is to slip a wedding ring on my finger?'

He stiffened before detecting sarcasm. 'Hardly,' he said.

She picked up her fork and hungrily began to eat. 'So why?'

Xan sucked in a long breath. Explanations he found

difficult. Almost as difficult as intimacy. It was in his nature to keep his thoughts and feelings to himself—or maybe that was just the way he'd been raised. His mother had been indifferent towards him and his father had been too busy trying to claw back his land and his heritage, to have any time for his only son. Either way, Xan had never let anyone close enough to worry about whether or not he trusted them. Yet to some extent he was going to *have* to trust Tamsyn Wilson if she agreed to his plan. And wouldn't that give her power over him? He swallowed, recognising that if he didn't want her abusing that power, he was going to have to reward her very handsomely.

'How much do you know about me?' he demanded.

She dabbed at her lips but the large linen napkin failed to hide her smile. 'You think I was so obsessed after our night in Zahristan that I hunted around to find out everything I could?'

'I don't know.' He sent her a look of challenge. 'Did you?'

'Funnily enough, no. I've had enough experience of lost causes to know when to quit. I certainly didn't waste any time mooning over someone who couldn't wait to get away from me. What do I know about you? Let me see.' She began to tap each finger, as if counting off the facts. 'Basically, you're loaded—my friend Ellie told me you were born mega-rich, though I think I could have worked that out for myself judging by your fancy suits and your swagger. My sister mentioned you were a hugely successful businessman—oh, and you're arrogant. I didn't need anyone to tell me that since that's a quality you seem to have in abundance.'

An unexpected smile touched the edges of Xan's lips. Clearly he wasn't going to have to worry about Tamsyn Wilson putting him on a pedestal!

'Anything else?' he questioned sardonically.

She shrugged. 'You don't seem as if you like me very much and yet now you're asking me to marry you?' She shook her red curls and scooped up another forkful of lobster. 'Forgive me if I sound confused—it's because I am.'

Discreetly, Xan gestured to the Sommelier, who returned moments later bearing a dusty bottle. A dark red liquid was dispensed into his glass and when Tamsyn shook her head in reply to the silent question in his eyes, he took a sip of the wine before continuing.

'There are only two things you need to know about me, Tamsyn,' he said. 'The first is that I believe there is no problem on this earth you can't buy your way out of, and the second is that there is a woman in Greece to whom I have been unofficially betrothed for many years.' He paused. 'Except I've realised that I cannot go through with it. I cannot marry her.'

He saw her eyes darken in distress. Saw the brief stabbing of her teeth into her lower lip before she displayed her more habitual air of nonchalance. 'Then don't. Just tell her. Dump her as comprehensively as you dumped me. She might be a bit upset but I should think one day she'll be grateful she isn't stuck with a misogynist like you for a lifetime. What's the problem, Xan? Has she found out you were sleeping with me—and maybe others—behind her back? Has she gone on the warpath in the way that only a jealous woman can?'

Angrily, Xan slammed his glass down on the table.

'Just for the record, I haven't had sex with anyone since the night I spent with you and I certainly haven't had sex with Sofia,' he growled. 'It's not that kind of relationship.'

At this, she put her fork down and the look she gave him was cynical. 'Let me guess,' she said tiredly. 'You play around and have your fun with women like me, is that right? And in the meantime there's a pure young virgin back home in Greece, just waiting for you? The age-old double standard of which so many men are guilty?'

Once again her perception startled him and she must have read the confirmation in his face because he could see her pushing her chair back as if preparing to walk out.

'You're disgusting!' she flared.

'Don't go,' he said urgently as he leant across the table towards her. 'Hear me out first. Please, Tamsyn.'

His words seemed to startle her but not nearly as much as they startled him because making pleas wasn't something he did very often. Had he thought she would be instantly malleable? So impressed by this introduction to a very different and glamorous kind of world, that she would leap at whatever he asked of her? Yes, he probably had thought exactly that. His lips flattened. How wrong he had been.

'What's there to hear?' she demanded.

'You said I was born wealthy but that certainly wasn't the case.'

'You mean you were born poor?' she questioned disbelievingly.

'Not poor but something in between. What is it they say? Asset rich, cash poor.' He met the question in her eyes and shrugged. 'My father inherited an island, a very beautiful island, called Prassakri. He was born there. Grew up there. Generations of his family lived and died there.' His voice tailed off as he recalled the story of how fortunes could wax, then wane without warning. 'Once many people inhabited that place, with enough work for all but gradually the work dried up and the young men began to leave, my father among them. Fortunately he had enough money to buy agricultural land on the mainland in Thessaly and for a while he was successful. But then came the drought, the worst drought the region had ever seen...'

His paused for a moment and she sat forward, genuine interest lighting up her freckled face. 'Go on,' she urged.

He grimaced. 'My father lost everything. And more. What the drought and resultant fires didn't take, bad investments soon took care of the rest. From being affluent, suddenly there wasn't enough food on the table. My mother took it badly.'

'How badly?' she questioned, her eyes narrowing.

'Badly enough.' He shut down her question sharply. Because he'd never talked about this with anyone. There hadn't really been the need to resurrect the pain and the discontent. Until now. 'The atmosphere of blame and recrimination in the house was unbearable,' he remembered suddenly, as he recalled walking into the house and seeing his mother's cold face and icy demeanour. 'My father was forced to sell the island to a neighbour and although it broke his heart to do so, he vowed that one day he would buy it back, because the bones of his ancestors are buried on that island and that means a great deal to a Greek.'

He took another mouthful of wine. 'Soon after that, land prices began rocketing and the purchase of Greek islands became beyond of the reach of most people. I could see my father's increasing powerlessness as he sensed the opportunity to buy back Prassakri slipping away from him. But his neighbour had a daughter—an only daughter—who just happened to be very beautiful. And I had just won a scholarship to an American college. It was a pretty big deal at the time and I was seen as someone who would one day make good. And that was when the neighbour made my father the offer.'

'What offer?' she breathed, her green eyes huge, her expression rapt.

'That if I were to marry Sofia, then he would allow my father to buy back the island at the original price.'

'And you agreed?' she breathed.

The facts when recounted now sounded like an extreme reaction but Xan recalled vividly that the offer had made perfect sense at the time. Hadn't he agreed in an attempt to bring about some sort of peace to his damaged family? To stop his mother haranguing his father with her bitter lament? *I didn't marry you in order to end up a pauper.'*

'I was nineteen,' he said harshly. 'And it didn't seem real at the time. Sofia was a sweet young girl who would make any man a good wife, and if it meant the end to my father's heartache, then why wouldn't I agree? With one stroke I could restore the pride which was so important to him and maybe stop my mother from withdrawing more and more.'

'Yes, I know—but even so.' Sitting back in her chair with her hair looking like living flame in the candlelight, she threw him a perplexed look. 'It seems very extreme.'

'To be honest, I thought that Sofia would back out of the offer before I did,' he said, he said with a shrug. 'That she would fall in love and want to marry someone else.'

'But that didn't happen?'

'No.' He shook his head. 'It didn't happen. I tried to convince myself that arranged marriages work in many countries. That we share a common language and upbringing. And as time went on I found it a useful deterrent to the ambitions of other women, knowing I had an arranged marriage bubbling quietly away in the background and therefore was not in a position to offer them anything.'

'But you're a modern Greek! This sounds positively archaic.'

'I am not so modern as I might appear on the surface, Tamsyn.' His voice grew silky as he corrected her. 'At heart I have many values which some might consider old-fashioned.'

At this she screwed up her face, but not before he had seen the brief shiver rippling over her skin. Was she remembering how it had been between them in bed that night? When he'd experienced an almost *primitive* pleasure as he had broken through the tight barrier of her hymen and given an exultant shout of joy? No, he had been anything but modern that night.

'And what about love?' she challenged. 'Isn't that supposed to lie at the foundation of every marriage?'

His laugh was bitter but at least now he was on familiar territory. 'Not for me, Tamsyn. Only fools buy into romantic love.'

For the first time since they'd started this extraordinary conversation Tamsyn experienced a moment of real connection as she recognised a sentiment which was all too familiar. She thought about her feckless mother and the way she'd hocked up with all those different men. Hadn't that been why she and Hannah had been left abandoned and taken in by a pair of dysfunctional foster parents—because their mother had fallen *in love* for the umpteenth time? 'Well, that's one thing we do have in common,' she said. 'Since I feel exactly the same.'

He gave a cynical laugh. 'You actually say that like you mean it.'

'Why, do people normally say things just to please you?''

'Something like that,' he agreed.

Tamsyn wondered what it must be like if everyone was tiptoeing around you all the time. Was that what made him so sure of himself? 'So what's the problem?' she questioned. 'It sounds like the perfect solution. You've played the field and now you're settling down. A practical union between two people who know exactly where the boundaries lie.'

'And that's exactly what I thought—until the theory became reality and I realised there was no way I could marry Sofia.' He met the question in her green eyes. ' Oh, she's still a nice enough woman, but she is not my type Most of all, I do not desire her.' His voice hardened. 'And there can be no marriage without desire.' There was a long pause. 'Which is where you come in,' he added, breaking into her unsettled contemplation.

She narrowed her eyes. 'How?'

'I don't want to hurt Sofia or tarnish her reputation by telling her I don't want her. If I do that there's no way her father will sell back the island, even if I offer him double what it's worth by today's values.' Cobalt eyes bored into her. 'But an acceptable way of breaking off the engagement is to explain that I've fallen in love with someone else and am planning to marry her instead. Which will allow Sofia the chance to walk away with her pride intact.'

'You mean a fake marriage?' Tamsyn frowned. 'Like fake news?'

'A temporary marriage,' he amended drily. 'With a very generous divorce settlement at the end of it. Sofia gets a dignified let-out clause. I get to buy the island and you end up with a hefty pay-out. This could make you a very wealthy woman, Tamsyn. You could have the kind of lifestyle most people only dream of.'

Tamsyn stared at him, trying not to be swayed by the thought of all that money—but for someone who'd always lived hand-to-mouth, that was easier said than done. She thought about not having to watch every single penny. About being able to buy clothes which didn't come from the local market, or thrift store. She thought about having food in the fridge which wasn't past its sell-by date. Being able to take buses instead of walking all the time. Yes, it was tempting—but not tempting enough. Didn't Xan's arrogant certainty that there was no problem money couldn't solve make her want to reject his offer? Because she wasn't some *commodity*. She shook her curls. 'Go and ask someone else,' she said coldly. 'There must be loads more suitable candidates who would happily masquerade as your wife.'

'Oh, there are,' he agreed benignly. 'But that's the whole point. You are so eminently *unsuitable* that everyone will believe it's true love.'

His words hurt. Of course they did. Tamsyn might have always thought of herself as someone who didn't conform. Who swam against the tide. But considering yourself a bit of a rebel was very different to the man who'd been your first lover, saying you were the most unsuitable person he could think of to marry. Her heart clenched with pain and this time she really *did* want to get up from that pristine white table. In a parallel universe—she might have upended it, letting the crystal and the silver cutlery cascade to the floor in a satisfying cacophony of sound. But she'd tried that kind of approach with him once before and all it had done was made her look stupid.

And something was keeping her rooted to her seat. She tried telling herself she should wait to see how much he was offering in return for accepting his extraordinary proposal, but deep down Tamsyn knew it was more than that. He was right. She *was* curious.

'So why didn't you fancy her?' she questioned, like someone determined to rub salt into an already raw wound. As if by hurting herself, it meant nobody else would be able to. 'If she's so beautiful?'

Xan stared at his lobster which had already congealed on his plate. There was no need to explain that somehow, Tamsyn Wilson made every other woman look almost *tame* in comparison. That he hadn't been able to shift the stubborn memory of how her skin had tasted or how it had felt to have her legs wrapped around his thrusting hips. Why flatter her with the knowledge that she was the fire which made every other woman seem like a mere flicker? He swallowed. That kind of information was irrelevant.

'Chemistry is intangible,' he said roughly. 'It's not like a shopping list you just tick off as you go along.'

For the first time during the entire conversation, she smiled. 'You do a lot of shopping do you Xan?' she questioned. 'Somehow I can't really imagine you pushing a trolley round the supermarket,. I've certainly never see anyone like you when I'm stacking the shelves.'

Xan was unable to stop the brief curving of his lips in response. 'I buy cars and planes and works of art. The purchase of food I leave to my housekeeper. But you're trying to change the subject, Tamsyn. Is that because you find my suggestion unpalatable?' he said softly.

Tamsyn shrugged. She wasn't sure *how* she felt. About anything. Something told her to walk away while she still could, but she couldn't deny that the delicious food had lulled her into a state of sluggishness. And wasn't Xan's powerful presence only adding to her languor? Wasn't she stupidly reluctant to turn her back and never see him again? 'It's a crazy idea,' she said weakly.

He leaned forward as if sensing a window of opportunity and suddenly she could see why he was such a successful businessman.

'Imagine no longer having to work unless you wanted to. You could go back to school—you are an intelligent woman,' he said, his Greek accent dipping into a sultry caress. 'Imagine being able to live somewhere which isn't a...

Tamsyn's shoulders stiffened as tactfully, his words faded away. 'Isn't a *what*?'

'It doesn't matter,' he said.

Somehow his careful diplomacy was more insulting than if he'd come right out and told her she lived in a slum. 'Of course it does! It matters to me. How the hell do you know where I live anyway?'

He gave her an odd kind of look. 'I had you checked out, of course.'

'You had me checked out,' she repeated slowly. 'By who?'

'There are people on my payroll who can find out almost anything. How else do you think I knew where you worked, Tamsyn?'

'I just assumed... I thought you might have asked the Sheikh.'

'No.' He shook his dark head. 'Kulal and Hannah know nothing about this.'

It was the mention of her sister's name which startled Tamsyn out of her lazy stupor. She had been about to tell Xan exactly what he could do with his offer— without letting him know how much he'd managed to hurt her. She would have told him that she mightn't have a job right now, but she would find one soon enough. She always did. Because one of the advantages of casual labour meant there were always vacancies for women like her. Women who had slipped through the net at school and at home. Who'd never had the comfort of regular meals or someone gently nagging at them to do their homework. She would get by because although she might not have any formal qualifications to her name, she was a graduate from the School of Survival. You didn't sleep in a room with winter frost inside the windows listening to sounds of arguments bouncing off the thin walls next door, without developing a tough exterior.

But what about Hannah? Her sister was in an entirely different situation. She might now be the wife of the world's richest men but that didn't necessarily mean she was safe. When she'd been in Zahristan for the wedding, Tamsyn had sensed all was not well in the new marriage. How could it be—when it had taken place between a powerful sheikh and someone as humble as Hannah? They had married because Hannah had been pregnant with the Sheikh's baby—but what if Kulal had only married her sister to get some kind of legal hold over his offspring? The Sheikh had all the power now that he had married her, didn't he? While Hannah had none. Not really. She might be the new Queen of a powerful desert region but she couldn't even speak the language of her adopted home.

Tamsyn folded up her napkin and placed it neatly on the table beside her empty plate. What if she agreed to Xan's crazy proposal, but on *her* terms? What if she demanded a whole load of money—more even than he'd probably contemplated giving her? Enough to bail out her sister, should the need ever arise. Wouldn't it be beyond fabulous to have enough cash to buy Hannah and her baby airline tickets out of Zahristan, if marriage to Kulal should prove intolerable? To give her a wad of that same cash to purchase a bolthole somewhere? Wouldn't it *mean* something to be able to do that—especially after everything her sister had done for her when they'd been growing up? To redress the balance a little. Even though...

Tamsyn swallowed down the suddenly acrid taste in her mouth.

Even though Hannah had been the reason Tamsyn had never met her father and it had taken her a long time to forgive her for that...

She looked up to find Xan watching her closely, the way she imagined a policeman might scrutinise a suspect from behind a piece of two-way glass. Well, he certainly wouldn't be able to read very much from *her* expression! Hadn't she spent all her formative years hiding her emotions behind the blasé mask she presented to the world?

'How long would this marriage last?'

'Not long. Three months should suffice. Any less than that and it will look like a stunt.'

She nodded. 'And how much money are you prepared to offer me?'

She saw him flinch—but that didn't surprise her either. Rich people never wanted to talk about money. They thought it was vulgar. Beneath them. Had Xan forgotten was it like to be poor, she wondered? Was that something else he'd blocked from his mind—like an agreement made by a teenage boy to marry a woman so his father could claw back an important piece of land?

'How much did you have in mind?' he questioned.

Her birth father had taught her everything she needed to know about desertion and rejection while her foster father's life lessons had been about infidelity and gambling. No wonder she distrusted men so much. But some of those lessons had been useful. She'd overheard enough bluster around card games to realise that you had to start high and be prepared to be knocked down whenever you were bargaining for something. So she mentioned an outrageous sum of money, prepared for yet slightly shamed by the brief look of contempt which hardened Xan's cobalt eyes. But it was gone almost immediately, because he nodded his head.

'Okay,' he said.

She blinked in disbelief. 'Just like that?'

He shrugged. 'You clearly want it. I can afford it. And obviously, the more I am prepared to pay—the more I get out of our brief union.'

The silky inference behind his drawled words made Tamsyn's stomach clench with anger. And something else. Something far more potent than anger. Because at times during his story she had wanted to reach out to him. To comfort him? Or to kiss him? Or both. Maybe both. Especially when his face had grown hard and hurt when he'd mentioned his mother. She could feel her breasts pushing against the fine wool of the cashmere dress as she directed him a heated look, forcing herself to be bold enough to ask the question. 'You think I'm going to have *sex* with you?'

'That's a pretty naive question, Tamsyn,' he answered softly. 'Why wouldn't I? We've had sex before and it was good. Very, very good.' He raised his eyebrows. 'And isn't it a very necessary part of the marriage contract?

There was a pause during which Tamsyn steeled herself against the shocking beauty of his face and her own even more shocking reaction to him…the heat of excitement in her blood and the soft throb of hunger between her legs. But somehow, using the kind of resilience which every abandoned child needed in order to survive, she managed to present to him a face devoid of expression. 'Not in this case, because it's only make-believe,' she said coolly. 'I'll marry you because I want your money. But it's nothing but a business arrangement and there's no way I'm being intimate with you again, Xan. Because it wouldn't be right. Not after everything that's happened.'

CHAPTER EIGHT

SOMEHOW THE FLOWERS woven into her hair stayed in
place, even though the sea breeze was whipping wildly
all around her. Tamsyn guessed that was one of the
benefits of marrying a billionaire—that he could afford to pay a top hairdresser to tame his prospective
wife's unruly curls into an elaborate style which had
miraculously stayed put all day. She clutched the rail-
ings of Xan's luxury yacht as it skimmed through the
sapphire waters, trying to get her head around the
fact that she was now the Greek tycoon's wife, and
that the shiny golden ring which glinted on her finger was for real.

Well, as real as a fake wedding would allow.

Determined not to let herself be led like a lamb
to the slaughter on her wedding day, she'd stated her
terms before the ceremony, insisting she didn't want
a big fuss—opting instead for something low-key and
pared down. She thought it would have felt *cheap* to
put on a big public show which meant nothing, and
there was no way she could have made hollow vows
in a place of worship. Most important of all, she didn't
want Hannah hearing about the marriage until it was
over, just in case she decided to do something dramatic

like arriving in a flurry of royal pomp to try and talk her out of it.

But keeping their nuptials quiet seemed to have appealed to Xan as well and in a quiet moment he'd admitted that he had no stomach for weddings in general and his own in particular.

'The details will be posted in the local town hall which is a requirement by law,' he said. 'But since the mayor is a friend, our privacy will be respected and there's no way word will get out to the press. At least, not until I am ready to issue a statement.' A hard glimmer of a smile had followed. 'And it adds a little passionate *authenticity* to our whirlwind romance if we keep it all very hush-hush don't you think, *agape mou*?

What Tamsyn thought wasn't really here nor there. It bothered her that Xan seemed to be almost *relishing* the clandestine nature of the wedding, until she forced herself to remember that most men enjoyed secrecy. This was nothing but an elaborate game to Xan, she reminded herself, and since they weren't planning to be married for very long, what was the point in objecting?

'We will have a big party straight after the honeymoon,' Xan had informed her the day after she'd accepted his proposal, when he had turned up unexpectedly at her tiny bedsit, his lips curving with distaste as he looked around, before announcing that from then on she would be staying at the Granchester until the wedding. 'A big, lavish party to which we will invite family and close friends, and announce that we are man and wife.'

'And Sofia?' Tamsyn's voice had asked, wondering how the Greek woman who had been Xan's bride intended would take the sudden news. 'When are you planning to tell her?'

'I will phone her after the ceremony, once I've spoken to my father.'

Something about the obvious omission made her tentatively ask the question. 'And what about…your mother?'

She had never seen his face so expressionless. As if it had been wiped clean of all feeling—his features looking as if they had been hewn from some dark and impenetrable marble. 'My mother died a decade ago.'

'Oh, Xan, I'm sorry.'

It had been an instinctive condolence on her part but he hadn't wanted it, cutting short the conversation with a cool determination she had come to recognise as Xan's way of doing things. And in a way she could understand his reluctance to talk. She didn't want to him delving into *her* past, did she? Didn't want him probing her own areas of painful memory. Why rake all that up, when this was a relationship which was never intended to last?

'But do you think Sofia will be upset?' she had persisted. 'The last thing I want is to cause another woman pain.'

His mouth had hardened. 'Let's hope not. Maybe she will have realised that she's better off without a man like me,' he'd added, his voice growing harsh. 'A man who cannot give her the love she deserves.'

Recalling those words, it was difficult for Tamsyn not to conclude that he considered her somehow unworthy of those things. In Xan's mind she was greedy and acquisitive. He thought of her as a gold-digger, just like her sister—she knew that. And although it wasn't necessary for him to have a high opinion of her, she couldn't deny it hurt that he thought so little of her.

They had married in a tiny ceremony outside Athens earlier that day—without fuss or fanfare, just two anonymous witnesses plucked from the street and a single photographer, who had captured the event for posterity. It was the first time she'd seen Xan smile all day.

'It will be no hardship to lose the obnoxious tag of "Greece's most eligible bachelor",' he had drawled, those thick, dark lashes shuttering the cobalt brilliance of his eyes. 'At least in future I might just be left alone to get on with my life and to live it as I please.'

His words had been arrogant enough to make Tamsyn bristle, but she'd bitten back her sarcastic response, deciding that having a stand-up fight right before the ceremony might not be the best way of portraying marital harmony. Instead, she'd concentrated on her appearance, determined to play her own part with aplomb. She'd chosen an extremely short white wedding dress in diaphanous layers of silk-chiffon which came to mid-thigh and defined the shape of her legs beneath. It was pretty and delicate as well as being slightly daring, but that was exactly what she wanted. She wanted people to look at her and tut. To remark that she really *was* an outrageous choice of bride for the Greek tycoon because that would pave the way for their speedy divorce.

What she hadn't banked on was Xan's reaction when he saw her walking towards him clutching a scented bunch of white flowers. He had looked her up and down as if he couldn't quite believe what he was seeing, his gaze lingering on her bare legs and a little muscle flickering at his temple. And when she'd enquired—a little anxiously—if the short dress was emphasising the freckles on her thighs, he had given her an odd kind of smile before shaking his head and guiding her towards the car waiting to take them to Piraeus.

'Not at all, *agape mou*.' His denial had been husky and the little muscle had still been flickering at his temple. 'Not at all.'

And now she and her new husband were skimming over the sapphire sea towards the Peloponnese penin- sula, because Xan had told her the best way to see his home for the first time was from the water. Almost as if was a *real* honeymoon and he was trying to im- press her!

She'd never been on a yacht before—just ferries— most memorably a day-trip to Calais when she'd been just seventeen. But Xan's sleek craft was worlds away from the lumbering ferry which had moved through the water with all the grace of a giant tractor. This boat gleamed silvery-white in the spring sunshine. It drew the eye of every passing yacht—especially with Xan at the helm. He had swapped his dark wedding suit for a pair of faded denims and a white T-shirt which em- phasised the contrasting gleam of his olive skin. The muscles in his arms bunched as he did impressive- looking things to the billowing sails and his raven- dark hair rippled in the Aegean breeze. With an effort, Tamsyn tried to concentrate on the horizon, trying to prevent her gaze from sliding to his powerful body as he tugged on a rope—as she wondered how difficult it was going to be to resist him during the fortnight's honeymoon which lay ahead.

'Tamsyn! Look over there.'

Over the white noise whoosh of the sea, Xan's voice broke into her thoughts and Tamsyn glanced up to follow the direction of his gaze. She hadn't really thought about what she might find at the end of her journey but now her heart contracted with something like yearning as suddenly she understood the meaning of the word paradise.

Xan's home was situated on a strip of land surrounded on three sides by the sea, like a green finger dipping into pot of blue water. A large, elevated modern house glinted in the bright sunshine of the spring morning but there were other buildings occupying the sprawling estate too, which made her realise just how vast it was. Outside seating areas with wicker chairs and tables and a long veranda, festooned with bright flowers and green climbers. In the distance was the seductive glitter of a sapphire swimming pool which blended into the ocean beyond, and impossibly smooth, emerald lawns sloping down a private beach, where a curve of sugar-white sand tempted the eye. Tamsyn watched as Xan expertly brought the yacht skimming into the small harbour where two fishermen were waiting, greeting him affectionately as they helped him anchor the boat.

Still in her wedding heels, Tamsyn consented to being lifted onto the sand by her new husband, which she supposed only added to the supposed romance of their arrival. And despite trying to convince herself that the gesture was functional rather than emotional, that didn't stop her skin from shivering in response when he briefly held her in his powerful arms. Did her eyes darken or some other barely visible response communicate itself to him? Was that why there was a speculative narrowing of his eyes? Tamsyn stiffened. Just because she *felt* desire, didn't mean she was going to act on it, did it? Even if it *was* difficult to shake the memories of just how good it had been between them…

'Let's go up to the house,' he said, indicating a steep flight of stone steps, before casting a doubtful look at her towering white heels. 'Think you can manage to walk in those, or would you like me to carry you?'

'I think I can manage,' she said, seeing the answering smile which curved his lips.

'I thought you might say that,' he commented drily.

But by the time they reached the top of the steps with Tamsyn panting slightly, Xan caught hold of her hand, lacing his fingers in hers as they began to walk towards the lawn.

She shot him a questioning glance, hating the sudden thrill of her hand as it was enclosed in the warmth of his. 'Xan?' she said breathlessly.

'My housekeeper is watching from the house,' he said. 'And I know how disappointed she would be if she thought we were anything other than a pair of deliriously happy newlyweds.'

His housekeeper was watching.

Well, what had she expected? That he had been suddenly overcome with emotion? Tamsyn tried to pull away but he stayed her with the feather-light circling of his thumb and instead she found herself shivering in response. What was the *matter* with her? Was she so starved of physical affection that even a tiny stroke could reduce her to such a state of longing? Maybe she was. Or maybe gestures like that mimicked *real* closeness and made her realise with a sudden shock just what she'd never had. No mother to cuddle her. No father to bounce her on his knee. Nobody except Hannah who back then had only ever given her the occasional half-hearted hug, because it was kind of embarrassing to cuddle your kid sister.

So remember why you're here, she told herself fiercely. Remember why you're doing this. Not for love, or scraps of affection, but for *money*. Money for Hannah—the only person who'd ever really been there for her.

But it was easy to forget reality when the housekeeper was standing in the doorway watching them approach, her face creased with pleasure as she clapped her gnarled hands together in delight. The greeting she gave Xan was a surprise—Tamsyn hadn't expected the tycoon to consent to being embraced so fervently by his elderly housekeeper. But neither was she prepared for the crushing embrace to which *she* was subjected afterwards and for a moment she stood, stiff as a board before gradually relaxing into the woman's cushioned flesh. And wasn't she secretly glad of that brief opportunity to compose herself and the chance to blink away the tears which had inexplicably sprung to her eyes.

'Tamsyn, this is Manalena,' Xan was saying as the woman relinquished her hold at last. 'Who has been with the family for a very long time.'

'Kalispera!' beamed Manalena, mimicking a rocking movement with her arms. 'I have known Kyrios Xan since he was a baby.'

It was difficult to imagine this towering man as a baby, thought Tamsyn. To picture him small and helpless and vulnerable. 'And was he a good baby?' she asked, with a smile.

Manalena gave a shake of her greying head. 'He never sleep and when he was a little boy, he never sit still. He is still like that now, and I am very happy he find a wife at last.'

Tamsyn remembered Xan telling her that his engagement to Sofia had been a private matter and for that she was grateful. Imagine if his staff regarded her as some kind of usurper and resented her, making her sense of isolation even more pronounced. She wondered how the housekeeper would feel if she knew the truth behind their whirlwind wedding and that Tamsyn was not the genuine and loving bride she must have hoped for. A flicker of discomfort washed over her as she glanced up at Xan while Manalena spoke to him in a torrent of rapid and babbled Greek.

'Manalena has just been explaining that a special wedding breakfast has been prepared for us,' he translated. 'She is also complaining that this morning a member of my staff arrived from Athens and is getting under her feet.'

As if on cue, a sleek brunette emerged from the house, talking excitedly into a cellphone, before quickly terminating the call. Slim and sophisticated, it was impossible to know exactly how old she was, though Tamsyn would have guessed mid to late thirties. Shiny shoulder-length hair swung in a raven arc around her chin and her linen trousers and pristine cream blouse made her appear the very definition of cool. In her too-short wedding dress with the flowers beginning to wilt in her windswept curls, Tamsyn felt inferior in comparison, even though the woman was smiling at her in a friendly manner.

'Hello! You must be Tamsyn,' she said, her perfect English tinged with a fetching Greek accent. 'I'm Elena and I'm very pleased to meet you and to offer my congratulations.'

'Elena is my personal assistant from the Athens office,' explained Xan. 'She's been overseeing all the wedding party preparations.'

'I hope everything will be to your satisfaction,' said Elena quickly. 'Xan gave me *carte blanche* to make decisions about food and drink and decorations, so I did. I would have communicated with you directly except—'

'I told Elena you were busy winding up your life in England,' said Xan, meeting Tamsyn's eyes with a bland look.

Tamsyn forced a smile because what could she say? That packing up her few miserable possessions had taken about five minutes and she might have welcomed having a little input into her own wedding party, rather than sitting around in the unfamiliar luxury of the Granchester Hotel, wondering what on earth she had let herself in for. Xan had given her a credit card and told her to buy an entire new wardrobe, one befitting the wife of a Greek tycoon. And although Tamsyn had half-heartedly done as he'd asked, she'd bought only what was strictly necessary, obsessively keeping all the receipts so that they could be included in a final tally when the divorce settlement came through.

Perhaps Xan had drafted Elena because he was afraid his new wife might prove incapable of choosing a sophisticated menu for their wedding party, despite holding her own that night they'd dined together at the Granchester. Or maybe he was worried she might let slip the true nature of their whirlwind romance—although he didn't seem to be doing anything to bolster the false fairytale himself. He wasn't exactly acting like a man who'd been swept away by passion, was he? She doubted whether that brief hand-holding exhibition would have convinced his housekeeper—or anyone else—that this marriage was for real.

'I'm very grateful for your help,' she told Elena brightly. 'For a start, I don't speak any Greek.'

'Well no, not *yet*,' said Elena with a friendly grin. 'But you will. Like your new husband, it isn't easy—but it's certainly possible to master.'

'I think you should kiss goodbye to your bonus, Elena,' said Xan mildly, propelling Tamsyn forward with the brief caress of his fingers. 'Come and meet the rest of the staff.'

The *rest* of the staff? Exactly how many people did he have working for him? Suddenly Tamsyn felt daunted by the line of workers who were waiting to meet her. Silently, she repeated their names before saying them out loud, terrified she would forget them before wondering why she was so anxious to please. There was Rhea the cook and pretty young Gia, who was in charge of the cleaning. A part-time driver named Panos, and Orestes the gardener, whose wife Karme helped Gia in the house when the need arose.

Tamsyn said hello to them all, using the few words of Greek she'd managed to learn before leaving England, but once again she felt faintly uneasy about deceiving these people who obviously adored her Greek husband and wanted the best for him.

Once again Manalena said something in Greek and Xan nodded, before glancing briefly at his watch.

'The meal is almost ready, but there are a couple of phone calls I need to make first,' he said. 'Manalena will show you where to freshen up and I'll meet you downstairs in the dining room in ten minutes.'

Feeling as if she'd been dismissed, Tamsyn followed the housekeeper up a sweeping staircase to the first floor, wondering how Xan was expecting to maintain the image of doting bridegroom if he couldn't even be bother to show her to the bathroom himself! Yet she couldn't deny a feeling of relief, that she would be spared the intimate reality of their shared marital space for at least a little while longer.

She walked down a wide and airy corridor, past walls covered with dramatic seascapes, until at last Manalena halted in front of a set of double doors. 'This is your room,' said Manalena, a note of pride creeping into her voice as she pushed open one of the doors.

Tamsyn walked into a room of breathtaking splendour with views right over the water, so that sunlight danced in an ever-moving lightshow over the pale walls. On the dressing table she could see the a pair of gold cufflinks set with sapphires which perfectly matched her new husband's eyes. Xan's room, she thought. And now hers, too. Her throat constricted. If it had belonged to anyone else she would have walked straight over to the window and feasted her eyes on the dark swell of the sea, but her attention was caught by something else. By the vast bed, on whose snowy covers someone had scattered pink rose petals—dozens of them—their scented splendour seeming to mock her.

Another reminder of a romance which wasn't real, she reminded herself, trying to erase the stupid sense of wistfulness which was clenching at her heart. Yet what could she do other than smile at the faithful housekeeper who stood anxiously in front of her, obviously awaiting her verdict on the honeymoon suite.

'It looks very beautiful, Manalena,' she said softly. '*Efkaristo.*'

Looking gratified, Manalena beamed and nodded. 'I wait for you outside.'

Alone at last, Tamsyn kicked off her high-heeled shoes and wiggled her newly liberated toes. And even though she could have happily thrown herself onto the bed and tried to blot out what was coming next, she freshened up in the lavish bathroom, helping herself from a selection of costly bath products which had obviously been acquired for the new bride. Pulling the wilting flowers from her hair, she raked a brush through her hair, gradually removing the tangles until it fell in a thick and vibrant curtain all the way down to her waist. She eyed the spindly wedding shoes doubtfully and decided against putting them back on. With a final tug at her short dress, she went back downstairs with Manalena, where Xan was waiting for her in the dining room.

And Tamsyn could do nothing about the overwhelming rush of desire which pulsed over her. It seemed incongruous to see the Greek tycoon standing there, still in his sailing clothes, his cobalt eyes darkening with unmistakable appreciation as he surveyed her. Her heart began to thunder as she realised that this powerful man was now her husband.

And she needed to keep it together. Not let desire

weaken her. To remember that this was nothing but an elaborate ruse. A business transaction, that was all.

'You don't look much like a bridegroom,' she commented lightly, in a vain attempt to defuse the sudden tension which seemed to have accompanied her into the room.

His gaze raked over her, lingering on the filmy white dress and focussing last on her bare feet whose toenails were painted a shimmering iridescent silver. 'Whereas you look exactly like a bride, *agape mou*,' he said unevenly. 'If a somewhat unconventional one.'

'Wasn't that the whole idea?' she questioned acidly.

Xan couldn't quite bring himself to answer, because he wasn't sure *where* his head had been when he'd asked Tamsyn Wilson to marry him. Had he thought she would be easily manipulated? That her humble status and the knowledge he was paying her a great deal of money, would give him the upper hand? Yes, he had. Guilty on all counts.

Pulling out a chair for her, he felt the silkiness of her loose curls brushing tantalisingly against his hand and his groin hardened. He hadn't believed her when she'd told him there was to be no sex, but her distant behaviour since they'd made their deal, had convinced him that she'd meant every word she said. He'd tried convincing himself that he wouldn't find it too much of a problem—and that three months enforced celibacy was easily doable. What he had failed to take into account was just how entrancing he would continue to find her, or that her stubbornness would act as an aching kind of aphrodisiac. His mouth hardened. He should have picked a bride from the type of woman with which he was familiar. The type who would jump when he snapped his fingers. Who would do whatever he asked of them, and do it with gratitude and pleasure. Not some feisty woman who seemed determined to oppose him every step of the way.

He poured two glasses of vintage champagne and handed her one, his throat drying with lust as their eyes met over the rims of the fine crystal. Suddenly he wished he'd told Manalena that they would eat something light on the balcony of his bedroom, so that he could have had Tamsyn all to himself. To test just how strong her resolve was. Too late, he thought grimly, knowing how much trouble his cook would have gone to.

But his expression betrayed none of his disquiet as he raised his glass to hers. 'So. What shall we drink to, Tamsyn?' he questioned.

For a moment she looked uncertain—like a small creature who'd strayed too far from her natural habitat. She stared down at the fizzing wine before lifting her gaze and chinking her crystal glass against his.

'To money, of course,' she said defiantly. 'That's what this is all about, isn't it? Money and land.'

And all that flippancy was back—the defiant tilt of her chin just daring him to challenge her, when ironically—all it made him want to do was kiss her.

CHAPTER NINE

It was the longest meal she'd ever endured but Tamsyn was determined to spin out her wedding breakfast as long as she could. Because eating and drinking would delay the inevitable—and she was terrified of accompanying Xan upstairs, to that vast bed scattered with pink rose petals. Terrified that she would give into the demands of her traitorous body and fall hungrily into his arms. Because that was the last thing she needed.

Dutifully she picked at course after delicious course, trying to give every impression of enjoying the food which had been so carefully prepared by Rhea, the cook. The Greek salad topped with fragrant basil, still warm from the herb garden. The fish with delicious sauce, followed by *giovetsi*—a dish of lamb baked in a clay pot, served with green beans stewed with tomatoes. Rhea's final flourish was a traditional wedding dessert called *diples*, a sweet fried concoction covered in a great deal of honey and crushed walnuts. The honey kept sticking to the roof of her mouth and she really didn't need another morsel, but Tamsyn was determined to eat it.

And each course had an accompanying wine—fine wines in different colours. Tamsyn rarely drank but today she sipped a little, so that by the time the sweet wine was served with dessert, she felt better than she had in days. It was as if a tight knot at the base of her stomach had slowly begun to unfurl, allowing her to relax at last.

Staring across the table at Xan, she tried not be affected by his rugged masculine beauty, but that was easier said than done. His skin gleamed like gold in the sunlight and the close-fitting jeans and T-shirt gave him a deceptively laid-back air. At times she was in danger of forgetting that he was a billionaire control freak who was calling all the shots, because right now he looked like some rippling-fleshed fisherman who'd just wandered up to the house for a bit of lunch.

'So,' she said, finally admitting defeat and putting her dessert spoon down. 'Here we are. Mr and Mrs Constantinides. How weird is that?'

A glint of amusement entered the cobalt eyes. 'Pretty weird,' he admitted.

'Have you issued your statement to the press yet? Is that what the phone call was all about?'

'I have no intention of speaking to the press today, Tamsyn. I will respond to questions if and when necessary. I was speaking to my father.' There was a pause. 'And Sofia.'

Tamsyn felt her heart lurch. 'And?'

'Sofia took it better than I expected. She seemed more resigned than upset. Which is a good thing.'

'Like I said,' Tamsyn observed. 'She's probably secretly pleased not to have to spend a lifetime with you.'

'Thanks for the vote of confidence, sweetheart,' he said drily.

She wanted to tell him not to tease her like that,

just like she wanted to tell him not to look at her with that sexy glint of amusement in his eyes. Mainly because she liked it. She liked it way too much. It made her want to do what she had vowed she wasn't going to do—mainly to rush upstairs and get up close and personal with him. She cleared her throat. 'And your father?'

For the first time, his face showed a flicker of darkness. 'My father took the news less well. He was angry, which didn't surprise me, but his concerns were focussed more on his island inheritance than on the people involved. No change there.' His laugh was tinged with bitterness. 'He seems to think that Sofia's father might refuse to sell me the island now that I've jilted his daughter. I think it will depend on Sofia's reaction, but better that than breaking her heart,' he added harshly.

'And if he's right? If Sofia's father won't sell?'

'Oh, if Sofia is okay, he'll sell—don't you worry about that.'

'How can you be so sure?'

'Because Tamsyn, everyone has their price' He gave a cynical smile. 'Even you.'

It was a timely reminder of her new husband's cold-heartedness but Tamsyn forced herself not to react, instead fixing him with a look of interest. 'Is your father coming to the wedding party?'

'He said not, but I know his bluster of old and he'll be there—if only because the cream of Athenian and international society will be attending and he'd hate to miss out.'

'And in the meantime, we have a whole two week honeymoon to get through.' Tamsyn resisted the temptation to chew on her fingernails which had been varnished silver to match her toes. 'Wasn't that a rather unnecessary addition to this sham marriage?'

'I told you. We don't want to make it look like a stunt.' He leaned back in his chair to study her. 'And we can make this as easy or as difficult as we like.'

Tamsyn wondered if he was out of his mind. Didn't he realise that there was a constant battle raging inside her? That while her head was telling her not to have sex with her new husband—her body was urging her in the opposite direction. Did Xan know that every time she looked at him she wanted to touch him, even though to do so would be madness. Or that at night she was haunted by the memories of his hard body thrusting into hers and giving her pleasure, over and over again? Running her trembling fingertip round the edge of her crystal glass, she struggled to find a neutral topic. 'Manalena seems very sweet,' she said at last.

'She is.' He took a mouthful of wine, his expression mocking her.

'Why did she used to look after you? Did your mother go out to work?'

'No. But motherhood appealed to her about as much as being poor, and she didn't care who knew it. Including me, just for the record. She went to great pains to assure me that some women simply weren't maternal, and she was one of them.'

His words were terse and he spoke them as if they didn't matter but they told her a lot, mainly that his mother had been emotionally distant. Tamsyn nodded, wondering just how far she could push him—without stopping to ask herself why she wanted to. 'Do you think that's what made you so...'

'So what, Tamsyn?' he questioned sardonically as her words tailed off.

'So... I don't know.' She straightened her napkin so that it lay at a ninety-degree angle next to her place-setting, just as she would have done if she'd been at work. 'So anti-love and marriage...'

He shrugged. 'That's what the psychologists would say, I guess.'

'And was it bad?' she questioned suddenly, her heart going out to him despite telling herself that he didn't need her sympathy. 'Your childhood, I mean?'

'Bad enough. But I happened to like the independence which came about as a result of having a mother who was never there for me. The thought of having to answer to someone every hour of every day filled me with horror and still does.' His eyes were like dark blue ice. 'In future all my bios will say, *he was briefly married*. And you, *agape mou*, will have liberated me from the expectation which society heaps on every wealthy man, that he is not complete until he finds himself a suitable wife. You will have done me a big favour, Tamsyn.' His lips curved into a reflective smile. 'And that in itself is worth the money I'm paying you to wear my ring.'

His mocking words effectively terminated the conversation, but it left Tamsyn thinking that maybe they were more similar than she'd imagined, despite the great difference in their lifestyles.

'So what now?' she questioned, aware that they couldn't sit amid the debris of their wedding breakfast all day.

His eyes gleamed. 'Now that you've made lunch last as long as you possibly could?'

'I was hungry.'

'Of course you were, *agape mou*,' he agreed, silkily. 'Hungry enough to pick at your food with marked indifference and then to push it around your plate? But your face is pale and your eyes strained, so I suggest you retire to the bedroom and take an afternoon nap. It's been a long day.'

His words made sense because Tamsyn *was* tired. But the memory of that petal-strewn bed kept flickering into her mind and she knew she couldn't keep skirting round the issue. In London she'd told him there was to be no sex and he needed to realise she meant it. But she couldn't discuss the subject here—not with Manalena poking her beaming head around the door and asking if they'd like coffee.

Her husband declined the offer, his drawled response bringing an instant smile to Manalena's face as she remained in the doorway, watching them. And when Xan walked around the table and held out his hand towards Tamsyn, she found herself taking it. She told herself she was doing this for the housekeeper's benefit and maybe she was. But she couldn't deny that she was enjoying the sensation of Xan's strong fingers encircling hers, as he led her upstairs towards the master bedroom. Of course she was. Because in those few moments she felt safe. As if nothing could ever harm her so long as she was with this powerful and charismatic man.

And that was nothing but an illusion. She was nothing but a bought bride, to be disposed of as soon as possible.

She was shivering as he closed the bedroom door behind them, acutely aware of the intimacy of the enclosed space. She ran her fingertips over the wilting bouquet she'd placed on a nearby table and then, when there was no room left for prevarication, looked into his face. 'Where am I sleeping?'

He raised his eyebrows. 'Judging by the amount of petals which seem to have been offloaded onto the bed, I'd say right here.'

She shook her head, hating the sudden hot prickle of her breasts. 'I told you I didn't want any intimacy, Xan, so therefore it makes more sense for me to have my own bedroom.'

'And if I were to grant you your wish, that would bring into question the validity of our marriage,' he answered coolly. 'Which kind of defeats the whole purpose of you being here.'

'So we've got to share a bed?'

'It's a very large bed.'

'I can see that for myself. But it doesn't matter how big it is,' she snapped. 'I don't want...'

'What don't you want, Tamsyn?'

She stiffened as she heard the soft mockery in his voice. Was he going to make her spell it out? And if he was, so what? She was no longer the shrinking little virgin who had given herself to him one starry desert night, even if right now she felt like it. This man knew her like no other. He had kissed her lips and suckled her breasts. He had shown her how he liked to be touched and stroked and had then thrust deep inside her hungry body. He had seen her vulnerable in the midst of her orgasm. Had heard her stumble out his name in a choking cry as she tumbled over the edge. Surely that gave her the right to say what was on her mind. 'Sex,' she managed, her cheeks growing hot.

'It isn't obligatory to have sex with me.' He shrugged. 'I'm not planning to demand my conjugal rights, if that's what you're worried about. Like I said, it's a big bed.'

'And you think it's possible for us to lie side by side and, and...' Her voice tailed off, unable to articulate the confusion of her feelings which were compounded by the sheer depth of her inexperience. Did he guess that? Was that why the look he slanted her seemed almost *compassionate*?

'I think it's possible,' he said slowly. 'It won't be easy and it certainly won't be enjoyable, but in the end the decision is yours, Tamsyn. Yet all you have to do is say the word and we could have one hell of a honeymoon.'

Her cheeks grew even hotter. 'I don't know how you can be...so...*callous*.'

'And I don't know why you're making such a big deal out of it. You think every time a couple have sex, there has to be some great big emotion underlying it?' His cobalt gaze seared into her. 'Didn't it ever occur to you that sexual gratification is just one of life's fundamental pleasures, Tamsyn?'

Tamsyn was aware of a sudden emptiness. A disappointment. As if he'd just burst some invisible bubble. As if the stories women told themselves about happy-ever-after really *were* a myth. 'And that's all there is to it?' she asked, in a small flat voice.

He shrugged. 'It exists for the procreation of children, but that's not going to be an issue for us, is it?'

'No,' she agreed, unprepared for another unexpectedly painful clench of her heart. 'It's not going to be an issue.'

'Don't take it so personally,' he advised softly. 'Sex doesn't have to be about love.'

'I realise that. I may be relatively inexperienced, but I'm not stupid!' she declared. 'I'm not looking for love but if I was, you'd be right at the bottom of my wish-list, Xan Constantinides!'

Her words sounded genuine and Xan gave the ghost of a smile because she really was surprising. Up-close contact with his enormous wealth didn't seem to have blunted her determination to do things *her* way, nor to subdue her feisty nature. She was behaving like his equal and that was doing dangerous things to his libido. He was used to female subjugation and was finding the lack of it a powerful aphrodisiac. Lust pulsed through him, hot and potent. She was such a contradiction in so many ways. Tough and outspoken—and yet at times he was certain he'd detected a glimpse of frailty beneath her waspish exterior. And didn't that intrigue him? Make him wonder what had put it there?

He stared out of one of the windows where he could see Orestes tending to the violet blooms of an exotic flower and he thought about the fortnight ahead, realising that this fabricated honeymoon would drag like hell unless he could find something pleasurable to fill the time. And sex with his fiery new bride would certainly while away the hours in the most delicious way.

She hadn't moved from where she'd been standing and he reached out to touch his fingertip against her mouth, instantly feeling it tremble. He could see her throat constricting and her eyes briefly closing as if she was trying to fight her own desire. And that turned him on even more, because he wasn't used to women fighting their attraction to him. 'You still want me, Tamsyn,' he observed thickly. 'And it's the same for me. I want you so much that I'm aching just thinking about it.'

He could see the uncertainty flickering in the depths of her green eyes. 'Nobody's denying the desire, Xan. Doesn't mean we're going to do anything about it though.'

'Why not?'

'Because....' She moved away from him then, wriggling her shoulders restlessly as the little white wedding dress shimmied provocatively over her bare thighs. 'It seems wrong to have sex just for the sake of it.'

'Says who? Why does it bother you so much?'

She stared at him and suddenly her eyes were very bright. 'It doesn't matter.'

'Oh, but it does. I'm interested in why you're such a fundamentally old-fashioned young woman at heart.'

Tamsyn gave a careless shrug which didn't quite come off, because it was difficult to remain indifferent to her past when he was looking at her so piercingly.

'I didn't realise I was.'

'Psychologists usually say it something to do with your parents and your upbringing,' he said wryly. 'So let's start with that.'

This is what she'd been trying to avoid telling him. But what difference did it make if she told him about her mother? This part of her life wasn't the part she had buried in a deep, dark place which she never ventured near.

'I don't remember my birth mother, because I was just a baby when she gave me and Hannah up for adoption,' she said baldly. 'But nobody wanted to adopt us because we were too much of a handful. Or rather, I was. Apparently it's quite common for abandoned babies to grow into troublesome children.' She shrugged. 'That's why we put up with so much from our foster parents, despite all their failings.' She shrugged as she met the question in his eyes. 'There was a terrible atmosphere in the house, mainly because my foster father used the grocery money to fund his card games, or to buy dinner for one of his many mistresses. We were terrified that if we complained we'd get split up. And neither Hannah or I could bear the thought of that.'

There was a silence during which she thought he was about to let it go. And didn't she *want* him to let it go?

'So what do you know about your birth mother, Tamsyn,' he prompted softly.

Tamsyn swallowed. If she told him he would judge her and she didn't want to be judged. Because that's what the girls at school had done, once they found out about her mum. They'd picked on her and bullied her and the strong skin she'd grown had been as a direct result of that. But talking about it would reinforce the certainty that there could never be any kind of future between her and Xan. And it might stop him from probing further—keeping him away from the stuff which was *really* unpalatable.

She shrugged. 'From what I understand, she was pretty liberal with her body. She liked men. A lot. And she wasn't that careful about contraception. Hannah and I have different fathers and apparently there's a younger brother out there, who we've never met.'

'And your father?'

'I never met him.' She moved away. 'And if you don't mind, I'd rather not discuss it any more.'

'Of course not.' He nodded slowly, his eyes gleaming with perception. 'It's no wonder you hung onto your virginity for so long. No wonder that behind that spiky exterior beats the heart of someone who only ever wanted to be a good girl. But you don't have to spend your whole life paying for the perceived sins of your mother, you know, Tamsyn. It won't make the slightest difference if you deny yourself pleasure, just for the sake of it.'

'You mean, now I've actually lost my innocence, I might as well capitalise on it?'

'That's one way of looking at it. If you could stop being so damned stubborn and think about the possibilities open to you, you might be able to see some of the benefits.'

'What kind of *benefits*?'

He gave a slow smile. 'Well, for a start I could teach you how to enjoy your body. I could show you just how sublime sex can be. Wouldn't you like that, Tamsyn? Wouldn't you like to walk away from this marriage knowing how to please a man, and how best *you* like to be pleased?'

Tamsyn shook her head because she hated his logic. For making it sound as if sex was just another new skill to learn—a bit like when she'd studied to be a silver-service waitress. His words reminded her that she was only here for a short while and soon she would be on her own again—back to her nomadic existence. It made sense to tell him no and to stick to her self-imposed celibacy.

So why couldn't she silence the memory of what it

had been like to be naked in his arms…how he'd made her glow and shout with pleasure and then tremble helplessly in his arms? Why not concentrate on how empty she'd felt afterwards, when he'd left her and gone away? 'It seems so…cold-blooded,' she breathed.

'Does it?' he said softly, as he walked towards her.

'Yes,' she whispered.

'On the contrary,' he husked, pulling her roughly into his arms. 'I would describe this as nothing but hot-blooded.'

The first kiss knocked some of the fight out of her and the second had her hungry for more. And when he cupped his trembling hand over her thrusting breast, Tamsyn moaned with pleasure.

Because it felt good. Way too good to resist. She knew she should tell him no. That being physically close again would put her in danger of something she couldn't understand. But how could she refuse something which felt like this? When he was sliding his hand up the filmy skirt of her dress and caressing the shivering skin of her inner thigh?

'Xan,' she moaned, as his finger edged inside her panties and she writhed with pleasure as he found her wet heat.

'You like that,' he observed thickly.

She was too het-up to reply, but maybe she communicated her need to him. Maybe that was why he halted his intimate caress and picked her up, carrying her effortlessly over to the bed. He unzipped her dress and dropped it to the floor, before laying her on top of the petal-strewn cover.

'I see you wore white lingerie for your wedding day,' he observed thickly, tracing a slow finger over the snowy lace edge of her balcony bra. 'How very traditional.'

'It was the only underwear which didn't show beneath my wedding dress,' she said defiantly.

Xan understood a little now of what had made her so defensive, but the thought left his mind the moment he brushed against the taut wetness of her panties, hearing her gasp as he encountered her sweet spot. He slid the zip of his jeans over his aching hardness and pulled off his own clothes before removing her underwear with hands which were inexplicably shaking, something which had never happened to him before. Yet as he climbed onto the bed beside her, he was forced to admit that this *did* feel different—and this time he couldn't blame it on her innocence. Had all the fuss made by his staff about their mock wedding somehow got to him? As if some of their thankful celebration had seeped into his system, kicking his habitual cynicism into touch, making what was happening between him and the little redhead seem especially intense.

Never had a woman seemed so responsive to his touch. She shivered as he reacquainted himself with every inch of her skin, his lips hungrily kissing her neck and breasts and belly as he began to finger her. He played with her until she was writhing and gasping his name, her fingernails clawing frantically at his shoulders. He remembered thinking that she was going to mark him and make him bleed—and that he didn't care.

His gasps became urgent as he entered her and she cried out with each deep thrust, soft thighs wrapped tightly around his back. And nothing had ever felt this good, thought Xan with delirious pleasure. Nothing.

He wanted it to last and last but she was too close, and so was he. He splayed his fingers over her peaking nipples as she began to spasm around him, and his own orgasm hit him like a speed train.

On and on it went, until at last he collapsed against her shoulder with his lips pressed against her damp and tumbled curls. It was a while before he could bring himself to withdraw from her, but just as soon as he did, her tiny fingers curled intimately around him and he could feel himself hardening again beneath her light touch. He slid inside her for a second time and before too long she was bucking wildly beneath him and crying out his name. Soon after his third orgasm, he lay stroking her head and realising that for the next two weeks of his honeymoon, it was just going to be him and Tamsyn.

He stared down at the satisfied slant of her lips. At the lazy flutter of her eyelashes as she gave a sleepy little sigh of contentment. She snuggled deeper into the crook of his arm and Xan felt the automatic stir of overpowering lust and something else. Something he couldn't seem to define....

Maybe it was panic.

CHAPTER TEN

THE MORNING SUN drifted in through the open windows of the bedroom but Tamsyn kept her eyes tightly shut, listening to the even sound of Xan's breathing. She needed to get her thoughts straight before he awoke. She needed to get her mask firmly in place, knowing he would baulk if he ever realised the truth. That their marriage of convenience was about to get a whole lot more complicated.

How the hell had it happened? At what point during this crazy honeymoon, had she started to care for her husband in a way which suddenly seemed unstoppable? She risked turning her head, to see his ruffled black hair lying against the pillow. Was she such a sucker for affection, that she'd fallen for a man just because he clearly enjoyed having sex with her and they spent long hours romping in bed together?

She swallowed. No. It was more than that. Xan could be *kind*, she had discovered. She'd seen that in the way he was with his staff, but he was also kind to her—and interested. In fact, he'd surprised her by wanting to know her views on all kinds of things. Things which nobody had ever bothered asking her about before—like politics and space travel and global warming. And Tamsyn had discovered how flattering it was when a powerful and successful man elicited the opinion of someone who didn't have a formal exam qualification to her name.

Nearly two weeks into her marriage and she had turned from being a reluctant bride to somebody who found joy in pretty much every moment she spent with her husband. But at least Xan didn't have a clue how she was feeling, because concealment was something she excelled at, when she put her mind to it. She'd had a lifetime's practice in emotional subterfuge. She might now want him, but he certainly didn't want her. That had never been part of the deal. No man had ever wanted her, she reminded herself grimly. Not even her own father.

This marriage couldn't last. It was never intended to last. *And the deeper she fell for him, the more painful their split was going to be…*

Dark lashes fluttered open and Tamsyn saw the cobalt gleam from between Xan's shuttered eyes. He gave a lazy stretch and yawned, before pulling her against his warm nakedness and kissing the top of her ruffled curls.

'And what would you like to do today, *sizighos mou*?' His voice deepened as his hand slipped beneath the sheet and he began to massage one erect nipple. 'Since it's the last day of our honeymoon.'

Tamsyn bit her lip, wishing he hadn't reminded her, especially since tomorrow was the day of their post-wedding party and one which his father had now announced he would definitely be attending. She wasn't looking forward to all his friends giving her the once-over and finding her wanting. Her thick skin seemed to have thinned these last few days and suddenly the thought of having to play the unsuitable wife was filling her with dread.

'We could spend the day on the beach,' Xan was saying, stroking the flat of his hand over her belly.

'Beach sounds good,' she agreed.

'Picnic or restaurant lunch?'

She tried to summon up some enthusiasm. 'Picnic, I think.'

'*Relios*.' He gave a slow flicker of a smile and bent his mouth to her nipple. 'My thoughts exactly.'

Reluctantly, she pulled away. 'I'll go and get showered—'

'Hey,' he protested, his hand reaching out to capture her waist. 'What's the hurry?'

Tamsyn's answering smile was tight as she wriggled free, because the last thing she needed was another example of an easy compatibility which meant nothing. 'I need to speak to Rhea about lunch,' she insisted, jumping out of bed before he could distract her again. 'If we're not careful, we'll end up spending the day in bed without actually having our picnic.'

'And would that be such a crime?' he grumbled. 'Isn't that what honeymoons are supposed to be about.'

'Today it would,' she said briskly. 'I need to speak to Elena about flowers for the party and to Rhea about all sorts of boring things, including canapés.'

There was a moment of silence. 'How quickly you have adapted,' he observed silkily, with a note of something she didn't recognise in his voice. 'You are beginning to sound like a real wife, Tamsyn.'

'And we wouldn't want that, would we?' she questioned brightly. 'Don't worry, Xan. I'll have re-adopted my wild-child persona by tomorrow. The shortest dress, the biggest hair and the most make-up. That should do the trick, don't you think? I can't wait to see the reaction of your friends and colleagues.' She forced a smile. 'And now I really *must* go and shower.'

Moodily Xan leaned back against the pillows and watched his wife sashay across the bedroom towards the bathroom, the globes of her buttocks paler than the tanned perfection of her shapely legs. Frustration heated his blood and his erection throbbed uncomfortably between his legs. Why hadn't he overridden her desire to help with the party and encouraged her to give into a far more satisfying kind of desire instead?

He was still engaged in silent contemplation when she returned, dabbing drops of moisture from her dewy body with a towel before slipping on a tiny yellow bikini, which she covered up with a green cotton dress.

His groin ached as he watched her. He had scheduled this honeymoon to give credibility to their whirlwind union, with the party tacked onto the end to indicate a return to normal life. He had planned to use this opportunity to slake himself of his seemingly inexhaustible appetite for his new wife, before she departed from his life for ever with her divorce settlement clutched tightly in her hand.

But his anticipation of all the sex he wanted had been tempered by caution, because he wasn't used to having a woman around full-time. Even during his longer relationships, he rarely stayed with a lover longer than twenty-four hours at a stretch, because by then he'd usually reached his boredom threshold. The thought of fourteen whole days and nights with one person had filled him with panic and he'd imagined he would be climbing the walls by day three. He'd planned to make an urgent visit to his office in Athens on some hastily constructed urgent business if necessary, using the trip as a badly disguised means of escape.

Only it hadn't turned out like that. He hadn't gone near his computer—not once—and the feeling of being trapped simply hadn't materialised. It turned out that Tamsyn liked her own space just as much as he did.

'Of course,' she had informed him carelessly when one day, frustrated at finding her curled up in the garden reading some lurid crime novel, he had enquired rather acidly whether she'd always been *quite* so independent. 'It's the way I was raised.'

Xan frowned. Was it contrary of him to find himself resenting the fact that she seemed intent on racing through the pile of novels she'd brought with her from England? Or excitedly informing him that his infinity pool gave her the ideal opportunity to perfect her breaststroke? And what about the afternoon when he'd fallen asleep beneath a pine tree and she had slipped away. He'd awoken up and gone looking for her and found her in the kitchen with Rhea, who was showing her how to make baklava which Tamsyn seemed to be alternating with colouring in a picture with Gia's young daughter Maria. This scene of domestic bliss should have spooked him but it hadn't, mainly because she had looked up at him with those big green eyes, and smiled and at that moment he had felt completely enslaved by her.

Xan scowled as he pushed away the rumpled sheet and got out of bed. The sooner he got back to work the better, he thought grimly. Work and distance would allow him to put this whole crazy marriage in perspective and to see it for what it really was.

Out on the sun-washed terrace, they breakfasted on fruit and honeyed yoghurt, served with strong black coffee. Afterwards Xan sailed his yacht to a sheltered cove—a favourite place whose inaccessibility always guaranteed privacy. Beneath the deep blue sky they spent the morning swimming and snorkelling in the crystal-clear waters and afterwards drank homemade iced lemonade. But although the food Rhea had stowed away in a cool box was carefully unpacked and looked delicious, he noticed Tamsyn seemed as disinterested in their picnic lunch as he was.

'Not hungry?' he murmured as he lay back on the soft sand.

She sat, ramrod-straight, looking out to sea. 'Not really.'

'Not for food?'

She cleared her throat. 'Something like that,' she agreed reluctantly, as if she resented his perception.

He smiled as a whispered fingertip down the entire length of her spine soon had the tension leaching from her shoulders and the touch of his lips which followed made her give an impatient little wriggle. He brushed his hand against her breasts and saw her lips open with hunger, clamping shut afterwards when he teased her by moving his fingers away from the thrusting nipple. He waited until he sensed complete readiness and then pulled her down next to him.

'Is there anything you want which I can give you?' he drawled lazily.

'Xan,' she said shakily.

'Neh?' he replied, as he stripped the tiny yellow bikini from her body and the sight of her naked in the sunshine made his blood roar. Tearing off his trunks with impatient hands, he parted her thighs and pushed deep inside her and she gasped as her hips lifted up to meet the hard slam of his. Never had she felt so hot or wet or deep and Xan could do nothing to stop the thoughts which flooded into his head as he drove into her. In a couple of days time he would be in his office in Athens, with back-to-back meetings and conference calls. He wouldn't see Tamsyn until he got home in the evening—probably not before eight at the earliest—because he always worked late. Was it that which made this seem so *poignant*? The sense of something ending which somehow increased the intensity, making his climax explode at exactly the same time as hers, which had never happened to them before.

They lay there afterwards, resting in the shade of rocky outcrop and for a moment he thought she was asleep. But no. He heard her sigh as, her eyes concealed by her shades, she stared up at the sky above.

'Was that good?' he questioned, with sleepy satisfaction.

'It's always good.'

'I don't know how you do it.' He gave another yawn. 'But every time I have you, I just want you all over again.'

'It's because you know it's only temporary,' she said lightly.

'Maybe.'

Tamsyn heard the sound of his breathing deepening and a quick glance at his supine form told her he'd fallen asleep. Reluctantly she dragged her gaze away from all the unleashed power of his magnificent body and stared out to sea. Out on the horizon was nothing but a deep slash of dark sapphire water and in front of it, the sugar-white grains of sand. The air was still and warm and fragrant and her body felt utterly satiated by Xan's sublime lovemaking. She wished she could capture that moment and keep it in a bottle.

But she couldn't.

She couldn't hold onto any of this. It was slipping through her fingers just like the fine sand on which she lay. She'd agreed to a three-month marriage but now she could see that her decision to put a time limit on their union might have been too hasty. Even reckless. How could she possibly endure another ten weeks of pretending that her feelings for Xan hadn't changed— when she was putty in his hands after a mere fortnight together?

Behind her dark glasses, Tamsyn blinked away the incipient threat of tears. She'd been told by men in the past that she was cold and frigid. That behind her vibrant exterior was nothing but ice—and she had believed it, because nobody before Xan had ever made her melt. But Xan had. How could she not grow closer to a man when he was inside her and they were staring deep into each other's eyes? When she became unsure where he began and she ended—as if they were both parts of the same body. That was when wishful thinking found an opportunity to creep into her mind and take root there. Started making her long for things which were never going to happen.

Because none of this was real, she reminded herself. They were just playing make-believe. Her Greek husband had embraced the physical, but his emotional barriers remained firmly in place. And so did hers, if she was being honest. Because otherwise, why hadn't she just come out and told him about her dad?

She swallowed. She'd never discussed her father, not even with Hannah. Especially not with Hannah—not after what had happened. Perhaps if she'd fallen in love with someone kind and approachable, she might have opened up her heart to him. But Xan wasn't that man. His lovemaking might be completely fulfilling—but that didn't detract from his hard and critical side.

He'd married her to get himself out of a tight corner.

An unsuitable wild-child bride he just happened to be sexually compatible with.

And the longer she stayed with him, the more vulnerable she made her already damaged heart.

CHAPTER ELEVEN

'So what's all this about?' questioned Xan softly.

Tamsyn didn't immediately look up from the mirror. She was going to need her best smile to get through the next few hours, so maybe she'd better practice composing her face accordingly. Straightening up, she slowly turned to face her husband, stupidly gratified by the instant desire she could read in his eyes. And she wasn't supposed to be feeling *gratified*. She was supposed to be distancing herself from the charismatic Greek billionaire, not revelling in the physical power she could still—unbelievably—wield over him.

'What's what all about?' she murmured absently.

'Don't act like you don't know what I'm talking about, Tamsyn,' he said, treating her to another assessing look. 'I'm just wondering why the sudden dramatic change of image for tonight's party.'

'Could you be a little more specific, Xan? What exactly are your objections?'

Objections? Xan's throat dried to dust. Who said anything about objections? It just wasn't what he'd been expecting, that was all. His wife was wearing a white dress—as befitting a new bride just freshly back from honeymoon—but the outfit was a world away from the flirty mini which had barely covered her bottom on the day they'd wed. This concoction was made from a rich, heavy silk which moulded every curve of her delicious body yet fell decorously to the knee. Her hair had been coiled into an elaborate style, the lustrous curls tamed and gleaming like silken flames, with only a few strands left dangling, drawing attention to the swan-like length of her neck. The strappy silver sandals which gleamed against her bare feet were the only frivolous thing about her tonight, but even they exuded a certain class and style. This was a Tamsyn he'd never seen before. Sophisticated. Elegant— and the very opposite of unsuitable.

'It doesn't look like you,' he observed unevenly. 'This isn't the edgy little redhead I know.'

A flash of colour flared into her cheeks. 'So you don't like it?'

He gave a short laugh. 'Tamsyn, you could wear sackcloth and I'd still want to rip it from your body. I'm just not sure what has prompted this sudden transformation.'

She wound a strand of hair around her forefinger, so that when she let it go, it sprang into a perfect little ringlet which brushed against her neck. He suddenly thought how slim she looked—and how breakable.

'I'm a chameleon,' she said flippantly. 'Didn't you know? I can be whatever people want me to be and tonight I've gone for the sleek and understated look.'

His mouth twitched. 'Any particular reason why?'

She shrugged. 'I've seen the guest list.'

He raised his brows. 'And?'

'And it was exactly as I could have predicted.' She tilted her chin defensively, her eyes momentarily uncertain, as if deciding whether or not to tell him. 'Rich people. Well-connected people. The current darling of the Greek cinema who just happens to be bringing two hulking great bodyguards with her. An international politician or two—including a man they're describing as the frontrunner candidate for the next-but-one US Presidential election.'

'What do you want me to say? I've known Brett since I was at college and to me he's just someone I learnt to play tennis with at Harvard.' He raised his brows. 'I offered to fly your friends over and put them up in a local hotel, but you refused.'

Tamsyn bit her lip. It was true, she *had* refused. Was that because she'd been terrified one of them might see past all the trappings and pick up on the heart-ache which was building inside her, minute by minute? Or because she was determined to keep her old enemy—pity—at arm's length? She wanted to remember this night as you might remember a particularly beautiful rainbow, or sunset—something amazing but short-lived.

Her sister wasn't coming either, citing a busy royal diary which was planned weeks in advance and didn't allow for last-minute invitations to rushed weddings. But Tamsyn had detected a strong sense of disapproval in Hannah's reply as well as disbelief that she'd actually tied the knot with Xan Constantinides. Tamsyn had wanted to write and tell her she was doing this mainly for her, but her sister suddenly seemed a very long way away.

'Those are the kind of people I associate with, Tamsyn,' continued Xan quietly. 'You knew that.'

'Yes. But it's one thing knowing something and another thing facing them all for the first and probably only time—and that includes meeting your father. I've realised I don't want to turn myself into some sort of spectacle—some caricature of a tart, who people can poke fun at and laugh about behind their back. I've realised I don't want to be *unsuitable*. Not tonight. If I do that it's going to make this evening even more of an ordeal.' She expelled a sigh. 'If you want to know the truth, I'm beginning to wish I'd never agreed to throw the wretched party in the first place.'

He gave an odd kind of laugh. 'Well, just for the record, so do I and if people weren't already on their way from halfway across the globe, I'd consider cancelling it. But we can't. Which means we just have to get through it and make the best of it.' An unwilling kind of admiration sparked in the depths of his dark blue eyes. 'And just for the record, it's a very beautiful dress. You look every inch the suitable bride.'

Trying not to be swayed by his soft praise, Tamsyn smoothed down the silk-satin bodice of the outfit she'd ordered online from a store in Athens and which Elena had smuggled in yesterday. It had given her a ridiculous amount of pleasure to see herself looking like the kind of bride she'd never thought she could be, but in the end—her clothes were irrelevant. All she wanted was for tonight to be over, so she could start thinking about her future.

She watched him walk over to the open windows of their terrace, thinking how much she was going to miss this. And him. She could hear the chink of glasses from out on the lawn as waiters began loading up their trays and in the distance, could see a long line of approaching headlights travelling along the coastal road.

Her eyes ran over Xan's powerful physique, trying to commit it to memory. The snowy white dinner jacket which contrasted vividly with the close-fitting dark trousers. She loved the way those coal-black tendrils of hair brushed against the collar of his shirt, reminding her that he looked as much at home on a sailing boat as he did a boardroom. But as he turned around she quickly wiped her face clear of emotion—eradicating all the yearning, so she was able to meet his cobalt gaze with nothing more telling than a look of cool enquiry.

'Let's go,' he said abruptly.

Xan felt the adrenalin pumping through his body as he took Tamsyn's hand and led her out into the garden, where burning flames lined the paths and fairy-lights were strung from the trees. The huge swimming pool had been illuminated with floating lights, which gleamed in the turquoise water like surreal water lilies and the front of the house had been floodlit in soft colours of rose and blue. He told himself it was pride in his beautiful home which was making him feel so pumped-up tonight, but it was more than that. He looked at the woman by his side, thinking that Tamsyn had never looked lovelier. The most beautiful woman he had ever seen.

Easily visible in her white gown, he watched men turning to stare at her, just as they had once done at Kulal's palace. Back then he remembered feeling nothing but a destabilising lust but now that had been over-ridden by a primitive satisfaction that she belonged to *him* and only him. His mouth hardened. But she didn't, did she? Not really. She was his only for a little while longer and he needed to accept that soon she would be free, because that was what the plan had always been.

Free for other men to pursue and to benefit from all that shining sexual promise which he had awoken. A powerful surge of jealousy coursed through him, even though jealousy had never been his thing. He told himself that the feeling would soon pass. That he'd never relied on a woman before and didn't intend to start now. His life had been fine before Tamsyn Wilson had fallen into it like some wayward star, and that state of affairs would resume once they'd split.

Slightly mollified by his own reasoning, he introduced her to a number of guests and she responded with a charm which was contagious. Everyone wanted to talk to her and she instantly hit it off with a European princess, herself a former wild-child, and he could hear the two of them giggling together. Soon she was deep in conversation with a sultan she'd met at her sister's wedding, and several other desert princes moved to join in with the conversation, so that very quickly she was at the centre of a significant power hub. At one point she looked up at him and he raised his glass in mocking salute, as if to silently remind her that her fears of blending in had been groundless. But something in the gesture made her eyes grow dark. He saw her bite her lip and a few moments later she murmured to him that she needed to speak to Elena, and slipped away.

Xan accepted a glass of champagne and looked around. A group of musicians were playing traditional Greek music and out of the corner of his eye, he noticed that Salvatore di Luca had arrived, with the requisite glamorous blonde hanging from his arm like a glittering accessory. But there was still no sign of his father.

He took a sip of his drink. Was the old man worried that Sofia's father would refuse to sell him the island after all—and would that be enough to make him cut Xan from his life for ever? His lips hardened into a humourless smile. What exquisite irony that would be—if an island coveted because of its precious links with his ancestors, should be the cause of alienating his father from his only son.

He looked around again, his eyes scanning the crowded lawn with dissatisfaction as he realised he was looking in vain for his wife. Xan scowled as he handed his half-drunk glass of champagne to a passing waiter, the memory of emerald eyes and fiery curls an image he couldn't seem to shift from his mind.

It was all about sex, he reassured himself heatedly. Nothing but sex.

Tamsyn melted into the shadows, trying to gather her thoughts together. Yes, the party was loads easier than she'd imagined—but it was still stressful, which was why she had sought a moment of quiet refuge at the darkened side of the house, at the top of a gentle sloping incline, which gave a fabulous view of the glittering estate. Carefully smoothing down the rich silk of her dress, she sat down on a bench—tempted to kick off her silver sandals but knowing if she did so, she would be reluctant to put them on again. And tonight there would be no barefoot bride, looking like she'd wandered in from a nearby rock festival.

She sat back against the wooden bench and sighed. It had been strangely gratifying that Xan's friends had seemed genuinely happy to meet her. Was that because she had taken charge of her own destiny, so that for once she actually *felt* as if she fitted in—in a way she'd never done before? Even at Hannah's wedding she'd worn her fancy gowns with a distinct air of resentment—probably because she'd been forced to wear them. But tonight she was revelling in the fact that she looked like a bride her husband could be proud of. She'd felt like a grown up and sophisticated version of the newest member of the Constantinides family. And weren't those thoughts dangerous?

A few times she'd found herself beguiled by the elusive possibility of something which could never happen, not in a million years. Of a life here, with Xan. A proper married life together—with a brood of babies and a golden future. And a shared love? Yes. Oh, yes. That was the ultimate dream. But Xan didn't want that. He'd told her so enough times. He didn't *do* love and he was okay with that. So she needed to be okay with it, too.

A sudden lump constricted her throat as she found herself thinking about her mother. About the paperwork which had been discovered after her death. Her mother had been a foolish dreamer, too—and where had it got her? All those stupid poems she'd written. And the letter addressed to her—the daughter she had abandoned. She mustn't forget that. The letter which Hannah had only shown Tamsyn a long while afterwards, which had told her something it might have been better not to have known. Something which for a long time had made her feel rotten to the core—and still could, if she wasn't careful.

She could see the powerful beam of headlights tracking along the road towards the house and from her secluded vantage point, could sense the excited bustle of the guests as a huge car drew to a halt and a man got out. Even from this distance, from the few photographs she'd seen of him, Tamsyn recognised the distinctive curved features of Andreas, Xan's father. She watched as Xan moved purposefully towards the car, but you didn't need to be a body language expert to notice the coolness between the two men. After a brief and business-like handshake, they began to walk towards the house, making no attempt to join the party.

Tamsyn sat on the bench, filled with indecision. She ought to go and meet him. Hadn't that been part of the deal? Her heart was pounding as she moved through the shadows towards the back of the vast house, away from the main party which was mostly happening poolside. For a moment she stood in silence, until she located the sound of voices which were coming from behind the closed doors of Xan's study. Tamsyn frowned. Xan and presumably Andreas were angrily talking over each other, the volume of their discussion getting louder and louder until she heard someone rasp out a curse. She meant to take a deep breath. To knock politely and walk in, but then she heard her own name and it halted her right in her tracks. Tamsyn froze. She almost wished they were speaking in Greek so she wouldn't understand what they were saying, but Xan had told her that after winning his American scholarship, English had been the language he and his father had conversed in, the older man refusing to be outdone by his fluent son.

'You know what kind of a woman she is?' came the ragged accusation. 'When you rang to tell me you'd married her, I had her investigated and discovered she's a nobody who can't even hold a job down. And she looks like a slut in every photo I've seen of her!'

Tamsyn flinched as she waited for Xan to reply and his next words came as such a shock that she had to put her hand against the wall to steady herself.

'She's no slut,' Xan said. 'She's honest and decent and true. And I will not have you speaking about her that way. Do you understand?'

'And you know her mother was no better than a whore?' continued the older man. 'That she has children by many different men?'

'Yes, I know that,' replied Xan slowly. 'But that isn't Tamsyn. She's never really had a chance, but now she's been given one, she's come into her own. She'd uneducated but she's bright. She reads. She plays with Gia's little girl—and that child thinks she's an angel. She's funny. You should meet her. I think you'll be surprised.'

'Oh, I'm not denying she's beautiful.' His father gave an ugly kind of laugh. 'But that's the main reason she's here, isn't it? You turned down the chance to marry a woman like Sofia, for her? I've heard she's hot, but so what? Whores usually are. You get what you pay for.'

There was a loud bang, which sounded like a fist being smashed against a desk and Tamsyn was vaguely aware of Xan's furious response, but by then she had started to run. To run and run until she had left the house and been swallowed up by the dense shadow of a fragrant pine tree.

Her brow felt hot and sticky by the time she came to a halt and it took a long while before she had calmed down enough to be able to think straight. Time for her breathing to slow and her heart to stop feeling as if it were going to burst out of her chest. Something made her tidy up the strands of hair which must have escaped during her run and to extract a slim tube of lipstick from the concealed pocket of her dress, before applying it to her trembling lips with shaky fingers. Her dress was smooth and she needed her features to mimic that smoothness, so that to the other guests it would appear as if nothing had happened.

Because nothing had.

Xan's father had simply told the truth—and he didn't know the half of it. And although Xan had sprung to her defence and her heart had melted slightly at his defence of her—it had still been lacking in emotion. He had still somehow managed to make her sound like piece of rock which had been carved into a rough approximation of a human being.

And suddenly she knew she couldn't endure any more. There was no way she could stay here, pretending to be someone she wasn't. If she did that, then these crazy feelings would keep building and building until she was ready to explode. She needed to walk away with Xan never guessing what had happened. To escape, and quickly—but not tonight. Tonight she would continue to play the role expected of her. The shining and loyal wife, basking in her newly-wed golden glow. The woman lucky enough to have finally snared the elusive Greek billionaire.

She drank a glass of champagne before going back to the illuminated swimming pool to join the other guests, chatting brightly and forcing herself to smile as she accepted congratulations. But her stupid heart turned over with sorrow when Xan reappeared and began to walk towards her.

Did he read something untoward in her expression?

Was that why a frown had creased his brow beneath the delicious tumble of his black hair?

'You okay?' he questioned.

She could tell him, of course. She could say she'd gone into the house to meet his father and heard him calling her a whore. But if she did that, the evening would be ruined—and for what purpose? The fact that Xan's father didn't like her should be regarded as a positive, surely? It meant he would be delighted when his son announced they were splitting up. Maybe their own relationship would even improve as a result. What was it they said? Every cloud has a silver lining.

You can do this, Tamsyn, she told herself fiercely. *You've had a lifetime of pretending everything's okay. Of acting like it doesn't matter when other people judge you, or look down their noses at you.*

'Yes, I'm fine,' she said, then cleared her throat. 'Did I see your father arrive?'

'You did.' An odd expression darkened his face. 'But he couldn't stay.'

'Oh? Was he—?'

'I don't want to talk about my father, Tamsyn,' he interrupted, and suddenly his voice sounded urgent. 'I just want to be alone with you.'

Her heart felt like it wanted to break when she heard the note of hunger she heard in his voice, but she couldn't stop herself from responding to it. 'Xan,' she said, mock-sternly. 'We have guests.'

'I don't care about the guests.' His voice dipped. 'There's only one thing I care about right now.'

His smile was hard and his eyes gleamed with an unspoken message. It reminded her that Xan remained a man who always got what he wanted, and right now he wanted sex. Tamsyn shivered as he traced a finger down her arm, knowing she should refuse to go along with it, especially in view of what his father had said earlier.

You get what you pay for.

But her mind was made up. She wasn't going to ruin the night by dwelling on the negative and besides, she wanted him just as much as he wanted her. Maybe even more. Xan had no idea this was going to be the last time, but she did—and wasn't it crazy not to want to make the most of every precious second with him?

'Then what are we waiting for?' she questioned huskily, as she went into his warm and waiting arms.

CHAPTER TWELVE

'WHAT ARE YOU talking about?' Xan stared at his housekeeper in disbelief. 'What do you mean, she's *gone*?'

But he barely listened to Manalena's distressed explanation as he stormed up to the bedroom because the evidence was there for him to see. He shook his head with disbelief as he pulled open one of the closet doors. Only the most basic of Tamsyn's clothes were missing—all the fancy ones remained. His throat dried as he reached out to touch the white gown she'd worn at their wedding party, which he'd almost torn in his eagerness to remove it from her body last night. Her unread books were no longer in a pile beside the bed-side table and that wide-toothed comb thing she used to rake through her unruly curls in the mornings was nowhere to be seen.

He dismissed the housekeeper as he saw a note she must have left lying on the pillow, striding across the room to pick it up and resisting the desire to crush it to a pulp within the palm of his hand. It was short and to the point. Was that deliberate? Was she mocking him for that terse note he'd once left *her* in a faraway desert palace?

Xan,
I've decided to go sooner rather than later and I
didn't want the bore of saying goodbye, I'm sure
you'll understand.
    Below you'll find all my bank details and I
look forward to hearing from your lawyer.
Yours, Tamsyn.

He stared at it, his eyes scanning the words in disbelief, as if there had to be some kind of mistake. But there was no mistake. There it was, in black and white. A stark farewell, which seemed mainly concerned with getting her payment for their short-lived marriage.

His mouth twisted. He'd gone back to the office this morning, strangely reluctant to leave the seductive warmth of his wife's body and the lazy caress of her arms after their surprisingly satisfactory honeymoon. The day had seemed to drag in a way he wasn't used to and several times he'd found himself picking up the phone to ring her, just to say hello, before reminding himself that wasn't his style and putting it down again. He'd told himself it was normal to be physically aching for her, because they'd been having so much amazing sex since the day of their marriage and they'd been together exclusively for fourteen days and nights. Elena had looked startled when he'd suddenly announced he was leaving early and his heart had been beating like a drum as his car had been driven at high speed to the estate, only to discover that his wife had gone. And to discover just how she had spent *her* day...

A bitter taste coated his throat. She must have

been silently planning her get-away. How long had she been plotting that, he wondered? While his own driver had been busy ferrying him around the city, she had persuaded Manalena to call her a cab to take her into Athens, supposedly on a shopping trip—before slipping away to the airport to catch a regular flight to London. Had she been laughing quietly as her lips had locked against his that morning, knowing what a surprise she was about to spring on him? Was that why her hand had slid between his legs to find his hardness—he was always hard for her—and guided him inside her slick, waiting heat for one last, bone-melting time?

He paced over to the window but the bright beauty of the Aegean failed to stir his heart, for his rage and incomprehension were all-consuming. Didn't she owe him the common courtesy of telling him she was breaking their agreement by leaving early, or at least explaining why?

He told himself not to do anything. To give himself time to calm down. But even as he thought it, he found himself lifting his phone and barking out instructions to Elena to have his private jet made ready. He didn't know what he was going to say to his runaway bride, all he knew was that he had to say *something*.

Tamsyn stared at the photograph, as if doing so could help. It was that old trick of voluntarily subjecting herself to pain before anyone else got the chance to do it. As if that could somehow make her immune to it.

Some hope. The photograph was from a gossip column and had obviously been taken at the wedding party. She didn't imagine Xan's friends were the type who sneaked photos at exclusive social events, but there had been a lot of outside caterers there that night and maybe one of them had captured the moment. And, oh, what a moment to have captured.

Beneath a headline which proclaimed *Greek Tycoon Weds at Last!* was a photo of her and Xan. She thought how dreamy she looked and how *happy* she seemed as she stared up into his face. And Xan? Tamsyn sighed. His darkly contoured features gave little away, but maybe it was good to recognise that. To reinforce that she'd done the right thing in running away from his luxury estate, because if she'd stayed around, growing fonder and fonder of him—then her heart would have been truly broken.

Yet didn't it feel a little bit broken now?

From a long way downstairs she heard the doorbell ring, but she didn't move. It wasn't her house—she was just lucky that her friend Ellie from the Bluebird Club had an attic room going free and had told Tamsyn she was welcome to stay there until she'd found her feet again. Funny expression, really. As if someone could lose their own feet. She couldn't imagine going back to waitressing, yet neither could she summon up the enthusiasm to enrol in college to get herself a late-in-the-day education, despite Xan's faith in her. And the craziest thing of all was that, having married just to get her hands on his money, she now found herself reluctant to take any of it. The deliberately cold note she'd left for him had been nothing but bravado—done to ensure that he would ultimately despise her and leave her in peace.

'Tamsyn!'

It was Ellie. With a sigh Tamsyn got up off the single bed, walked across the tiny room and stuck her head outside the door. 'Yep?' she yelled down.

'There's somebody here to see you.'

Tamsyn blinked. Nobody other than Ellie knew she was back, because that was how she wanted it. Time to lick her wounds and recover—even if right now that seemed like an impossibility. She'd told Hannah she was here, in a rushed phone call to the palace in Zahristan when she'd tried her very best—and somehow succeeded—in not sobbing her heart out as she explained that her brief marriage was over. Surely her heavily pregnant sister hadn't impulsively flown over to see her?

'Who is it?' she called back.

'Me,' said a dark, accented voice which carried up the stairs. 'Your husband.'

Tamsyn clutched onto the door handle, trying not to react as she saw a glimpse of the top of Xan's dark head as he walked up the stairs. A lurch of joy and fear made her feel almost dizzy, but most of all she could feel an overwhelming sense of yearning as his broad shoulders came into view. But she wasn't going to let him know that, because one thing she knew was that there could be no going back. She could be strong, yes—she'd spent her life trying to be strong in the face of adversity. Just not strong enough to stay with a man who was never going to care for her.

'Xan,' she croaked, as he drew closer. 'What…what are you doing here?'

'Not now,' he said grimly as he reached the top of the stairs. 'In private.'

'Everything okay?' called Ellie's anxiously from the bottom of the stairs.

'Everything's just fine,' said Xan, in the kind of tone which broached no argument.

Tamsyn felt even more dizzy as he reached the top of the stairs and gestured for her to proceed him into the room, still with that same grim expression on his face. She told herself she didn't have to let him in. After all, it was *her* room, not his—and technically he could even be described as trespassing. She could tell him to leave and only to contact her through her lawyers, but deep down she knew that wasn't an option—and not just because she didn't actually *have* any lawyers. It was more because she wanted to feast her eyes on him one last time. To file away the memory of those cold blue eyes, that hot body, and the sensual mouth which had brought her so much pleasure.

'So, Tamsyn,' he said, once he was inside the miniscule room and completely dominating it, having flicked a dismissive glance at the tiny bed and the view out over an alley which was lined with overflowing dustbins. 'Are you going to explain why you decided to run off without telling me?'

Her heart was beating very fast as she sucked in a deep breath. No, she wasn't. Because she didn't owe him anything. Nothing.

But the defensiveness which had always been second nature to her wasn't coming as easily as usual and she wondered how convincing her nonchalant shrug was. 'We both knew it had to end sometime,' she said carelessly. 'I just made an executive decision to end it early. It was a fake marriage, Xan. It was conceived to get you out of a tight spot and as far as I'm concerned, I've performed my part of the bargain.'

'Why, Tamsyn?' he said simply.

Once again, she shrugged, even though when he said her name like that it made her want to cry. 'I heard… I heard you talking with your father.'

His eyes narrowed in comprehension and then he nodded. 'Did you now? So you will have heard me defending you.'

'Yes, I heard you. Thanks.'

He looked at her. 'And that's it?'

She nodded. 'Yep, that's it. There's nothing more to say. I don't even know why you're here.'

'Because I don't understand. And I need to understand.'

She shook her head so that her unruly curls flew all around her shoulders and impatiently she pushed them away. 'No,' she negated heatedly. 'You don't *need* to understand, Xan. You *want* to understand—and there's a difference. I know you're rich and powerful, but even you have got to realise that you can't always get what you want. So will you please go?'

He shook his head. 'There's something you're not telling me, Tamsyn.'

'And? What if there is? You're not privy to my innermost thoughts—even if we were a real married couple, which we're not! You have no right to expect explanations.'

'I disagree,' he said coolly. 'I think I do, and I'm not going anywhere until you start talking to me. I want the truth, Tamsyn. I think you owe me that, at least.'

Did she? Did she owe him *anything*? For the sexual awakening, or for making her realise that she was as capable of love as anyone else? As she stared into his resolute face, Tamsyn recognised she was in real danger here. She wanted her heart to stop hurting but the only way that was going to happen was if Xan went away and left her alone, and he wasn't showing any sign of doing that. She could see the look of determination on his face and realised he meant it when he'd said he wouldn't be satisfied with anything but the truth.

So should she tell him and witness his disgust when he realised what kind of person he'd really married? Watch his gorgeous face freeze with fastidious horror when he learned the truth about her gene pool? And that might that be the best outcome of all, because then he really *would* say goodbye and she could begin the long process of getting over him. If she pushed him away first—at least he wouldn't be able to turn round and do it to her. She sucked in an unsteady breath. 'You described me as honest and decent and true,' she said quietly. 'But I'm not. At least, I'm not honest.'

'What are you talking about?'

Don't let your voice shake. And, above all, don't cry.

'You only know half the truth. That my mother was a groupie—'

'Yes, yes. That's old news,' he said impatiently.

She shook her head, but her determination not to cry was failing her. She felt her eyes brimming with tears and saw Xan flinch, as if he found such a spectacle distasteful. He probably did. He didn't like emotion. It was messy and he wasn't used to it. Well, neither was she if it came to that, but for once in her life Tamsyn was finding it impossible to hold back the shuddering sob which seemed to erupt from the very bottom of her lungs.

'Well, here's some hot-off-the-press news!' she snarled. 'My father was a rock star. A very famous rock star. His name was Jonny Trafford.'

'Jonny Trafford? Wow.' He frowned. 'But he—'

'I'm not interested in how many albums you had of his. You want to know what happened?' she rushed on, waving her hand impatiently to silence him in her determination to tell him the facts. The unvarnished facts—not the version which everyone knew. It was the only thing she had left of Jonny Trafford—her few brief and bitter memories. 'He had a one-night stand with my mother.' Her voice shook with something like shame. 'According to his official biography, he had similar nights with lots of women. Sometimes with more than one at the same time...'

'Tamsyn—'

'Shut *up*!' she declared as the tears now began to stream down her cheeks and the words came choking out. 'You know my mother had us fostered because we got in the way of her latest love interest? I know. Shocking, isn't it? And after she died Hannah came into possession of her paperwork, including a letter addressed to me which contained the bombshell discovery that Jonny Trafford was my father. But Hannah didn't tell me that. At least, not straight away.'

He narrowed his eyes. 'Why not?'

'She was trying to protect me, just like she'd always done.' Tamsyn stabbed at her wet cheeks with a balled-up fist. 'She thought I'd been through enough hurt and wanted to make sure I wasn't going to endure any more. So she went to see him.' Her voice tailed off but his face was intent as he leaned forward.

'Tell me, Tamsyn.'

She shook her head as she looked at him, knowing this was it. The words tasted sour as she began to speak them but she forced herself to keep looking at the man she had married, no matter how much it hurt. No matter how much disgust he showed when he heard the truth. 'He was a full-blown junkie by then, of course. She said she'd never seen anyone look so pathetic, in his huge mansion with all those great big mirrors and shaggy rugs, and the dusty platinum discs on the walls. But when she told him about me, she said she thought she saw a light in his eyes. He told her straight off he was going to go into rehab, like his manager had been nagging at him to do for years, and he did. And that was when she told me about him.'

'Well, that was good, wasn't it?' Xan questioned.

Tamsyn shrugged. 'Yeah, I suppose so. He wasn't allowed any contact with the outside world for six weeks, not until he was properly clean, but he was allowed to write letters. He wrote to me and said he was looking forward to seeing me and I can remember how excited I felt. I had no real memories of my mother, but here was the chance to connect with my roots at last. I know it sounds stupid but I wanted to see if I had the same nose, or eyes, or if we walked in a similar way. I wanted to feel *connected*.'

'It doesn't sound stupid.' There was a pause and his eyes were very steady as he looked at her. 'What happened?'

'We arranged to meet in a famous London hotel, for tea, but...' She swallowed, then shook her head and it took a couple of moments before she could compose herself enough to continue. 'He couldn't face it—or maybe the lure of heroin was stronger than the thought of meeting his daughter for the first time. I sat in that fancy hotel for ages with barely enough money to pay the inflated price of the pot of tea I'd had to order.

I remember getting lots of pitying looks—probably because of the way I was dressed. Or maybe people thought I'd been stood up. Which I had, I g-guess.' She swallowed again, but now the tears were like hot rivers coursing down her cheeks and the pain in her heart was fierce and intense as she relived a scenario she hadn't allowed herself to think about for years. 'When I came out it was dark and the evening news bulletins were flashing up on TV screens in a nearby department store—and the lead story was that Jonny Trafford had been found dead in a hotel room with a needle hanging out of his arm.'

'Tamsyn—'

'No!' she interrupted, her voice trembling as she fished a tissue out of the back of her jeans and loudly blew her nose. 'Don't say all the things you think you're supposed to say. Because words won't change anything, Xan. I know it was terrible but I've come to terms with the fact that neither my father nor my mother wanted me, and that's why I'm so screwed up. Whichever way you look at it, I'm not the right type of wife for you. My unsuitability runs deeper than you thought and it's far better we split now, rather than later. So just go, will you? Go now and leave me in peace.'

He shook his head. 'But I don't want to go.'

'When will you get it into your thick skull that I don't care what *you* want?' she flared back. 'I'm telling you my wishes and since this is my home, for now at least, you will have to listen to them!'

But Xan didn't move. There was silence for a moment as he glanced over his shoulder to survey the bleak view outside the window and then looked back at her, the woman he had married. He saw the way her lips quivered with belligerence and pride and shame. Her cheeks were wet and streaky and fiery strands of hair were matted with tears. Her expression was defiant but wary as she returned his gaze—like a dog which had spent its life being kicked but had just enough spirit left to fight back. And that was Tamsyn all right. He admired her spirit and always had done.

He hadn't been expecting yet another layer to her tragic life story. He hadn't realised just how deeply she'd been damaged. He'd imagined coming here today and after some token resistance, the two of them having some pretty urgent sex up against the wall, since that bed looked way too small to accommodate two people. Unwilling to let her go just yet, he'd planned to take her back to Greece, thinking that a few months more of his feisty spouse would be enough to get her out of his system.

But now he recognised that he couldn't do that. He couldn't pick her up and put her down, using her like his own sexy little toy. To do that would be to dishonour and disrespect her—and damage her further. Didn't she deserve every bit of his respect after what she'd been through? His heart clenched, knowing that if he wanted this to work—he was going to have to give more than he'd ever given before. He was going to have to have the courage to open up and confront his feelings—just as she had done with him.

'You know that with you, it's like it's never been for me before,' he said softly.

Her emerald eyes clouded with suspicion. 'What are you talking about?'

'I'm talking about you. How different it is with you.

It's been different from the start, Tamsyn—in every way. You're fresh and feisty and original—and more fun than any other woman I've ever known. And we're alike. I see that now. We both grew up rejected by our mothers. We didn't know how to express love because nobody had ever shown us how.' He sucked in a deep and unsteady breath. 'The thing is that I think we could be good together. Not for three months, or a year—but for ever.'

'For ever?' she echoed, as if this was a concept beyond her comprehension.

He nodded. 'It won't always be easy and it won't always be fun. There'll be bad times as well as good, because my married friends tell me that's what life is like. But I think we can be strong for each other and supportive of each other, if the will is there.'

He saw the brief hope which flared in her face before it was banished by that determined little expression of mutiny once more. 'No. It won't work. It can't work,' she husked. 'It'll all end in tears, I know it will. So do yourself a favour, Xan—and get away from me.'

'Sorry.' He shook his head again. 'No I can't do that. You aren't going to sabotage this, Tamsyn—no matter how hard you try. And even if you continue to glare at me and send me away—I'll just keep coming back until you give me the answer that both of us really want. Which is that you will be my wife for real.'

She chewed on her bottom lip as her eyes swam with green tears and it took a full minute before she could form the words. 'You...you really mean it?' she whispered.

He slammed his palm against the left side of his sternum. 'From the bottom of my heart.'

At this she started crying again but this time the tears were different and her mouth was trying to smile instead of wobbling with pain and Xan pulled her into his arms and kissed her with a tenderness he hadn't known he possessed. For a long while they just stood there, locked in each other's arms as their mouths connected in kiss after kiss, and not long after that, Xan made the discovery that the bed was plenty big enough for what he had in mind.

Efficiently, he stripped off all their clothes and it wasn't until he had filled her with his seed and heard her choke out her own cry of fulfilment, that he finally felt as if he was exactly where he needed to be in the world. That everything he'd ever wanted was right here, right now. They lay there, quiet and contented and Xan was stroking Tamsyn's tumbled curls when he tilted her chin to look at him.

'One thing interests me,' he said.

Dreamily, she looked up into his face. 'Mmm?'

'Why didn't you make a claim on Jonny's estate, which presumably you didn't? You could have been a very wealthy woman.'

Tamsyn shook her head. Even Hannah had told her she should try to get something from Jonny Trafford's property portfolio and his back catalogue of songs,, but Tamsyn hadn't wanted to know. 'It all just seemed too sordid,' she said slowly. 'I knew there would be publicity and DNA tests and inevitable opposition to my claim and I couldn't…'

'You couldn't face them?'

'That's right. It wasn't worth it. All the money in the world wouldn't have tempted me to put myself through an ordeal like that.'

He flinched. 'Yet you were willing to marry me for a price.'

She met the question in his eyes and shrugged. 'To be honest, it wasn't for me. I was worried about my sister.'

'Hannah?' He looked at her in bemusement. 'Who's married to one of the wealthiest men on the planet?'

She nodded. 'At the time I wasn't sure if her marriage to the Sheikh was going to last and realised I needed funds to help her if she needed to get away from him. That's why I did it.'

He pulled her closer and his eyes were darkly blue. 'Oh, I love you, Tamsyn Constantinides. I love you because you're strong and brave and loyal. You are the bright fire in my life, my love—and the world would be a very dark and cold place without you.'

Tamsyn swallowed, knowing that there was one thing more which needed to be addressed. 'It doesn't matter what my reasons were, Xan,' she said quietly. 'I still married you for money, didn't I? All your life you've been pursued by women who know how wealthy you are and maybe at heart, you think we're all gold-diggers. I can't blame you for that, Xan. If I were you, I might even think the same!'

He traced his finger thoughtfully over the trembling outline of her mouth. 'Okay. Let's sort this out once and for all. Will you answer me just one question, Tamsyn, with all the honesty you have already demonstrated today?'

She hooded her eyes suspiciously. 'Just one?'

'Just one.' He looked her straight in the eyes. 'If I didn't have a cent in the world, would you be lying with me now, like this?'

It wasn't a fair question because there could be no equivocation about her answer and more stupid tears sprang to Tamsyn's eyes as she nodded. 'Of course I would,' she whispered. 'Because I love you for you, Xan—you and only you. All the other stuff simply doesn't matter.'

His face was serious as he kissed away her tears and only when her cheeks were dry did he turn his attention to her mouth. And the kiss which followed was like no other. It wasn't about sex, or ownership or possession. It was seeking and tender. It spoke of compassion and true intimacy. It spoke of the powerful trust which existed between them now. It spoke of sanctuary and a golden future.

And for the first time in her life, Tamsyn felt safe.

EPILOGUE

'IT'S SO *BEAUTIFUL*,' breathed Tamsyn as the sun sank slowly into the sea, turning the surrounding water into contrasting shades of deep purple and gold.

'I know,' said Xan softly. 'Utterly beautiful.'

Tamsyn looked up to find her husband's gaze fixed not on the magnificent spectacle taking place over the Aegean but on her. 'Xan,' she said, in mock-reprimand. 'I was talking about the view.'

'So was I. But in my mind there's no contest. The sunset on this island is always magnificent—but its blaze is nothing compared to the colour of your hair, *agape mou*.'

Tamsyn gave a shiver of delight as his silken words washed over her. 'If only I'd realised I was marrying a poet.'

'There were a lot of things we didn't know about each other back then.'

Their eyes met. 'But we do now,' she said.

'Yes.'

He walked over to where she stood, on the strip of land not far from the beach. Behind her was the small stone house where their son lay sleeping and in front of her was the endless potential of the night ahead. This was their fourth day on Prassakri, where the bones of Xan's ancestors lay. They'd spent lazy hours walking and talking and teaching their son how to swim. They'd built sandcastles and eaten picnics as they explored the stunning island, where little had changed over the centuries.

But it had been a rollercoaster three years since their wedding.

After initially refusing to sell Xan the island, Sofia's father had eventually agreed on a deal. A deal prompted by the discovery that his daughter was in love with one of his farm labourers, and had been for years—and they needed an injection of cash to start up on their own. Sofia had met Tamsyn and Xan for lunch in Athens and told them everything.

'I knew Papa would never allow me to marry Georgiou because he was so poor,' she'd explained, looking down at her plain gold wedding band with an expression of delight. 'Which was why my long-term engagement to Xan worked so well. It's why I was so happy to go along with it. As a kind of smokescreen, I guess.'

Xan had smiled and so had Tamsyn, glad that no hearts had been broken during the fictitious understanding.

The reconciliation with Xan's father had happened slowly—bolstered by the knowledge that his ancestral island was back under the ownership of the Constantinides family. But the real rapprochement had come after the birth of Tamsyn and Xan's child. Andreas had unexpectedly turned up on the doorstep with a jar of honey—which apparently was a Greek tradition—his eyes filling with tears as he had gazed down at his newborn grandson. These days he came to their house on the Peloponnese peninsula often, enjoying the kind of warm family life he'd never really experienced before.

Tamsyn glanced up at the sky. The sun had almost disappeared and in the darkening indigo sky was the first faint sprinkle of stars.

'I think it's time for us to go to bed, *agape mou*,' observed Xan throatily. 'Don't you?'

Leaning back against his broad chest, Tamsyn nodded. 'Mmm,' she agreed. 'Let's.'

It was still early but they liked to retire early for they enjoyed nothing better than the endless discovery of each other's bodies. The ancient stone steps absorbed the sound of their footsteps as they went upstairs and peeped in on their toddler son who lay contentedly sleeping and sucking his thumb.

'He's worn out,' said Xan approvingly.

'Are you surprised?' She wrinkled her nose. 'He seems a bit young to start playing tennis.'

'That's not what his godfather says.'

'No.' There was a pause while Tamsyn considered the very real chance that her son's godfather would one day be president of the United States of America. She looked down and smiled as she studied the unruly black curls which looked so dark against the sheet. Andreas Alexandros Iohannis. She'd known that another tradition was to call the first born son after his paternal grandfather, but it had been Xan who had suggested including the Greek version of John among his names. At first Tamsyn hadn't known how she felt about that, until a sudden rush of emotion had reminded her that nobody could deny their roots, even if those roots had been allowed to wither, and die. Nobody knew that Jonny Trafford was her father, but echoes of him would live on in her child. She hoped that Andreas inherited some of his undoubted talent, and prayed that they could nurture him with enough love to defeat his demons.

She drew in a deep breath as she stared up at Xan, her heart suddenly beating very fast. 'We won't make the mistakes our own parents did,' she said unsteadily.

'No,' he agreed, his watchful gaze understanding. 'We'll make our own. But we'll try to limit them.'

'Yes,' she agreed as he pulled her into his arms.

'And we'll be honest enough to say if we think either of us is stepping out of line.' He tilted her chin to look directly into her eyes. 'Because we love each other and we're completely honest with each other, Tamsyn—and nothing is ever going to change that. Do you understand?'

Clamping her lips together, she nodded. 'Oh, Xan,' she said eventually, as she touched her fingertips to the roughened shadow at his jaw. 'I must have done something very good in a previous life, to have ended up with you.'

His eyes glinted as he led her from the nursery. 'I like the thought of you being good,' he murmured, as he began to undo the sarong which was knotted around her hips. 'But I like the thought of you being bad much better.'

'Do you really?' she said, tugging eagerly at the zip of his jeans. 'Then I'd better do as my husband desires.'

And she could hear nothing but his growl of contentment as she climbed on top of him in the silver moonlight, and day gave way to night.

* * * * *

THE CONSEQUENCE OF HIS VENGEANCE

JENNIE LUCAS

To Pippa Roscoe, with best wishes
for a brilliant future.

You are going to rock it!!

THE GREEK'S BACK IN HIS BED... IN SECRET!

Letitia stood recently frozen into coolness in a shiny. You would still be in a crust.

Her heart, her flesh had said. Dallas's love, of and Letty think it any—a tangent. She lived Darjanian-ish... to be here, to me.

CHAPTER ONE

LETTY SPENCER HUNCHED her shoulders against the frosty February night as she pushed out of the Brooklyn diner, door swinging behind her. Her body was exhausted after her double shift, but not half as weary as her heart.

It had not been a good day.

Shivering in her threadbare coat, Letty lowered her head against the biting wind on the dark street. Snow flurries brushed against her exposed skin.

"Letitia." The voice was low and husky behind her. Letty's back snapped straight.

No one called her Letitia anymore, not even her father. Letitia Spencer had been the pampered heiress of Fairholme. Letty was just another New York waitress struggling to make ends meet for her family.

And that voice sounded like...

He sounded like...

Gripping her purse strap tight, she slowly turned around. *And lost her breath.*

Darius Kyrillos stood against a glossy black sports car parked on the street. Dark-haired and dark-eyed, he was devastatingly handsome and powerful in his well-cut suit and black wool coat, standing beneath the softly falling snowflakes illuminated by a streetlight.

For a moment, Letty struggled to make sense of what her eyes were telling her. Darius? Here?

"Did you see this?" her father had said excitedly that morning, spreading the newspaper across their tiny kitchen counter. "Darius Kyrillos sold his company for twenty billion dollars!" He looked up, his eyes unfocused with painkillers, his recently broken arm awkward in a sling. "You should call him, Letty. Make him love you again."

After ten years, her father had said Darius's name out loud. He'd broken the unspoken rule. She'd fled, mumbling that she'd be late for work.

But it had affected her all day, making her clumsily drop trays and forget orders. She'd even dumped a plate of eggs and bacon on a customer. It was a miracle she hadn't been fired.

No, Letty thought, unable to breathe. This was the miracle. Right now.

Darius.

She took a step toward him on the sidewalk, her eyes wide.

"Darius?" she whispered. "Is it really you?"

He came forward like a dark angel. She could see his breath beneath the streetlight like white smoke in the icy night. He stopped, towering over her. The light frosted his dark hair, leaving his face in shadow. She half expected him to disappear if she tried to touch him. So she didn't.

Then he touched her.

Reaching out, he stroked a dark tendril that had escaped her ponytail, twisted it around his finger. "You're surprised?"

At the sound of that low, husky voice, lightly accented from his early childhood in Greece, a deep shiver sent a rush of prickles over her skin. And she knew he wasn't a dream.

Her heart pounded. Darius. The man she'd tried not to crave for the last decade. The man she'd dreamed about against her will, night after night. Here. Now. She choked out a sob. "What are you doing here?"

His dark eyes ran over her hungrily. "I couldn't resist."

As he moved his head, the streetlight illuminated his face. He hadn't changed at all, Letty thought in wonder. The same years that had nearly destroyed her hadn't touched him. He was the same man she remembered, the one she'd once loved with all her innocent heart, back when she'd been a headstrong eighteen-year-old, caught up in a forbidden love affair. Before she'd sacrificed her own happiness to save his.

His hand moved down to her shoulder. Feeling his warmth through her thin coat, she wanted to cry, to ask him what had taken so long. She'd almost given up hope.

Then she saw his gaze linger on her old coat, with its broken zipper, and her diner uniform, a white dress that had been bleached so many times it was starting to fray. Usually, she also wore unfashionable nylons to keep her legs warm while she was on her feet all day in white orthopedic shoes. But today, her last pair had been unwearable with too many rips, so her legs were bare.

Following his gaze, she blushed. "I'm not really dressed for going out…"

"Your clothes don't matter." There was a strange undercurrent in his voice. "Let's go."

"Go? Where?"

He took her hand in his own, palm to palm, and she suddenly didn't feel the snowflakes or cold. Waves of electricity scattered helter-skelter across her body, across her skin, from her scalp to her toes.

"My penthouse. In Midtown." He looked down at her. "Will you come?"

"Yes," she breathed.

His sensual lips curved oddly before he led her to his shiny, low-slung sports car and opened the passenger door.

As Letty climbed in, she took a deep breath, inhaling the scent of rich leather. This car likely cost more than she'd earned the past decade waiting tables. She moved her hand along the fine calfskin, the color of pale cream. She'd forgotten leather could be so soft.

Climbing in beside her, Darius started the engine. The car roared away from the curb, humming through the night, leaving her neighborhood to travel through the gentrified areas of Park Slope and Brooklyn Heights before finally crossing the Manhattan Bridge into the New York borough that most catered to tourists and the wealthy: Manhattan.

All the while, Letty was intensely aware of him beside her. Her gaze fell upon his hand and thick wrist, laced with dark hair, as he changed gears.

"So." His voice was ironic. "Your father is out of prison."

Biting her lip, she looked at him hesitantly beneath her lashes. "A few days ago."

Darius glanced back at her old coat and fraying uniform. "And now you're ready to change your life."

Was that a question or a suggestion? Did he mean that *he* wanted to change it? Had he actually learned the truth about why she'd betrayed him ten years ago?

"I've learned the hard way," she said in a low voice, "that life changes, whether you're ready or not."

His hands tightened as he turned back to the steering wheel. "True."

Letty's eyes lingered on his profile, from the dark slash of eyebrows to his aquiline nose and full, sensual mouth. She still felt like she was dreaming. *Darius Kyrillos.* After all these years, he'd found her at the diner and was whisking her off to his penthouse. The only man she'd ever truly loved...

"Why did you come for me?" she whispered. "Why today, after all these years?"

His dark gaze was veiled. "Your message."

She hadn't sent any message. "What message?"

"Fine," he murmured, baring his teeth in a smile. "Have it your way."

Message? Letty felt a skitter of dark suspicion. Her father had wanted her to contact Darius. For the last few days, since he'd broken his arm in mysterious circumstances he wouldn't explain, he'd been home on painkillers, sitting next to her ancient computer with nothing to do.

Could her father have sent Darius a message, pretending to be her?

She glanced at Darius, then decided she didn't care. If her father had interfered, all she could be was grateful, if this was the result.

Her father must have revealed her real reasons for betraying Darius ten years ago. She couldn't imagine he would even be talking to her now otherwise.

But how to know for sure?

Biting her lip, she said awkwardly, "I read about you in the paper this morning. That you sold. Your company, I mean."

"Ah." His jaw set as he turned away. "Right."

His voice was cold. No wonder, Letty thought. She sounded like an idiot. She tried to steady herself. "Congratulations."

"Thank you. It cost ten years of my life."

Ten years. Those two simple words hung between them in silence, like a small raft on an ocean of regret.

Their car entered Manhattan, with all its wealth and savagery. A place she'd avoided since her father's trial and sentencing almost a decade before.

Her heartbeat fluttered in her throat as she looked down at her chapped hands, folded tightly in her lap. "I've thought of you a lot, wondering how you were. Hoping you were well. Hoping you were happy."

Stopping at a red light, Darius abruptly looked at her.

"It was good of you to think of me," he drawled in a low voice, once again with that strange undercurrent. In the cold night of the city, headlights of passing cars moved shadows across the hard lines of his face.

The light changed to green. It was just past ten o'clock,

and the traffic was starting to lessen. Heading north on First Avenue, they passed the United Nations plaza. The buildings had started climbing higher against the sky as they approached Midtown. Turning off Forty-Ninth onto the gracious width of Park Avenue, they approached a newly built glass-and-steel skyscraper on the south side of Central Park.

As he pulled his car into the porte cochere, she was craning her neck back in astonishment. "You live here?"

"I have the top two floors," he said casually, in the way someone might say, *I have tickets to the ballet.*

His door opened, and he handed the keys to a smiling valet who greeted him respectfully by name. Coming around, Darius opened Letty's door. He held out his hand.

She stared at it nervously, then put her hand in his.

He wrapped it tightly in his own. She felt the warmth and roughness of his palm against hers.

He had to know, she thought desperately. He had to. Otherwise, why would he have sought her out? Why wouldn't he still hate her?

He led her through the awe-inspiring lobby, with its minimalist furniture and twenty-foot ceilings.

"Good evening, Mr. Kyrillos," the man at the desk said. "Cold weather we're having. Hope you're staying warm!"

Darius held Letty's hand tightly. She felt like she might catch flame as he drew her across the elegant, cavernous lobby. "I am. Thank you, Perry."

He waved his key fob in front of the elevator's wall panel and pressed the seventieth floor.

His hand gripped hers as the elevator traveled up. She felt the warmth of his body next to hers, just inches away, towering over her. She bit her lip, unable to look at him. She just stared at the electronic numbers displaying the floors as the elevator rose higher and higher. *Sixty-eight, sixty-nine, seventy...*

The bell dinged as the door slid open.

"After you," Darius said.

Glancing at him nervously, she stepped out directly into a dark, high-ceilinged penthouse. He followed her, as the elevator door closed silently behind them.

The rubber soles of her white shoes squeaked against the marble floor as she walked through the foyer beneath the modern crystal chandelier above. She flinched at the noise, embarrassed.

But his handsome face held no expression as he removed his long black overcoat. He didn't turn on any lights. He never looked away from her.

With a gulp, she turned away.

Gripping her purse strap, she walked forward into the shadowy main room. It was two stories high, with sparse, angular furniture in black and gray, and floor-to-ceiling windows twisted around the penthouse in every direction.

Looking from right to left, she could see the dark vista of Central Park, the high-rise buildings to the Hudson River, and the lights of New Jersey beyond it, and to the south, the skyscrapers of Midtown, including the Empire State Building, all the way to the Financial District and the gleaming One World Trade Center.

The sparkling nighttime view provided the only light in the penthouse, aside from a single blue gas fire that flickered in the stark fireplace.

"Incredible," Letty breathed, going up to the windows. Without thinking, she leaned forward, putting her overheated forehead against the cool glass, looking down at Park Avenue far below. The cars and yellow cabs looked tiny, like ants. She felt almost dizzy from being so high off the earth, up in the clouds. It was a little terrifying. "Beautiful."

His reply was husky behind her. "*You* are beautiful, Letitia."

Turning, she looked at him in the soft blue glow of firelight. Then, as she looked more closely…

Her lips parted with an intake of breath.

She'd thought Darius hadn't changed?

He'd changed completely.

At thirty-four, he was no longer a slender youth, but a powerful man. His shoulders had broadened to match his tall height, his body filling out with hard muscle. His dark hair had once been wavy and tousled, like a poet's, but was now cut short, as severe as his chiseled jawline.

Everything about Darius was tightly controlled now, from the cut of his expensive clothes—a black shirt with the top button undone, black trousers, black leather shoes—to his powerful stance. His mouth had once been expressive and tender and kind. Now his lips had a hard twist of arrogance, even cruelty.

He towered over her like a king, in his penthouse with all of New York City at his feet.

At her expression, his jaw tightened. "Letitia…"

"Letty." She managed a smile. "No one calls me Letitia anymore."

"I have never been able to forget you," he continued in a low voice. "Or that summer we were together…"

That summer. A small noise came from the back of her throat as unwanted memories filled her mind. Dancing in the meadow. Kissing the night after her debutante ball. Escaping the prying eyes of servants in Fairholme's enormous garage, steaming up the windows of her father's vintage car collection for weeks on end. She'd been ready to surrender everything.

Darius was the one who'd wanted to wait for marriage to consummate their love.

"Not until you're my wife," he'd whispered as they strained for each other, barely clothed, panting with need in the backseat of a vintage limousine. "Not until you're mine forever."

Forever never came. Their romance had been illicit, forbidden. She was barely eighteen, his boss's daughter; he was six years older, the chauffeur's son.

After a hot summer of innocent passion, her father had been infuriated when he'd discovered their romance. He'd ordered Darius off the estate. For one awful week he and Letty had been apart. Then Darius had called her.

"Let's elope," he'd said. "I'll get a day job to support us. We'll get a studio apartment in the city. Anything as long as we're together."

She'd feared it would hurt his dream of making his fortune, but she couldn't resist. They both knew there was no chance of a real wedding, not when her father would try to stop the marriage. So they'd planned to elope to Niagara Falls.

But on the night his car waited outside the Fairholme gate, Letty never showed up.

She hadn't returned any of his increasingly frantic phone calls. The next day, she'd even convinced her father to fire Eugenios Kyrillos, Darius's father, who'd been their chauffeur for twenty years.

Even then, Darius had refused to accept their breakup. He'd kept calling, until she'd sent him a single cold message.

I was only using you to get another man's attention. He's rich and can give me the life of luxury I deserve. We're engaged now. Did you really think that someone like me would ever live in a studio apartment with someone like you?

That had done the trick.

But it had been a lie. There had been no other man. At the ripe old age of twenty-eight, Letty was still a virgin.

All these years, she'd promised herself that Darius would never know the truth. He could never know how she'd sacrificed herself, so he'd be able to follow his dreams without guilt or fear. Even if it meant he hated her.

But Darius must have finally found out the truth. It was the only explanation for him seeking her out.

"So you know why I betrayed you ten years ago?" she said in a small voice, unable to meet his eyes. "You forgive me?"

"It doesn't matter," he said roughly. "You're here now."

Her heart pounded as she saw the dark hunger in his eyes.

She looked down at the coffee stain on her uniform, the smear of ketchup near the cheerful name tag still on her left breast: LETTY! She whispered, "You can't still…want me?"

"You're wrong." He pulled her handbag off her shoulder. It felt unspeakably erotic. He pulled off her coat, dropping it to the marble floor. "I wanted you then." Cupping her face with both hands, he whispered, "I want you now."

Electricity ran up and down her body. Involuntarily, she licked her lips.

His gaze fell to her mouth.

Tangling his hands in her hair, he pulled out her ponytail, and her long dark hair tumbled down her shoulders. He stroked down her cheek, tilting back her head.

He was so much taller. He towered over her in every way.

She felt crazy butterflies, like she'd gone back in time and was eighteen again. Being with him now, all the anguish and grief and weariness of the last ten years seemed to disappear like a bad dream.

"I've missed you for so long," she choked out. "You're all I've dreamed about…"

He pressed a finger to her lips. At the contact, fire flashed from her mouth and down to her breasts. Sparks crackled between them in the shadowy penthouse, as she breathed in his woodsy, musky scent. Tension coiled low and deep in her belly.

Pulling her body tight against his own, he lowered his mouth to hers.

His kiss was hot and demanding. The stubble on his rough jawline scratched her delicate skin as he gripped her hard against him. She kissed him back with desperate need.

A low growl came from the back of his throat, and he pushed her back against the wall. His hands ran down her body to rip apart the front buttons of her white dress. She gasped as her naked skin was exposed, along with her plain white bra and panties.

"Take this off," he whispered, and he pulled her white dress off her body, dropping it to the floor. Kneeling in front of her, he pulled off her white shoes, one by one. She was nearly naked, standing in front of the floor-to-ceiling windows that revealed the whole city.

Rising to his full height, he kissed her. His mouth plundered hers, searing her to the core. She realized her hands were unbuttoning his black shirt to feel the warmth of his skin, the hard muscles of his body. She stroked his chest, dusted with dark hair, and trembled. He felt like steel wrapped in satin, hard and soft.

She desperately wanted to feel him against her, all of him. She wanted to be lost in him—

As he kissed her, his hands roamed over her shoulders, her hips, her breasts. Her fingers twisted in his hair. She felt dizzy with longing as he pressed her against the wall, kissing her with savage desire, nipping at her lips until they bruised.

He kissed down her throat, reaching beneath the white cotton fabric of her bra to cup her bare breasts. She felt his rough warm hands against her naked skin, and her taut nipples ached, until with a low curse he reached around and unhooked the clasp of her bra.

She heard his intake of breath as it fell to the floor. She now wore only panties, while he was still fully dressed, with his black shirt unbuttoned to reveal his bare chest. As he lowered his head, taking her exposed breasts fully in his hands, her head fell back, hair tumbling down, as she gripped his bare, muscular shoulders.

She gasped as she felt the wet heat of his mouth envelop a taut nipple. Lightning shot down her body as he suckled her in his stark, shadowy penthouse, with its spectacular view of nighttime New York at their feet. She moaned softly.

Abruptly, he pulled away. She opened her eyes, feeling dizzy. Her lips parted to ask a question, but before she could remember it, he lifted her into his arms.

She didn't try to resist as he carried her through the great room into an enormous bedroom in the opposite corner. That, too, had windows on both sides, twenty feet high. She could see all of Midtown, from the Chrysler Building to the Empire State, a forest of skyscrapers between two dark rivers with their bright, moving barges.

Manhattan sparkled coldly in the dark night as Darius spread her across his bed, his expression half shadowed. He undid his cuffs and dropped his shirt to the floor.

For the first time, Letty saw the full strength of his hard-muscled torso and powerful arms. His shoulders were broad, narrowing to tight, hard abs. Removing his belt, he kicked off his shoes. Wearing just low-slung black tailored trousers, he climbed onto the bed.

Lowering his head, he kissed her against the pillows, his lips hard and rough. She felt his desire for her; she felt his heavy weight over her. Darius wanted her... He cared...

Something broke, deep inside her heart.

All this time, Letty had thought their love had ended forever. But nothing had changed, she thought in wonder, tangling her hands in his dark hair. *Nothing.* They were the same two people, still young and in love...

He slowly kissed his way down her body, his hands

stroking her. She quivered, helpless beneath his touch. He dropped kisses here and there as he traversed the softness of her belly to the top edge of her white cotton panties. Drawing up, he looked down at her.

"You're mine, Letty," he whispered. "At last."

Then his heavy, hard body crushed hers deliciously, sensually. Her fingertips moved down the warm skin of his back, feeling his muscle, his spine. He moved his hips against hers, and she felt how huge and hard he was for her. Desire coiled low and deep in her belly.

He slid her white cotton panties down her thighs, down her legs. Like a whisper, they were gone.

Pushing her legs apart, he knelt at the foot of the bed. She held her breath, squeezing her eyes shut in the shadowy bedroom as he kissed the tender hollow of each foot. He moved up her calves, his fingertips caressing her skin as he lifted each knee for a slow kiss in the hollow beneath. She shivered as she felt the warmth of his breath on her thighs.

His hands moved beneath her, cupping her backside. Her thighs melted beneath his breath, hips trembling.

Finally, with agonizing slowness, he lowered his head between her legs.

Moving his hands, he kissed her inner thighs, one then the other. She felt his breath against the most intimate part of her and tried to squirm away, but he held her firmly.

Spreading her wide, he took a long, deep taste. The pleasure was intense. She choked out a gasp.

Holding her hips down against the bed, he forced her to accept the pleasure, working her with his tongue, twirling against her aching nub for long exquisite moments, then lapping her with the full width of his tongue.

She forgot to breathe, held by ruthless pleasure like a butterfly pinned to a wall. Her hips lifted involuntarily off the bed as she soared, and she gripped the white bedspread so she didn't fly up into the sky.

Waves of pleasure crashed against radiating joy. She'd never stopped loving him. And now he'd forgiven her. He wanted her. He loved her, too…

Twisting and gasping beneath his mouth, she exploded with a cry of pure happiness that seemed to last forever.

Instantly lifting his body, he pushed her arms above her head, gripping her wrists against the pillow, and positioned his hips between her legs. As she was still soaring between ecstasy and joy, he ruthlessly impaled her.

She felt him push all the way inside her, the entire enormous length of him going deep, to the heart. Her eyes flew open in shock and pain.

His back straightened at the moment he tore through the barrier that he clearly had not expected. Feeling her flinch, he looked down at her in shock.

"You were—a virgin?" he panted.

She nodded, closing her eyes and twisting her head away so he couldn't see the threatening tears. She didn't want to mar the beauty of their night, but the pain cut deep.

He held himself still inside her.

"You can't be," he said hoarsely. "How, after all these years?"

Letty looked up at him, her throat aching. And she said the only thing she could say. The words that she'd repressed for ten years, but that had never stopped burning inside her.

"Because I love you, Darius," she whispered.

CHAPTER TWO

DARIUS STARED DOWN at her. Letitia Spencer, a virgin?

Impossible. Not in a million years.

But her words shocked him even more.

"What do you mean, *you love me*?" he choked out.

Her dark eyelashes trembled against her pale skin. Then those big, beautiful hazel eyes shone up at him from the shadows of the bed as she whispered, "I never stopped loving you."

Looking down at her beautiful heart-shaped face, Darius was overwhelmed by emotion. Not the good kind, either.

He felt the cold burn of slow-rising rage.

Once, he'd loved Letty Spencer so much he'd thought he'd die without her. She'd been his angel. His goddess. He'd put her on such a pedestal, he'd even insisted they wait to make love. He'd wanted to marry her.

The memory made him writhe with shame.

How far she'd fallen. Today, she'd sent him a message—her first direct communication with him since she'd dumped him so coldly ten years before—offering him her body. For money.

All afternoon, Darius had tried to ignore her message, to laugh it off. He'd gotten over Letty years ago. He wasn't interested in paying a hundred thousand dollars to have her in his bed tonight. He didn't pay for sex. Women fought for his attention now. Supermodels fell into his bed for the price of a phone call.

But the part of him that still couldn't completely forget the past relished the idea of seeing her one last time.

Only this time, she'd be the one begging. He'd be the one to reject her.

As he'd signed the contracts that afternoon to formally sell his company, built on a mobile messaging app with five hundred million users worldwide, to a massive tech conglomerate for the price of twenty billion dollars, he'd barely listened to his lawyers droning on. Holding 90 per-cent of equity in the company made him the beneficiary of an eighteen-billion-dollar fortune, minus taxes.

But instead of rejoicing in the triumphant payoff of ten years of relentless work, he'd been picturing Letitia, the woman who'd once betrayed him. Imagining her trying to seduce him with an exotic dance of the seven veils. Pic-turing her wearing nothing but a black negligee. Begging him to take her to bed, so she could perform Olympic-level sexual feats for his pleasure.

After the papers were signed, he practically ran out of the office, away from all the congratulations and celebra-tions. All he could think about was Letty and her offer.

He'd spent hours trying to talk himself out of it. Then, gritting his teeth, he'd driven to the Brooklyn diner when the message said she'd be getting off work.

He didn't intend to actually sleep with her, he told himself. He'd only wanted to make her feel as small and ashamed as he'd once felt. To see her humiliated. To see her beg to give him pleasure.

Then he'd planned to tell her he no longer found her at-tractive, and toss the money in her face. He'd watch her take it and slink away in shame. And for the rest of his life he'd know that he'd won.

What did he care about a hundred thousand dollars? It was nothing. It would be worth it to see her abject humili-ation. After her savagely calculated betrayal, he craved vengeance far more than sex.

Or so he'd thought.

But so far nothing had gone according to plan. Seeing her outside the diner, he'd been shocked at her appearance.

She didn't look like a gold digger. She looked as if she were trying to be invisible, with no makeup, wearing that ridiculous white diner uniform.

But even then, he'd been drawn to her. She managed to be so damn sexy, so sweetly feminine and warm, that any man would want to help her, to take care of her. *To possess her.*

Bringing her back to the penthouse to enjoy his vengeance, Darius had allowed himself a single kiss.

Big mistake.

As he'd felt the soft curves of her body press against his, all his plans for vengeance were forgotten against the ruthless clamor of his body. For ten years, he'd desired this woman; and now she was half-naked in his arms, willing to surrender everything.

Suddenly, it all came down to two simple facts.

She'd sold herself.

He'd bought her.

So why not take her? Why not enjoy her sensual body as a way to finally excise her memory, once and for all?

She'd lied her way through the evening, pretending it was a romantic date, instead of a commercial transaction. He'd almost been surprised.

Until now.

Naked beneath him, Letty looked up, her eyes luminous in that lovely face he'd never been able to forget.

"Say something," she said anxiously.

Darius set his jaw. After her heartless betrayal, followed by ten years of silence, she'd just told him out of the blue she loved him. What could he say in response? Go to hell?

Letitia Spencer. So beautiful. So treacherous. So poisonous.

But now, at last, he understood her goal. She wasn't just playing for a hundred thousand dollars tonight. No. Tonight was just the sample that was supposed to leave him wanting more.

Because he'd seen her face as she left that diner. She was tired. Tired of working. Tired of being poor. Perhaps her father, newly free from prison, had been the one to suggest how to easily change her life—by becoming Darius's wife.

She must have seen his company's sale trumpeted in the newspaper today and decided it was time she made a play for his billions. He almost couldn't blame her. She'd been holding on to her virginity all these years—why not cash in?

She loved him.

Cold, sardonic anger pulsed through him.

She thought he'd learned nothing all these years. She actually thought, if she told him she loved him, he would still swoon at her feet. That he was still the lovesick idiot of long ago.

If Darius had despised her before, it was nothing compared to how he felt about her now.

And yet, he still desired her. Holding himself motionless inside her hot, tight sheath, he was still so hard, he was close to exploding.

That fact enraged him even more.

He wanted to make her pay. Not just for this last insult, but for everything that had gone before. Suddenly, causing her one night of humiliation wasn't nearly enough.

Darius wanted *vengeance*.

He wanted to raise her up, give her hope, then bring it crashing down as she'd once done. Fantastical plans coursed through his skull. He wanted to marry her, fill her with his child. He wanted to make her love him, then coldly spurn her. He wanted to take everything, and leave her penniless and alone.

That wouldn't be revenge. It would be *justice*.

"Darius?" A shadow of worry had crossed her face as she looked up at him, naked on the bed.

Lowering his head, he kissed her almost tenderly. She trembled in his arms, her plump breasts crushed against his naked chest, her amazing hips spread wide for him. Seeing her stretched out on his bed, with the play of shadows and light on the sexy curves of her tantalizing breasts, stretched the limits of his self-control.

"I'm sorry I hurt you, *agape mou*," he said in a low voice. Lie. His lips brushed the sensitive flesh of her cheek. As lightly as a butterfly setting down, he kissed the two tears that had overflowed her lashes. "But the pain won't last." Another lie. He would make sure it lasted the rest of her life. He smiled grimly. "Just wait."

She looked up at him, the picture of wide-eyed innocence. Then sighed, relaxing in surrender.

The kiss he gave her then was anything but tender. It was demanding, rough, fierce. He had experience, and she did not. He knew how to lure her. How to master her.

Unless—she could be feigning her desire?

No, he thought coldly. He would make sure she did not. That would be one insult he'd not allow her to pay. He would make sure every bit of her pleasure was real.

He stroked her soft body, taking his time, caressing her, until, slowly, she started kissing him back.

She wrapped her arms around his shoulders, pulling his weight back down on her. He shifted his hips, testing her ability to accept him, still rock hard and huge inside her. She whimpered, then exhaled, swaying her hips.

He moved expertly, drawing back slowly, then pushing inside her a second time. She gripped his shoulders, closing her eyes. He suckled a nipple, watching her face carefully. It wasn't until he saw the glow of ecstasy return to her face, and felt her muscles start to tighten around him, that he knew he'd succeeded. Triumph filled him as he began to ride her.

Filling her so deeply, this woman he'd desired for almost a third of his life, he felt light-headed. His body started to shake with pleasure so intense that it was almost like pain. They were so intertwined it was hard to know where one ended and the other began.

Pleasure and pain.

Hatred and desire.

As he thrust into her, sweat covered his body with the effort of keeping control. Her breasts swayed as he thrust inside her, all the way to the hilt. Gasping, she put her hands against the headboard, bracing against the force of his thrust. Her breathing became shallow as her body twisted beneath him with building need.

Her eyes were closed, her head tilted back, as she panted for breath. She moved her hands to his shoulders. He barely noticed her fingernails digging into his skin. He was lost in the sensation of possessing her, filling her, owning her, the glory of her flesh, the sweetness of her skin.

He felt simultaneously lost and found. Every corner of his soul that had ever felt hollow was miraculously filled. His body was pure light.

From a distance, he heard a low ragged shout and realized the sound was coming from his own mouth, releasing emotion he'd kept locked up for a decade. Her voice joined his as she cried out her own joy and grief and pain.

His body spasmed with a final, violent thrust and he poured himself into her, collapsing over her on the bed, their bodies slick with sweat, fused together.

It was much later when he opened his eyes and discovered Letty was sleeping in his arms. He stared down at her in wonder.

He wondered how he'd ever been satisfied by those pallid, skinny supermodels who had filled his bed till now.

Those affairs had been insipid, hollow, dull compared to this fire. Tasting her, feeling her shake, hearing her cry of pleasure had pushed him to the limit.

It's hatred, he realized.

Hatred had made him utterly lose self-control in a way he'd never done before, in a way he'd never imagined possible. As he'd taken possession of her body, after ten years of frustrated desire, he'd slaked his ache in a dark, twisted fantasy of vengeance.

It had been the single best sexual experience of his life.

But as he pulled away from her, he sucked in his breath.

The condom had broken.

He'd worn one, of course. No matter how he might fantasize about revenge, no matter how much he hated her, the last thing he would want was to actually get her pregnant and drag an innocent child into this.

Now he stared down, unable to believe his own eyes. How could the condom have broken?

Had he been too rough, forgetting everything in his need to possess her, to relieve the savage, unrequited desire of ten years?

He'd wanted to brand her forever with the deepest mark of his possession. Had he actually wanted to fill her with his child?

A curse filled his heart.

Unraveling himself from her, he pulled away, rising naked from the bed.

He walked to the window and looked down at the bright skyscrapers of this dark city. His throat was tight as he pressed his hand against the cold glass. Catching his own reflection in the window, he was startled by the cold rage in his eyes.

Disaster. He hadn't done anything like he'd planned. He'd actually slept with Letty. And now…it might be so much worse. His hand tightened against the window. He looked back, and his jaw tightened.

Her fault, he thought. All hers.

"Are you up?" Letty murmured. "Come back to bed."

She was beneath the blankets now, looking sleepy and adorable with her dark hair tumbling over his pillows. She'd covered herself with the comforter. As if he hadn't seen everything, touched everything, tasted everything already.

His body hardened against his will, already desiring her again. He'd just had her, and he already wanted more. He wanted to take her on the bed. Against the wall. Against the window. Again and again. He stared at her in bewildered fury. Truly she was poison.

But did he really imagine after everything that had gone wrong tonight, the gold digger couldn't achieve her ultimate goal—marriage and total command, not just of his fortune, but of his body and soul?

He clawed a hand through his hair.

"Darius, what's wrong?"

He repeated flatly, "You love me?"

"It's true," she whispered.

He took a step toward the bed.

"What is it, Letty?" he said in a low voice. "Did you plan all along to renegotiate the deal? One night isn't enough, is that it? You don't want to be a rental, but a permanent sale?"

She frowned. "What are you talking about?"

Darius's jaw felt so tight it ached. Grabbing gray sweatpants from a sleek built-in drawer, he pulled them up over his naked body. He forced his shoulders to relax, forced himself to face her. When he spoke, his voice was like ice.

"You don't love me. You don't even know what the word means. When I think of how I once adored you, it sickens me. Especially now—now we both know what you really are."

Her forehead creased. "What are you talking about?"

"This night. This whole night. Don't pretend you don't know."

"I don't!"

"Don't play the outraged innocent. You sold your virginity to me for the price of a hundred thousand dollars."

For a moment, his hard words echoed in the shadowy bedroom. The two of them stared at each other in silence.

"What are you talking about?"

"Your email," he said impatiently. "Claiming you needed to pay off some mobster who'd broken your father's arm and threatened to break his whole body if he didn't come up with a hundred thousand dollars within the week." He tilted his head curiously. "Is it true? Or just a convenient excuse?"

Her eyes were wide. "My father's broken arm..." She seemed to shudder as she pulled the blankets up higher against her neck. "I never sent any message."

His lips curved sardonically. "So who did?"

Letty's cheeks were bright red. "I..." Running her hand over her eyes, she said, "So that's why you came for me? You were buying a night in bed?"

"What did you think?"

"I thought..." She faltered. "I thought you'd forgiven me for what I did..."

He snorted. "Ten years ago? You did me a favor. I've been better off without you. Your other fiancé must have realized that fast, since he didn't bother to stick around, either." His jaw set. "What I'll never forgive is what you and your father did to my dad. He died an early death because of you. Lost his job, his life savings. He lost everything, had a heart attack and died." He bared his teeth in a shark-like smile. "Because of you."

"Darius, it's not what you think," she blurted out. "I..."

"Oh, is this the part where you come up with an explanation that makes you look like an innocent saint?" he drawled. "Go on, Letty. Tell me how your betrayal was actually a favor. Explain how you destroyed my family at great personal sacrifice, because you loved me so much." His voice dripped contempt. "Tell me all about your *love*."

She opened her mouth.

Then snapped it closed.

Darius's lip twisted coldly. "That's what I thought."

She blinked fast, her beautiful eyes anguished. She took a deep breath and spoke one small word. "Please..."

But mercy had been burned from his soul. He shrugged. "I thought it would be amusing to see you again. I didn't actually intend to sleep with you, but you were so willing, I finally thought, why not?" He sighed as if bored. "But though I paid for the whole night, I find I've already lost interest." Leaning forward, he confided, "And just as one entrepreneur to another, you sold yourself too cheaply. You could have bartered for a higher price with your virginity. Just a suggestion as you go forward with your new career. What is it called now? Paid mistress? Professional girlfriend?"

"How can you be so cruel?" She shook her head. "When you came to the diner tonight, I saw the same boy I loved..."

"Really?" He tilted his head, quirking a dark eyebrow. "Oh. Right. Since you'd kept your virginity in reserve all these years, you thought if you tossed in a little romance, I'd fall for you like a stone, just like I did back then. 'I love you, Darius. I never stopped loving you,'" he mimicked mockingly.

"Stop!" she cried, covering her ears with her hands. "Please stop!"

Some of her blanket had slipped where she sat on his bed, revealing a curvy breast. He could see the faint pink tip of her nipple, and he could still taste the sweetness of her, still remember how it had felt to be deep inside her.

His breath came hard. Sleeping with her hadn't satiated his desire. To the contrary. He only wanted her more.

The fact she still had such power over him was infuriating.

Turning sharply, he went to his desk. He pulled a cashier's check from a leather binder. Returning to the bed, he tossed it toward her.

"There. I believe this concludes our business."

Letty's lovely face looked dazed as she picked up the cashier's check from the bed. She looked at it.

"If you have another client tonight, don't let me keep you," he drawled.

She briefly closed her eyes and whispered, "You're a monster."

"*I'm* a monster." He barked a low, cruel laugh. "Me?"

Turning away, she rose naked from the bed. He waited, wondering for a split second if she'd toss the check in his face and prove him wrong. If she did...

But she didn't. She just picked up her panties from the floor and walked to the door. He sneered at himself for being naive enough to even imagine the possibility she'd give up her hard-earned money for the sake of honor, or even pride!

She left the bedroom, going out into the great room of the penthouse. He followed, watching as she collected her bra and shoes, then scooped her white dress from the floor. Putting it on after slipping on her panties, she buttoned the dress quickly, leaving gaps where he'd ripped off buttons in his haste to get it off her. She wouldn't meet his eyes.

Darius wanted to force her to look at him. He wanted her humiliated. He wanted her heartbroken. His pride demanded something he couldn't name. *More.*

She stuffed her bra in her handbag and put her bare feet into her shoes and turned to go.

"It's just a shame the condom broke," he said.

She froze. "What?"

"The condom. Of course I was wearing one. But it broke.

So if you wind up pregnant, let me know, won't you?" He gave a hard smile. "We will negotiate a good price."

He was rewarded. She finally turned and looked at him, aghast.

"You'd pay me? For a baby?"

He said coldly, "Why not, when I paid you for the act that created it?" His expression hardened. "I will never marry you, Letty. So your attempt at gold digging ends with that check in your bag. If by some unfortunate chance you become pregnant, selling me our baby would be your only option."

"You're crazy!"

"And you disgust me." He came closer to her, his eyes cold. "I would never allow any child of mine to be raised by you and that criminal you call a father. I would hire a hundred lawyers first," he said softly, "and drive you both into the sea."

For a moment, Letty looked at him, wide-eyed. Then she turned away with a stumble, but not before he saw the sheen of tears in her eyes. She'd become quite the little actress, he thought.

"Please take me home," she whispered.

"Take you home?" Darius gave a sardonic laugh. "You're an employee, not a guest. A temporary employee whose time is now done." His lip curled. "Find your own way home."

CHAPTER THREE

LETTY SHIVERED IN the darkest, coldest hours of the night as she walked to the Lexington Avenue subway station and got on the express train. It was past one in the morning, and she held her bag tightly in the mostly empty compartment, feeling vulnerable and alone.

Arriving at her stop in Brooklyn, she came numbly down the stairs from the elevated station and walked the blocks to her apartment. The streets were dark, the shops all closed. The February—no, it was March now; it was past midnight—wind was icy against her cheeks still raw with tears.

She'd thought it was a miracle when she saw Darius again. She'd thought he'd found out the truth of how she'd sacrificed herself, and he'd come back for her.

Telling him she loved him had felt so right. She'd honestly thought he might tell her the same thing.

How could she have been so wrong?

You disgust me.

She could still hear the contempt in his voice. Wiping her eyes hard, she shivered, trembling as she trudged toward her four-story apartment building.

While many of the nearby buildings were nice, well kept, with flower boxes, hers was an eyesore, with a rickety fire escape clinging to a crumbling brick facade. But the place was cheap, and the landlord had asked no personal questions, which was what she cared about. Plugging in a security code, Letty pushed open the door.

Inside, the temperature felt colder. Two of the foyer's lights were burned out, leaving only a single bare lightbulb to illuminate the mailboxes and the old delivery menus littering the corners of the cracked tile floor.

Even in the middle of the night, noises echoed against the concrete stairwell, a Doppler tangle of tenants yelling, dogs barking, a baby crying. A sour smell came up from beneath the metal stairs as she wearily climbed three flights. She felt wretched, body and soul, torn between her body's sweet ache from their lovemaking and her heart's incandescent grief.

The fourth floor had worn, stained carpet and a bare lightbulb hanging from the ceiling. Going past the doors of her neighbors—some of whom she'd never met even after three years—she reached into her handbag, found her keys and unlocked the dead bolt. The door creaked as she pushed it open.

"Letty! You're back!" Her father looked up eagerly from his easy chair. He'd waited up for her, wrapped in both a robe and a blanket over his flannel pajamas, since the thermostat didn't work properly. Turning off the television, he looked up hopefully. "Well?"

As the door swung shut behind her, Letty stared at him in disbelief. Her handbag dropped to the floor.

"How could you?" she choked out.

"How could I get you and Darius back together so easily?" Her father beamed at her. "All I needed was a good excuse!"

Her voice caught on a sob. "Are you kidding?"

Howard frowned. "Are you and Darius not back together?"

"Of course we're not! How could you send him a message, pretending to be me? Offering me for the night!"

"I was trying to help," he said falteringly. "You've loved him for so long but refused to contact him. Or he you. I thought…"

"What? That if you forced us together, we'd immediately fall back into each other's arms?"

"Well, yes."

As she stared at him, still trembling from the roller coaster of emotion of that night, anger rushed through her.

"You didn't do it for me!" Reaching into her bag, she grabbed the cashier's check and shoved it at him. "You did it for this!"

Her father's hands shook as he grasped the cashier's check. Seeing the amount, his eyes filled with visible relief. "Thank God."

"How could you?" She wanted to shake her father and scream at him for what he'd done. "How could you sell me?"

"Sell you?" Her father looked up incredulously. "I didn't sell you!" Struggling to untangle himself from his blanket, he rose from his chair and sat beside her on the sofa. "I figured the two of you would talk and soon realize how you'd been set up. I thought you'd both have a good laugh, and it would be easier for you each to get over your pride. Maybe he'd send money, maybe he wouldn't." His voice cracked. "But either way, you'd be together again. The two of you love each other."

"You did it for love." Letty's eyes narrowed skeptically. "So the fact that you read about Darius's billion-dollar deal this morning had nothing to do with it."

He winced at her sarcasm, then looked down at the floor. His voice trembled a little as he said, "I guess I thought there was no harm in also trying to solve a problem of my own with a…dissatisfied customer."

Glaring at him, Letty opened her mouth to say the cruel words he deserved to hear. Words she'd never be able to take back. Words neither one of them would ever be able to forget. Words that would take her anguish and rage, wrap them up into a tight ball and launch them at her father like a grenade.

Then she looked at him, old and forlorn, sitting beside

her on the sagging sofa. The man she'd once admired and still absolutely loved.

His hair had become white and wispy, barely covering his spotted scalp. His face, once so hearty and handsome, was gaunt with deep wrinkles on his cheeks. He'd shrunk, become thin and bowed. His robe was too big on him now. His near decade in prison had aged him thirty years.

Howard Spencer, a middle-class kid from Oklahoma, had come to New York and built a fortune with only his charm and a good head for numbers. He'd fallen in love with Constance Langford, the only daughter of an old aristocratic family on Long Island. The Langfords had little money left beyond the Fairholme estate, which was in hock up to the eyeballs. But Howard Spencer, delirious with happiness at their marriage, had assured Constance she'd never worry about money again.

He'd kept his promise. While his wife had been alive, he'd been careful and smart and lucky with his investment fund. It was only after his wife's sudden death that he'd become reckless, taking bigger and bigger financial risks, until his once respected hedge fund became a hollowed-out Ponzi scheme, and suddenly eight billion dollars were gone.

The months of Howard's arrest and trial had been awful for Letty, and worrying about him in prison had been even worse. But now, as she looked at the old man he'd somehow become, was the worst of all.

As she looked at his slumped shoulders, his heartbroken eyes—at his broken arm, still hanging uselessly in the cast—she felt her anger evaporate, leaving in its place only grief and despair. Her mouth snapped shut.

Slumping forward, she covered her face with her hands.

The memory of Darius's words floated back to her. *You needed to pay off some mobster who'd broken your father's arm and threatened to break his whole body if he didn't come up with a hundred thousand dollars within the week.*

Chilled, she looked up. "Why didn't you tell me someone broke your arm, Dad? Why did you let me think it was an accident?"

Howard looked down at the floor guiltily. "I didn't want you to worry."

"Worry?" she cried.

His wan cheeks turned pink. "A father's supposed to take care of his daughter, not the other way around."

"So it's true? Some thug broke your arm and threatened you if you didn't pay him back his money?"

"I knew I could handle it." He tried to smile. "And I have. Once I sign over this check, everything will be fine."

"How do you know you won't have more thugs demanding money, once it's known you actually paid someone back?"

Her father looked shocked. "No. Most of the people who invested in my fund were good, civilized people. Not violent!"

Letty ground her teeth. For a man who'd been in a minimum-security federal prison for nine years, he could be surprisingly naive.

"You should have told me."

"Why? What would you have done except worry? Or worse—try to talk to the man yourself and put yourself in danger?" He set his jaw. "Like I said, I didn't know if Darius would actually send the money. But I knew, either way, you would be safe because you'd be with him." He shook his head, trying to smile. "I really thought you and Darius would take one look at each other and be happy again."

Letty sagged back against the sofa cushions. Her father'd really thought he was doing her a favor. That he was reuniting her with a lost love. That he was protecting her, saving her.

She whispered bleakly, "Darius thought I was a gold digger."

Howard looked indignant. "Of course he didn't! Once you told him you hadn't sent the message…"

"He didn't believe me."

"Then…then…he must have believed you were just a good daughter looking out for your father. Darius has so much money now, you can't tell me he'll miss such a small amount. Not after everything you did for *him*!"

"Stop," she choked out. Just remembering how Darius had looked at her when he handed her the cashier's check was enough to make her want to die. But after he'd told her about the threat against her father's life, what choice had she had?

Her father looked bewildered. "Didn't you tell him what happened ten years ago? Why you never ran away with him?"

She flinched as she remembered Darius's acid words. *Go on, Letty. Tell me how your betrayal was actually a favor. Explain how you destroyed my family at great personal sacrifice, because you loved me so much.*

"No," she whispered, "and I never will. Darius doesn't love me. He hates me more than ever."

Howard's wrinkled face looked mournful. "Oh, sweetheart."

"But now I hate him, too." She looked up. "That's the one good thing that happened tonight. *Now I hate him, too.*"

Her father looked anguished. "That was never what I wanted!"

"It's good." Wiping her eyes, she tried to smile. "I've wasted too many years dreaming of him. Missing him. I'm done."

She was.

The Darius Kyrillos she'd loved no longer existed. She saw that now. She'd tried to give him everything, and he'd seduced her with a cold heart. Her love for Darius was burned out of her forever. Her only hope was to try to forget.

But four weeks later, she found out how impossible that would be. She'd never be able to forget Darius Kyrillos now.

She was pregnant with his baby.

She'd taken the pregnancy test, sure it would be negative. When it was positive, she was shocked. But shock soon became a happy daze as Letty imagined a sweet fat baby in her arms, to cuddle and adore.

Then she told her father.

"I'm going to be a grandfather?" Howard was enraptured at the news. "That's wonderful! And when you tell Darius—"

That caused the first chill of fear. Because Letty suddenly recalled this baby wouldn't just be hers, but Darius's.

He hated her.

He'd threatened to take her baby from her.

Letty shook her head violently. "I can never tell him about the baby!"

"Of course you will." Her father patted her on the shoulder. "I know you're angry at him. He must have hurt you very badly. But that's all in the past! A man has a right to know he's going to be a father."

"Why?" She turned to him numbly. "So he can try to take the baby away because he hates me so much?"

"Take the baby?" Her father laughed. "Once Darius finds out you're pregnant, he'll forget his anger and remember how much he loves you. You'll see. The baby will bring you together."

She shook her head. "You're living in a dream world. He told me…"

"What?"

Letty turned away, hearing the echo of that coldly malevolent voice. *I would never allow any child of mine to be raised by you and that criminal you call a father.*

"We need to start saving money," she whispered. "Now."

"Why? Once you're married, money will never be a worry for you again." Howard looked ecstatic. "You and my grandchild will always be cared for."

Letty knew her father couldn't believe Darius wanted to hurt her. But she knew he did.

I would hire a hundred lawyers first and drive you both into the sea.

They had to leave this city as soon as possible.

Under the terms of her father's probation, Howard was required to remain in the state of New York. So they'd go north, move to some little town upstate where no one knew them, where she could find a new job.

There was just one problem. Moving required money. First and last month's rent, a security deposit and transport for Letty, Howard and all their belongings. Money they didn't have. They were barely keeping their heads above water as it was.

Over the next few months, Letty's fears were proved true. No matter how hard she worked, she couldn't save money. Howard was always hungry or needed something urgently. Money disappeared. There were also the added expenses of medical co-payments for Letty's doctor visits, and physical therapy for her father's arm.

There was some good fortune. After Howard had paid off the mobster, no other angry former investors had threatened him, demanding repayment.

But there, their luck ended. Just when Letty was desperate for overtime pay, all the other waitstaff suddenly seemed to want it, too. But warmer summer weather meant fewer customers at the diner craving the fried eggs and chicken fried steak that were the diner's specialties. Her work hours became less, not more.

Each morning when she left for work, her father pretended to look through job listings in the paper, looking shifty-eyed and pale. Pregnancy exhausted her. Each night when she got home from work, almost falling asleep where she stood, she cooked dinner for them both. She'd do the dishes and go to bed. Then the whole day would start again.

Every day, she anxiously counted the savings she kept in her old chipped cookie jar on the kitchen counter. And every day, she looked at the calendar and felt more afraid.

By late August, amid the sticky heat of New York City, Letty was growing frantic. She could no longer hide her baby bump, not even with her father's oversize shirts. Everyone at the diner knew she was pregnant, including her friend and coworker Belle Langtry, who kept teasing her about it.

"Who's the father?" Belle demanded. "Is it Prince Charming? I swear I saw you leave here once with a dark-haired man in a sports car."

No. It wasn't Prince Charming, Letty thought numbly. Her baby's father was no prince, but a selfish, coldhearted beast who wanted to steal her child away.

Finally, as her yearlong lease on the apartment ended, she knew she couldn't wait any longer. She gave two weeks' notice at the diner. She still hadn't saved enough money, but time had run out.

On the first of September, Letty splashed cold water on her face in the darkness before dawn, then looked at her drawn face in the mirror.

Today was the day.

They couldn't rent a truck to move their belongings. No money for that. Instead, they'd just take what would fit in two suitcases on the bus.

They'd have to leave behind all the final memories from Fairholme. From her childhood. From her mother.

The thought made her throat ache.

But Letty was six months pregnant now. Her heart pounded as she put her hand protectively over her baby bump. She knew from the ultrasound at the doctor's office that she was expecting a boy. How had time fled so quickly? In less than three months, by late November, she'd be cuddling her sweet baby in her arms.

Or else she'd be weeping as the baby's coldhearted father took him away from her forever. She still remembered Darius's cold, dark eyes, heard the flat echo of his voice.

If by some unfortunate chance you become pregnant, selling me our baby would be your only option.

She was suddenly terrified she'd waited too long to leave New York.

Going into the tiny kitchen, she tried to keep her voice cheerful as she said, "Dad, I'm going to pick up my last paycheck, then buy bus tickets."

"I still don't understand why Rochester," he said with a scowl.

She sighed. "I told you. My friend Belle knows someone who knows someone who might be able to get me a job there. Everyone says it's nice. I need you to start packing."

"I have other plans today." His voice was peevish.

"Dad, our lease is up in two days. I know it's not fun, but whatever you don't pack, I'm going to have to call the junk dealer to take." Her throat ached. Maybe all their leftover stuff *was* junk, but it was all they had left. Of Fairholme. Of her mother. Her voice tightened. "Look, I know it won't be easy."

Sitting at the peeling Formica table where he was doing the crossword, Howard glared at her with irritation. "You just need to tell that man of yours you're pregnant."

They'd been having this argument for months. She gritted her teeth. "I can't. I told you."

"Poppycock. A man should be given the opportunity to take care of his own child. And you know, Letty," he added gruffly, "I won't always be here to look after you."

Howard—look after her? When was the last time that

had been true, instead of the other way around? She looked at her father, then sighed. "Why don't you believe me?"

"I knew Darius as a boy." Fiddling with his untouched coffee mug, he looked at her seriously. "If you'd just help him see past his anger, he's got a good heart—"

"I'm not gambling on his *good heart*," she said bitterly. "Not after the way he treated me."

Her father looked thoughtful. "I could just call him…"

"No!" Letty shouted. Her eyes blazed. "If you ever go behind my back like that again, I will never talk to you for the rest of my life. Do you understand? *Never.*"

"Okay, okay," he grumbled. "But he's your baby's father. You should just marry him and be happy."

That left her speechless for a minute.

"Just be packed by the time I return," she said finally, and she went out into the gray, rainy September morning. She picked up her last check at the diner—for a pitiful amount, but every dollar would help—and said farewell to her fellow waitress Belle, who'd moved to New York from Texas the previous Christmas.

"Anytime you need anything, you call me, you hear?" Belle hugged her fiercely. "No matter where you are, Rochester or Rome, remember I'm only a phone call away!"

Letty didn't make friends easily, so it was hard to say goodbye to the only real friend she'd made since she'd left Fairholme. The thought of going to yet another new apartment in a new town where she didn't know anyone, in hopes of starting a job that might not even exist, filled her with dread. She tried to smile.

"You too, Belle," she managed. Then, wiping her eyes, she said goodbye to everyone else at the diner and went back out into the rain to deposit her check at the bank and get two one-way bus tickets to Rochester.

When Letty got back home, her hair and clothes were damp with rain. Her father wasn't at the apartment, and his suitcases were empty. All their belongings were still untouched, exactly where she'd left them.

She'd just sort through everything herself, she thought wearily. Once she'd figured out how many boxes they'd have to leave behind, she'd call the junk dealer.

Of the eight billion dollars her father's investment fund had lost, three billion had since been recovered. But the authorities had been careful not to leave him with anything of value. Their possessions had been picked over long ago by the Feds and bankruptcy court.

What was left was all crammed into this tiny apartment. The broken flute her mother had played at Juilliard. The ceramic animals Constance had painted for her daughter as gifts, starting with her first birthday. The leather-bound classic books from her grandfather's collection, water-damaged, so worthless. Except to them. Her great-grandfather's old ship in a bottle. Her grandma Spencer's homemade Christmas ornaments. All would have to be left.

We'll get through it, Letty told herself fiercely. They could still be happy. She'd raise her baby with love, in a snug cottage overlooking a garden of flowers. Her son would have a happy childhood, just as Letty had.

He wouldn't be raised in some stark gray penthouse without a mother, without love...

Letty started digging through the first pile of clutter. She planned to stay up the whole night scrubbing down the apartment, in hopes their landlord might actually give back her security deposit.

Hearing a hard knock at the door, she rose to her feet, overwhelmed with relief. Her father had come back to help. He must have forgotten his key again. Sorting through their possessions would be so much easier with two of them—

Opening the door, she gasped.

Darius stood in her doorway, dressed in a black button-down shirt with well-cut jeans that showed the rugged lines of his powerful body. It was barely noon, but his jaw was dark with five-o'clock shadow.

For a moment, even hating and fearing him as she did, Letty was dazzled by that ruthless masculine beauty.

"Letty," he greeted her coldly. Then his eyes dropped to her baby bump.

With an intake of breath, Letty tried to shut the door in his face.

He blocked her with his powerful shoulder and pushed his way into her apartment.

CHAPTER FOUR

SIX MONTHS AGO Darius had wanted vengeance.

He'd gotten it. He'd ruthlessly taken Letitia Spencer's virginity, then tossed her out into a cold winter's night. He'd seduced her, insulted her. He'd thrown the money in her face, made her feel cheap.

It had been delicious.

But since then, to his dismay, he'd discovered the price of that vengeance.

In Darius's childhood, back on the Greek island where he was born, his grandmother had often told him that vengeance hurt the person who committed it worse than the one who endured it. When the kids at school mocked his illegitimate birth, sneering at his mother's abandonment— *Even your own* mitéra *didn't want you*—his grandmother had told him to ignore them, to take the high road.

He'd tried, but the boys' taunts had only grown worse until he was finally forced to punch them. They'd all been bloodied in the fight, but especially Darius, since it had been one against four.

"So you see I'm right," his grandmother had said gravely, bandaging him afterward. "You were hurt worse."

In Darius's own opinion, that vengeance had been not only justified, but strategic. The boys at school had never taunted him again.

But this time, his grandmother had been proved right. Because Darius's vengeance against Letty had hurt him more than he'd ever imagined.

Instead of quenching the flame, that night together had only built his desire for her into a blazing fire.

He wanted her. Every night for the last six months, he'd

half expected Letty to contact him. Once her prideful anger had faded, surely she would want him back—if not for his body, then obviously for his money.

But she never had. And when he'd remembered the haunted look on her beautiful heart-shaped face the night she'd told him she loved him, the night he'd taken her virginity and tossed her ruthlessly into the dark, he'd had moments when he'd wondered if he might have been wrong.

But how could he be wrong? The evidence spoke for itself.

Still, in the months since their night together, his continual raw desire for her had made him edgy. He'd intended to remain as his company's CEO for a year, guiding his team in the transition after the sale. Instead, he'd gotten into an argument with the head of the conglomerate and left within weeks. Darius could no longer endure working for someone else, but he'd signed a noncompete clause, so couldn't start a new business in the same field.

Bereft of the twenty-hour workdays that had been the entirety of his life for a decade, he hadn't known how to fill his hours. He tried spending some of his fortune. He'd bought a race car, then ten cars, then a race track. He'd bought four planes, all with interiors done in different colors. No. Next he'd tried extreme sports: skydiving, heliskiing. Yawn.

Worst of all, he'd been surrounded by beautiful women, all keen to get his attention. And he hadn't wanted a single one of them.

He'd been *bored*. Worse. He'd felt frustrated and angry. Because even with the endless freedom of time and money, he couldn't have what he really wanted.

Letty.

Now, seeing her in the flesh, so beautiful—so *pregnant*—he hated himself for ever taking his vengeance. No matter how richly she'd deserved it, look where that thrill of hatred and lust had led.

Pregnant. With his baby.

Even wearing an oversize white T-shirt and baggy jeans, Letty was somehow more sensual, more delectable, than any stick-thin model in a skintight cocktail dress. Letty's pregnancy curves were lush. Her skin glowed. Her breasts had grown enormous. With effort, he forced his gaze down to her belly.

"So it's true," he said in a low voice. "You're pregnant."

She looked frozen. Then she squared her shoulders, tossing her dark ponytail in a futile gesture of bravado. "So?"

"Is the baby mine?"

"Yours?" Her eyes shot sparks of fire, even though she had dark shadows beneath, as if she hadn't been sleeping well. "What makes you think the baby's yours? Maybe I slept with ten men since our night. Maybe I slept with a hundred—"

The thought of her sleeping with other men made Darius sick. "You're lying."

"How do you know?"

"Because your father told me."

The fight went out of her. She went pale. "My...my father?"

"He wanted me to pay for the information, but when I refused, he told me everything. For free."

"Maybe he was lying," she said weakly. She looked as if she might faint.

"Sit down," Darius ordered. "I'll get you a glass of water. Then we'll talk."

She sank into the old pullout sofa, her cheeks pale. It wasn't hard for him to find the kitchen. The apartment was pathetically small—just a postage-stamp-sized living room, surrounded by an even smaller bedroom, bathroom and kitchen.

He looked around him, amazed that the onetime heiress of Fairholme, born into a forty-room mansion, was now living with her father in an apartment the same size as the room her mother had once used to arrange flowers off the solarium.

Old boxes and mementos were packed everywhere. The leftovers of her family's former life—items that obviously weren't valuable enough to be sold, but too precious to be thrown away—were clustered around the old television and piled tightly along the walls. A pillow and folded blanket sat beside the pullout sofa.

Darius walked across the worn carpet to the peeling linoleum of the telephone-booth-sized kitchen. Dust motes floated in the weak gray sunlight. The barred window overlooked an air shaft that faced other apartments, just a few feet away. With the bars across the window, it felt like prison.

It's better than they deserve, he told himself firmly. And it was still nicer than his childhood home in Heraklios. At least this place had electricity, running water. At least this place had a parent.

Darius's own parents had both left him, in different ways, two days after he was born. His unemployed father had discovered his newborn son crying in a basket by his door, left out in the rain by his former lover, a wealthy, spoiled heiress who'd abandoned the child she'd never wanted.

Fired from his job, Eugenios Kyrillos found himself unable to get another. No other rich Greek fathers, it seemed, wanted to risk their daughters' virtue to a chauffeur who didn't know his place. Desperate to find work, he'd departed for America, leaving his baby son to be raised by his grandmother in the desolate house by the sea.

The first time Darius had spoken to his father in person had been at his grandmother's funeral, when he was eleven.

Then his father had taken him from Greece, away from everything and everyone he'd ever known, and brought him to America.

Fairholme had seemed like an exotic palace, where everyone spoke a language he couldn't understand. His father had seemed just as strange, the emotionally distant chauffeur of this grand American king—Howard Spencer.

And look what the Spencers had come to now.

Darius had long ago torn down his grandmother's shack in Heraklios and built a palatial villa. He had a penthouse in Manhattan, a ski chalet in Switzerland, his private race track outside London. His personal fortune was greater than anything Howard Spencer ever dreamed of.

And the Spencers were now living in this tiny, threadbare apartment.

But instead of feeling a sense of triumph, Darius felt strangely unsettled as he walked through her dreary kitchen and poured a glass of water from the tap. Returning to the equally depressing living room, he handed Letty the glass, then looked at the folded blankets and pillow on the floor.

"Who sleeps on the sofa?"

Letty's cheeks turned pink as she looked down at the sagging cushions. "I do."

"You pay all the rent, and your father gets the bedroom?"

"He hasn't been sleeping well. I just want him to be comfortable."

Darius looked at her incredulously. "And you're pregnant."

"What do you care?" she said bitterly. "You're just here to take my baby away."

Well. True. His eyes fell on the empty suitcases. "Where were you planning to go?"

"Anywhere you couldn't find us."

Darius stared down at her grimly. After his conversation with Howard Spencer, he'd had his investigator check up on Letty and found she'd only recently left her job as a waitress. She was still broke. None of the other employees remembered seeing any men around her, except one waitress, Belle, who had described Darius himself.

It seemed that, contrary to all previous assumptions, Letty wasn't a gold digger. Not with other men.

Not even with Darius.

In that, he'd misjudged her. After the way Letty had crushed him so devastatingly ten years ago, informing him that she was leaving him for a richer man, he'd believed Letty was a fortune hunter to the core.

It made sense. His own mother had abandoned him as a two-day-old newborn for the exact same reason. To Calla, Darius had been the embarrassing result of a one-night liaison with her wealthy family's chauffeur. She'd been determined to marry as befitted her station. She'd cared only about money and the social position that went with it.

But Letty wasn't the same. At least not anymore.

Darius abruptly sat down on the sofa beside her. "Why didn't you come to me when you found out you were pregnant? You had to know I would give you everything you needed and more."

"Give? I knew you'd only take!" she said incredulously. "You threatened me!"

He ground his teeth. "We could have come to some arrangement."

"You threatened to buy my baby, and if I tried to refuse, you would take the baby from me and—what were your words?—drive me into the sea?"

Darius didn't like to be reminded of what he'd said six months ago. He'd rationalized his cruelty on the grounds of justice. But now…strictly speaking, he might have sounded a little less than civil, if not outright crazy. Irritated, he glared at her. "Drink your water."

"Why? What did you put into it?" She sniffed the glass.

"Some drug to make me pass out so you can kidnap me to a Park Avenue dungeon?"

He snorted a laugh in spite of himself. "The water came from your tap. Drink it or not. I just thought you looked pale."

She stared at him for a moment, then took a tentative sip.

He looked around the tiny apartment. "Why are you living here?"

"Sadly, the presidential suite at the St. Regis was already booked."

"I mean it, Letty. Why did you stay in New York all these years? You could have just left. Moved west where no one would know you or care about what your father did."

She blinked fast. "I couldn't abandon him. I love him."

The man was a liar and a cheat, so of course Letty loved him. And she'd intended to raise their baby with him in the house, the man Darius blamed for his own father's death. He ground his teeth. "Are you even taking care of yourself? Do you have a doctor?"

"Of course," she said, stung. "How can you ask me that?"

"Because you've been working on your feet all day, until recently. And living in a place like this." He gestured angrily around the threadbare, cluttered apartment. "It never occurred to you I'd want better for our child?"

She glared at him. "*I* wanted better! I wanted my baby's father to be a good man I could trust and love. Instead, I got you, Darius, the worst man on earth!"

"You didn't think so ten years ago."

He immediately wished he could take the words back, because they insinuated that he still cared. Which he didn't.

"Oh, you're actually willing to talk about ten years ago? Fine. Let's talk about it." She briefly closed her eyes. "The reason I never showed up the night we were supposed to elope was because I was protecting you."

His lip curled scornfully. *"Protecting* me."

"Yes." Her expression was cool. "The day we were going to elope, my father told me his investment fund was a fraud. It had stopped making money years before, but he'd continued making payouts to old investors by taking money from new ones. The Feds were already on his tail. I knew what was going to happen." She lifted her luminous gaze. "I couldn't let you get dragged into it. Not with all your big dreams. You'd just started your tech company…" She took a deep breath and whispered, "I couldn't let my father's crime ruin your life, too."

For a moment, Darius's heart twisted as he looked at her beautiful face, her heartbreaking hazel eyes. Then he remembered that he no longer had any heart vulnerable enough to break.

"You're lying. You left me for another man. A rich man who could—how did you express it?—*give you the life of luxury you deserved."* He snorted. "Though obviously he wasn't much good. He must have dumped you the moment your father was arrested."

"He couldn't dump me." She gave a low laugh. "He never existed."

"What?"

"It was the only way I knew you'd let me go." She lifted her chin and added with deliberate lightness, "I knew your weakness, even then."

"Weakness?" he growled.

"You always said a man could be measured by his money. I knew you wouldn't accept my just breaking up with you without explanation. So I gave you one. I told you I wanted someone richer. I knew you'd believe that."

He stared at her. "It's not true."

"I've always been a terrible liar." She looked sad. "But you still believed it. And immediately stopped calling me."

Darius's cheeks burned as he remembered how he'd felt that day. She was right.

He had loved her beyond reason, had been determined to fight for her at any cost. Until she'd told him she didn't want him because he was poor. He'd believed it instantly. Because money made the man. No money, no man.

His throat felt tight as he looked at her, struggling not to believe she was telling the truth when every fiber of him believed her.

"And my father?" he said hoarsely. "Were you protecting him, too—getting him fired?"

"It's true. I did have him fired. I told Dad I couldn't bear to look at Eugenios because he reminded me of you. I did it because I was afraid my dad might ask him to invest his life savings in the bankrupt investment fund. My dad still believed he could fix everything then. I knew your father would give him his savings. He was loyal to the core."

"Yes, he was," he bit out. His father had always made his employer his top priority, even over his own son.

Darius couldn't remember when his father had ever put his son first, over his job. He hadn't attended Darius's school events, not even his high school graduation. Being eternally at Howard Spencer's beck and call, keeping the ten luxury cars all gleaming and ready, had been Eugenios's total focus in life.

Oh, his father had fed and clothed him and given him a place to live in the two-bedroom apartment over the Fairholme garage that went with his job. But emotionally, they were oceans apart. The two men never talked.

Until that one awful day Darius told his father what he really thought of him...

But that memory was so white-hot with pain, he pushed it from his mind with all the force of a ball thrown from the earth to the moon.

Letty sighed beside him on the sofa. "I was trying to get

your father away from Fairholme before he lost everything. But it was too late. He'd already invested his life savings years before. My dad had accepted it for his fund, even though it was such a small amount," she said in a small voice. "As a favor."

A small amount? His father's life savings! The arrogance of them! Darius's dark eyebrows lowered in fury.

"Howard Spencer is a liar and cheat," he said harshly. "He destroyed people's lives."

"I know," she whispered, looking down. She bit her full, rosy lower lip. "He never meant to."

"He deserves to suffer."

She looked up. "He has suffered. During his arrest and trial, I tried so hard to be strong for him. When he was in prison, I was there every visiting day. I cheered him up. Encouraged him. And all the time, I felt so scared. So alone." She gave him a watery smile. "Sometimes the only thing I had to cling to was you."

"Me?"

"At least I hadn't dragged you down with me," she whispered. "At least you were able to follow your dreams."

Darius stared at her in shock.

Then he narrowed his eyes. She was trying to take credit for his accomplishments. To claim that if not for her sacrifice, he never would have made his fortune. She thought so little of him. Ice chilled his heart.

"And you expect me to be grateful?"

She looked startled. "I—"

"When you found out about your father's crime," he said tightly, "you should have come to me. I was your future husband. Instead, you lied to me. You cut me out of your life. Rather than asking for my help, you apparently believed I was so incompetent and useless, you felt you had to sacrifice yourself to save me."

"No," she gasped, "you've got it all wrong..."

"You never respected me." He forced his voice to remain calm when his shoulders were tight with repressed fury. "Not my intelligence, my judgment or my strength."

"Respected you?" she choked out. "*I loved you.* But I knew what was about to happen. I couldn't let you drown with us. You had nothing—"

"You're right," he said coldly. "I had nothing. No money. No influence. You knew I couldn't pay for lawyers or speak to politicians on your behalf. So you decided I was useless."

"No." She looked pale. "I just meant you had nothing to do with it—"

"You were my fiancée. I had *everything* to do with it. I would have tried to protect you, to comfort you. But you never gave me the chance. Because you believed I would fail."

Her voice sounded strangled. "Darius—"

He held up his hand sharply. "But now I have made my fortune. Everything has changed. And yet you still intended to disappear and keep my child secret from me for the rest of your life." A new, chilling thought occurred to him. "What story did you intend to tell the baby, Letty?"

"I don't know," she whispered.

"What were you going to raise my child to believe? That he or she had no father? That I hadn't wanted him?" An old childhood grief he'd thought long buried suddenly shook the ground beneath his feet, like an earthquake threatening to swallow him whole. "That I'd purposefully abandoned him?"

"I don't know!" Letty cried. "But you said you'd take the baby from me. I had no choice but to run!"

Darius stared at the woman he'd known for most of his life. He'd loved her for such a short, sweet time. He'd hated her far longer.

He himself had been abandoned by everyone who should

have loved him as a child. His whole young life he'd never felt like he really belonged anywhere.

And then there was Letty.

He'd loved her so wildly, so truly, so recklessly. She had finally destroyed what was left of his heart. That had been Darius's final lesson.

He was determined that his child would never learn such a lesson.

Darius's jaw tightened. His child would be surrounded by love from the beginning. His son or daughter would have a solid place in the world and never doubt their worth.

The blindfold of rage and hurt pride lifted from his eyes. He looked at Letty, and suddenly everything became crystal clear. Calm settled over him like rain.

Their child needed both of them.

For the last decade, he'd tried to forget about the Letty he'd once known. About her character. About her kind heart.

He saw now that in Letty's mind, her hurtful lies a decade before hadn't shown disrespect, but love. She really had been trying to protect him. As she still was trying to protect her father.

As she was trying now, in her own misguided way, to protect their child.

Letty hadn't betrayed him. She'd loved him, as recently as February, the night they'd conceived their child. Yes, she'd shown bad judgment ten years ago, lying to him, hiding the truth about her father. She'd continued to show bad judgment today, planning to run away with his child. A chill went down his spine to think of what might have happened if her father hadn't called him today.

But it wasn't entirely her fault. Her love blinded her. It made her weak. And after the cold way he'd treated her, and his threats to take the child, he couldn't blame her for being afraid.

It didn't make her a monster. It wasn't enough of a reason to brutally separate her from their child. Not after he himself had known what it was to have no mother. No father. No real place in the world.

Their baby would have both parents and a secure, settled home.

Darius knew he had to rebuild Letty's trust in him. He had to find a way to strengthen her occasionally faulty judgment with his own. If Darius was wiser, it was because he never allowed love to blind him. He always focused on the bottom line. So what was it here?

The answer was simple.

He had to make Letty his wife.

It was the only way to properly secure their child's future. It would guarantee the stability of two parents and a permanent home.

And also, his body suddenly whispered, marrying Letty would permanently secure her in his bed.

The thought electrified him. That settled it.

"I misjudged you," he said.

Letty glared at him. "Yes!"

"I treated you badly."

"You think?"

"So let me make up for it now." Leaning toward her on the sofa, Darius said, "I want you to marry me, Letty."

Her jaw dropped. "Marry you!"

"I've realized now I blamed everything on you. It wasn't your fault…"

"No."

"It was your father's," he finished grimly. "He's ruined your life. I won't let him ruin our child's."

Her eyes were wide as she put her hands over her large belly. "You're crazy. My father loves the baby, just as he loves me!"

"And what about the next time some thug decides to attack him? What if that man decides to hurt your father's family instead?"

Letty's expression became troubled. Swallowing, she whispered, "That wouldn't happen…"

"No. It won't. Because you and the baby will be miles away from Howard Spencer and safe with me." He rose abruptly to his feet. "You will have to sign a prenuptial agreement…"

"I won't, because I'm not going to marry you."

She wasn't joking or playing coy. She actually sounded serious.

Darius stared down at her in confusion. So many women were dying to marry him, he'd assumed that Letty—jobless, penniless, faced with threats on all sides—would be thrilled at the thought of being his bride. "Of course you want to marry me."

"Marry someone I hate? Who hates me back? No, thanks."

He couldn't believe she was trying to fight him when it was the only practical solution. He gritted his teeth. It was that idea of *love*, once again interfering with all common sense!

"Have you thought this through?" Folding his arms, he regarded her coolly. "I could take you to court. Have you declared an unfit mother, selfishly placing our child at risk."

Letty rose to her feet in turn, matching him toe-to-toe, though he was bigger by a foot in height and at least sixty pounds of muscle. She narrowed her eyes. "You could *try*."

In spite of himself, he almost smiled. Another thing he'd forgotten about her character. She fought harder for others than she ever did for herself.

"You really think you can handle a custody battle? You think there are waves of lawyers out there, willing to support Howard Spencer's daughter pro bono, when all they'd get for their trouble is a lot of bad PR?"

Her cheeks flushed, even as she lifted her chin defiantly. "We'll see, won't we?"

But beneath her bravado, her expression was soft and sad. Her long dark ponytail gleamed in waves down her back, and his eyes strayed to the roundness of her belly and full breasts, voluptuous beyond belief. In this moment, Darius thought she looked like everything desirable in a woman—the perfect image of what any man would dream of in a wife.

He suddenly imagined how she might look in court. Whatever her father's sins, if she did find a good attorney, she could be packaged and sold to the presiding judge as the poor, innocent, poverty-stricken waitress threatened by the cold, power-hungry billionaire. No matter how many legal sharks he hired, Darius wasn't guaranteed to win. There was some small possibility he might lose.

He abruptly changed tack.

"Does our baby deserve to have parents at war? Living in here—" he motioned to the peeling wallpaper, the cracked ceiling "—instead of my penthouse? Does he deserve to grow up in poverty without the protection of his father's name? Without my love?"

Letty looked stricken. "Our baby could still have your love."

"He deserves everything I can provide. Are you really so selfish as to make our child suffer for the sake of your own angry pride?"

He saw emotions struggle on her face. She really was a terrible liar. He knew he was very close to getting what he wanted—her total surrender.

"We could make our marriage work," he murmured. "Our son or daughter would be our priority, always."

"Son," she said unwillingly.

He looked at her sharply.

She took a deep breath, then slowly smiled. "We're having a boy."

"A boy!" The nebulous idea of a baby suddenly solidified in Darius's mind. He could imagine his son smiling, playing soccer, laughing, hugging him. And the fact that she'd revealed that detail proved how close she was to agreeing to his proposal. His resolve solidified. Stepping closer, he said softly, "Marry me, Letty."

Looking uncertain, she bit her lip. "It would be a disaster. Not just for me. For you. Don't you know how much people hate me?"

"Not once you're with me," he said confidently.

"You don't understand how bad it is…"

"I'm sure you're exaggerating." He'd all but won. Now that his unborn child was secure, he was already jumping ahead to the thought of enjoying Letty's surrender in full, imagining her naked and writhing with desire in his arms. He wanted to take her back to the penthouse immediately. Then he remembered. "I am hosting a charity event tonight. The Fall Ball."

She looked impressed in spite of herself. "You're hosting that this year?"

"We can announce our engagement to all of New York."

"It's a mistake!"

"Let me worry about that."

"Okay, but…"

"But what?"

A shadow crossed her face. "But I don't love you anymore."

He felt a strange emotion, deep down inside. He crushed it down before he could identify what it was.

"I do not need your love. I can assure you that you'll never have mine. Love is for children. I just need your compliance." When she still hesitated, he took a deliberate step back. "Or I can walk out that door and go straight to my lawyer."

Letty looked wistful in the gray light from the small window. She sighed sadly. "Have it your way."

"You'll marry me?"

She nodded.

He felt a surge of smug masculine triumph. "Good choice."

Pulling her roughly into his arms, he did what he'd yearned to do for six months and kissed her.

From the moment he felt her lips against his and tasted her sweetness—her mouth, her tongue—he was lost, and at the same time, found. Her lips parted, and as she melted against him, he savored her surrender. His body and long-dead soul roared back to life.

Letty wrenched away. "But first, you'll take me to your charity ball tonight. And see firsthand what it would be like to actually have me as your wife."

"Good—"

"Just remember." She gave him a crooked smile. "You asked for it."

CHAPTER FIVE

LETTY ALMOST DIDN'T leave a note for her father. Her anger at his betrayal was too high. But in the end she didn't want him to worry, so she scribbled a note and left it on the counter.

Out with Darius, and I'm never talking to you again.

Darius had taken one look at her closet and told her he was taking her shopping for the ball. She'd tried to protest, but he'd retorted, "There's no point in announcing our engagement if you turn up at the ball dressed in rags. No one would believe it."

"Fine," she said sulkily. "Waste your money on a ball gown. See if I care."

But she had the sudden disconcerting feeling that her life was no longer her own.

As she climbed into his sports car, her stomach growled with hunger. But she vowed she wasn't going to say a word about it. It was bad enough he was buying her a dress. She wasn't going to ask him for food, like a beggar!

But as Darius climbed into the driver's seat beside her, all her senses went on high alert. Having him so close did strange things to her insides. As he drove through the busy traffic, she glanced at him out of the corner of her eye. His dark hair wasn't even mussed, and his powerful body was relaxed in the leather seat. He looked so much calmer than she felt.

But why wouldn't he be relaxed?

He'd won.

She'd lost.

Simple as that.

Or so Darius thought. Letty clasped her hands together in her lap as she looked out the window. Once he actually saw what life would be like for him with her at his side, he wouldn't be able to get rid of her fast enough. Maybe she and her father could still be on that bus to Rochester tomorrow.

Darius didn't yet see that her family's scandal wasn't something he could master or control. That was why he'd been so angry that she'd protected him ten years ago with her silence. He still somehow thought, if he'd known the truth back then, he could have prevented disaster.

She looked up through the window, seeing flashes of blue sky between the skyscrapers like a strobe light. Darius would get a dose of reality today. He'd discover how toxic the Spencer name was, even now. It had been even worse at the time of her father's arrest and trial, when reporters and angry, tomato-throwing hecklers had camped outside her father's pied-à-terre on Central Park West!

Let Darius get just a glimpse of what he would have been up against if she'd actually followed her heart and married him ten years ago instead of setting him free. He didn't appreciate the way she'd tried to protect him? Fine. Still staring out the window, she wiped her eyes hard. Let him just see.

The rain had stopped. The sky was blue and bright on the first of September. As they drove through Manhattan, puddle-dotted sidewalks were full of gawking tourists, standing still like islands as a current of New Yorkers rushed past them, coming up from the subway, hurrying back to work after lunch.

When their car stopped at a red light, Letty glanced at a fancy chauffeured town car stopped beside them. In the backseat, she saw a man speaking angrily into his phone and staring at a computer tablet, totally wrapped in his own bubble. Rich people lived in a separate world. Letty hadn't fully realized that.

Not until she'd fallen out of it.

After her father's confession that awful night long ago, after she'd tried her best to protect Darius and his father by getting them away from the manor, she'd begged Howard to go to the police and throw himself on their mercy.

He'd loved her, so a few months later he'd done it.

The police and Feds had descended on him like the hardcase criminal they believed him to be. Within six months, he was in prison on a nine-year sentence.

Letty had tried to remain in one of the exclusive small towns on Long Island near Fairholme. But it proved impossible. Too many people recognized her and didn't hesitate to yell or even—more than once—physically take the few dollars in her wallet, saying her father owed them. Manhattan had been even worse, and anyway was way out of her price range. So she'd moved to a working-class neighborhood in Brooklyn where she could be anonymous. No one bothered her. Mostly, people were kind.

But without money or family or friends, Letty had learned the hard way what it meant to struggle and always have too much month at the end of her paycheck.

No one likes self-pity. Help someone else, baby. Letty could almost hear the whisper of her mother's voice, so kind, so warm, so loving. Almost see her mother's eyes glowing with love. *The best way to feel better when you're sad is to help someone who's hurting more.*

Good advice.

Taking a deep breath, Letty turned to Darius in the sports car. "So tell me about your charity, the one benefiting from the Fall Ball tonight."

Driving, he glanced at her out of the corner of his eye. "It provides college scholarships for foster kids."

"Nice," she said, surprised. "But I never pegged you as the society-ball-hosting type."

He shrugged. "I have the time. Might as well use it."

"You could just waste your days dating beautiful women and spending your obscene amounts of money."

He pulled his car to a curb where a valet waited. "That's exactly what I plan to do today."

"You're going on a date?" Then she saw his look and realized he meant her. She blushed. "Oh."

The door opened, and Letty stepped out onto Fifth Avenue, which was lined with exclusive designer shops from famous international brands to quirky boutiques less well-known but every bit as expensive. The last time she'd shopped on this street she'd been a pampered seventeen-year-old looking for a white dress for the graduation ceremony at her private school, Miss Parker's. She hadn't fit into society, even then. She'd been too bookish, too tenderhearted, too socially awkward.

But now Letty was actually scared. She glanced at the people coming out of an exclusive department store, almost expecting one of them to tell her to get lost, that she no longer belonged here.

"Which shop first?" Darius asked, his dark eyes smiling.

"I changed my mind," she muttered. "I don't want to go."

The smile disappeared. "Too late for that."

"Darius..."

Ignoring her protests, he grabbed her hand. Letty tried not to notice the sizzle of electricity from their touching palms as he pulled her into a famous luxury store.

As soon as they passed the doorman into the store's foyer, a salesgirl came up to them, offering a tray of champagne. "Monsieur?"

He took a glass. "Thank you."

Noting Letty's pregnant belly, the salesgirl didn't offer

champagne. "And for madame? Some sparkling water, perhaps, some juice of *pamplemousse*?"

"No, thanks," Letty said, pulling away from Darius. Ducking her head, she pretended to look through the nearest dress racks, sparsely and expensively filled with garments that seemed to be designed for a size zero.

"We require assistance," he said.

"Sir?"

He turned to an elegant white-haired woman, apparently the manager, dressed in an expensive-looking tweed suit. "I need a ball gown for my fiancée."

Fiancée. The word made Letty shiver. But it was true, in a way. She'd agreed to his marriage proposal.

It's not a real engagement, she told herself firmly. She glanced down at her bare left hand. There was no ring. No ring meant it wasn't real. Anyway, the engagement would be over before the end of the night.

"Couture or ready-to-wear, Mr. Kyrillos?" The white-haired woman somehow already knew who he was.

"It's for tonight."

"We can, of course, do any last-minute alterations that madame may require. If you'll please come this way?"

They were led to a private area with a white leather sofa and a three-way mirror, as a succession of salesgirls, under the sharp-eyed direction of the manager, brought in clothes.

"She'll try on everything," Darius said, standing in front of the sofa as his cell phone rang. Lifting it from his pocket, he told Letty, "Come out when you have something to show me."

As salesgirls filled her arms with gowns and gently pushed her toward the changing room, she hesitated. "What do you want to see?"

Looking her body over slowly, Darius gave her a heavy-lidded sensual smile. "Everything."

Beneath his hot gaze, somehow, he made her feel like

a goddess of sex—even at six months pregnant, in her old T-shirt and jeans!

Darius sat down calmly on the white leather sofa, talking into his phone and sipping champagne. She turned away with a sigh to try on gowns for a ball that she was dreading.

Maybe it wouldn't be all bad, she tried to tell herself. She couldn't remember the last time she'd had new clothes. Everything in her closet was either from high school or purchased from the bargain bin at the thrift store. It might be fun to get a dress that was not only pretty, but actually fit.

Then she saw the price tag of the first gown.

Darius looked up expectantly when she came out of the dressing room. His expression changed to a scowl. "Why are you still in your old clothes?"

"The price of these gowns is ridiculous! We can go to the local thrift shop and find a barely used prom dress…"

"Letty."

"I mean it. It's foolish for you to throw money away when you might never see me again after tonight."

"Now you're talking nonsense." He tilted his head, looking her over critically. "Are you not feeling well? Are you hungry? Thirsty? Tired?"

She wasn't going to say a word about being hungry. Wild horses couldn't drag it out of her!

Her stomach growled again.

"Um. I might have missed breakfast."

It wasn't her fault! The baby made her say it!

He looked mad. "You should have told me." He grabbed a glass of sparkling mineral water from a salesgirl. "Here," he said gravely, pushing it into her hand. "Start with that. Breakfast or lunch?"

The cool water tasted delicious, and did make her feel slightly better. "Breakfast?"

Turning to one of the hovering assistants, he ordered, "Have a large breakfast sent down from your café."

"Oh, sir." The salesgirl looked sorrowful. "I'm afraid that's impossible…"

"Of course it's possible for Mr. Kyrillos," the white-haired manager snapped, turning to them with a bright smile. "A pregnant woman must never go hungry. What would madame like?"

"Everything," Darius said. "Send down a tray or two. We'll be here a while. We need a ball gown, but also a great deal more. Shoes, accessories, maternity clothes. Price is no object. We may be here for hours."

"Yes, sir," the woman replied happily, clapping her hands at her assistants, who rushed to obey.

"Darius, you don't need to make a fuss!"

"You're wrong. I can see all too well that I need to be in charge. Because you've always been better at taking care of others than yourself." He drew Letty gently to the white sofa. "Here. Sit down. Take a breath."

"But I left all those dresses in the changing room—"

"They will wait. Relax. You do not have to shop hungry. Breakfast is on its way."

The white leather cushion shifted beneath them, tipping her toward him on the sofa. The edge of her thigh brushed against his. She jumped away with an intake of breath, looking up at him with big eyes.

"I'm not your responsibility."

"You are now." Reaching out, he tucked a long tendril of her dark hair back behind her ear and said softly, "And taking care of you will be my pleasure."

His…pleasure?

A sudden terrifying thought occurred to her.

"Darius," she said haltingly, unable to meet his eyes. "You surely can't think…"

"Think what?"

Taking her courage in her hands, she looked into his dark wicked eyes. However charming he might seem at the moment, she couldn't forget the heartless man he'd revealed himself to be. She couldn't let herself confuse him with the boy she'd once loved. No matter how much Darius's dark eyes, his smile, his kindness might seem the same. *He was nothing like the man she'd loved.*

"You can't think…" She took a deep breath. "That our marriage would be real."

"Of course it will be real. Legal in any court."

"I mean…" She licked her lips, hating him for making her spell it out. "It would just be a marriage of convenience, nothing more. For our baby. We wouldn't… You and I, we would never…"

"You will sleep in my bed, Letty." His dark eyes burned through her. "Naked. Every single night."

His sensual voice swirled around her body like a hot wind, making her toes curl.

She had to resist. She had no intention of sleeping with him again, no matter how seductive he might be. She'd been a virgin till twenty-eight, waiting for love. That love was gone.

"I loved you the night we conceived our baby. Everything has changed. Unlike you, I can't have sex with a cold heart," she said in a low voice. "No love, no sex."

He wrapped her hand in his larger one. She felt his palm against hers, and a shiver ricocheted through Letty's body, deep, to blood and bone. He leaned forward.

"We'll see," he whispered.

CHAPTER SIX

LETTY WAS SAVED when the salesgirls interrupted them with trays of pastries and fruit and juices, followed closely behind by yet more racks of clothes for her to consider.

A proper breakfast tray soon followed with maple bacon pancakes drizzled in maple syrup, hash brown potatoes and hot fried sausages. Thus fortified, Letty spent another hour trying on all the clothes she liked in that luxury store. Then they moved to a designer boutique. Then an exclusive department store.

By the end of the afternoon, Darius had bought her so many bags of clothes, he'd had to call his bodyguard and driver down to Fifth Avenue to carry everything back to the penthouse.

He took her to a world-famous jewelry store where they were ushered to an exclusive, private floor. She tried to protest, for about the thirtieth time. "You really don't need to keep spending more money on me!"

Darius held up a twenty-carat diamond necklace with a critical eye. "You're going to be my wife. Of course you need clothes."

"Those are diamonds."

He grinned. "Hard, sparkling clothes."

She harrumphed. "You're wasting your money."

"So let me waste it. What do you care?" Lifting his eyebrow, he said mildly, "I seem to recall your saying you hate me. So why not make me suffer?"

Why not indeed? Put that way, it didn't sound so unreasonable. "You do have it coming."

Setting the necklace down, he looked at her with a heavily lidded gaze.

"And I intend to take it." Turning back to the jeweler, he nodded toward the diamond necklace. "Starting with that."

But though Darius insisted on buying her an entire wardrobe of fancy clothes, he was never satisfied by any of the ball gowns she tried on. Truth be told, even Letty thought most of them hideous. A hoop skirt on a baby bump? She looked like a cartoon hippo.

In spite of Letty's misgivings, the afternoon flew by in an irresistible whirlwind of small pleasures. Her new wardrobe wasn't comprised of minimalist black and gray clothes as he had originally suggested, currently popular with chic society women, nor were they the plain, sensible, washing-machine-ready clothes she'd worn for the last ten years. No.

Darius had watched her carefully as she'd tried on each outfit, and he seemed to notice the colors that made her face light up with joy. Bright, vivid jewel tones—emerald green, cerulean blue, fuchsia, ruby red—in impractical sensual fabrics like silk.

"We'll take it," he would say immediately.

Letty felt guilty revealing her own pleasure, but she couldn't help herself. For so long, survival had been her only goal. She couldn't remember the last time that her happiness had mattered to anyone, least of all her.

But Darius treated her as if her happiness was actually the main goal.

Because I carry his baby inside me, she told herself, as she changed her clothes yet again in a private dressing room.

But his hot dark gaze had told her it was more than that. He didn't just want custody over their baby.

He wanted to possess Letty, too.

You will sleep in my bed. Naked. Every single night.

She shivered, then tried on yet another formal gown, this one made of a slinky knit fabric in a delicious shade of hot pink, her favorite color.

The dress fell softly over her body. Reaching back, she couldn't quite zip it all the way. She looked at herself in the mirror.

The long stretchy gown fit perfectly over her pregnant body, curving over her full breasts and huge belly. She liked it, but weren't pregnant women supposed to wear tent dresses?

"I want to see," Darius's voice commanded outside the dressing room. She took a deep breath, then came out, her cheeks hot.

"What do you think?" she said timidly.

His expression said everything. He walked slowly around her, looking up and down her body in a way that made her shiver inside.

"That," he said softly, "is the dress."

She bit her lip. "I'm afraid it's too formfitting…"

"It's perfect."

"I couldn't zip it all the way up…"

Drawing close, he wrapped his arms around her. She felt his arms brush against her body as he pulled on the zipper. His eyes never left hers as he towered over her, so close. He made her breathless.

A hint of a smile lifted the edges of his cruel, sensual mouth. He cupped her cheek, then stroked down her throat. "The necklace will be perfect here. Against your skin."

Looking down, she realized how low cut the gown was. Her cheeks went redder. "I shouldn't wear this."

"Why?"

"It's too revealing. Everyone will stare."

"They will stare regardless."

"Because I'm the daughter of a criminal."

"Because you're an incredibly beautiful woman."

At his soft words, Letty's throat suddenly hurt. "You don't realize how much they hate me." Her eyes stung as she pushed away. "When they see me…it'll be like dropping raw meat in a shark tank. And the more they notice me, the more they'll rip me apart." She took a deep breath, tried to smile. "I sound like I'm complaining. I'm not. I can handle it. I'm used to it. But…"

"But what?"

She looked down at the floor.

"Letty?"

She said in a small voice, "I don't want them to say rude things about you at your own party. And they will if I'm your date."

Reaching out, he lifted her chin. "I can take care of myself, *agape mou*," he said in a low voice. "When will you learn that?"

His dark gaze fell to her mouth, and Letty's whole body tightened as, for a moment, she wondered if he was going to kiss her, right there in the luxurious store. For a wild moment, it didn't seem like such a bad idea.

He turned to the nearest salesgirl. "We'll take this dress. Wrap it up. We need shoes to match."

Letty tried on ten pairs before she found stiletto heels that made her gasp at their outrageous beauty.

"Those," Darius said, looking at Letty's face.

"No, I couldn't possibly. They're too impractical. I'll never wear them again!" She looked doubtfully at her feet, wobbling in the high heels. "I'm not even sure I can wear them now."

But even as she protested, she couldn't look away from the beautiful shoes, which were encrusted with glittery pink crystals and had a red sole.

"We'll take them," he told the salesgirl firmly.

Though they pinched Letty's toes and made her wobble ever so slightly, she was filled with joy as she sat down and handed the precious pink crystal stilettos to the salesgirl. She couldn't remember the last time she'd had anything so outrageous, just because of their beauty. And their cost! She was trying not to think about owning shoes worth three months' rent. And when would she ever wear them again? Working as a waitress? Going to the grocery store?

It was wicked, letting him buy her these shoes. Letting him buy her so many things, when after tonight, he'd likely never want to see her again.

She would just leave everything behind, she decided. Most of the clothes could be returned, unworn, with tags. She'd have nothing to feel guilty about when he tossed her out of his life. Nothing!

"Now—" Darius's gaze lingered on her lips, then dropped lower "—lingerie."

Letty made a sound like a squeak. "Forget it!"

"Ah. You intend to wear nothing beneath your gown tonight? I approve."

Her cheeks burned. "Of course I'm going to wear something!"

"Then you need undergarments." He nodded toward three hovering salesgirls. "Get us a selection of lingerie that would suit the gown."

They departed in a rush to obey.

"I hope you don't expect me to try *those* on for you," Letty said sulkily.

"No?" He looked at her lazily. "Maybe later."

Her blush deepened.

Right here, in the exclusive department store, with strangers everywhere, Darius was looking at Letty as if he wanted nothing more than to drag her into a changing room and roughly make love to her. Possibly while she was wearing nothing but those pink crystal stilettos. Not a bad idea...

She blinked, realizing she'd been licking her lips. She put her hand unsteadily to her head. What was happening? Was she losing all her morals over a pair of beautiful shoes and for the body of a dangerously beautiful man?

Except Darius wasn't just beautiful. He was also the only man she'd ever slept with. The only man she'd ever been in love with. She was even now carrying his child deep inside her. He wanted her in his bed. He wanted to marry her. All of those things together were likely to distract any woman.

And with every moment, she felt herself being drawn into his world. Remembering what it was like when money was no object. To be without worry or care.

To be cherished.

It had been a long time since she'd felt that way. She'd been a lonely teenager, far happier spending her time with the estate staff, pets or books instead of other debutantes. At fourteen, she'd fallen hopelessly for Darius, the chauffeur's son, six years older and totally out of her league. Funny now to recall that she'd actually imagined herself to be unhappy then.

She'd discovered soon after what unhappiness really meant, when her beloved mother, the heart of their home, had suddenly fallen ill. She'd wasted away and died within months.

Her father had been gutted. A few years later, he'd gone to prison. Letty had tried to be tough. She'd tried to be strong. She'd hadn't let herself think. Hadn't let herself feel.

But now…

For the first time in years she realized how it felt to be truly looked after. To be cared for. As the salesgirls wrapped up a thousand dollars' worth of silky lingerie, she tried to tell herself it was just an illusion. Exactly like Cinderella. After midnight tonight it would all disappear.

Darius signed the credit card receipt, smiling at her out of the corner of his eye. "Is there anything else you desire?"

Letty looked at him, her heart in her throat. Then she just shook her head.

"It's growing late." He took her hand. "We have one more place to go."

The bodyguard had already left in Darius's sports car filled with bags. As his driver walked ahead, weighed down by yet more bags, toward the waiting town car, Darius never let go of her hand. His dark eyes glowed down at her as the sun slipped down between the skyscrapers, toward a horizon she couldn't see.

Maybe it was the pregnancy hormones, but as they climbed into the back of the elegant car, emotion squeezed her heart as she looked at him. All day, Darius had been beside her, ready to push through any crowds, to make sure that she got—in his opinion—proper attention. When she was thirsty, when she was hungry, when she was tired, he seemed to know even before she did, and like a miracle, whatever she desired would instantly appear.

It was as if she were no longer alone. Someone else was looking out for her. Someone tough and strong. Someone who made her feel safe.

Safe?

She shook herself hard. Darius was dangerous. Selfish. Arrogant and cold.

He frowned at her in the backseat. "Are you crying?"

She wiped her tears. "Nope."

"Letty."

"I'm sorry. I just…" She faltered. "You've been so kind."

"Buying you clothes?" he said incredulously. He gave a low laugh. "Is that all it takes?"

It was more than the clothes, far more, but she couldn't explain. She said miserably, "I shouldn't go with you to the ball tonight."

His mouth turned down grimly. "You're going."

"Don't you understand? It'll only cause you trouble."

"Stop trying to protect me," he said evenly. "I mean it."

"But—"

"It's not your job to protect me. It's my job to protect you now. And our baby. Never again insult me by insinuating

I am incapable of it." At her expression, he said more gently, "Don't you understand, Letty? I will watch over you. I'll make sure no one ever hurts you again. You'll always be taken care of now. You're safe."

She was suddenly shaking as the town car drove down the street. How she wished it were true! How she wished she could believe in him, as she had so long ago.

The car door opened. Looking up in surprise at Darius's driver, who was holding it open, Letty looked back at Darius. He gave her a cheeky grin.

"I'm just dropping you off. This is the best day spa in the city. Collins is bringing your gown and everything else you'll need for the ball tonight. I'll collect you here at eight."

"A day spa? Why?"

"You deserve some pampering. Enjoy yourself." He leaned forward in the car's backseat. She felt his warmth and breathed in his scent as he brushed back her hair and whispered in her ear, "I'll be back for you soon."

As he drew back, her heart beat rapidly, and she felt prickles of sensation and desire course through her body, down her spine and over her skin.

And all he'd done was whisper in her ear!

Oh, this was bad.

Her legs were shaky as she stepped out of the car and was whisked into the gorgeously bright day spa with its tall windows, green plants and kitschy pink furniture. A team of specialists, including massage therapists, beauty therapists, stylists and more, surrounded her, moaning about Letty's cuticles, her tense shoulders, her dry skin…

Hours passed in a flash. Her nails were done and her muscles rubbed and her skin freshened until dewy. Hairstylists and makeup artists came next, and once they were done, it was nearly eight.

Letty put on the new silk bra and panties, the perfectly

fitting pink gown and sparkly stiletto heels. She looked at herself in the mirror.

Her long, freshly shaped dark hair was now glossy and shiny and bouncy from the hairstylist's efforts. Red lipstick made her look glamorous, and her eyes were emphasized with dark liner and even a few false eyelashes for drama. Her full breasts, pushed up by the bra, were laid out like a platter in the knit pink dress, her hips thrust forward by the stilettos, her voluptuous belly the star.

She was dazzled by her own image. She barely recognized herself.

"Wait until Mr. Kyrillos sees you," the proprietress of the spa said with a broad smile. "Our finest creation!" There was a whisper, then a gasp. "He's here!"

Nervously, Letty came down into the foyer. She wondered if he would think she looked silly. She couldn't bear it if her appearance embarrassed him, on top of everything else.

But as Darius came into the foyer, she saw his face. And she knew he approved. Deeply.

"You look incredible," he whispered. "So beautiful."

She gave him a shy smile. "You don't look so bad yourself."

The truth was, she couldn't take her eyes off him. His hard jaw was freshly shaved, and his dark eyes wickedly bright. He looked impossibly handsome, tall and broad-shouldered in his sophisticated black tuxedo, which was obviously tailored. No tuxedo off the rack could have fit his muscled body so perfectly.

Wordlessly, Darius held out his arm.

Wrapping her hand around his hard, thick bicep, she shivered, remembering how six months ago, she'd felt his naked, powerful body over hers. Inside hers. She nearly stumbled at the memory.

He stopped.

"Sorry, I'm still getting the hang of my shoes," she lied. She couldn't explain that it wasn't the stilettos that had made her stumble, but the memory of that hot February night they'd conceived their baby.

A night that would never happen again, she thought wistfully. After tonight, he'd run away from her so fast that there would be flames left on the ground, like in a cartoon.

This time, a limousine waited for them. Collins, the driver, wore his formal uniform with a peaked cap as he held open her passenger door.

"Where is the ball this year?" she asked Darius.

"The Corlandt," he said, naming a venue that was nearly as famous as the Met or Frick or Whitney.

She gulped. It was even worse than she'd thought. As the limo took them uptown, she felt sick with dread. She looked out the window, frantically trying to build ice around her heart and get herself back into a place where she was too well armored to feel any attack.

But her newly scrubbed skin felt far too thin now. Wearing this beautiful dress, and being with Darius, she felt vulnerable. She felt visible. She felt raw.

Even though she no longer loved him, she still didn't want him hurt because of her. She tried to tell herself it would be for his own good, so he'd realize they had no future. But she couldn't bear the thought of what was about to happen.

All too soon, the limo arrived. Looking out at the crowds and red carpet and paparazzi, Letty couldn't breathe. Collins got out and opened their door.

Darius went first. There was a low roar from the crowds, watching from behind the cordons of the red carpet, at seeing Darius Kyrillos, the host of the evening and currently New York's most famous billionaire bachelor, get out of the limo, gorgeous in his tuxedo. As cameras flashed in the darkening twilight, he gave a brusque wave.

Looking at the photographers, Letty felt so weak she wasn't sure she could get out of the limo.

Turning back, Darius held out his hand to where she sat quivering in the backseat. He lifted a challenging eyebrow.

Shaking, Letty put her hand in his.

As she exited the limo, a low murmur started amid the photographers and press waiting outside the red carpet as someone recognized Letty.

Then it spread.

There was a gasp of recognition traveling among the photographers and crowd like a rumble of thunder rolling across the ground. The camera flashes went crazy as journalists and celebrity bloggers started screaming at her.

"Letitia Spencer!"

"Where have you been for the last ten years?"

"How does it feel now that your father's out of prison?"

"Do you feel guilty for your father's victims as you're coming to a ball in diamonds?"

"Are you two together?"

"Mr. Kyrillos, with all the city at your feet, why would you date a jailbird's daughter?"

Darius responded only with a glower as he arrogantly walked past them, Letty gripping his hand tightly. He led her past the reporters and inside the magnificent beaux-arts-style granite building. Only after she'd walked up the steps and past the imposing columns through the oversize door, and he'd shut it behind them, did she exhale. Immediately, he pulled her close. Letty closed her eyes, still shaking as she breathed in his strength, his warmth, his comfort.

"It's over," he said softly as he finally drew back, tucking back a dark tendril of her hair behind her ear. "That wasn't so bad, was it?"

"You think it's over?" She gave him a trembling smile. "It's only just begun."

Darius's expression darkened, but they were interrupted

as a famous white-haired society matron covered in jewels entered the foyer behind them. Her face brightened when she saw Darius. She immediately left her much younger date to come forward and give him air-kisses.

"Darius, how lovely to see you! Thank you again for hosting this important event." She simpered. "Though I think there will be many broken hearts when they see you brought a date—"

But as the matron turned to Letty, her smile froze. Her expression changed to shock, then outrage.

"Hello, Mrs. Alexander," Letty said bashfully. "I don't know if you remember, but I used to go to school with your daughter, Poppy. We were both debutantes at the—"

"Stop." The woman's eyes blazed. "Don't you dare speak to me." Looking back at Darius, she hissed, "Do you know who this girl is? What she's done?"

He looked at her coldly. "Of course I know who Letty is. We've been friends since childhood. And as for what she's done—I think you have her confused with her father."

The woman turned to Letty with narrowed eyes. "You have some nerve coming here. Your father stole money from nearly every person attending tonight." She looked at Darius incredulously. "And you are insane to bring her. Take my advice. Send Letitia Spencer straight out the door. Or you might find that you suddenly have no guests, and your charity will suffer. For what? So you can get that little tart in your bed?" She looked pointedly at Letty's belly. "Or perhaps you did that already?"

Letty's cheeks went hot. She suddenly felt like a tart, too, wearing this low-cut, formfitting pink dress that showed off every curve. Beneath the society matron's scrutiny, even her beautiful sparkly shoes lost their gleam, and suddenly just pinched her feet.

"It's only out of respect for those poor foster children that I'm not leaving here right now." The woman glared between them, then flounced away in her jewels and fluttering silk sleeves.

Letty was left paralyzed from the ambush.

"Don't listen to her," Darius said, putting his hand on her shoulder. "She's a witch."

"I don't blame her for being mad," Letty said in a low voice. "Her family lost a lot of money. Tens of millions."

"It obviously hasn't cut into her jewelry and plastic-surgery budget. Forget her. Let's go in."

Wrapping her arm securely over his, he marched her into the ballroom as cheerfully as a revolutionary leading a French aristocrat to the guillotine.

But it was no good. The rest of the evening was just as Letty had feared. As lovely and magical as the afternoon had been, the ball sucked the joy out of everything.

Darius insisted on keeping her by his side as he greeted his society guests, each of whom had paid thousands of dollars to attend this ball, ostensibly for the benefit of college scholarships for foster kids but mostly just to have a good excuse to party with friends and show off new couture.

Letty felt their hostile stares, though with Darius beside her, none were as brave or foolhardy as Mrs. Alexander. None of them said anything to her face. Instead, the cream of New York society just stared at her in bewildered horror, as if she had a contagious and fatal disease, then looked at Darius as if they were waiting for him to reveal the punch line of whatever joke had inspired him to bring a pariah like Letitia Spencer to the Fall Ball when he could have had any beauty in the city for the asking.

She heard whispers and felt their hard stares as she and Darius passed through the crowds in the ballroom. When he briefly left her to get drinks, she felt vulnerable, alone. She kept her eyes focused on the floor, trying to be quiet and invisible, as if facing wild animals. If they didn't notice her, they might not tear her to shreds with their teeth and claws.

It didn't work.

Within moments, three former debutantes blocked her like bouncers at a bar.

"Well, well, well." A skinny young woman in a designer gown gave her a hard-edged smile. "Letitia Spencer. This is a surprise. Isn't it, Caroline?"

"A big surprise."

Letty vaguely recognized the two women from her school, where they'd been a year older. They were looking at her now with the cold expressions of mob enforcers. She could suddenly imagine how her father must have felt right before that thug had broken his arm.

But the third woman stood a slight distance from the first two. It was Poppy Alexander. She and Letty had once been study partners, sophomore year. Poppy just stood there, looking pale and uneasy.

"Excuse me." Letty backed away. "I don't want any trouble."

"You don't want trouble?" The first woman's lip twisted scornfully. "How very amusing."

"Amusing," Caroline echoed with a sneer.

"You shouldn't be here."

"You're a disgrace to society."

"If you had any decency, you'd disappear or die."

Poppy stood silently beside her friends, looking faintly sick, as if she wished she were a million miles away. Letty sympathized with that feeling.

The first woman continued with a sneer, "You might think you're safe on Darius Kyrillos's arm, but…"

"Ah, there you are, Letty," Darius said smoothly, coming up behind them. "I brought your drink." Turning to the other women, he gave a charming smile. "Ah. Augusta. Caroline. And Poppy Alexander. How lovely to see you."

"Hello, Darius," they cooed with weak smiles, then departed, the first two with a final venomous glance at Letty, Poppy hanging her head, looking guilty and ashamed.

Emotions Letty knew well.

"Everything all right?" Darius murmured after they left.

She exhaled, blinking fast. "Fine. Just fine."

The night only got worse. It was past ten when the formal dinner was finally served, and Letty felt half-starved as she sat down beside Darius at the prestigious head table. But as she felt the glares from the four other couples at the table, she could barely eat a bite of salad or the lobster with white truffle cream. At any moment, she half expected one of the hedge fund millionaires or society wives might smash a three-hundred-dollar champagne bottle against the table and attack her with it.

That might have been preferable to the waves of unspoken hatred overtaking her like a blast of heat from all sides. During the unendurably long meal, Darius tried several times to start conversations with the others at the table. Each time, he succeeded. Until he tried to include her. Then the conversation instantly died.

Finally, Letty could stand it no longer.

"Excuse me," she breathed, rising from her seat. "I have to—"

She couldn't finish her sentence. Turning, she rushed past all the other tables and out of the ballroom. Going down the long hall, she found a ladies' bathroom, where she was violently sick. Going to the sink, she washed out her mouth. She looked at herself wanly in the mirror. She felt like she'd rather die than go back into that ballroom and see Darius trying to stick up for her.

Better for her to just leave quietly. Better for both of them.

After lingering as long as she could in the cool quiet of

the empty, marble bathroom, with the old-fashioned elegance of a more genteel era, she went out into the hallway.

She found Darius waiting for her, smolderingly handsome in his tuxedo, leaning against the wall with his arms folded and his jaw tight.

"Are you all right?"

He was angry. She could hear it in his voice. She stopped, barely holding back her tears. "Have you seen enough?" she choked out. "You're surely not enough of an idiot to marry me."

He came closer in the empty hallway, with its plush carpets and gold light fixtures. She tensed, waiting for him to tell her he'd obviously made a mistake, bringing her to his ball, and that there was no way he would marry her now or in fact ever wanted to see her again. She waited for him to give her what she'd wanted and set her free.

Except in this moment the thought didn't make her as happy as it once did.

He narrowed his eyes. "I didn't realize how bad it was for you."

She'd successfully fought back tears all night. But she could do it no longer. Not now, when the illusion of having a protector—even for a night—was coming to an end.

Letty took a deep breath, trying to ignore the lump in her throat, wiping her eyes before he'd see the tears. She tried to smile. "But now you know. So tomorrow I'll go to Rochester with my father. You can continue to be rich and famous and popular here. You can visit our baby anytime you want…" Something in his eyes made her voice trail off uncertainly. "If you even want to see our baby anymore," she whispered.

His eyes suddenly blazed with cold fury. "No."

"What?"

He gripped her arm. "I said no."

She tried to pull away, but couldn't. "What are you doing?"

"What I should have done the moment we arrived here."

He pulled her grimly down the hall, back toward the ballroom.

"No," she choked out, struggling. "Please. I can't go back in there. Don't make me…"

Darius was merciless. He dragged her back into the enormous ballroom, with its high ceiling and crystal chandeliers. He gripped her wrist as she limped behind him in the tight stiletto shoes and pink dress, going past all the big round tables, where a thousand people were now drinking after-dinner brandies and coffees and the men, at least, were eating desserts. Letty felt each ten-person table fall silent as they went by. She felt everyone's judgment. Their blame. Their hatred.

Ruthlessly, Darius pulled her through the ballroom, leaving people silent in their wake. As he walked past their own table, he grabbed his glass of champagne. Crossing the small dance floor, he dragged her up the stairs to the stage, where, still holding her wrist, he took the microphone at the podium. He cleared his throat.

Letty's knees were trembling with fear. She wished she'd never come here—wished she'd never taken a single risk—would have given twenty years of her life to be back at her tiny apartment, snug on the sofa with a blanket over her head!

"Good evening," Darius said into the microphone. His husky, commanding voice rang over the ballroom. A spotlight fell on him. "For those of you I haven't yet met personally, I'm Darius Kyrillos. Thank you for coming to my party, the event kicking off the New York fall social season, and thank you for supporting scholarships for kids in need. It's because of you that many deserving youngsters will be able to go to college or learn a trade."

A smattering of applause ensued; much less enthusiastic than it would have been if Letty hadn't been standing with him on stage. She was ruining everything, she thought unhappily. Even for those kids who needed help. She hated herself. Almost as much as she hated him.

Darius deliberately turned away from the microphone to give her a searching glance, and her stomach fell to the floor. *Here it comes*, she thought. *He's going to announce that he brought me here as a joke and have me thrown me out.* She was social poison, so he really had no choice but to distance himself. This was exactly what she'd expected.

She just hadn't expected it to hurt so much when it happened.

Darius's lips twisted. He turned back to the microphone. "Most of you know this beautiful woman on stage with me. Miss Letitia Spencer." There was a low hiss across the ballroom, a rumble of muffled booing. He responded with a charming smile. "Since we're all friends, I wanted you to be the first to know…I just asked her to marry me."

Letty's eyes went wide. What? Why would he say that? Was he insane?

"And she has accepted," he finished calmly. "So I want you all to be the first to wish us joy."

This time, the gasp came from Letty. Forget insane. Was he suicidal?

The low hisses and boos changed to ugly muttering across the ballroom, angry, obscene words that made Letty squirm. Instinctively, she covered her belly with her arms to protect her unborn baby from the cruel words.

But Darius's smile only widened as he put his large hand over hers, on her belly.

"We're expecting a baby, too. All of this has left me so overwhelmed with joy, I want to share it with all of you. Now. Some of you might know of her father's troubles…"

A white-haired man, unable to contain himself any longer, sprang up from his table. "Howard Spencer defrauded my company of millions of dollars!" he cried, shaking his fist. "We were only repaid a fraction of what we lost!"

A low buzz of rage hummed around him.

"Letty's father is a criminal," Darius agreed. "He abused your trust, and I know over half of what he stole is still unaccounted for. But *Letty* did nothing wrong. Her only crime was loving a father who didn't deserve it. That's why I've decided, in my future bride's honor, to make amends."

Suddenly, it was dead quiet across the tables.

Darius held his champagne glass high. "I will personally pay back every penny her father stole."

A collective gasp ripped through the ballroom.

The white-haired man staggered back. "But that's...*five billion dollars!*"

"So it is," Darius said mildly. He looked over the crowd. "So if your family is still owed money by Howard Spencer, I personally guarantee repayment. All in honor of my beautiful...innocent...unfairly hounded...bride." Turning back toward Letty on stage, he held up his champagne glass and said into the microphone, "To Letitia Spencer!"

As photographers rushed forward, Letty felt faint. Camera flashes lit up everywhere. There was a rumble of noise, of shouts and gasps and chairs hastily pushed aside as a thousand people scrambled to their feet and lifted their champagne glasses into the air.

"Letitia Spencer!" they cried joyfully.

CHAPTER SEVEN

IT WASN'T EVERY day a man spent five billion dollars on a whim.

Darius hadn't intended to do it. He'd had a different surprise in mind for Letty tonight: a black velvet box hidden in the pocket of his tuxedo jacket, which he'd planned to spring on her as soon as the evening was over and all her overblown fears had proved unfounded.

Instead, he'd realized how much she'd endured over the last ten years. Alone. While he'd been happily free to live an anonymous life and make his fortune.

Standing in the hallway, when he'd seen her come out of the bathroom looking shattered and as pale as a ghost, he'd finally realized the toll it had taken on her. And if this was how people treated Letty now, how much worse had it been ten years ago, when their rage had been white-hot?

He'd been forced to ask himself: If Letty had actually shown up the night they were going to run away together and told him about her father's confession, what would have happened?

Darius would have of course insisted she marry him anyway. After all, what did her father's stupid investment fund have to do with their love?

But as her husband, he would have been at her side throughout the scandal and media circus of a trial. He might not have received the critical early loan that enabled him to build his software, to hire employees, to lease his first office space. He would have been too tainted by association as Howard Spencer's son-in-law.

If Letty hadn't set him free, he might have been unemployable, unable to easily provide for his wife or children.

He might be living in that tiny Brooklyn apartment, too, struggling with the loss of his dreams. Struggling to provide for his family. Struggling not to feel like a failure as a man.

It was Letty's sacrifice ten years ago that had made his current success possible.

While he'd been triumphantly building his billion-dollar company, she'd lived in poverty, suffering endless humiliations for a crime that wasn't even hers. And she'd kept her sacrifice a secret, so he'd never once had to feel guilty about deserting her.

Even now, she continued to protect him. She'd warned him what would happen if he brought her as his date. And now he'd finally seen how the members of the so-called upper class had treated her all this time. He'd watched Letty bear their insults without complaint. And he'd realized her stigma was so bad that, in spite of his arrogant earlier assumption, his presence alone wasn't enough to shelter her.

He knew how it felt to be treated badly.

He'd once been the poorest child in his village, mocked as an unloved bastard. He was now the most beloved, feared man of Heraklios. He did pretty well in Manhattan, too. And London. And Paris and Rome, Sydney and Tokyo.

Money could buy everything from houses to souls.

Money made the man.

It astonished him that not everyone realized this. Some people seemed to think love was the most important thing. They were either fools, Darius thought grimly, or gluttons for punishment. He'd learned his own lesson well. The sick truth was that love only led to pain.

Love was a pale facsimile of money. Love begged.

Money demanded.

So when Darius had seen how badly New York society had treated Letty for all these years—these people who didn't have a fraction of her kindness or her loyalty or her heart—ice had seized his soul.

Especially when he'd realized that he'd treated her even worse. After a decade of ignoring her, he'd taken revenge for her so-called sins through cold seduction, insults and threats.

His jaw tightened. He would pay that debt.

Darius didn't love her. The part of his heart that had once craved love had been burned away. Love wasn't something he ever wanted to feel for anyone.

But there were other qualities Darius did believe in.

Honor.

Loyalty.

Protecting his woman.

So he'd settled the matter, once and for all.

Now Letty would be the most popular girl in the city. Every person who'd once treated her shabbily would be begging for an invitation to their wedding. Begging to be her friend.

At the moment of Darius's triumph, as he toasted her on stage, he turned to face Letty at the podium. Rough, raw desire surged through his body as he looked at her—his woman now, *his*—lush and pregnant and obscenely beautiful in that pink gown, which slid over her breasts and belly like a caress.

She stood unsteadily in those ridiculous stiletto heels, beneath the blinding spotlight, as a thousand people applauded from the darkness. People who had treated her like garbage just minutes before started chanting her name. Camera flashes lit up the darkness as reporters shouted questions.

"Miss Spencer, what's it like to be loved to the tune of five billion dollars?"

"When's the wedding?"

"When's your baby due?"

"How does it feel to suddenly be the most popular girl in New York?"

Letty looked at Darius with the expression of a terrified deer, and he realized she wasn't enjoying this as much as he was.

Turning back to the microphone with a smile, Darius answered for her. "The wedding will be soon. No plans yet. Our baby will be born soon, too." He looked past the reporters to the well-heeled crowd. "That's all. Thank you for your support! Enjoy your night. And since you're now all so much richer, don't forget to be generous to the scholarship fund—it's for the kids." Setting his empty champagne glass on the podium, he glanced at the full orchestra. "Let's start the music!"

"Kick off the dancing, Darius!" someone shouted from the back.

"Yes, the first dance to you and Letty!" someone else cried.

Darius led her down the steps from the stage, and as they reached the dance floor, the music started, a slow, romantic song he'd purposefully requested from the orchestra earlier because he knew Letty would remember it from that long-ago summer.

He was right. She stopped when she heard it, eyes wide.

Darius looked down at her with a crooked half smile. "What do you say? Will you dance with me, Letty?"

She looked around at all the people who had treated her with such contempt for the last ten years, now beaming at her as if they were best friends.

"Why are they acting as if they like me?" she said softly, for his ears alone.

"People love to talk about character and loyalty and love. They mean money." He allowed himself a grim smile. "Now the money's been paid, so they can love you again."

Letty's head snapped back to look at him. Her big hazel

eyes, fringed with dark lashes, were wide, as if he were a superhero who'd flown down from the sky. "Why did you do it, Darius? Why pay five billion dollars for a debt that isn't yours?"

The music swirled around them like a whirlwind. "Do you remember our old waltz?"

Her forehead creased. "Of course…" She looked back at the people yelling encouragement for them to dance. She bit her lip. "But not in front of everyone…"

"Now." Darius pulled her against his tuxedo-clad body. "Dance with me."

Letty's long dark hair was falling softly around her beautiful face to her shoulders, nestling against the diamonds sparkling around her neck. He'd already wanted her, but as he felt her body in his arms, and the crush of her belly and swollen breasts against his chest, he wanted her even more.

Just like that long-ago summer…

"Come on, Letty," he said in a low voice. "Let's show them all we don't give a damn."

He moved commandingly onto the dance floor, leading her in the first steps of the waltz he'd helped her practice for her debutante ball long ago, the spring of her senior year. They'd practiced the waltz over and over in the sunlit spring flower meadow on the Fairholme estate, overlooking the sparkling bay, as music sang from her phone.

They'd started out as friends and ended as something else entirely.

When she'd left for her debutante ball in Manhattan that May, looking beautiful beyond belief in her white dress, Darius spent the whole evening prowling the meadow in a rage, hating the Harvard boy who was her date.

He'd been shocked when Letty came back early, whispering, "I didn't want to dance with anyone but you…"

Darius had taken one look at Letty's joyous, upturned face surrounded by spring flowers, and then he, the chauffeur's son, had done the unthinkable: he'd wrapped her in his powerful arms and kissed her…

Now, as he swirled her around in that waltz, it was like going back in time. The audience standing on the edge of the dance floor clapped their approval. In this moment, in this place, Darius and Letty were the king and queen of the city, the pinnacle of all his youthful dreams.

But he barely noticed the crowds. There was only Letty. He was back in that meadow, a young man so sure of his own heart, so naively enthusiastic about his future, dancing with the beautiful princess he'd dreamed about, the one he could never deserve. And, oh, how he'd craved her to his very core…

Now, Darius pulled her more indecently close to his hard, aching body than any waltz allowed. She lifted her luminous gaze to his, visibly holding her breath. The electricity between them suddenly sizzled with heat.

He stopped dancing. Louder than the music, he heard the rush of his blood in his ears, the pounding of his own heart.

He needed her in his bed.

Now.

The music abruptly ended, and the ballroom exploded in applause echoing from the high ceiling. Without a word, Darius led her from the dance floor. He pulled her through the crowds, which parted for them like magic. Compliments and cheers followed them. Everywhere, people were apologizing to Letty for how badly they'd treated her. He recognized Poppy Alexander.

"I'm so sorry, Letty," the girl blurted out. "I was afraid to be your friend. I knew it wasn't your fault, what happened, but I was a coward…"

"That's all right, Poppy," Letty replied gently. She looked around at everyone else. "I don't blame anyone."

Darius thought about the dragon Poppy had for a mother, and he couldn't blame her for being scared. Until he thought of how bad Letty's life had been for the last decade, and he didn't think any of them deserved another minute of Letty's time.

He swept Letty away without looking back. He didn't care about anyone or anything right now, except getting her into his bed.

Darius pulled his phone from his tuxedo jacket pocket. By the time they exited the stately beaux-arts building, his limo was waiting at the curb. Collins leaped out and opened the passenger door.

The second they were in the backseat, and the door closed behind them, Darius pulled Letty roughly into his arms and kissed her.

Her lips were sweet as sin. She trembled, her curves melting against him. His whole body was hard with need. He had to have her.

"Sir?" said Collins from the driver's seat.

"Home," he said hoarsely. "As fast as you can."

Then he pressed the button that raised the barrier between front and back seats. Just those few seconds were agony. But he was not willing to share Letty with anyone. He'd shared her enough.

She belonged to him now. To him alone.

Once they had privacy in the backseat, he kissed her passionately as the limo moved through the sparkling streets of the lit-up city at midnight. But all he could see was her sensual beauty. All he could feel was the soft brush of her long dark hair, and her warm skin like silk beneath his hands. He pushed her back against the leather seat, devouring her soft lips, kissing her neck, running his hands over her full breasts overflowing the tight pink bodice of her dress.

He kissed her savagely, biting and sucking her lower lip. A gasp of need came from her throat as she returned his kiss with matching fire, gripping his shoulders through his tuxedo jacket. He kissed slowly down her neck as her head fell back, her eyes closed, her expression one of ecstasy.

When he saw that, it was all he could do not to take her, right here in the back of the limo. He was unconsciously reaching for his fly when he realized they'd stopped.

Resurfacing from his haze of desire, he saw the limo was parked beneath the porte cochere in front of his building. Just in time, too. He glanced at Letty, stretched back against the smooth calfskin leather seat. Her big hazel eyes were smoky with passion, her dark hair mussed, her pink dress disheveled. Another moment and he would have yanked up her dress and roughly pushed inside her.

That wasn't how he wanted this night to be, fast and brutish in the back of a limo. No. After the disaster of their first night together, when he'd taken her virginity then insulted her and tossed her out of the penthouse into the snow, he wanted this night to be perfect.

He would finally treat Letitia Spencer, the forbidden princess of his youth, as she deserved to be treated.

He would enjoy her as he deserved to enjoy her.

Thoroughly.

Reaching over, he smoothed the fabric of Letty's bodice modestly back over her breasts just as the passenger door opened behind him.

Taking her hand, he led her out of the limo and into the elegant lobby, where the doorman greeted him. "Good evening, sir."

"Good evening, Jones." Such civilized words. Wearing a tuxedo, Darius knew he must appear civilized on the outside. On the inside, he felt anything but.

Gripping Letty's hand, he desperately kept himself in check. Neither of them looked at each other as they went through the high-ceilinged lobby, past the front desk to the elevator. Civilized.

But as soon as the door closed behind them, they were

in each other's arms. He pushed her against the wall, kissing her hungrily, desperately.

She breathed against his skin, "I still can't believe you're doing this."

"Kissing you?"

"Giving five billion dollars away. Why did you do it?"

"Don't you know?" he growled, his lips against hers. "Can't you guess?"

Panting, she shook her head. "You hate my father…"

Darius's lip curled as he drew back. "I didn't do it for him."

"For your friends?"

"Those aren't my friends."

"For the other victims, then. All those hardworking people with pensions. Firemen. Nurses…"

"I'm not that noble."

The elevator door opened. The floor-to-ceiling windows flooded the penthouse with moonlight. Taking her hand, he led her inside. He could hear the tap of her stiletto heels against the marble.

She stopped, staring up at him.

"Then why?" she whispered.

"I couldn't stand to see you treated badly," Darius said huskily, "when all you've done is give your love and loyalty to someone who doesn't deserve it."

She bit her lip. "I know my father isn't perfect—"

"Perfect?" His jaw tightened. "He's a criminal—" He cut himself off, then said, "You're under my protection now."

She looked troubled. "Your protection—or your rule?"

"It is the same. I protect what is mine."

"Our baby."

His eyes met hers. "And you."

Letty stared at him, her eyes wide, as if she had no idea how to react. As if she had forgotten what it was like to have anyone properly look after her.

He wondered how long it had been since anyone had tried to take care of her, rather than the other way around. He suspected Letty always sacrificed herself to take care of others—especially that father of hers—while her own heart bled.

"But I'm not yours," she said quietly. "Not truly. We got pregnant by accident. I didn't think you were serious about marriage."

"I am."

"That commitment is serious, Darius. It means…forever."

"I know," he said.

She swallowed, searching his gaze. "I was sure after tonight you'd never want to see me again."

Taking her hand, he lifted it slowly to his lips. She seemed to hold her breath, watching as he kissed the back of her hand, breathing against her skin. Straightening, he held her hand tightly in his own. "I want to see you tomorrow, and every other tomorrow for the rest of our lives."

"Darius…"

"You will marry me, Letty," he said in a low voice. "You know it, and I know it. In your heart, you were always meant to be mine."

Marry him? For real?

How could she?

Even if Darius no longer hated her, he certainly didn't love her. And she was starting to fear she could love him again. Perhaps all too easily.

What hope could they have of happiness?

He'd never love her back. All he wished to do was possess her. He offered sex and money, and in return, he'd expect sex and total devotion. For her, those things went together. He wouldn't have just her body, but her soul.

So why was she still so tempted?

She shivered, caught between fear and desire.

"Are you cold?" he asked huskily, his eyes dark.

"No, I...I..." Hugging her baby bump, she gasped, "I need some fresh air."

He smiled. "Come with me."

Still holding her hand, he led her through the moon-bathed penthouse, and she thought dimly how she was getting in the habit of following where he led. But with his hand enveloping hers so protectively, she didn't want to do anything else.

She still couldn't believe what he'd done, announcing their engagement, defending her in front of all those people—and then telling the world he intended to pay billions of dollars of his own money to repay what her father had stolen.

She'd been dazed. Then she'd danced with him, the same routine he'd helped her learn so long ago, and she'd been back in that spring meadow, practicing the waltz not for the pimply-faced Harvard boy, who was the nephew of her father's lawyer, but for Darius, always for him, only for him. As they'd danced in the ballroom, she'd felt time melt away.

Darius was right. She was his. From the very beginning, Darius Kyrillos had been the only man she'd ever wanted. The only man she'd ever loved.

I don't love him anymore, she told herself desperately. She wouldn't let him buy her!

Darius led her up an elaborate staircase, then pushed open a glass door that led out onto a private rooftop garden.

Letty gasped at the beauty of the ivy-covered pergola decorated with fairy lights near a lit lap pool gleaming bright blue in the warm September night.

Above them, distant stars sparkled like diamonds across a dark velvety sky. Past the glass walls of the terrace, the night skyline of Manhattan glittered.

She kept her distance from the edge, afraid to go too

close. But Darius went right to it. He leaned against the short glass wall, totally unfazed and unafraid of plummeting seventy floors to his death. He looked out at the city.

Letty crept closer, her heart pounding. "This terrace is amazing."

"All the flowers remind me of home," he said simply. She wondered if he meant Greece or Fairholme, but didn't have the nerve to ask. She slowly turned her head, marveling at the lavish beauty of a rooftop garden that treated all of Manhattan as nothing but a backdrop.

"You're king of the mountain now," she said softly. "Looking down on a valley of skyscrapers."

Turning to her, he came forward. Then he abruptly fell to one knee in front of her astonished eyes.

Reaching into his tuxedo jacket pocket, he pulled out a small black velvet box.

"Rule it with me, Letty," he said quietly. "As my wife."

Shivering, she put her hand on her heart. "I already said…"

"You said yes when you thought I'd back out. This is a real proposal. I expect a real answer." He held up the black velvet box. "Letty Spencer, will you do me the honor of marrying me?"

He opened the lid. Inside the black velvet box was an enormous pear-shaped diamond set in platinum. It was the hugest, most outrageous ring she'd ever seen.

But that wasn't what made her lose her breath.

It was Darius's face. His dark, yearning eyes. As he looked at her in the moonlight, she saw the man who'd just bruised her with the intensity of his kisses. Who'd just defied all of Manhattan and paid five billion dollars for her. The man whose child she carried.

In his eyes, she saw the shadow of the younger man she'd once loved, strong and kind, with such a good heart. The one who'd loved her so fervently. *They were the same.*

Letty's heart skipped a beat.

It's an illusion, she told herself desperately. *He's not the same.* But as she reached out and brushed her fingers against the diamond engagement ring, it sparkled like the stars. Like the lights of this powerful city.

Like the smolder in Darius's dark eyes.

"It would destroy us," she said shakily, but what she really meant was *it would destroy me.*

Darius slowly rose in front of her, until his tall, powerful body towered over hers. Waves of blue light from the pool reflected against him as the warm wind moved across the water. Putting his hand on her cheek, he lowered his head.

"Say yes," he whispered. "Say you'll be mine."

His kiss was tender at first. She felt the rough warmth of his lips, the gentle hold of his arms.

Then his grip tightened. His embrace became hungry, filled with need. Spirals of heat twisted through her body, and she gripped his shoulders. Until he pulled away.

"Say it," he demanded.

"Yes," she choked out.

A flash of triumph crossed his starkly handsome face. "You will?"

She nodded, tears in her eyes.

"There will be no going back," he warned.

"I know." She tried to ignore the thrill that crept into her heart. Excitement? Terror?

Right or wrong, disaster or not, there was nothing to be done. What he'd said was true. She'd always been his. In many ways, this decision had been made for her long ago.

He slid the diamond ring over the third finger of her left hand. It fit perfectly. She looked down at it, sparkling in the moonlight. "How did you know my ring size?"

"It's the same ring."

She frowned. "What?"

"It's the same I bought for you ten years ago." His voice was low. "I had it set with a different stone."

The thought that he'd kept their original ring all these years made her heart ache. Whatever he might say, didn't that mean he might still care for her, at least a little?

Could love, once lost, ever be regained?

Looking at him with tears in her eyes, she breathed, "Darius…"

"You're mine now, Letty," he whispered, kissing her forehead, her eyelids, her cheeks. "You belong to me. Forever."

Then he kissed her lips as if those, too, were his possession.

Sparks of pleasure went up and down Letty's body, coiling low and deep inside her, and she felt his hands running down her bare arms, her sides, cupping her breasts over the pink dress.

She fell back against the ivy-covered stone wall. Above them, fairy lights swayed gently in the warm wind, the skyscrapers of Manhattan illuminating the moonlit sky.

Letty's eyes closed as he kissed his way down her throat. She felt breathless, like she was lost in a dream.

He kissed over the diamond necklace to her bare clavicle and the valley between her full breasts, half revealed above the low-cut bodice of her gown.

Picking her up, he carried her past the sweeping ivy into a half-enclosed room protected on two sides by walls, with a rustic chandelier hanging over a long table. Two leather sofas were arranged around a fireplace and well-stocked bar.

He flicked a switch, and the gas fire lit up. She saw Darius's face clearly in the flickering firelight as they faced each other silently. The soft wind blew against her hair, her skin.

Slowly, Darius removed his tuxedo jacket and dropped it to the flagstone floor. Coming closer, he unzipped her pink dress. She felt the brush of his fingertips, then the warm night air against her bare skin as her gown dropped to the floor beside his jacket. She stepped out of the fabric, wearing only the diamonds, a lace bra, panties and the wicked pink crystal stiletto heels.

He stepped back, looking at her.

"Incredible," he breathed in deep masculine appreciation, and she realized that, just as he'd promised, he was seeing her in the lingerie. She scowled.

"Do you always get what you want?" she said accusingly.

"I do," he said, caressing her cheek. "And now, so will you."

She licked her lips and felt a thrill of delight as his expression changed to raw desire. Reaching up, she saucily loosened his tuxedo tie, before tugging on it, drawing him closer for a kiss.

It was the first time she'd ever made the first move, and he growled fierce approval. Holding her tight, he kissed her back hungrily.

His hands caressed her naked skin, her arms, her shoulders, the small of her back. And suddenly she couldn't remove his clothes fast enough. His tie, cuff links, shirt. They all dropped to the floor.

His tanned body, laced with dark hair, looked like sculpted marble in the flickering firelight, all hard muscles and taut belly. She brushed her hand lightly against his chest. His skin felt like silk over steel. Biting her lip, she lifted her eyes to his.

"If I'm yours, Darius," she whispered, standing in front of him in the half-enclosed room, "you're mine."

Brushing back long dark tendrils of her hair, he pulled her roughly into his arms. His hard-muscled chest moved against her full, aching breasts and pregnant belly. The soft wind whispered against her bare skin as he unhooked her silk lace bra, and her breasts sprang free. He looked down at her body and gave a quick breath.

Pressing her breasts together, he cupped their weight in his hands before he lowered his head to suckle one pink, full nipple, then the other.

Shuddering with pleasure, she closed her eyes.

His hands stroked gently, reverently, down her body to her naked belly to her hips, still covered with the tiny silk panties.

Running his hand down her legs, he knelt before her and pulled off one stiletto, then the other, as she balanced against him, her hands gripping his shoulders. She remained standing—barely—as he caressed upward from her manicured toes, to the tender hollows of her knees, and higher still. She swallowed, holding her breath as he stroked up her thighs.

She closed her eyes, heart pounding as he pulled her panties down her legs. She couldn't move fast enough. He impatiently ripped them off in his powerful hands, tossing the flimsy silk aside.

"Those were expensive—" she protested.

He looked up, and the edges of his cruel, sensual mouth curved upward. "They served their purpose."

An icy fear suddenly crept through her heart as Letty wondered if she, too, might someday have served her purpose. If he might someday rip her apart, then discard her.

Then all her rational thought fled as, still on his knees, he gripped her hips and moved between her legs.

She felt the warmth of his breath on the most sensitive, intimate part of her body, as she stood naked with the warm night breeze swirling against her skin, as one of New York's most famous billionaires knelt before her in the firelight, beneath the ivy walls of a rooftop garden.

Holding her tight, he lowered his mouth between her thighs and tasted her with a soft moan. He licked her as if she were a melting ice cream cone in his favorite flavor, creamy and sweet. As she gasped, his rhythm intensified, until he worked her with his tongue, sliding sensuously against her. Pleasure exploded through her body almost immediately, and he gripped her hips, keeping her firmly against his mouth as her body twisted with the sudden intensity of pleasure that left her knees weak and sent spasms all over her body.

She was still dizzy in the heights of pleasure as he rose to his feet and drew her toward the sofa. He lay down first, stretching out naked against the black leather, hard and ready for her. She took a step, then hesitated, biting her lip.

"What is it?"

She tried not to look at how huge he was, his hard shaft jutting arrogantly from his body. She blushed, feeling shy. "Um, what do I do?"

He gave a low, lazy laugh, then pulled her over him.

"I'll show you," he said huskily.

He spread her across him on the sofa, her thighs over his hips, his arousal pressing low against her pregnant belly. He reached up, cupping her cheek. As he drew her down for a kiss, her long dark hair fell like a veil against his skin.

The kiss was tender at first. She relaxed into it with a sigh, her body curving over his as his hands roamed gently over her back, her arms, her belly, her breasts. Then his kiss deepened, turning urgent and fierce. Placing his hands on her hips, he lifted her up, positioning himself beneath her.

He slowly lowered her down on him, filling her, inch by delicious inch, in tantalizing slow motion.

She gasped as she felt him inside her, going deep, then deeper still. Her whole body started to tighten, more savagely than it had before.

Lifting her hips, he lowered her again, showing her the rhythm, until her body started to move of its own accord.

Closing her eyes with fervent intensity, she rode him, slowly at first, then faster. The pleasure built and built…

Her lips parted in a silent cry as joy burst like fireworks shaking through her body. She heard his low gasp as he, too, exploded, pouring inside her.

She collapsed, falling softly against him on the black leather sofa.

For long moments, he held her tenderly, as if her weight were nothing. Their bodies were still fused, slick with sweat, as he leaned up to kiss her. He felt so solid and strong beneath her. Like a foundation that could never be shaken.

She shivered in his arms. In the half-enclosed outdoor room, the September night was growing cool. But that wasn't the reason.

The idea of being Darius's wife had seemed like a recipe for disaster, if not outright doom. And so it would be, if she were tempted into giving him her heart, while in return, he gave her only money.

Letty looked down at the heavy diamond ring, now shining dully on her left hand.

If only Darius could again be the young man she remembered, with the kind nature and forgiving heart. She would willingly give him everything. Not just her body, not just her name, but her heart.

CHAPTER EIGHT

HE WAS A GENIUS, Darius thought as he woke in his bed the next morning with sunlight flooding in through the windows. He looked down at Letty sleeping beside him and smiled. A damn genius. Best five billion dollars ever spent.

And he would spend the rest of his life being thrilled, if it continued paying off like it did last night. The sex had been spectacular. And even more. Something had changed in the way Letty looked at him. He loved the mixture of gratitude and shy hope he saw in her eyes.

He kissed Letty's temple tenderly. She yawned, stretching like a cat.

"What time is it?" she murmured, her eyes still closed.

"Late," he said, amused. "Almost noon."

Her eyes flew open. "Oh, no! I'm late for—" Then she seemed to remember how much had changed in the last twenty-four hours, and that being late for work was no longer an issue. "Oh. Right." She bit her lip, blushing and looking so adorable that he was tempted to keep her in bed another hour.

It was incredible how much he still wanted her, when they'd made love *four times* last night—on the rooftop terrace, here in bed, and in the shower when they decided to wash off. Only to promptly get all sweaty again when they returned to bed.

Letty was meant to be his, Darius marveled. He'd never felt so sexually satisfied in his life.

And yet already he wanted more. How was it possible?

He smiled down at her. "Hungry?"

"Starving," she admitted. "And thirsty."

"I can solve that." Rising from the bed, he got a white

terry cloth robe and handed her one, too. "Come out to the kitchen."

She gave a sudden scowl, and even that was adorable. "You didn't tell me you had staff staying at the penthouse. What if they heard us last night? What if they—"

"There are no live-in staff. I have a housekeeper who comes in four times a week, that's it."

She blinked in confusion. "Then who's going to cook?"

"I'm not totally useless."

She looked at him with unflattering shock in her eyes. "You can't cook, Darius."

"No?" His smile widened to a grin. "Come see."

She ate her words shortly afterward, sitting in the brightly lit kitchen at the counter, as he served her an omelet to order with tomatoes, bacon and five kinds of cheese, along with orange juice over ice. When she took the first bite of the omelet, her eyes went wide.

"Good, huh?" he said smugly, sitting beside her with his own enormous omelet of ham and cheese, drenched in salsa. Being a sexual hero all night definitely had built his appetite.

And hers, as well. If he felt like a hero, Letty was a sex *goddess*, he thought. Even now, he felt aware of her, just sitting companionably beside her at the counter with its dazzling view of the city through floor-to-ceiling windows. But he wasn't looking at the view. He was watching her.

"Delicious," she moaned softly as she gobbled it down, bite after bite. "We should serve omelets at our wedding."

He gave a low laugh. "I appreciate the compliment, but I don't see myself whipping up omelets for a thousand."

She froze. "A thousand? *Guests?*"

Gulping black coffee, he shrugged. "Our wedding will be the social event of the year, as you deserve. All of New York society will come and grovel at your feet."

She didn't look thrilled. She took another bite of omelet. "That's not what I want."

"No?" he said lazily, tucking back a tendril of her dark hair. His eyes traced the creamy skin of her neck, down to the smooth temptation of her clavicle and swell of her breasts above the luxurious white cotton robe. He glanced down to her belt, tied loosely between her breasts and pregnant belly. He had the sudden impulse to sweep all the dishes to the floor, tug open her robe and lean her back naked against the counter.

"A wedding should be a happy occasion." She shook her head. "Those society people aren't my friends. They never really were. Why would I invite them?"

"To rub your new status in their faces? I thought you'd glory in your return to status as the queen of it all."

"Me?" Letty snorted. "I was never queen of anything. As a teenager I never knew the right clothes to wear or understood how to play the society game. I was a total nerd."

He frowned. "I never saw you that way. I just assumed…"

"That I was a spoiled princess?" She gave him a funny smile. "I *was* spoiled, though not the way you mean. I always knew I was loved." Her face was wistful. "My parents loved each other and they loved me."

Revenge wasn't Letty's style, Darius realized. She never showed off or tried to make others feel bad. Even when she was younger, she'd always been most comfortable reading the dusty leather-bound books in Fairholme's oak-paneled library, baking cakes with the cook in the kitchen or playing with the gardener's kittens in the yard. Letty never wanted to be the center of attention. She was always more worried about other people's feelings than her own.

In this respect, Darius thought, the two of them were very different.

"And I had a real home," she whispered.

Memories of that beautiful gray stone manor on the edge of the sea, surrounded by roses, came to his mind. He said gruffly, "You still miss Fairholme after all this time?"

She gave him a sad smile. "I know it's gone for good. But I still dream about it. My mother was born there. Four generations of my family."

"What happened to it?"

She looked down at her plate. "A tech billionaire bought it at a cut-rate price. I heard he changed everything, added zebra-print shag carpeting and neon lights, and turned the nursery into his own private disco. Of course that was his right. But he wouldn't let me take a picture of my great-grandmother's fresco before he destroyed it with his sand-blaster."

A low growl came from Darius's throat. He remembered the nursery fresco, a charming monstrosity picturing a sad-eyed little goose girl leading ducks and geese through what looked like a Bavarian village. Not his cup of tea, but it was part of the house's history. "I'm sorry."

She looked up with a bright, fake smile. "It's fine. Of course it couldn't last. Good things never do."

"Neither do bad things," he said quietly. "Nothing lasts, good or bad."

"I guess you're right." She wrapped her arms around her pregnant belly. "But I don't want a big society wedding, Darius. I think I'd just like you and me, and our closest family and friends. I don't need ten bridesmaids. I just want one."

"An old friend?"

She smiled. "A new one. Belle Langtry. A waitress at the diner. How about you? Who would you choose as your best man?"

"Ángel Velazquez."

"Ángel?"

"It's a nickname. His real first name is Santiago, but he

hates it, because he was named after a man who refused to recognize him as his son."

"How awful!"

Darius shrugged. "I call him by his last name. Velazquez hates weddings. He recently had to be the best man for a friend of ours, Kassius Black. He complained for months. All that tender love gave him a headache, he said."

Letty was looking at him in dismay. "And you want him at our wedding?"

"He needs a little torture. When you meet him you'll see what I mean. Completely arrogant, always sure he's right."

"Hard to imagine," she said drily.

"So Velazquez. And my extended family."

Her eyes brightened. "Your family?"

"My great-aunt, Theia Ioanna, who lives in Athens. Assorted uncles, aunts and cousins, and the rest of my village on Heraklios, the island I'm from."

"Could we bring them all over from Greece? And of course we'll have my father…"

Darius stiffened. "No."

"No?" She frowned. "We could get married on Heraklios, if they can't travel. I've always wanted to visit the Greek islands…"

"I mean your father. He's not invited."

"Of course he's invited. He's my father. He'll walk me down the aisle. I know you don't like him, but he's my only family."

"Letty, I thought you understood." His jaw was taut, his voice low and cold. "I don't want you, or our baby, within ten feet of that man ever again."

"What?"

"It's not negotiable." Swiveling to face her at the counter, Darius gripped her shoulder. "I will pay back everything he stole. But this is the price." His dark eyes narrowed.

"You will cut your father completely and permanently out of our lives."

She drew back. "But he's my father. I love him—"

"He lost the right to your loyalty long ago. Do you think I want a con artist, a thief, around my wife…my child…my home?" He looked at her in tightly controlled fury. "No."

"He never meant to hurt anyone," she tried. "He always hoped the stock market would turn and he'd be able to pay everyone back. He just lost his way after my mom died. And he hasn't been well since he got out of prison. If you just knew what he's been through…"

"Excuses on top of excuses! You expect me to feel sympathy?" he said incredulously. "Because he was sick? Because he lost his wife? Because of him, you and I were separated. Because of him, my own father never had the chance to grow old! After he'd worked for him with utter devotion for almost twenty-five years. And that's how your father repaid him!"

"Darius, please."

"You expect me to allow that man to walk you down the aisle? To hold my firstborn child in his arms? No." He set his jaw. "He's a monster. He has no conscience, no soul."

"You don't know him like I do…"

Remembering her weakness where her father was concerned, her senseless loyalty at any cost, Darius abruptly changed tack. "If you truly love him, you will do as I ask. It will benefit him, as well."

"How can you say that?"

"Once I've paid all his debts, he'll never need to be afraid of someone breaking his arm again. He'll be treated better by his probation officers. By potential employers."

"He can't work. No one would hire him. He would starve in the street."

Revulsion churned in Darius's belly, but he forced himself to say, "I will make sure that does not happen. He can remain in your Brooklyn apartment and his rent will be paid. He will always have food and any other necessities he might require. But he must face the consequences of what he's done. He's taken enough from you, Letty. Your future is with me."

Pushing away the breakfast plates, he stood up from the kitchen counter and went to her handbag on the entryway table. Pulling out her phone, he held it out to her.

"Call him," he said quietly. "See what he tells you to do."

Sitting at the counter in her white robe, Letty stared at the phone with big, stricken eyes, as if it were poison. She snatched it up, and with an intake of breath, dialed and held it up to her ear.

"Hi, Dad." She paused, then said unhappily, "Yes. I'm sorry. I don't blame you for worrying. I should have... Ooh? You saw that?" She looked up and said to Darius, "Your announcement about repaying the five billion is already all over the news. Our engagement, too. Dad is thrilled."

"Of course," he said acidly.

"What?" She turned her focus back to her father. "Oh, yes," she whispered, looking up at Darius with troubled eyes. "We're very happy." She bit her lip. "But, Dad, there's this one thing. It's a big thing. A big horrible thing—" her voice broke a little "—and I hardly know how to say it..." She took a deep breath. "I won't be able to see you any-more. Or let you see the baby."

Darius watched her face as she listened to her father's response. Her expression was miserable.

He blocked all mercy from his soul. He was being cruel to be kind. Saving her from her own weak, loving heart.

"No," she whispered into the phone. "I won't abandon you. It's not..."

She paused again, and her expression changed, became numb with grief. Finally, she choked out in a voice almost too soft to hear, "Okay, Dad. All right. I love you, too. So much. Goodbye."

Tears were streaming down her face. Wiping them away, she handed Darius the phone. "He wants to talk to you."

He stared down at the phone in dismay. He hadn't expected that. He picked it up and put it to his ear.

"What do you want?" he said coldly.

"Darius Kyrillos." He recognized Howard Spencer's voice. Though the voice had aged and grown shaky, he could almost hear the older man's smile. "I remember when you were a little boy, just come to Fairholme. You barely spoke English but even then, you were a great kid."

Unwanted memories went through him of when he'd first come to Fairholme with a father who was a stranger to him, a lonely eleven-year-old boy, bereaved by his grandmother's death. He'd felt bewildered by America and homesick for Greece. Back then Howard Spencer had seemed grand and as foreign as a king.

But he'd welcomed the bereft boy warmly. He'd even asked his five-year-old daughter to look after him. In spite of their six-year age difference, Letty, with her caring and friendly heart, had swiftly become his friend, sharing her toys and showing him the fields and beach. While her father had given Darius Christmas presents and told him firmly he could do anything he wanted in life.

In an indirect way, Howard Spencer had even helped start his software company. As a teenager, Darius had been fascinated by computers. He'd taught himself to tinker and code, and soon found himself responsible for every tech device, security feature and bit of wireless connectivity at Fairholme. It was Howard Spencer who'd hired him as the estate's first technical specialist and allowed him to continue to live there. He'd even paid for Darius to study computer science at the local community college...

Darius felt a twist in his gut. Like...guilt? No. He rushed

to justify his actions. All right, so Spencer had encouraged him and paid for his schooling. Using stolen money from his Ponzi scheme!

"Yes, a good kid," Howard continued gruffly. "But stubborn, with all that stiff-necked Greek pride. Always had to do everything yourself. Letty was the only one you really let help you with anything. And even then, you always thought you had to be in charge. You never recognized her strength."

"Your point?" Darius said coldly.

He heard the other man take a deep breath.

"Take good care of my daughter," he said quietly. "Both Letty and my grandchild. I know you will. That's the only reason I'm letting them go."

The line abruptly cut off.

"What did he say?" Letty's miserable face came into view.

"He said…" Darius stared down in amazement at the phone in his hand.

He ground his teeth. Damn the old man. Taking the high road. He must be playing the long game. Trusting that Letty would wear him down after their wedding and make him relent. Make him forgive.

But Darius would never forgive. He'd die before he let that man worm his way back into their lives.

"Tell me what he said," Letty pleaded.

He turned to her with an ironic smile. "He gave our marriage his blessing."

Her shoulders slumped.

"That's what he said to me, too," she whispered.

So his theory was correct. Clever bastard, he thought grudgingly. He really knew how to pull his daughter's heartstrings.

But Howard Spencer had finally met someone he couldn't manipulate. The old man would end his days alone, in that tiny run-down apartment, with no one to love him. Just as he deserved.

While they—they would live happily ever after.

Darius looked at Letty tenderly.

After their marriage, after she was legally his forever, she would come to despise her father as Darius did. At the very least, she would forget and let him go.

She would love only Darius, be loyal only to him.

He wouldn't love her back, of course. The childish illusion that love could be anything but pain had been burned out of him permanently. But love was still magic to Letty, and he realized now it was the only way to bind her and make her happy in their marriage. For the sake of their children, he had to make her love him.

This was just the beginning.

"You did the right thing," Darius murmured. Pulling her into his arms, he kissed the top of her head, relishing the feel of her body against his, the crush of her full breasts and her belly rounded with his child. "You'll never regret it."

"I regret it already."

Leaning forward, he kissed the tears off her cheeks. He kissed her forehead, then her eyelids. He felt her shudder and pulled her fully into his arms. He whispered, "Let me comfort you."

He lowered his mouth to hers, gripping her smaller body to his own, and kissed her passionately. A sigh came from her throat as she wrapped her arms around him. He opened the belt of her robe and ran his hands down her naked body. Then with a large sweep of his arm, he knocked all the dishes to the floor with a noisy clatter.

Lifting his future bride up onto the countertop, Darius did what he'd wanted to do for the last hour. He made love to her until she wept. Tears of joy, he told himself. Just tears of joy.

* * *

Letty had never been the sort of girl to dream about weddings. At least not since she was eighteen, when her one attempt at elopement had ended so badly.

But she'd vaguely thought, if she ever did get married, she'd have a simple wedding dress, a cake, a bouquet. And her father would give her away.

This wedding had none of that.

Two days after Darius's proposal, they got married in what felt like the worst wedding ever.

Her own fault, Letty thought numbly, as she stood in front of a judge, mumbling vows to honor and cherish. She had no one to blame but herself.

Well, and Darius.

After her phone call with her father, Letty had been too heartsick to care about planning a wedding ceremony. Even Darius ruthlessly taking possession of her body on the kitchen counter hadn't cheered her up. Her heart felt empty and sad.

Darius had tried to tempt her with outrageous ideas for a destination wedding. "If you don't want a big society wedding, there's no reason to wait. The sky's the limit! Do you want a beach wedding in Hawaii? A winter wedding in South America? If you want, I'll rent out the Sydney Opera House. Just say the word!"

She'd looked at him miserably. "What I want is for my father to be there. Without love, what difference does the wedding make?"

The temperature in the room had dropped thirty degrees. "Fine," he said coldly. "If that's how you feel, we might as well just get married at City Hall."

"Fine," she'd said in the same tone.

So they'd gone to the Office of the City Clerk near Chinatown this afternoon, where they'd now been killing time for three hours, surrounded by happy couples all waiting for their turn.

Letty felt exhausted to the bone. She hadn't slept at all the night before. Neither she nor Darius had even bothered to dress up for the ceremony. She wore a simple blouse and maternity pants. Darius wore a dark shirt, dark jeans and a dark glower.

Nor had it helped that the two friends they'd brought to be their witnesses had hated each other on sight. The constant childish bickering between Belle Langtry and Santiago Velazquez, who'd introduced himself as Ángel, had been the final nail in the coffin of Worst Wedding Ever.

It could have been so different, Letty thought sadly. If her father had been there, if she and Darius had been in love, nothing else would have mattered.

But there was no love anywhere on this wedding day.

As she and Darius had sat waiting, listening to their best man and maid of honor squabble, she couldn't stop tears from falling. Darius's glower only made them fall faster.

Their number was the very last to be called in the late afternoon. The four of them had gone up to the desk. As the officiant swiftly and matter-of-factly spoke the words that would bind her to Darius forever, Letty couldn't stop thinking about how she was betraying her father. The man who'd taught her to roller-skate down Fairholme's long marble hallways, who'd taught her chess on rainy days. The man who'd told her again and again how much he loved her.

"I screwed everything up," Howard had told her sadly when he got out of prison. "But I swear I'll make it up to you, Letty. I'll get you back the life you lost…"

He'd never once criticized her for getting pregnant out of wedlock. He'd just been delighted about a future grandchild. Even when she'd phoned him before the wedding, and told him she was marrying Darius, she'd felt his joy.

Though it had been abruptly cut off when she'd tearfully told him the rest of the deal.

Then he'd said quietly, "Do it, sweetheart. Marry him. It's what you've always wanted. Knowing you're happy, I'll be at peace."

Now, as she watched Darius speak his marriage vows, Letty's heart twisted. She blinked as she heard the officiant solemnly finish, "...I now pronounce you man and wife."

The whole ceremony had taken three minutes.

She dimly heard Belle clapping and hooting wildly as Darius leaned forward to kiss her. Some instinct made her turn away and offer him only her cheek.

His glower turned radioactive.

After signing the marriage certificate, their small party of four trundled out of the City Clerk's Office to discover the cold gray September skies pouring rain.

"Such a beautiful ceremony. I'm so happy for you," Belle sighed, obviously caught up in some romantic image that had nothing to do with reality. "You make a perfect couple."

"You're living in a fairy tale," Santiago Velazquez muttered. "They can obviously barely stand each other."

Belle whirled on him irritably. "Just once, could you keep your bad attitude to yourself?" Her voice was shrill. "I'm sick of hearing it!"

He shrugged, glancing at Darius. "You got married because she's pregnant, right?"

"Velazquez, don't make me punch you on my wedding day."

"See?" Belle crowed. "Even *Darius* can't stand you."

The Spaniard looked superior. "Just because I'm the only one who is willing to speak the truth..."

"The truth is that marriage is about love and commitment and a whole bunch of sophisticated emotions you obviously can't handle. So keep your opinions to yourself.

You might think you're being all deep, but talking like that at a wedding is just plain tacky!"

The Spaniard's eyes narrowed and for a moment Letty was afraid that the constant bickering between them was about to boil over into something truly unpleasant. But to her relief, the man abruptly gave a stiff nod.

"You are right."

Belle stared at him wide-eyed, then tossed her hair, huffing with a flare of her nostrils. "Course I'm right. I'm always right."

Letty exhaled as they seemed to drop the matter.

"Except for when you're wrong," came his sardonic response, "which is every other time but now, since you're obviously living in some ridiculous romantic dream world."

Belle glared at him, then whirled on Letty with a beaming smile. "Are you having a good wedding day, sweetie? Because that's what I care about. Because I'm not rude like some people. We learn manners in Texas."

"I have a ranch in Texas," the Spaniard rejoined. "And I learned an expression that I believe applies to you, Miss Langtry."

"The meek shall inherit the earth?"

He gave her a sensual half smile. "All hat, no cattle."

Belle gave an outraged intake of breath. Then she said sweetly, "That's a lot of big talk for a man with a girl's name."

He looked irritated. "You're saying it wrong. An-hel. And it is a man's name. In every Spanish-speaking country…"

"Aaain-jel, Aaain-jel!" she taunted, using the pronunciation that involved harps and wings. She blinked. "Oh, look, the limo's here."

Letty almost cried in relief.

"Finally," Darius muttered. The limo had barely slowed down at the curb before he opened the back door for his bride. Letty jumped in, eager to escape.

"Where are we going?" Belle said, starting to follow, the Spaniard coming up behind her. Darius blocked them from the limo.

"Thank you so much. Both of you. But I'm afraid Letty and I must leave immediately for Greece."

Belle frowned. "I thought you weren't leaving until tomorrow. We were going to take you out for dinner…"

"Unfortunately, we must get on the plane immediately. My family is waiting to meet my new bride."

"Oh," Belle said, crestfallen. "In that case… Of course I understand." Leaning into the back of the limo, she hugged Letty. "Have a wonderful honeymoon! You deserve every bit of your happiness!"

Belle was right, Letty reflected numbly as the limo pulled away from her friend still beaming and waving on the sidewalk. She'd get all the happiness she deserved after abandoning her father to marry Darius: none.

Letty stared out at the gray rain. Darius sat beside her silently for the hour and a half it took to drive through the evening rush-hour traffic to the small airport outside the city. As they boarded his private jet, he continued to ignore her.

Fine. Letty didn't care. She felt exhausted and miserable. Walking to the separate bedroom in the back of the jet, she shut the door behind her. Climbing into bed, she pulled the blanket up to her forehead, struggling to hold back tears. She closed her eyes.

And woke up in a different world.

Letty sat up with an intake of breath.

She was no longer on the jet. She found herself in a big, bright bedroom, empty except for a king-size wrought-iron bed.

Brilliant sunlight came through the open windows, leaving warm patterns against the white walls and red tiled floor. She heard laughter outside and conversation in an exotic language and the sweet singing of birds.

She looked down at the soft blanket and cotton sheets. Where was she? And—her lips parted in a gasp. She was wearing only her bra and panties! Someone had undressed her while she was asleep! The thought horrified her.

How had she gotten into this bed?

The flight across the Atlantic had been lonely and dark. She remembered crying herself to sleep on the plane. After her sleepless night before their wedding, she'd slept deeply.

She dimly remembered Darius carrying her, the warmth of his chest, the comforting rumble of his voice.

"So you're awake."

Looking up with an intake of breath, Letty saw her husband now standing in the open doorway, dressed more casually than she'd ever seen him, in a snug black T-shirt and long cargo shorts. Sunlight lit him from behind, leaving his expression in shadow.

"Where are we?"

"The island of Heraklios. My villa."

"I barely remember arriving."

"You were exhausted. Overwhelmed from the happiness of marrying me," he said sardonically.

"What time is it?"

"Here? Almost two in the afternoon." He motioned to a nearby door. "There's an en suite bathroom if you'd like a shower." He indicated a large walk-in closet. "Your clothes have already been unpacked."

"Are you the one who took off my clothes?"

"Just so you'd sleep more comfortably."

She bit her lip as she looked down at the bed. "Um. And did you...did we...uh, share this bed?"

His shoulders tensed. "If you're asking if I took advantage of you in your sleep, the answer is no."

She took a deep breath. "I didn't mean..."

"Get dressed and come out on the terrace when you're ready. My family is here to meet you."

Letty stared at the empty doorway in dismay, then slowly rose out of bed. Her body felt stiff from sleeping so long.

Going into the elegant marble bathroom, she took a hot shower, which refreshed her. Wrapping herself in a towel, she wiped the steam off the mirror. Her face looked pale and sad.

A fine thing, she thought. When she was about to meet his family. They'd take one look at Letty's face and assume, as Santiago Velazquez had, that she and Darius had gotten married only because of her pregnancy. Why else would someone as handsome and powerful as Darius Kyrillos ever choose a penniless, ordinary-looking woman like her?

He was taking a risk even bringing her to meet them. She could embarrass him, treat them disrespectfully. She could even explain how he'd blackmailed her into marriage.

Letty looked at her eyes in the mirror. She didn't want to hurt Darius. She just wanted him to forgive her dad.

Maybe she could start by treating his family with the same respect she wanted for her father.

Letty dressed quickly and carefully, blow-drying her long dark hair and brushing it till it shone. She put on lipstick, and chose a pretty new sundress and sandals from the closet. Her knees shook as she went down the hallway. A maid directed her toward the terrace.

With a deep breath, she went outside into the sunshine.

Bright pink bougainvillea climbed the whitewashed walls of the Greek villa, above a wide terrace overlooking the mountainous slopes of the island jutting out of the Ionian Sea.

Against the blue horizon, she saw the shaded forest green of a distant island. The whole world seemed bright with color: blue and white buildings, sea and sky, pink flowers, brown earth and green olive, fig and pomegranate trees.

She felt the warm sun against her skin, and pleasure

seeped through her body. Then she saw the group of people sitting at a long wooden table.

Darius rose abruptly from the table. Silence fell as the others followed his gaze.

Wordlessly, he came over to her. His dark eyes glowed as he lowered his head to kiss her cheek. Turning back to the others, he said in English, "This is Letty. My wife."

An elderly woman got up from the table. Standing on her tiptoes, she squinted, carefully looking Letty over from her blushing face to her pregnant belly. Then she smiled. Reaching up, she patted Letty on the cheek and said something in Greek that she didn't understand.

"My great-aunt says you look happy now," Darius translated. "Like a beautiful bride."

"How sweet… Did she see me before?" Letty asked.

"When I brought you in. She said you looked like death warmed over."

She stared at him in horror, then narrowed her eyes accusingly. "She never said that."

He gave a sudden grin. "She says our island has obviously revived you, all our sun and sea air. Plus, clearly—" he quirked a dark eyebrow " marriage to me."

The elderly woman said something quickly behind him. He glanced back with an indulgent smile. *"Nai, Theia Ioanna."*

"What did she say?"

Darius turned back to Letty. "She said marriage to you seems to agree with me, as well." Looking down at her, he hesitated. "Our wedding was…"

"Horrible."

"Not good," he agreed. His dark eyes caressed her face, and he leaned forward to whisper, "But something tells me our honeymoon will make up for it."

Letty felt his breath against her hair, the brush of his lips against her earlobe, and electricity pulsed through her at the untold delights promised by a honeymoon in the Greek villa. In that enormous bed.

She tried not to think about that as he introduced her to the other people around the table, aunts and uncles and innumerable cousins. She smiled shyly, wishing she could speak Greek as one Kyrillos family member after another hugged her, their faces alight with welcome and approval.

One of the younger women grabbed her arm, motioning for her to take the best seat at the table. On learning she was hungry, other relatives dished her out a lunch from the tempting dishes on the table. Tangy olives, salad with cucumbers, tomatoes and feta, vine leaves stuffed with rice, grilled meats on skewers, fresh seafood and finally the lightest, flakiest honey pastries imaginable. After sleeping so long, and having no appetite yesterday, Letty was ravenous and gobbled it all up as fast as she could get it.

The women around her exclaimed approvingly in Greek. Darius sat beside her, smiling, his dark eyes glowing beneath the warm Greek sun.

"They like how you eat," he told her.

She laughed in spite of herself. In this moment, beneath the pink flowers and warm Greek sun, with the blue sea beyond, she felt suddenly, strangely happy. Finally, she pushed her chair away from the table, shaking her head as his relatives offered yet more plates. "No, thank you." She turned anxiously to Darius. "How do I say that?"

"Óchi, efharisto."

"Óchi, efharisto," she repeated to them warmly.

One by one, his family members hugged her, speaking rapidly, patting her belly, then hugging Darius before they hurried into the villa.

"Your family is wonderful."

"Thank you." He lifted a dark eyebrow. "By the way, some of them speak English quite well. They're just hoping if you don't realize that, you'll be inspired to learn Greek."

She laughed, then looked around the terrace at the flowers and sea view. "I'm feeling very inspired, believe me."

"They already love you. Because you're my wife." He put his arm along the back of her chair. "Not only that, you're the first woman I've ever brought home to meet them."

Her eyes went wide. "Really?"

He grinned, shaking his head. "For years, they read about my scandalous love life and despaired of me ever settling down with a nice girl." He sipped strong black coffee from a tiny cup. "Great-aunt Ioanna is delirious with joy to see me not only sensibly married, but also expecting a child. And she remembers you."

Letty's smile fell. "She does?"

"Yes."

"Does she blame me for—?"

"No," he cut her off. "She remembers you only as the girl that I loved and lost long ago. In her mind, that means our marriage is fate. *Moíra.* She believes our love was meant to stand the test of time."

Letty blinked fast. *Our love was meant to stand the test of time.*

Leaning forward, he took her hand. "You are part of the family. You are a Kyrillos now."

It was true, she realized. She had a new last name. When she updated her passport, she'd no longer be Letitia Spencer, the daughter of the famous white-collar criminal, but Letitia Kyrillos, the wife of a self-made billionaire. Just by marrying, she'd become an entirely different person. What a strange thought.

But maybe this new woman, Letitia Kyrillos, would know how to be happy. Maybe their marriage, which had been so bleak at the start, could someday be full of joy, as her own parents' marriage had been.

She just had to change Darius's mind about her father. It wouldn't be hard.

Like making it snow in July.

One of Darius's female cousins came back out of the villa and pulled on his arm, talking rapidly in Greek, even as she smiled apologetically at Letty.

"They need to move the big table," he explained. "To get the terrace ready for the party tonight."

"What party?"

"They wouldn't let us come all this way without making a big fuss." He grinned. "There's a party tonight to welcome you as my bride. Only family and friends from the village have been invited…"

"Good," she said, relieved.

"Which, naturally, means the entire island will be here, and a few people from neighboring islands, as well."

Her heart sank to her sandals at the thought of all those people judging her, possibly finding her unworthy of being Darius's bride. She whispered, "What if they don't like me?"

Reaching out, Darius lifted her chin. "Of course they will," he said softly. "They will because I do."

As the hot Greek sun caressed her skin in the flower-dappled terrace, the dark promise in his gaze made her shiver.

As his relatives bustled back out on the terrace, with maids following them, they started clearing dishes, wiping the table and sweeping the terrace.

Letty looked around anxiously. "Ask them how I can help."

He snorted. "If you think they'll allow either of us to lift a finger, you're out of your mind."

"We can't just sit here, while they do all the work!"

"Watch this." Pushing his chair back, Darius rose from

the table and said casually in English, "Hey, Athina, hand me that broom."

"Forget it, Darius," his cousin replied indignantly in the same language, yanking the broom out of his reach. "You sent my sons to college!"

"You gave me a job when I needed work," a man added in heavily accented English, as he lifted fairy lights to dangle from the terrace's leafy trellis. "We're doing this. Don't think you're getting out of it!"

They all gave a low buzz of agreement.

Looking at Letty, Darius shrugged. She sighed, seeing she was outmatched. His great-aunt was now, in fact, shooing them away with a stream of steady Greek, a mischievous smile on her kindly, wizened face.

Letty drew closer to him. "So what should we do with ourselves?"

Darius's eyes darkened as he said huskily, "We *are* on our honeymoon..."

She shivered at his closeness and at the tempting thought of going back to the bedroom. But she was distracted by the sweep of the brooms and the loud cries of the relatives and house staff bustling back and forth across the villa as they cleaned and set up for the party, all the while watching Darius and Letty out of the corners of their eyes with frank interest and indulgent smiles.

"I couldn't," Letty whispered, blushing beneath all the stares. "If we stay, I'll feel like we should help cook and clean."

"Then let's not stay." He took her hand. "Let me show you the island."

He drew her out of the enormous, luxurious villa, past the gate and out onto unpaved road. Looking around, she saw the rural rolling hills were covered with olive and pomegranate trees, dotted with small whitewashed houses beneath the sun. But there was one thing she didn't see.

"Where are all the cars? The paved roads?"

"We don't have cars. Heraklios is too small and mountainous, and there are only a few hundred residents. There are a few cobblestoned streets by the waterfront, but they're too winding and tight for any car."

"So how do you get around?"

"Donkey."

She almost tripped on her own feet. She looked at him incredulously. "You're joking."

He grinned. "I managed to put in a helicopter pad, and also a landing strip, at great expense, and it isn't even usable if the wind is too strong. Here we transport most things by sea." As they walked closer to an actual village clinging to a rocky cliff, he pointed to a small building on a hill. "That was my school."

"It looks like one room."

"It is. After primary school, kids have to take a ferry to a bigger school the next island over." As they continued walking, he pointed to a small *taverna*. "That's where I tasted my first sip of *retsina*." His nose wrinkled. "I spit it out. I still don't like it."

"And you call yourself a Greek," she teased. His eyebrow quirked at her challenge.

"I'd take you in and let you taste it, except—" he looked more closely at the closed door "—it looks like old Mr. Papadakis is already up at the villa. Probably setting up drinks."

"The whole town's closing—just for our wedding reception?"

"It's a small island. I don't think you realize how much pull I have around here."

Letty slowed when she saw a ruined, lonely-looking villa at the top of the hill, above the village. "What's that?"

His lips tightened, curled up at the edges. "That was my mother's house."

"Oh," she breathed. She knew his mother had abandoned him at birth. He'd never talked much about her, not even when they were young. "No one lives there anymore?"

"My mother left the island right after I was born, her parents soon after. It seems they couldn't stand the shame of my existence," he added lightly.

She flinched, her heart aching. "Oh, Darius."

"My mother moved to Paris. She died in a car crash when I was around four." He shrugged. "I heard her parents died a few years ago. I can't remember where or how."

"I'm so sorry."

"Why? I didn't love them. I don't mourn them."

"But your mother. Your grandparents…"

"Calla Halkias died in a limousine, married to an aristocrat." His voice was cold as he looked back to the ghostly ruin on the hill. "Just as I'm sure she would have wanted. The prestigious life her parents expected for her."

A lump rose in her throat as she thought of Darius as a child on this island, looking up at the imposing villa of the people who'd tossed him out like garbage. She didn't know what to say, so she held his hand tightly. "Did you ever forgive them?"

"For what?"

"They were your family, and they abandoned you."

His lips pressed down. "My mother gave birth to me. I'm glad about that. But I wouldn't call them *family*. From everything I've heard, they were a total disaster. Like…" He hesitated. But she knew.

"Like my family?" she said quietly.

He paused. "Your mother was a great lady. She was always kind. To everyone."

"Yes," she said over the lump in her throat.

"My *yiayiá* raised me. Our house didn't have electricity or plumbing, but I always knew she loved me. When I finally made my fortune, I had the old shack razed and built a villa in its place. The biggest villa this island has ever seen." Looking up at the ruin, he gave a grim smile. "When I was young, the Halkias family was the most powerful here. Now I am."

She noticed he'd never said if he forgave them. She bit her lip. "But, Darius…"

"It's in the past. I want to live in the present. And shape the future." Taking both her hands in his own, Darius looked down at her seriously on the dusty road beneath the hot Greek sun. "Promise me, Letty. You'll always do what's best for our family."

"I promise," she said, meaning it with all her heart.

Lowering his head, he whispered, "And I promise the same."

He softly kissed her, as if sealing the vow. Drawing back, he searched her gaze. Then he pulled her back into his arms and kissed her in another way entirely.

Feeling the heat of his lips against hers, the rough scrape of the bristles on his chin, she clung to him, lost in her own desire. He was her husband now. *Her husband.*

He finally pulled away. "Come with me."

He led her to the end of the dusty road, through the winding cobblestones of the small village of whitewashed houses. On the other side, they went through a scrub brush thicket of olive trees. She held his hand tightly as the branches scraped her arms, and they went down a sharp rocky hill. Then suddenly, they were in a hidden cove on a deserted white sand beach.

Letty's eyes went wide in amazement. The popular beaches of the Hamptons and even around Fairholme would have been packed on a gloriously warm September day. But this beach was empty. "Where is everyone?"

"I told you. They're at the villa, getting ready for the party."

"But—" she gestured helplessly "—there must be tourists, at least?"

He shook his head. "We don't have a hotel. The tourists are at the resorts up in Corfu. So we all know each other here. Everyone is a friend or relative, or at least a friend of a relative. It's a community. One big family."

No wonder this island felt like a world out of time. She felt her heart twist. Turning away, she looked around at the hidden cove with the white sand beach against the blue Ionian Sea and tried to smile. "It's wonderful."

"You're missing Fairholme," he said quietly.

She looked down at the white sand. "It's been ten years. It's stupid. Any psychiatrist would tell me it's time to let it go."

"I miss it, too." He grinned. "Do you remember the beach at Fairholme? Nothing but rocks."

"Yes, and the flower meadow where you taught me to dance."

"What about the pond where I tried to catch frogs and you always wanted to give them names and take them home—?"

Suddenly their words were tumbling over each other.

"The brilliant color of the trees in autumn—"

"Roller-skating down the hallways—"

"The secret passageway behind the library where you'd always hide when you were upset—"

"Your mother's rose garden," Darius said with a sudden laugh, "where she caught me that time I tried a cigarette. My first and last time—"

"And how Mrs. Pollifax scolded us whenever we tracked mud into her freshly cleaned kitchen." Letty grinned. "But she always gave us milk and cookies after we'd made it right. Though it took a while. You weren't very good at mopping."

"We always turned it into a game."

The two of them smiled at each other on the deserted beach.

Letty's smile slipped away. "But we'll never see Fairholme again."

Darius stared at her for a long moment, then abruptly started taking off his shoes. "The sea should be warm."

She lifted her eyebrows. "What are you doing?"

"I'm getting in." He leaned over to unbuckle her sandals. "And you're coming with me."

Barefoot, they went splashing out into the sea. Letty delighted in the feel of the water caressing her feet, then her calves and finally knees. She was tempted to go deeper into the water, to float her pregnant body in the seductive waves that would make her feel light as air. She took a few more steps, until the sea lapped the hem of her white sundress.

Splashing behind her, Darius suddenly pulled her into his arms.

As the waves swirled around them, he kissed her, and there was no one to see but the birds soaring across the sky. For hours, or maybe just minutes, they kissed in the hidden cove, between the bright blue sea and sky, beneath the hot Greek sun. He ran his hands over her bare shoulders, over her thin cotton sundress, as the salty sea spray clung to their skin and hair.

Waves swirled around them, sucking the sand beneath their toes, as the tide started to come in. The waves crashed higher, moving up against their thighs.

Finally pulling away, Darius looked down at her intently. She felt his dark gaze sear her body. Sear her heart.

"Letty, the house we grew up in might be gone," he whispered. "But we still have each other."

The lowering afternoon sun shone around the edges of his dark hair, making Darius shimmer like the dream he was to her.

And it was then Letty knew the worst had happened.

The doom and disaster. And it had happened more swiftly than she'd ever expected.

She loved him.

All of him.

The man he'd been.

The man he was.

The man he could be.

Since the February night they'd conceived their child, Letty had tried to convince herself that he'd changed irrevocably. That she hated him. That he'd lost her love forever.

It had all been a lie.

Even in her greatest pain, she'd never stopped loving him. How could she? He was the love of her life.

Glancing back at the lowering sun, Darius sighed. "Can't be late for our own party. We'd better get back to the villa." He glanced down at his shorts, now splattered with sand and seawater. "We might have to clean up a little."

"Yes," she said in a small voice.

"We'll finish this later," he said huskily, kissing her bare shoulder. He whispered, "I can hardly wait to make love to you, Mrs. Kyrillos."

As they splashed their way to the beach, and made their way up the shore, Letty stumbled.

He caught her, then frowned, looking at her closely. "Did you hurt yourself?"

"No," she said, hiding the ache in her throat, struggling to hold back tears. It wasn't totally a lie. She wasn't hurt.

But she knew she soon would be.

One day married, and her heart was already lost.

CHAPTER NINE

DARIUS NEARLY GASPED when he first saw Letty at the party that night. When she came out onto the terrace, she looked so beautiful she seemed to float through the twilight.

She wore a simple white maxi dress, which fit perfectly over her full breasts and baby bump. The soft fabric showed off the creamy blush of her skin and bright hazel of her eyes. Bright pink flowers hung in her long dark hair.

As the red sun was setting into the sea below the cliffs, three hundred people on the terrace burst into spontaneous applause amid a cacophony of approving Greek.

Darius's heart was in his throat as he looked at her. He was dazzled. He thought she'd put Aphrodite, freshly risen from the sea, completely to shame.

And the fact that he'd even have such a ridiculously poetic thought stunned him.

As she came closer, he cleared his throat awkwardly. "You look nice."

"Thank you," she said, smiling shyly.

He did not touch her. He was almost afraid to. She was simply too desirable, and after their hours of kissing on the beach, he did not know how much more temptation his self-control could take. They'd been married for over twenty-four hours, but had not yet made love.

The party was torture. It lasted for hours, testing his resolve. If it had been any other situation, he would have told everyone to go to hell and taken his bride straight to bed.

But this was his family. His village. He couldn't be rude to them or reject the warm welcome they gave his bride.

His whole body ached to possess her. He could think of nothing else. It was causing him physical pain. He was just glad he was wearing a long, loosely tailored jacket and loose trousers so the whole village could not discuss with amused approval his obvious desire for his bride.

The party was over the top, as only village affairs could be, with music, drinking and dancing. A feast had been lovingly prepared by his family and all the rest of the village. So many people rushed to Letty and started talking excitedly in Greek that she'd announced she planned to start taking Greek lessons as soon as possible. Some of his cousins immediately started cheering, and when Darius translated her words for his elderly great-aunt, Theia Ioanna actually stood on tiptoe to kiss Letty on both cheeks. His family loved her.

Of course they did. Letty Kyrillos was the perfect bride. She would be the perfect wife and mother. Now he'd gotten her away from her father, there would be no bad influences in her life.

Darius would be the only one to claim her loyalty. And the expression in Letty's eyes as she looked at him now—a mix of longing, hero worship and fear—did strange things to his insides. It made him feel oddly vulnerable, reminding him of the insecure, lovesick youth he'd once been for her.

No. He just desired her, he told himself firmly. He was appreciative that she was comporting herself as a proper Greek wife, with kindness and respect to his family. And he hoped—expected—that she would soon love him. It would make all their lives easier.

Darius did not intend to love her in return. He would never leave himself that vulnerable again. As the protector of their family, as a husband, as a father, as a man, it was his duty to be strong.

Letty's heart was her weakness. It would not be his.

His great-aunt went to bed at midnight, and the rest of the older generation soon after, but with the ouzo flowing and loud music and enthusiastic dancing, his cousins and many of the younger villagers remained well into the wee hours. It wasn't until the ouzo was gone and the musicians were falling asleep over their instruments that the last guests finally took the hint and departed, after many congratulations and kisses for the newly married couple.

Darius and Letty were finally alone on the terrace, surrounded by streamers and empty champagne glasses.

She looked at him, her eyes huge in the moonlight, the pink flowers wilting in her dark lustrous hair.

Without a word, he took her hand.

Leading her to their bedroom suite at the farthest end of the south wing, he closed the door behind them and opened the windows and sliding glass door to the balcony. The wind blew from the sea, twisting the translucent white curtains, illuminated by moonlight.

Turning back to her, he lifted her long dark hair from the nape of her neck and slowly unzipped her dress. In the hush of the night, it felt like an act that was almost holy.

Her dress dropped to the floor. She turned to him, her eyes luminous in the silvery light. Reaching up, she pulled off his jacket. She unbuttoned his shirt. He felt the soft brush of her hands against his chest and caught them in his own. She looked up at him questioningly.

A strange feeling was building in his heart. *Desire*, he reminded himself fiercely. *I desire her.* He kissed her hands—first one, then the other.

The wind blew against her hair, causing pink flower petals to float softly to the floor like a benediction. Without a word, he pulled her to the enormous bed.

This time, as they made love, there were no words beyond the language of touch. There was only pleasure and delight.

He'd thought he'd known ecstasy the night they'd made love over and over in his Manhattan penthouse.

But this was something else. It felt different.

Why? Because they were married now, and she was permanently his? Because she knew him better than anyone on earth? Because she'd truly joined his family?

Whatever the reason, as he made love to her on this, their first true wedding night, it felt sacred.

It felt like…

Happiness.

After they'd both joined and shattered like a supernova in each other's arms, Darius held her as she slept. As he stared at the ceiling, her words on the beach floated back into his mind.

We'll never see Fairholme again.

Her voice had been quietly despairing. As if she'd accepted bleak loss as her due.

Darius scowled. He didn't accept that.

He suddenly wanted to give Letty back everything she'd lost. And more.

Careful not to wake her, he rose from the bed in the gray light of dawn. Going out onto the balcony, with its view of the wild gray sea, he made a quiet phone call to his long-suffering executive assistant in New York. Mildred Harrison had worked for him for seven years, so she didn't even sound surprised that he'd be rude enough to call her so late.

"Pity you left New York right when you're the city's hero," she said drily. "Your picture is on the cover of the *Daily Post*. Apparently you're some kind of Robin Hood figure now, robbing from your own fortune to pay back Howard Spencer's victims."

"Glad I'm not there, then. We'll be back in two weeks, by which time I expect the papers will all be insulting me again. Anything else?"

"That Brooklyn apartment building has been purchased as you requested. Your father-in-law—"

"Never call him that again," Darius said tersely.

She cleared her throat. "Um, Mr. Spencer has been advised that he will be allowed to remain in the apartment for as long as he wishes, free of charge."

"Good," he said, already bored with the subject.

She paused. "There's something else you should know."

"Well?"

"The investigator following him says Spencer has been visiting an oncologist. Apparently he's sick. Maybe dying."

Darius's eyes widened. Then he gave a snort. "It's a trick."

"Mr. Green didn't think so. He managed to get his hands on the medical records. It seems legit."

"Spencer must have paid the doctor off."

"Maybe." Mildred sounded doubtful. "But if it were my father, I'd still want to know."

Yes, Darius thought. He looked back at the shadowy form of Letty sleeping in his bed. She would want to know. But there was no way he was telling her. Not when the old man was probably just trying once again to cause trouble between them.

At worst, Spencer probably had a cold and thought he could use it to get out of his well-deserved punishment. Darius was not going to let it happen.

"I won't have my wife bothered," he said shortly. "Spencer must have known he was being followed."

"As you say, Mr. Kyrillos."

He set his jaw. "I called you for another reason. I want to buy my wife a wedding gift."

"Beyond the billions you're already putting in trust for her father's victims? We've had a whole team of accountants coming through here, by the way, working with the Feds to determine accurate payments, including those for third-party clients. We're not really staffed for this…"

"You'll sort it out. And at the end, I'll send you and your husband to Miami for a week of well-deserved rest."

"Rome," she said firmly. "For three."

He grinned. Mildred knew what she was worth. He respected that.

"Three," he agreed. "But I need you to do something first. I want to buy a home."

"Your penthouse is too small?"

"I have a special place in mind. Find out what it would cost."

He explained, and she gave a low whistle. "All right, boss. I'll call you soon as I know. What's your ceiling?"

"Whatever it takes."

After he hung up the phone, Darius went back to the king-size bed he shared with his pregnant bride. Joining her under the blankets, he wrapped his arm around her as she slept. He heard the birds singing as, outside the window, the sun started to rise.

Holding Letty in his arms, he suddenly saw the reward for everything he'd done right in his life. He had Letty. He'd have the rest. Home. Children. Joy. All the things he'd stopped dreaming about long ago. He would have it all.

And nothing, especially not her criminal of a father, would come between them.

As their private jet began its descent through the clouds toward New York City, Letty felt a mixed sense of relief and regret.

She was glad to be returning closer to her father. Darius had assured her that Howard was fine and living rent-free in their old apartment with a stipend to supply his needs. "Your father is spending his days playing chess with friends down at the park," he'd told her irritably. She could only assume Darius had someone watching him, but she didn't even mind because she was glad to know he was all right. It felt so wrong never to see him, never to call him.

But at least now she'd know her dad was only a quick

drive away, if needed. And soon she hoped he'd be back in their lives for good.

The heart attack that had caused the death of Darius's father was a tragic accident. But surely he couldn't hate her dad forever? She loved Darius too much to believe that. Soon they would all be a family again.

And family was all Letty cared about. As she'd promised her husband in Greece, she would always put her family above everything else.

She already felt wistful for the tiny Greek island where she'd been immediately accepted into Darius's extended family. Their honeymoon had been the happiest two weeks of her life. She'd loved everything about Heraklios. The village. The beach. The vivid colors and bright sun. The villa. The people. Her eyes met Darius's across the airplane cabin.

The man.

He was sitting in a white swivel chair and had spent much of the flight typing on his laptop, with some idea he'd had for a new business venture. But as his gaze caught hers, she felt every bit of his attention. She always felt it to her toes when he looked at her.

Lifting a dark eyebrow, he teased, "We could still turn the plane around."

"I loved our visit," she said wistfully, then glanced out the window. "But it'll be nice to be back home." She paused, biting her lip. She knew she shouldn't ask, but she couldn't help it. "Now we're back in the city, maybe you could talk to my dad. Then you'd see his side…"

"Forget it," he said flatly.

"He never meant to hurt anyone, he—"

Darius closed his laptop with a thud. "Stop."

"Forgiveness frees the soul. You never know—" her voice sounded desperate even to her own ears "—*you* might have to ask someone for forgiveness one day!"

He snorted. "I don't intend to commit any crimes, so I think I'm safe."

"Darius—"

"No."

Disappointment filled her heart. Clenching her hands, she told herself she'd just have to be patient. She forced herself to take a deep breath and change the subject. "I loved spending time with your family. Maybe your great-aunt could come visit us in New York."

His expression relaxed and he smiled. "Theia Ioanna hates planes. She thinks of them as newfangled machines, a dangerous fad. She's waiting for everyone to come to their senses. But after our baby's born we could go back to Heraklios."

"I'd like that." Outside the window, the plane was descending through clouds that looked like white cotton candy. "In the meantime, I'm going to start learning Greek." She looked at him coyly beneath her lashes. "You'd like to teach me your native tongue, wouldn't you?"

His eyes darkened with interest. He started to rise from his seat, but as the plane broke beneath the clouds, the pilot announced over the intercom that they should buckle their seat belts for landing. Letty smiled.

Then she looked through the porthole window. "That's not Teterboro."

Now he was the one to smile. "No."

Staring down, she suddenly recognized the airport. Long ago, her family had landed here every time they went on a trip. She looked up with a frown. "Long Island? Is there a problem?"

"Wait and see."

After the plane landed at the small airport, the two of them came down the steps. A town car waited on the tarmac, and his driver and bodyguard swiftly loaded their suitcases from the plane.

"But why are we here?" she asked Darius helplessly in the backseat of the car a few minutes later as it pulled away from the airport.

"You'll see."

"You're really vexing."

His dark eyebrows lifted. "Vexing?" he teased, then moved closer as he whispered, "Is that what I am?"

Then he kissed her senseless in the backseat, until she was forced to agree rather unsteadily that he did have one or two good qualities, as well.

But she tensed when the limo turned onto the coastal road that she'd once known very, very well. Her suspicions were confirmed as they drove down the same country lane that she knew led to the massive 1920s beachfront estate that had once been her home. She turned on Darius angrily.

"Why would you bring us here?" she choked out. "Just to torture me? You can't see the house from the road." She felt a sudden ache in her throat as she looked out toward the gray-blue bay that led to the Atlantic. "The gate is guarded. That tech billionaire is serious about privacy. So if you're hoping to get a peek of the house, it won't happen."

"You tried?"

"A month after it was sold at auction. As I told you, I just wanted a picture of my great-grandmother's fresco. His guard did everything but set the dogs on me."

"That won't be a problem today."

Letty pointed at the road ahead. "See? I told you—"

Then her eyes went wide.

The gate was wide open. Their limo drove right past the empty guardhouse, up the wide driveway to the glorious windswept oceanfront manor that had been built by Letty's great-great-grandfather, a steel baron named Edwin Langford.

Fairholme.

Letty's breath caught in her throat as she leaned out the

car window, and her eyes were dazzled as she saw, for the first time in ten years, her beloved home.

Tears swelled in her eyes as she looked up at the gray stone mansion with its turrets and leaded glass windows soaring against the sky. Looking back at her husband, she breathed, "What have you done?"

He was smiling. "I've given you what you want most."

The limo had barely stopped before she flung open her car door and raced eagerly into the house. Pushing aside the stately front door—unlocked!—she hurled herself into the foyer where she'd played as a child.

"Dad?" she cried out. "Dad, where are you?"

Letty ran from room to room, calling his name, overwhelmed with happiness that somehow, while pretending he was never going to forgive her father, Darius had seen the desperate desire of her heart.

I've given you what you want most.

"Dad!" she cried, moving from one elegant, empty room to the next. Memories followed her with every step.

There she had played pirates with her father.

There she had slipped down the marble floor in socks as the two of them competed to see who could slide farthest and make her mother laugh loudest.

There she'd played with the gardener's kittens.

There she'd played hide-and-seek with Darius when they were kids...

There—every Saturday in summer—she'd tucked roses into the priceless Ming dynasty vase to make her mother smile.

But where was her dad? Where?

As Letty finished going through the main entrance rooms, she ran up the sweeping staircase toward the second floor. She stopped halfway up the stairs, realizing she was hearing only the echo of her own voice.

Her dad wasn't there.

Letty's shoulders sagged with savage disappointment. Turning back down the stairs, she saw Darius standing in the front doorway, watching her. The happy, smug expression had disappeared from his handsome face.

He said tightly, "Why do you think I would invite your father here?"

"You said—you said," she faltered, biting her lip, "you were giving me what I wanted most."

"This house." His expression now could only be described as grimly outraged. "Your childhood home. I arranged to buy it for you. It wasn't easy. I had to pay the man a fortune to leave before we arrived. But I wanted you to have all your dreams. Everything you'd lost."

Everything she'd lost...

Gripping the banister for support, Letty sagged to sit on a stair. Heartbreaking grief was thundering through her, worse than if she'd never gotten her hopes up at all.

She struggled to hide it. She knew she was being churlish. Her mother would be ashamed of her. Here Darius had given her the stars and she was crying for the sun.

She should be overjoyed.

Fairholme.

Letty took a deep breath, looking up at the high painted ceilings, at the oak-paneled walls. *Home.* She was really here. Darius had given her back the home that had raised generations of Langfords, her mother's family.

What an amazing gift.

Wiping her eyes, Letty looked at Darius and tried to smile.

His handsome face was mutinous.

She couldn't blame him. He'd gone to a lot of trouble and expense to give her this incredible surprise, and she'd been completely ungrateful.

Rising unsteadily to her feet, she walked down the stairs to the foyer where he stood with a scowl, his arms folded.

"Thank you," she whispered. "I love your wonderful gift."

He looked distinctly grumpy. "It didn't look like it."

Feeling ashamed at her bad manners, she wrapped her arms around his neck and kissed him.

"I love it," she said softly. "It's a miracle to be here."

Looking mollified, he accepted her embrace. "I've also hired Mrs. Pollifax to come back as our housekeeper."

"You have!"

He smiled, clearly pleased by her reaction. "Along with as many of the original staff who were available. Giving them a big raise, naturally. I've also established a bank account in your name."

"Whatever for?"

Darius gave her a sudden grin. "You obviously haven't seen the stripper pole the last owner put up in the library. I knew you'd want to oversee the remodeling personally. Perhaps the fresco can be repaired? I've instructed the bank to give you unlimited funds. Use the money however you please."

"For the house?"

"Yes."

"The baby?"

"Of course. And you, Letty. Anything you want, jewelry, cars, furniture. You don't have to ask me. Buy anything you desire."

Biting her lip, she blurted out, "Could I send some money to my father?"

She knew immediately it was a mistake.

His expression turned icy. "I weary of your constantly bringing up this topic. We have an agreement."

"I know, but—"

"Your father already has far more than he deserves."

"If I could only just see him, so I could know he's all right…"

"He's fine."

Letty searched his gaze, hoping for reassurance. "He's fine? You know for sure?"

He paused. Then he finally said, "Yes."

He wouldn't meet her eyes.

"I miss him," she whispered. She took a deep breath, reminding herself of everything she had to be grateful for. Taking Darius's hand, she pressed it to her cheek and looked up at him with gratitude. "But what you've done for me today, buying Fairholme back… I'll never forget."

For a long moment, the two of them stood together in the foyer, with sunlight pouring in through the open door. She breathed in scents she'd craved so long, the tangy salt of the ocean, the honeyed sweetness of her mother's rose garden. The salt and sweetness of a lifetime of memories.

"Thank you," she whispered. "For bringing me home."

He cupped her cheek. "You're worth it, Letty," he said huskily. "For you, I would pay any price."

Lowering his head, he kissed her, claiming her lips as he'd already claimed her body and soul. Words lifted unbidden to her throat. Words she hadn't tried to say since that horrible night in February. Words straight from her heart.

"I love you, Darius," she said softly.

He gave her an oddly shy smile. "You do?"

Smiling back through her tears, she nodded. Her blood was rushing through her ears, pounding through her veins, as she waited for what he'd say next.

Without a word, he kissed her.

As she stood in the Fairholme foyer, her heavily pregnant belly pressed between them as her husband kissed her so tenderly, miracles seemed to be spinning around her like a whirlwind.

They were married now. Expecting a baby. He'd paid off her father's debts. He'd just brought her home. She loved him.

And someday, he would love her.

Letty was suddenly sure. They'd already had so many miracles. Why not more?

Darius would soon forgive her father and let him back into their family. He was too good a man not to forgive, especially when it meant so much to her. It was the only thing he hadn't given her. That, and those three little words.

It was the same thing, she realized. When he forgave her father, that was how she would know that he truly loved her.

When he finally pulled away from their embrace, she looked up, still a little dazzled. "Is there really a stripper pole in the library?"

Darius gave a low laugh. "Come with me."

Taking her hand, he drew her down the long marble hallway to the oak-paneled library. When she saw the gleaming stripper pole set in the brand-new white shag carpeting, she burst into horrified snorts of laughter.

"I told you," he said.

"I'll get it removed. Don't worry. I'll make this house just like it was," Letty said. "Just like we remember."

"All those memories." He pulled her against his chest, his dark eyes intense as he whispered huskily, "But as I remember, there's one thing we've never done in this house."

And as her husband pulled her against him in a hot, fierce embrace, Letty knew all her deepest dreams were about to come true.

CHAPTER TEN

HOME. LETTY LOOKED around with satisfaction. Was there any sweeter word?

The remodel was finished just in time, too. The former owner's monstrous decor had been removed—the shag carpeting, the stripper pole, the "ironic" brass fixtures and all the rest of it—and everything at Fairholme had been returned to its former glory.

The sitting room felt cozy, especially compared to the cold November weather outside. A fire crackled in the fireplace. Polished oak floors gleamed beneath priceless Turkish rugs. The sofas and chairs were plush and comfortable, the lamps sturdy and practical. Family photos now decorated the walls.

Letty snuggled back against the sofa. Her husband was sitting at the other end, tapping away on his laptop, but periodically he would rub her feet, so she made sure they were strategically available. Earlier, they'd had a delicious hearty meal of lamb stew and homemade bread, her favorite meal from childhood, prepared by Mrs. Pollifax.

The housekeeper had just left, saying that she needed to go visit a friend at a Brooklyn hospital. She'd had a strange expression when she said it, causing Letty to reply with a sympathetic murmur, "Please take all the time you need for your friend."

"I just might," the housekeeper had replied tartly, "since his own family can't be bothered to go see him."

"Poor man," Letty had sighed, feeling sorry for him. She couldn't imagine what kind of family wouldn't visit a sick man in the hospital.

That reminded her of how much she missed her father

after more than two months of not seeing him or talking to him. Darius still refused to forgive him. But surely, after their baby was born, his heart would be so full, he would have a new capacity to forgive? To love.

Letty looked at her husband hopefully. With the departure of Mrs. Pollifax, and the rest of the staff in their outlying cottages on the estate, the two of them were now completely alone in the house. The room felt snug and warm with her afghan blanket, the crackling fire and Darius's closeness as outside the cold November wind blew, rattling the leaded glass windows.

She was getting close to her due date, and happier than she'd ever imagined.

The nursery was ready. She'd been overjoyed to discover that her great-grandmother's precious fresco hadn't been completely destroyed. A well-known art restorer had managed to bring a good portion of it back to life. The ducks and geese were far fewer in number, and the Bavarian village mostly gone, but the little goose girl no longer looked so sad. It was a joy to see it again, and though Darius pretended to mock it and roll his eyes as he called it "art," she knew he was happy for her.

The nursery was the most beautiful room in the house, in Letty's opinion, the place where she'd slept as a baby, as had her mother and her grandfather before. It was now freshly painted and decorated, with a crib and rocking chair and brand-new toys. All they needed was the baby.

"Soon," she whispered aloud, rubbing her enormous belly. "Very soon."

"Talking to the baby again?" Darius teased.

Holding up a tattered copy of a beloved children's book, she responded archly, "I'm just going to read him this story."

His dark eyebrows lifted. "Again?"

"The pregnancy book said..."

"Oh, have you read a pregnancy book?"

Letty's lips quirked. Her constant consultation of pregnancy books and blogs was a running joke between them. But as a first-time mother and an only child, she had little experience with children and was anxious to do it right.

"It's been scientifically proven," she informed him now, "that a baby can hear, and therefore obviously listen to stories, from the womb."

He rolled his eyes, then put his large hand tenderly on her belly. "Don't worry, kid," he said in a whisper. "I have something to read you that I know you'll find way more interesting than the bunny story."

"Oh, you do, do you?" she said, amused.

"Absolutely." Turning back to his laptop, he clicked a few buttons and then started reading aloud, with mock seriousness, the latest business news from overseas.

Now she was the one to roll her eyes. But she found Darius's low, deep voice soothing, even when he was describing boring tech developments. Sipping orange spice herbal tea, she nibbled on the sugar cookies she'd made earlier that afternoon. She'd been eating so much lately she felt nearly as big as a house herself.

But Darius didn't seem to mind. Her cheeks grew hot as she recalled how he'd made love to her all over the house. Even the bathrooms—those with showers, at least. Almost forty rooms.

"We have to make this house ours," he'd growled, and she'd loved it.

Now as she felt his gentle hand resting on her belly, she grew drowsy listening to his low voice reading news stories to their baby and punctuating them with exclamations when he felt the baby kick.

"Letty," Darius said in a low voice, "are you awake?"

"Barely." She yawned. "I was just going to head up to bed. Why?"

He was quiet for a long moment, then said quietly, "Never mind. It'll wait. Good night, *agape mou*."

The next morning, she kissed Darius goodbye as he left for lower Manhattan, as was his usual schedule Monday through Thursday. He'd set up an office for a new business he was excited about, to create software that would teach math and coding skills. Each day, Darius hired more employees, paying for their salaries out of his own pocket. There hadn't been any profits. "And there might never be any," he'd confessed sheepishly. But he wanted to make a difference in the world.

She'd never been so proud of him. He had a new spark in his eyes as he left Fairholme for his ninety-minute commute to the office.

Letty went up to the nursery, her favorite room, to fold all the cute tiny baby clothes one more time and make sure everything was ready. She'd had a dull ache in her lower back all morning. She went down to the kitchen, intending to ask Mrs. Pollifax if she knew of any natural remedy for back pain.

Instead she found the housekeeper crying.

"What's wrong?" Letty cried, going up to her in the enormous, gleaming kitchen. "What's happened?"

"My friend." The woman wiped her eyes with the edge of her apron. "He's dying."

"I'm so sorry," Letty whispered.

Mrs. Pollifax's eyes looked at her accusingly. "You should be. Since it's your own father."

Letty stared at her in shock. For a long minute, she couldn't even make sense of the words.

"I'm sorry—I can't be silent any longer," the housekeeper said. "Whatever caused you to be estranged from him, you're wrong to let him die alone. You'll regret it the rest of your life!"

"My father…?" Letty said slowly. "Is dying?"

Mrs. Pollifax's expression changed. "You didn't know?"

Shocked, she shook her head. "There must…must be some mistake. My father's not sick. He's fine. He's living without a care in the world…going to the park every day to play chess…"

"Oh, my dear." Coming closer, the housekeeper gently put her hand on Letty's shoulder. "I'm sorry. I judged you wrongly. I thought you knew. He collapsed a few weeks ago and has been in the hospital ever since. When I visited him yesterday, he didn't look well. He might have only weeks left. Days."

A loud rushing sound went through Letty's ears.

"No," she said numbly. "It has to be a mistake."

"I'm so sorry."

"You're wrong." Shaking off the housekeeper's hand, Letty reached for her phone. She dialed Darius's number first. When it went to voice mail, she hung up.

She took a deep breath. Her hands shook as she deliberately broke her vow to her husband for the first time. Her father had always hated cell phones, disparaging them as "tracking devices," so she called him at their old apartment number.

That, too, went to voice mail. But it was no longer Letty's voice on the phone greeting. Her father had replaced it with his own. For the first time in two months, she heard his recorded voice, and it sounded different. Fragile. Weak.

Terror rushed through her.

Her body was shaking as she looked up at Mrs. Pollifax. "Which hospital?"

The housekeeper told her. "But you're in no fit state to drive. I'll have Collins bring around the car. Shall I come with you?"

Letty shook her head numbly.

The older woman bit her lip, looking sad. "He's in room 302."

The drive to Brooklyn seemed to take forever. When they finally arrived at the large, modern hospital, Letty's body shook as she raced inside.

She didn't stop at reception, just hurried to the elevator, holding her heavy, aching belly. On the third floor, she followed the signs toward room 302.

Her steps slowed when she saw a man sitting in the waiting area. He looked up and saw her, too. She frowned. She recognized him from somewhere…

But she didn't stop, just headed straight for her father's room.

"Miss!" a nurse called anxiously as she passed the third-floor reception desk, barreling toward the corner room. "Please wait just a moment."

"It's all right," Letty said. "I'm his daughter." She pushed open the door. "Dad. Dad! I'm—"

But the room was empty.

Letty stared around in shock. Was she in the wrong room? Had she misunderstood?

Was he—oh, God—surely he couldn't be…?

"I'm sorry," a woman said behind her.

"You should be!" her father's gruff voice retorted.

With a sob, Letty whirled around.

In the doorway her living, breathing father was sitting in a wheelchair, glaring back at the dark-haired nurse struggling to push him through the doorway.

"You practically ran me into a wall. Where'd you learn how to drive?"

Letty burst into noisy tears. Her father turned his head and saw her, and his gaunt, pale features lit up with joy.

"Letty. You came."

Throwing her arms around his thin frame in the wheelchair, she choked out, "Of course I came. As soon as I heard you were sick. Then when I didn't see you in the bed, I thought…"

"Oh, you thought I was dead? No!" Glancing back at the nurse, he added drily, "Not for *some* people's lack of trying."

"Hmph." The nurse sniffed. "That's the last time I agree to help you win a wheelchair race, Howard."

"Win! We didn't win anything! Margery crushed us by a full ten seconds, in spite of her extra pounds. After all my big talk, too—I'll never live this down," he complained.

Letty drew back with astonishment. "Wheelchair race?"

"Admittedly not one of my best ideas, especially with Nurse Crashy here."

"Hey!"

"But it's what passes for fun here in the hospice wing. Either that or depress myself with cable news."

"It's totally against hospital protocol. I can't believe you talked me into it. Ask someone else to risk their job next time," the nurse said.

He gave her his old charming grin. "The race was a good thing. It lifted the spirits of everyone on the wing."

Looking slightly mollified, she sighed. "I guess I'd better go try convince my boss of that." She left the room.

Her father turned back to Letty. "But why are you crying? You really thought I was dead?"

She tried to smile. "You're crying, too, Dad."

"Am I?" Her father touched his face. He gave her a watery smile. "I'm just glad to see you, I guess. I was starting to wonder if you'd ever come."

"I came the instant I heard," she whispered, feeling awful and guilty.

Howard gave a satisfied nod. "I knew he'd eventually tell you."

"Who?"

"Darius. Sure, I promised I'd never contact you. But there was nothing in our deal that said I couldn't contact *him*. I left him a message four weeks ago, when I woke up in the hospital. I'd collapsed in the street, so an ambulance brought me here."

Four weeks? Letty was numb with shock. Darius had known for a *month* that her father was in the hospital, just an hour away from Fairholme?

Her father stroked his wispy chin. "Though I'm pretty sure he knew even before that. He's had me followed since the day you ran off with him. The guy must have noticed me going to my doctor's office three times a week."

She sucked in her breath, covering her mouth. Not just one month, but two? Darius had known her father was sick, dying, but he'd purposefully kept it from her?

Your father is spending his days playing chess with friends down at the park.

A lie!

Last night, when she and Darius had been cuddled by the fire, dreaming about their child, even then, her husband had been lying to her. While Letty had been eating cookies and drinking tea, her father had been spending yet another night in this hospital. Alone. Without a single word of love from his only daughter.

A cold sweat broke out on her skin. She trembled as if to fight someone or flee. But there was no escaping the horrible truth.

Darius had lied to her.

The man she'd loved since childhood. The center of all her romantic dreams and longings. He'd known her father was dying, and he'd lied.

How could Darius have been so callous? So selfish, heartless and cruel?

The answer was obvious.

He didn't love her.

He never would.

A gasp of anguish and rage came from the back of her throat.

"He never gave you the message, did he?" her father said, watching her. When she shook her head, he sighed. "How did you know I was here?"

"Mrs. Pollifax."

"I see." He looked sad. Then his eyes fell to her belly and he brightened as he changed the subject. "You're so big! You're just a week or two from your due date, aren't you?"

"Yes."

"I've almost made it." His voice was smug. "The doctors said I was a goner, but I told them I wasn't going anyplace yet."

Letty's body was still shaking with grief and fury. In the gray light of the hospital room, she turned toward the window. Outside, she saw November rain falling on the East River, and beyond it she could see the skyscrapers of Manhattan. Where Darius was right now.

Howard said dreamily behind her, "I was determined to see my grandbaby before I died."

She whirled back to her father. "Stop talking about dying!"

His gaunt face sagged. "I'm sorry, Letty. I really am."

"Isn't there any hope?" Her voice cracked. "An operation? A—a second opinion?"

Her father's eyes were kind. He shook his head. "I knew I was dying before I left prison."

She staggered back. "Why didn't you tell me?"

He rubbed his watery eyes. "I should have, I guess. But I didn't want you to worry and take all the stress on yourself like you always do. I wanted, for once, to take care of you. I wanted to repair the harm I did so long ago and get you back where you deserved to be. Married to your true love."

True love, Letty thought bitterly. Her stomach churned every time she thought of Darius lying to her all this time. The unfeeling bastard.

"It was my only goal," her father said. "To make sure

you'd be looked after and loved after I was gone. Now you and Darius are married, expecting a baby." He grinned with his old verve and said proudly, "Getting my arm broken by that thug was the best thing that ever happened to me, since it helped me bring you back together. I can die at peace. A happy man."

"Darius never told me you were sick," she choked out, her throat aching with pain. "I'll never forgive him."

Her father's expression changed. "Don't blame Darius. After all my self-made disasters, it just shows his good sense. Shows me he'll protect you better than I ever did." He looked up from the wheelchair. "Thank you, Letty."

She felt like the worst daughter in the world. "For what?"

"For always believing in me," he said softly, "even when you had no reason to. For loving me through everything."

She looked at her dying father through her tears. Then looked around the hospital room at the plain bed, the tile floor, the antiseptic feel, the ugly medical equipment. She couldn't bear to think of him spending his last days here, whiling away his hours with wheelchair races.

Her eyes narrowed. "Do you really need to be in the hospital?"

Howard shrugged. "I could have gone to full hospice. Other than pain meds, there's not much the doctors can do for me."

Her belly tightened with a contraction that felt like nothing compared to the agony of her heart. She lifted her chin. "Then you're coming home with me."

Howard looked at her in disbelief. "Back to that apartment? No, thanks. At least the hospital isn't cold all the time and someone brings me meals…"

"Not the apartment. I'm taking you to Fairholme."

His eyes looked dazzled.

"Fairholme?" he breathed. She saw the joy in his

wrinkled face. Then he blinked, looking troubled. "But Darius—"

"I'll handle him." Wrapping her arms around her father's thin shoulders, she kissed the wispy top of his head. Her father's last days would be happy ones, she vowed. He would die in the home that he'd adored, where he'd once lived with his beloved wife and raised his child, surrounded by comfort and love.

Letty would take care of him as he'd once taken care of her.

And, she thought grimly, she'd also take care of Darius.

She'd loved her husband with all her heart. Now she saw that all the sacrifices she'd made, all of her trust, had been for nothing. For an illusion. Darius didn't love her. He would never love her.

It was his final betrayal. And for this, she would never forgive him.

Darius walked into his office near Battery Park with a smile on his face and a spring in his step. He was late but had an excellent reason. He'd stopped at his favorite jeweler's on Fifth Avenue to buy a push present for his wife.

He'd read about push presents in a parenthood article. It was a gift that men gave the mothers of their children after labor and delivery, in celebration and appreciation of all their hours of pain and hard work. Since Letty's due date was so close, Darius had known he had no time to lose. He'd found the perfect gift—exquisite emerald earrings, surrounded by diamonds, set in gold, almost as beautiful as her hazel eyes. They'd even once belonged to a queen of France. With Letty's love of history, he knew she'd get a kick out of that, and he could hardly wait to give them to her. And even more amazing: when he did, their son would be real at last, and in their arms.

Darius realized he was whistling the same hokey lullaby that his wife had sung in the shower that morning to their unborn baby.

He loved Letty's voice.

He loved their home.

And he loved that he'd been able to blow off half a morning of work in order to get her a gift. It was supposedly one of the perks of being a boss, but at his last company, he'd been too grimly driven to do anything but grind out work. So he could build his fortune. So he could be worth something.

But even after he'd succeeded, even when he'd finally been rich beyond imagination, he'd been unhappy. He realized that now. He'd spent ten years doing nothing but work, and when he'd sold his company he'd felt lost. Money hadn't fulfilled him quite as much as he'd thought it would.

But now, everything had changed. Both in his work and his life.

He was building a new company. A free website would teach software coding, math and science skills, so others could have the opportunities he'd had, to get good jobs or perhaps even start their own tech companies someday.

His goal wasn't to build a fortune. He already had more than he could spend in a lifetime. When he'd paid out billions of dollars to Howard Spencer's victims, he hadn't even missed it.

Letty was teaching him—reminding him? —how a good life was lived.

Throughout their marriage, as Fairholme had every day become more beautiful, so had his pregnant wife. She was huge now, and she glowed. Every day she told him how much she loved him. He could feel it, her love for him, warming him like a fire in winter.

There was only one flaw.

One secret he was keeping.

And he knew it might ruin everything.

Darius's steps slowed as he crossed through the open office with the exposed brick walls.

Letty's father was dying. And Darius didn't know how to tell her.

He hadn't wanted to believe it was true at first. For weeks, he'd insisted it was all an elaborate con. "Call me when he's dead," he'd told his investigator half-seriously.

Then he'd gotten a message from Howard Spencer himself, saying he was in the hospital. Even then, for a few days, Darius had told himself it was a lie. Until his investigator had combed through the hospital records and confirmed it was true. Darius had no choice but to face it.

Now he had to tell Letty.

But how? How could he explain to her all his weeks of silence, when he'd known her father was dying in a Brooklyn hospital?

Darius still believed he'd done the right thing. He and Letty had made a deal at the start of their marriage: no contact with her father. There hadn't been any fine print or "get out of jail free" card if the man decided to die. All Darius had done was uphold their deal. He had nothing to feel guilty about. He hadn't just paid Spencer's debts, but also his living expenses and even his medical bills. He'd practically acted like a saint.

Somehow, he didn't think Letty would see it that way.

Darius dreaded her reaction. He'd halfheartedly started to tell her last night, but stopped, telling himself he didn't want to risk raising her blood pressure when she was so close to delivery. He didn't want to risk her health, or the baby's.

After the baby's born, he promised himself firmly. Once he knew both mother and baby were safe and sound.

She would be angry at first, he knew. But after she'd had some time to think it over, she'd realize that he'd only been trying to protect her. And it was in her nature to forgive. She had no choice. She loved him.

Feeling calmer, he walked past his executive assistant's desk toward his private office. "Good morning, Mildred."

Lifting her eyebrows, she greeted him with "Your wife is on the line."

"My wife?" A smile lifted unbidden to his face, as it always did when he thought of Letty.

"She said you weren't answering your cell."

Instinctively, Darius put his hand to his trouser pocket. It was empty. He must have left it in the car.

"Mrs. Kyrillos sounds pretty stressed." His executive assistant, usually stern and no-nonsense, gave him a rare smile. "She said it's urgent."

Letty never called him at work. His smile changed to a dazed grin. There could be only one reason she'd call now, so close to her due date!

"I'll take it in my office," he said joyfully and rushed inside, shutting the door behind him. He snatched up the phone. "Letty? Is it the baby? Are you in labor?"

His wife's voice sounded strangely flat. "No."

"Mildred said it was urgent—"

"It is urgent. I'm leaving you. I'm filing for divorce."

For a long moment he just gripped the phone, that foolish grin still on his face, as he tried to comprehend her words. Then the smile fell away.

"What are you talking about? Is this some kind of joke?"

"No."

He took a deep breath. "I've read about pregnancy hormones…"

Anger suddenly swelled from the other end of the line.

"Pregnancy hormones? *Pregnancy hormones?* I'm divorcing you because you lied to me. You've been lying for months! My father is dying and you never told me!"

Darius's heart was suddenly in his throat.

"How did you find out?" he whispered.

"Mrs. Pollifax couldn't understand how I could be such a heartless daughter to just let my father die alone. Don't worry. I've let her know that the heartless one is you."

He looked up, past his desk to the window overlooking the southern tip of Manhattan, and the Atlantic beyond it. Outside, rain fell in the gray November morning.

He licked his lips and tried, "Letty, I don't blame you for being upset—"

"Upset? No. I'm not upset." She paused. "I'm happy."

That was so obviously not true he had no idea how to react. "If you'll just give me a chance to explain."

"You already explained to me, long ago, that you wouldn't love me. That love was for children. You told me. I just didn't listen," she said softly. "Now I really, truly get it. And I want you out of my life for good."

"No—"

"I've brought my father to Fairholme."

Gripping the phone, he nearly staggered back. "Howard Spencer—in my house?"

"Yes." Her voice was ice-cold. "I'm not leaving him in the hospital, surrounded by strangers. He's going to spend his last days surrounded by love, in the home where he was married to my mother."

"It's not just your decision. I bought that house and…" He stopped himself, realizing how pompous he sounded. But it was too late.

"Right." Her voice was a sneer. "Because money makes the man. You think you can buy your way through life. That's what you do, isn't it? Buy things. You bought my virginity, and ever since, you've kept buying me. With marriage. With money. You didn't realize it was never your money I wanted." Her voice suddenly broke to a whisper. "It was you, Darius. My dream of you. The amazing boy you were." She took a breath. "The man I actually thought you still were, deep down inside."

"I'm still that man," he said tightly. "I was going to tell you. I just didn't want you upset…"

"Upset by my father dying!"

Darius flinched at the derision in her voice. "Perhaps I made a bad decision, but I was trying to look after you."

"And you assumed I would forgive you."

He felt shaken. "Forgiveness is what you do."

She gave a hard laugh. "How convenient for you. Only the idiots who love you have to forgive. But since you never love anyone, you never have to worry about that. You're free to hurt whomever you please."

She didn't sound like his wife at all, the kindhearted woman who greeted him every day with kisses, who gave so much of herself and asked for very little in return.

Except for him to forgive her father, Darius realized. That was the one thing she'd actually asked for. And the one thing he'd refused, again and again.

He, who was never afraid of anything, felt the first stirrings of real fear. "If you'll just listen to me—"

"I've had suitcases boxed up for you. Collins is taking them to your penthouse in Midtown. Don't worry. I won't stay here forever. You can have Fairholme back after…" Her voice was suddenly unsteady. "After. I don't want anything from you in our divorce. The baby and I will be leaving New York."

"You can't be serious."

"Poppy Alexander lives in Los Angeles now. She offered me a job a while back. I told her no. Now I'm going to say yes."

"No."

"Try and stop me. Just try." He could hear the ragged gasp of her breath. "You called my dad a monster. You're the real monster, Darius. Because you know what it was like to have your father die alone. That was the reason for all your vengeance and rage, wasn't it? That was the big reason you wouldn't let me see my dad. Well, you know what? My dad nearly died alone, too. Because of you."

The pang of fear became sharper, piercing down his spine. He licked his lips. "Letty—"

"Stay away from us," she said in a low voice. "I never want to see you again. Better that our son has no father at all than a heartless one like you."

The line went dead. He stared down at the phone in his hand.

Numb with shock, Darius raised his head. He looked blankly around his office, still decorated with his wife's sweet touches. A photo of them on their Greek honeymoon. A sonogram picture of their baby. He stared in bewilderment at the bright blue jeweler's bag on his desk. The push present for his wife, the emerald earrings once owned by a queen that he'd bought to express his appreciation and joy.

Above him, he could hear the rain falling heavily against the roof. Loud. Like a child's rattle.

And felt totally alone.

He'd known this would happen. Known if he ever lowered his guard and let himself care, he would get kicked in the teeth. Teeth? He felt like his guts had just been ripped out. For a second, he felt only that physical pain, like the flash of lightning before thunder.

Then the emotional impact reached his heart, and he had to lean one hand on his desk to keep his balance. The pain he felt then was almost more than he could bear.

Standing in his office, in the place he'd been happily whistling a lullaby just moments before, anguish and rage rushed through him. Throwing out his arm, he savagely knocked the jewelry bag to the ground.

Suddenly, he could almost understand why Howard Spencer had turned criminal when he'd lost his wife. Because Darius suddenly wanted to set fire to everything in his life, to burn it all down.

Slowly, as if he'd gained fifty years, he walked out of his office.

"Everything all right, sir?" Mildred Harrison said serenely from her desk. "Are you headed to the hospital for Mrs. Kyrillos?"

Mrs. Kyrillos. He almost laughed at the name. She'd never been his wife, not really. How could she, when she'd seen through him from the start?

You always said a man could be measured by his money.

He looked slowly around the bustling office loft, with its exposed brick walls, its high ceilings, the open spaces full of employees busily working on computers or taking their breaks at the foosball table. He said softly, "No."

His executive assistant frowned. "Sir?"

"I don't want it anymore." Darius looked at her. "Take the company. You can have it. I'm done."

And he left without looking back.

He spent the afternoon in one of Manhattan's old dive bars, trying to get drunk. He could have called Santiago Velazquez or Kassius Black, but they weren't exactly the kind of friends who shared confidences and feelings. Darius had only really done that with Letty. He told himself Scotch would keep him company now.

It didn't.

Finally he gave up. He was alone. He would always be alone. Time to accept it.

Dropped off by the taxi, Darius came home late that night to his dark penthouse. All the bright lights of Manhattan sparkled through the floor-to-ceiling windows. He saw nothing but darkness and shadows.

And three expensive suitcases left in his foyer. Suitcases Letty had packed for him when she'd taken his measure, found him completely lacking and tossed him out of their family home.

You think you can buy your way through life. That's what you do, isn't it? Buy things.

Slowly, Darius looked around the stark, impersonal penthouse at the sparse, expensive furniture. Everything was black and white. He'd bought this place two years ago, as a trophy to show how far he'd come from the poverty-stricken village boy he'd once been. A trophy to prove to himself that Letitia Spencer had made a fatal error the day she'd decided he wasn't good enough to marry.

This penthouse was not his home.

His home was Fairholme.

Darius closed his eyes, thinking of the windswept oceanfront manor with its wide windows over the Great South Bay and the Atlantic beyond. The roses, fields and beach. The sun-drenched meadow where he'd taught Letty to dance. Where he'd first learned to love.

Letty.

He opened his eyes with a slow intake of breath.

Letty was his home.

Even during their brief marriage, he'd experienced happiness he'd never known before. The comfort and love of having a wife who put him first, who waited for him every night, who kissed him with such passion. Who slept warm and willing beside him every night in bed.

More than that. She'd reminded him who he'd once been.

You didn't realize it was never your money I wanted. It was you, Darius. My dream of you. The amazing boy you were. The man I actually thought you still were, deep down inside.

Numbly, he looked out the two-story-high windows that overlooked the twinkling lights of the city.

Letty was always determined to protect those she loved.

Now she was trying to protect their child from him. Just as he'd once tried to protect Letty from her father.

You called my dad a monster. You're the real monster.

He leaned his forehead against the cold window glass.

Howard Spencer had been a good man once. He'd been a good employer to Darius's father and kind to everyone, including the scared eleven-year-old boy newly arrived from Greece. Then he'd changed after he'd lost his beloved wife.

What was Darius's excuse?

He took a deep breath, looking out bleakly into the night. Why had he been so determined to wreak vengeance on her father? So determined that he hadn't even cared how badly it might hurt Letty as collateral damage?

He should have told her the truth from the start.

He should have taken her in his arms. He should have fallen to his knees. He should have told her he was sorry, and that he'd do whatever it took to make it right.

Why hadn't he?

What the hell was wrong with him?

Darius had convinced himself he was justified for his actions, because he blamed Howard Spencer for his father's early, unhappy death.

Letty was right. He was a liar. And he'd lied to himself worst of all.

The truth was, deep in his heart, there had always been only one person Darius truly blamed for his father's death, and it had been too painful for him to face till now.

Himself.

He closed his eyes as a memory that he'd pushed away for over a decade pummeled him. But today, he could no longer resist the waves of guilt and shame as he remembered.

Eugenios had called Darius in the middle of the day.

"I've lost everything, son." His Greek father, usually so distant and gruff, had sounded lost, bewildered. "I just got a certified letter. It says all my life savings—everything I invested with Mr. Spencer—it's all gone."

Darius had been busy working in his first rented office, a windowless Manhattan basement. He'd only gotten three hours of sleep the night before. It was the first time the two men had talked in months, since Letty had dumped him and caused Eugenios to be fired and tossed from Fairholme. Just hearing his voice that day had reminded Darius of everything he was trying so hard to forget. A lifetime of resentment had exploded.

"I guess that pays you back for all your loyalty to Spencer, huh, Dad? All those years when you put him first, even over your own family."

Darius had been so young, so self-righteous. It made him feel sick now to remember it.

"That was my job." His father's voice had trembled. "I wanted to make sure I never lost a job again. Never felt again like I did that awful day we found you on the doorstep…"

The awful day they found him? Darius's hurt and anger blocked out the rest of his father's words as Eugenios continued feebly, "I had no money. No job. I couldn't let my family starve. You don't know what that does to a man, to have nothing…"

It was the most his father had ever spoken to him. And Darius's cold reply had haunted him ever since.

"So you had nothing then, huh, Dad? Well, guess what? You have nothing now. You ignored me my whole childhood for nothing. You have nothing. You *are* nothing."

He'd hung up the phone.

An hour later, his father had quietly died of a heart attack in his Queens apartment, sinking to his kitchen floor, where he was found later by a neighbor.

Darius's hands tightened to fists against the window.

His father had never been demonstrative. In Darius's

childhood, there had been no hugs and very little praise. Even the attention of criticism was rare.

But Darius and his grandmother hadn't starved. Eugenios had provided for them. He'd taught his work ethic by example. He'd worked hard, trying to give his son a better life.

And after all his years of stoically supporting them, after he'd lost his job and money, Darius had scorned him.

Remembering it now, he felt agonizing shame.

He hadn't wanted to remember the last words he'd spoken to his proud Greek father. So instead he'd sought vengeance on Howard Spencer, carefully blaming him alone.

Darius had thought if he never loved anyone, he'd never feel pain; and if he was rich, he'd be happy.

Look at me now, he thought bitterly, surveying the elegant penthouse. Surrounded by money. And never more alone.

He missed Letty.

Craved her desperately.

He loved her.

Darius looked up in shock.

He'd never stopped loving her.

All these years, he'd tried to pretend he didn't. Tried to control her, to possess her, to pretend he didn't care. He'd hidden his love away like a coward, afraid of the pain and shame of possible loss, while Letty let her love shine for all the world to see.

He'd thought Letty weak? He took a shuddering breath. She was the strongest person he knew. She'd offered him loyalty, kindness, self-sacrifice. She'd offered him every bit of her heart and soul. And in return, he'd offered her money.

Darius clawed back his hair. She was right. He'd tried to buy her. But money didn't make the man.

Love did.

Darius loved her. He was completely, wildly in love with

Letty. He wanted to be her husband. To live with her. To raise their baby. To be happy. To be home.

His eyes narrowed.

But how? How could he show her he had more to offer? How could he convince her to forgive him?

Forgiveness. His lips twisted with the bitter irony. The very thing he'd refused to give her all these months, he would now be begging for...

But for her, he'd do anything. He set his jaw. With the same total focus he'd built his empire, he would win back his wife.

Over the next month, he tried everything.

He respected her demand that he stay away from her, even after his friend Velazquez sent him a link to a birth announcement, and he saw his son had been safely born, weighing seven pounds and fourteen ounces. Both mother and baby were doing well.

Darius had jumped up, overwhelmed with the need to go see them in the hospital, to hold them in his arms.

But he knew bursting into her room against her express wishes would have only made things worse, not better. So he restrained himself, though it took all his self-control. He cleaned out a flower shop and sent all the flowers and toys and gifts to her maternity suite at the hospital. Anonymously.

Then he'd waited hopefully.

He'd found out later that she'd immediately forwarded all the flowers, toys and gifts straight to the sick children's ward.

Well played, he'd thought with a sigh. But he wasn't done. He'd contacted Mildred and she'd sent him via courier the jewelry bag he'd left in his office. He'd sent it to Fairholme, again anonymously.

A few days later he received a thank-you card from Mrs. Pollifax, stating that the earrings had been sold and the money donated to the housekeeper's favorite charity, an animal shelter on Long Island.

He'd ground his teeth, but doggedly kept trying. Over the next week, he sent gifts addressed to Letty. He sent a card congratulating her on the baby. On Thanksgiving, he even had ten pies from her favorite bakery delivered to her at Fairholme.

Pies she immediately forwarded to a homeless shelter.

As the rain of November changed to the snows of December, Darius's confidence started to wane. Once, in a moment of weakness, he drove by Fairholme late at night, past the closed gate.

But she was right. He couldn't even see the house.

After the pie incident, Darius gave up sending gifts. When she continued to refuse his calls, he stopped those, too. He kept writing heartfelt letters, and for a few weeks, he was hopeful, until they were all returned at once, unopened.

His baby son was now four weeks old. The thought made him sick with grief. Darius hadn't seen him. Hadn't held him. He didn't even know his name.

His wife wanted to divorce him. His son didn't have a father. Darius felt like a failure.

In the past, he would have taken his sense of grief and powerlessness and hired the most vicious, shark-infested law firm in Manhattan to punish her, to file for full custody.

But he didn't want that.

He wanted her.

He wanted his family back.

Finally, as Christmas approached, he knew he was out of ideas. He had only one card left to play. But when he went to see his lawyer, the man's jaw dropped.

"If you do this, Mr. Kyrillos, in my opinion you're a fool."

He was right. Darius was a fool. Because this was his last desperate hope.

But was he brave enough to actually go through with it? Could he jump off that cliff, and take a gamble that would either win him back the woman he loved, or cost him literally everything?

The afternoon of Christmas Eve Darius got the package from his lawyer. He was holding it in his hands, pacing his penthouse apartment like a trapped animal when his phone rang. Lifting it from his pocket, he saw the number from Fairholme.

His heart started thudding frantically. He snatched it up so fast he almost dropped it before he placed it against his ear. "Letty?"

But it wasn't his wife. Instead, the voice on the line belonged to the last person he'd ever imagined would call him.

CHAPTER ELEVEN

"IT'S YOUR VERY first Christmas," Letty crooned to her tiny baby, walking him through Fairholme's great hall. She was already dressed for Christmas Eve dinner in a long scarlet velvet dress and soft kid leather bootees. She'd dressed her newborn son in an adorable little Santa outfit.

She'd asked Mrs. Pollifax to make all her father's holiday favorites, ham, plum pudding, potatoes, in hopes of tempting him to eat more than his usual scant bites. They'd even brought the dining table into the great hall, beside the big stone fireplace, so they could have dinner beneath the enormous Christmas tree.

Letty wanted this Christmas to be perfect. Because she knew it would be her father's last. The doctor had said yesterday that Howard's body was failing rapidly. It would likely be only days now.

Her heart twisted with grief. Her only comfort was that she'd tried her best to make his last few weeks special.

A lump rose in Letty's throat as she looked up at the two-story-high tree, decorated with sparkling lights and a mix of ornaments, old and new. Some of them Letty had treasured since childhood. And now they were back here, where they belonged. Funny to think she had Darius to thank for that. If he hadn't found her in Brooklyn and stopped her from taking that desperate bus ride out of the city, the ornaments would have been long lost to a junk dealer or the landfill.

Without him, she wouldn't be here now. Her father couldn't have come to Fairholme for his last Christmas, nor would her baby be here for his first one. It was because of Darius.

She missed him. No matter how much she denied it. No matter how she tried not to.

Every time some thoughtful gift had arrived at the house, she'd pictured how her father had looked in the hospital, so pale and alone. She'd remembered how Darius had taken her love for granted, and selfishly lied. She'd told herself she was done loving someone who could never love her back.

But as the gifts tapered off, and the phone calls stopped, and the letters stopped arriving in the mail, she hadn't felt triumphant. At all.

"I hate him," she said aloud. "I never want to see him again." She wasn't sure she sounded convincing, even to her own ears. So turning to her son, she held out one of the homemade ornaments. "Look!"

"Gah," the baby replied, waving his little hands unsteadily.

"You're so smart!" She let him feel the soft fabric of the dove against his cheek, then put it back on the tree before he tried to eat it. "Your grandma Constance made that," she said softly. "I just wish she could have met you."

Her six-week-old baby smiled back, Letty would swear he did, even though her father continued to rather annoyingly claim it was only gas. Letty knew her own baby, didn't she?

Even though Darius didn't.

The thought caused an unpleasant jolt. She'd thought she was doing the right thing to exclude him. She couldn't allow such a heartless man near her baby. Even if he *was* the father.

But Darius hadn't even laid eyes on their baby, or held him, or heard the sweet gurgle of his voice or his angry cry when he wasn't fed fast enough. Darius had already missed so much. Six weeks of sleepless nights, of exhaustion and confusion.

But also six weeks of getting to know this brand-new little person. From the moment her son had been placed in her arms at the hospital, Letty had felt her heart expand in a way she'd never known before.

Darius didn't know that feeling. He didn't know his son at all. Because of her actions.

Two weeks ago, her baby had been irritable and sleepless at midnight, so she'd wrapped him in a warm blanket and put him in the stroller to walk him up and down the long driveway, behind the gate. Then she'd seen a dark sports car driving slowly by.

Darius! She'd practically run to the gate, panting as she pushed the stroller ahead of her. But by the time she reached the gate, the car was long gone. For long moments she stared through the bars of the gate, looking bleakly down the dark, empty road, hearing only the waves crashing down on the shore. And she'd realized for the first time how empty the house felt without him, even with her father and her baby and all the household staff. She missed him.

No. I don't, she told herself desperately. And if she hadn't filed for divorce yet or hired an attorney, that was only because she just hadn't had the time. Taking care of a newborn, caring for her father and decorating for Christmas would be enough to keep anyone busy, wouldn't it?

Letty's lips twisted downward. She'd said things that would never be forgiven. She'd made her choice clear. She'd used his every olive branch as a stick to stab him with.

That car probably hadn't even been his. He'd probably moved on entirely, and if she ever heard from him again, it would be only via his lawyer, demanding custody. She stiffened at the thought.

Carrying her baby up to the nursery, she fed him, rocking him for nearly an hour in the glider until he slept and she was nearly asleep herself. She smiled down at his sweet little face. His cheeks were already growing chubby. Tucking him gently in his crib for his late afternoon nap, she turned on the baby monitor and crept out of the darkened nursery.

She closed the door softly behind her. Light from the leaded glass windows reflected against the glossy hardwood floors and oak paneling of the second-floor hallway, resting with a soft haze on an old framed family photo on the wall. She looked at her own chubby face when she'd been just a toddler with two parents beaming behind her.

Trying to ignore the ache in her throat, Letty started to turn toward the stairs. Then she heard low male voices coming from down the hall.

Her father's bedroom was the nicest and biggest, the room he'd once shared with her mother, with a view of the sea. He rarely got up from his bed anymore, except when Letty managed to cajole him into his wheelchair and take him down in the elevator for a stroll around the winter garden, or to sit in a comfortable spot near the fire, beneath the Christmas tree, as the baby lay nearby.

But the male voice Letty heard talking to her father didn't sound like Paul, his nurse. Who was it? Frowning, she drew closer.

"Yes," she heard her father say, his voice a little slurred. "Always a good kid."

"I can't believe you're saying that, after everything."

Hearing the visitor's voice, low and clear, Letty's knees went weak outside her father's door. What was Darius doing here? How had he gotten into Fairholme?

"You weren't so bad. Just prickly, like your father. Eugenios was the best employee I ever had. We used to talk about you. He loved you."

"He had a funny way of showing it." Her husband's voice wasn't bitter, just matter-of-fact.

Howard gave a laugh that ended in a wheeze. "In our generation, fathers showed love differently."

"Yet Letty always knew you loved her."

"I didn't grow up with your father's fears." Howard paused. "From the age of fifteen, he was your grandmother's sole support. When you came along, he lost any chance of a job in Greece."

"I know."

"His greatest fear was of not providing for you." Coughing a laugh, Howard added, "Maybe if I'd been a little more careful about that myself, I wouldn't have left my daughter destitute while I spent years in prison. It's only because of you that we're back home now. That's why I called. I'm grateful."

Darius's voice was suddenly urgent. "Then convince Letty to stay."

"Stay? Where would she go?"

"She says as soon as you're dead, she's leaving New York."

Howard gave a low laugh. "That sounds like her. Foolish as her old man. Can't see the love right in front of her eyes, has to flee her own happiness because she's afraid. Actually, now that I think about it, she sounds like you."

Letty's heart was pounding as she leaned against the oak-paneled wall beside the open door, holding absolutely still as she listened intently.

Silence. Then Darius said in a voice so low she almost couldn't hear, "I'm sorry I blamed you for my father's death all these years. The truth is, the person I really hated was myself. I said something terrible to my dad right before he died. I'll never forgive myself."

"Whatever it was," Howard said simply, "your father forgave you long ago. He knew you loved him. Just as he loved you. He was proud of you, Darius. And seeing that you were brave enough to come here today, I am, too."

Her father was proud of the man who'd treated her so

badly, who'd lied to her? Letty sucked in her breath with an astonished little squeak.

There was a pause.

"Letty," her father said drily, "I know you're there. Come in."

Her heart was in her throat. She wanted to flee but knew she'd only look foolish and cowardly. Lifting her chin, she went into her father's room.

His bedroom was full of light from the bay window. Her father was stretched out beneath the blankets, propped up by pillows, his nightstand covered with pill bottles. His gaunt face smiled up at her weakly, his eyes glowing with love.

Then, with a deep breath, Letty looked at the man standing beside the bed.

Tall and broad-shouldered and alive, Darius seemed to radiate power. For a moment, her eyes devoured his image. He was dressed simply in a dark shirt, dark jeans. His hands lifted, then fell to his sides as he looked at her, as if he had to physically restrain himself from touching her. But his dark eyes seared her. Their heartbreak and yearning cut her to the bone.

Her body reacted involuntarily, stumbling back as her heart pounded with emotion. Fury. Regret. Longing...

"What are you doing here?" she whispered.

"He's here to meet his son," her father said.

She whirled on her father, feeling betrayed. "Dad!"

"And I want him to stay for Christmas Eve dinner," he continued calmly.

She stared at him in shock. "No!"

Her father gave her a weakened version of his old charming smile. "Surely you wouldn't refuse your dying father his last Christmas wish?"

No. Of course she couldn't. She ground her teeth. "He kept me from you for two months!"

Her father stared her down. "Only a little longer than you've kept him from his son."

"I would like to meet him," Darius said quietly. "But if you don't want me around after that, I won't stay."

Trembling, she tossed her head defiantly. "Did he tell you the baby's name?"

"No."

"It's Howard." She lifted her chin, folding her arms. "Howard Eugenios Spencer."

To her shock, Darius didn't scowl or bluster. He didn't even flinch. He just looked at her with that same strange glow of longing in his eyes.

"That's not the name I would have chosen." Triumph surged through her as she waited for him to be sarcastic and show his true colors in front of her father. Instead, he just said quietly, "His last name should be Kyrillos."

Darius was upset only about the surname? Not about the fact that she'd named their precious baby son after her father—his hated enemy?

"Aren't you furious?" she said, dropping her arms in bewilderment.

His lips curved as he looked down at her father, then slowly shook his head. "Not as much as I used to be."

Darius came toward her. It took all Letty's willpower not to step back from him as he towered over her. It wasn't him she was afraid of, but herself. Her whole body was trembling with her own longing. Her need. She missed him.

But she couldn't. She'd made her choice! She wouldn't be married to a man who didn't love her!

"Please let me see my son," he said humbly. He bowed his head, as if waiting for her verdict.

"Let him," her father said.

Looking between the two men, she knew she was outnumbered. She snapped, "Fine."

Turning on her heel, she walked out. She didn't look

back to see if Darius was following her. Her hands were trembling.

All these weeks when she'd pushed him away, she'd pictured him as angry, arrogant, heartless. It was why she hadn't been tempted to open his letters—why would she, when she knew he'd only be yelling at her?

She'd never once imagined Darius looking at her the way he did now, with such heartbreaking need. But it wasn't just desire. He had an expression in his eyes that she hadn't seen since—

No! She wasn't going to let her own longing talk her into seeing things in his eyes that weren't there, things that didn't exist.

Pressing a finger to her lips, she quietly pushed open the nursery door and crept into the shadowy room, motioning for him to follow. Darius came in behind her.

Then, as they both stood over the crib, Letty made the mistake of looking at her husband when he saw their son for the very first time.

Darius's dark eyes turned fierce, almost bewildered with love when he looked at their sleeping baby. Tenderly, he reached out in the semidarkness and stroked his dark downy head as he slept.

"My son," he whispered. "My sweet boy."

A lump rose in her throat so huge it almost choked her. And she suddenly knew that Darius wasn't the only one who'd been heartless.

What had she done?

Blinded by furious grief at his lie about her father, Letty had actually kept Darius from his own firstborn son. *For six weeks.*

Anguish and regret rushed through her in a torrent of pain. Even if Darius could never love her, she had no doubt that he loved their baby. Especially as she watched him now, gently stroking their baby's small back through his

Santa onesie as the sleeping child gave a soft snuffle in the shadowy room.

She'd had no right to steal his child away.

"I'm sorry," she choked out. He looked up.

"You're sorry?"

Unable to speak for misery, she nodded.

Reaching out in the shadowy nursery, beneath the hazy colors of the goose girl fresco, Darius put his hand gently on Letty's shoulder, and she shuddered beneath his touch.

"Letty...there's something you should know."

Their eyes locked, and she saw something in his black eyes that made the world tremble beneath her feet.

Panic rushed through her heart. Seeing Darius make peace with her father, seeing him look so lovingly at their baby, had cracked open her soul and everything she hadn't wanted to feel had rushed in.

She'd painted him so badly in her mind. She'd called him a monster. And yes, he never should have lied about her father.

But when she'd said horrible things and threatened to take his child permanently away, he hadn't hired some awful lawyer to fight her. He'd done what she asked, and stayed away. Obviously at great emotional cost.

Now, she saw his sensual lips part, heard his hoarse intake of breath and knew whatever he was about to say would change her life forever. He was going to tell her he was done with her. She'd won. He'd given up. Now he wanted to talk like reasonable adults about sharing custody of their son.

She'd destroyed their marriage with her anger and pride. She'd told herself she'd rather be alone than married to a man who didn't love her. Now she suddenly couldn't bear to hear him speak the words that would end it...

"No," she choked out.

Turning, she fled the nursery. She ran down the hall, down the stairs, her heart pounding, gasping for breath.

She heard him coming down after her. "Letty!"

She didn't stop. Pushing off the stairs, she ran outside, into the snow.

Her mother's rose garden was barren in winter, nothing but thorny vines and dead leaves covered in a blanket of white. Letty's soft black boots stumbled forward, her long red dress dragging behind, scarlet against the snow.

But he swiftly caught her, roughly pushing her wrists against the outside wall of the greenhouse with its flash of exotic greenery behind the steamy glass. She struggled, but he wouldn't let go.

She felt his heat. His power. She felt the strength of her own longing for this man, whom she continued to love in the face of despair.

"Let me go," she cried.

"Forgive me," Darius choked out. He lowered his head against hers. She heard the heavy gasp of his breath. "You were right, Letty. About everything. I'm so sorry."

Her lips parted. She looked up at him in shock.

"*You're* sorry?" she whispered. "I kept you from our baby."

"You were right to kick me out of your life." He cupped her face in both his hands. "I blamed you and your father for so much. I blamed everyone but the person really at fault. Myself."

"Darius—"

"No." He held up his hand. "Let me say this. I don't know if I'll get another chance."

All around them in the silent white garden, soft snow began to fall from the lowering gray clouds. Letty's heart was suddenly in her throat. Now he was going to tell her that they were better off apart...

"You're right, Letty," he said in a low voice. "I did try

to buy you. I thought money was all I had to offer anyone. I thought I could selfishly claim your love, while being cowardly enough to protect my own heart. But I failed." He gave a low laugh. "The truth is, I failed long ago."

His dark eyes had a suspicious gleam. Surely Darius Kyrillos, the ruthless Greek billionaire, couldn't have tears in his eyes? No. It must be the cold winter wind, whipping against his skin.

"I loved you, Letty. It terrified me. My whole life, all I've ever known of love is loss. Losing you all those years ago almost destroyed me. I never wanted to feel like that again. So I buried my soul in ice. Then when I saw you again, when I first took you to my bed, everything changed. Against my will, the ice cracked. But even then I was afraid." Taking a deep breath, he lifted his eyes to hers. "I'm not afraid anymore."

"You're not?" she whispered, her heart falling.

With a little smile, he shook his head. He took her hand in his larger one. "Now I know the truth is that love never ends. Not real love. The love your father has for you and my father had for me. The love your parents had for each other." His hand tightened over hers as he said softly, "And even if you divorce me, Letty, even if you never want to see me again after tonight, I can still love you. And it won't bring me pain, but joy, because of everything you've brought to my life. You saved me. Made me feel again. Taught me to love again. Gave me a son." Stroking her cheek, he whispered, "No matter what happens, I will always be grateful. And love you."

His hand was warm over hers. With him so close, she didn't even feel the snow. Trembling, she whispered, "Darius…what are you saying?"

His jaw tightened. "If you still want to divorce me, you won't need a lawyer." He reached into his shirt pocket, where a single page was folded in quarters. "Here."

Opening the paper, she looked down at it numbly. She tried to read it, but the words jumbled together. "What's this?"

"Everything," he said quietly. "Fairholme. The jets. My stocks, bonds, bank accounts. It's all been transferred to your name. Everything I possess."

She gasped, then shook her head. "But you know money doesn't mean anything to me!"

"Yes, I know that." He looked at her. "But you know what it means to me."

Letty's eyes went wide.

Because she did know what Darius's fortune meant to him. It meant ten years of twenty-hour workdays and sleeping in basements. It meant working till he collapsed, day after day, with no time to relax or see friends. No time to even *have* friends. It meant borrowing money that he knew he'd have to pay back, even if his business failed. It meant taking terrifying risks and praying they would somehow pay off.

Those dreams had been fulfilled. Through work and will and luck, a poverty-stricken boy whose mother had abandoned him as a baby had built a multibillion-dollar empire.

This was what she now held in her hand.

"But I'm not just offering you my fortune, Letty," he said quietly. "I'm offering everything. My whole life. Everything I've been. Everything I am." Lifting her hand, he pressed it against his rough cheek and whispered, "I offer you my heart."

Letty realized she was crying.

"I love you, Letitia Spencer Kyrillos," he said hoarsely. "I know I've lost your love, your trust. But I'll do everything I can to regain your devotion. Even if it takes me a hundred years, I'll never…"

"Stop." Violently, she pushed the paper against his chest. When he wouldn't take it, it fell to the snow.

"Letty," he choked out, his dark eyes filled with misery.

"I don't want it." She lifted her hand to his scratchy cheek, rough and unshaven. Reaching her other arm around his shoulders, she whispered, "I just want you, Darius."

The joy that lit up his dark eyes was brighter than the sun.

"I don't deserve you."

"I'm not exactly perfect myself."

He immediately began protesting that she was, in fact, perfect in every way.

"It doesn't matter." Smiling, she reached up on her toes to kiss him, whispering, "We can just love each other, flaws and all."

Holding her tight, he kissed her passionately against the greenhouse, with the hot wet jungle behind the glass, as they embraced in the snow swept bare garden. They kissed each other in a private vow that would endure all the future days of sunshine and snow, good times and bad, all the laughter and anger and pleasure and forgiveness until death.

Their love was meant to be. It was fate. *Moira.*

They clung to each other until he broke apart with a guilty laugh.

"Ah, Letty, I'll never be perfect, that's for sure," Darius murmured, smiling down at her through his tears. "But there's one thing you should know…" Cupping her cheek, lightly drawing away the cold wet tendrils of her hair that had stuck to her skin, he whispered, "For you, I intend to spend the rest of my life trying."

Spring came early to Fairholme.

Darius had a bounce in his step as he came into the house that afternoon with a bouquet of flowers. He'd had to work on a Saturday because it was crunch time developing the new website. But he was hoping the flowers would make her forgive the fact that he'd missed their new Saturday morning family tradition of waffles and bacon.

Darius had started that tradition himself, in the weeks he'd taken to focus only on Letty and their beloved son, whom they'd nicknamed Howie. After that, encouraged by Letty, he'd sheepishly called Mildred and apologized, then asked if there was any way she could try to reassemble his team at the office.

"The office is still in fine fettle," she'd replied crisply. "I've been running everything just as you requested. I knew whatever you were going through you'd soon come to your senses. I haven't worked for you all these years for nothing."

He choked out a laugh, then said with real gratitude, "What would I do without you?"

"You'll find out next summer," she'd said firmly, "when you send my husband and me on a four-week first-class cruise through Asia. It's already booked."

Darius grinned to himself, remembering. He was grateful to Mildred. Grateful to all the people around him, his employees and most of all his family, who saw through all his flaws but were somehow willing to put up with him anyway.

Money didn't make the man. He knew that now. What made a man was what he did with his life. With his time. With his heart.

His father-in-law had died in January, surrounded by family, with a smile on his drawn face. Right before he died, his eyes suddenly glowed with joy as he breathed, "Oh. There you are..."

"He saw my mother before he died," Letty told Darius afterward, her beautiful face sparkling with tears. "How can I even be sad, when I know they're together?"

Darius wasn't so sure, but who was he to say? Love could work miracles. He was living proof of that.

Now he looked around his home with deep contentment. The oak floors gleamed and fresh-cut flowers from the greenhouse filled all the vases.

Fairholme was about to be invaded by more of the Kyrillos family. He'd sent his private plane to Heraklios, and tomorrow, Theia Ioanna, along with a few cousins, would arrive for a monthlong visit. His great-aunt's desire to meet her great-great-nephew had finally overcome her fear of flying.

He relished the thought of having his extended family here. Heaven knew Fairholme had plenty of room.

Love was everywhere. Love was everything. His son was only five months old, but he'd already collected toys from all the people who loved him around the globe. His wife did that, he thought. With her great heart, she brought everyone together with her kindness and loyalty. She was the center of Darius's world.

"Letty!" he called, holding the flowers tightly.

"She's outside, Mr. Kyrillos," the housekeeper called from the kitchen. "The weather's so fine, she and the baby went for a picnic in the meadow."

Dropping his computer bag, he went outside, past the garden, where even though the air was cool beneath the sunshine, tulips and daffodils were starting to bloom. He walked the path through the softly waving grass until he reached the meadow where he'd first taught his wife to dance. Where she'd first taught him to dream.

He stopped.

The sky was a vivid blue, the meadow the rich gold-green of spring, and in the distance, he could see the ocean. He saw Letty's beautiful face, alight with joy, as she sang their five-month-old baby a song in Greek, swinging him gently in her arms as he giggled and shrieked with happiness. Behind them on the hillside, a blanket was covered with a picnic basket, teething toys and that well-worn book

about the bunny rabbit. But now, as always, Letty was dancing. Letty was singing.

Letty was love.

Darius stared at them, and for a moment the image
caught at his heart, as he wondered what he'd ever done to
deserve such happiness.

Then, quickening his steps, he raced to join them.

* * * * *

THE GREEK'S
NINE-MONTH
REDEMPTION

MAISEY YATES

To Jackie, Megan and Nicole
for listening to me say,
'This is weird. I'm not doing it right.
I don't think this is good enough!'
every time I work on a book, and
helping me through it. Every time.

CHAPTER ONE

SOMETIMES ELLE ST. JAMES imagined taking a pen and stabbing it straight through Apollo Savas's chest. Not to kill him of course. He didn't have a heart so the wound would hardly be fatal. Just to hurt him.

Still, other times she fantasized about crossing the boardroom, wrenching free the knot on his tie and tearing the front of his shirt open, scraping her fingernails down his heated skin and feeling all those hard muscles beneath her hands. Finally. After nine long years of resisting him, resisting the heat that roared through her body every time their eyes met.

That one was *way* more disturbing than the stabbing thing.

It was also far too frequent.

They were sitting in a crowded meeting and she should be paying attention. But all she could think about was what she would do to him if she had five minutes with him, alone, behind a locked door.

It would either be violent or naked.

He was talking about budgets and cuts. And she hated those words. It would mean scaling down her team again. As had been the story of the past twelve months, ever since he'd bought her out from her father's holding company. A company that had since sunk into bankruptcy.

Just another moment in a long line of Apollo undermining her. Finally, her father had been forced to give her responsibility. Since his stepson had finally proven to be a viper in the nest, so to speak.

She'd been installed as CEO. Then Apollo had come down like a hammer.

It was his fault. At least in part. And nothing would convince her otherwise.

She had a plan. A plan he seemed intent on thwarting at every turn. She knew she could rescue Matte without all of these sweeping staff changes, but he wouldn't give her a chance.

Because—just as he'd always done—he was making it his mission to undermine her. To prove he was better even now.

But that didn't stop her eyes from following his hands as he gestured broadly, from wondering what those hands might feel like on her skin.

She could write what she knew about sex on a napkin. The sad thing was, it would be two words.

Apollo Savas.

He'd been sex to her from the moment she'd understood what the word *sex* meant. From the moment she'd understood why men and women were different, and why it was such a wonderful thing.

The dark-haired, dark-eyed son of the woman her father had married when Elle was fourteen. He had been fascinating. So different from her. Rough around the edges, a product of his upbringing in a class of society Elle herself had had no contact with. His mother had been a maid prior to her marriage to Elle's father. The culture shock had been intense. And very, very interesting.

Of course, since then he'd grown into a dark-hearted

man who'd betrayed her family and put her under his boot heel.

Still, she wanted him.

The Big Bad Wolf of the business world, huffing and puffing and blowing your dreams down.

"Don't you agree, Ms. St. James?"

She looked up, her eyes locking with Apollo's, her heart thudding a dull rhythm. The last thing she needed was to admit she'd missed what he was saying. She would rather admit to having fantasies of killing him than the alternative.

"You'll have to repeat the question, Mr. Savas. My attention span for repetition isn't infinite. This is the same song you've been singing for months, and it isn't any more effective or logical than it was last time."

He stood, his movements liquid silk. She could see from the black glitter in his eyes that she was going to pay for her words. The thought sent a shiver down her spine. Fear mingled with unaccountable lust.

"I am sorry you find me boring. I shall endeavor to make myself more interesting. You see, I was speaking of the fact that for a company to be successful it must be sleek. Well oiled. Each cog functioning at top capacity. Extraneous cogs are unnecessary. Sluggish cogs are unnecessary. I was attempting to be delicate with my metaphor." He began to walk down the length of the boardroom table, the postures of each person he moved behind straightening as he did. "Perhaps I would have held your attention a bit better if I would have simply said that if I identify a portion of your company functioning at less than optimum capacity I will start slashing and burning your employees like they were dry brush."

Her entire face felt like it was on fire, her heart pounding harder now. She clenched her shaking hands into fists. "Everyone in this company—"

"I'm sure your speech is about to be inspiring and truly emotional, but since this is not a feel-good underdog sports movie, you should perhaps save your breath, Ms. St. James. You can say what you will, but I have seen the numbers. Conviction doesn't equal profits. I will be reviewing everything closely and making cuts at my discretion. With that, I think the meeting is adjourned. Ms. St. James has a very low tolerance for my droning, I hear. If it is the same for the rest of you, you should be pleased to be sent on your way."

The collective surge of bodies making their way out of the room reminded Elle of a herd of wildebeests fleeing a lion.

A big, bored lion who wanted nothing more than to scare them by flashing his teeth. He wasn't going to give chase. Not now.

No, now his focus had turned to her.

"You are in rare form today, Elle."

"I am in exactly the appropriate form, *Apollo*," she said, reverting to the use of his first name.

They were *family*, after all.

Not that she'd ever seen him as a brother. A sexual fantasy she didn't want. Her biggest competitor. Her darkest enemy. He was all of those things, but not a brother.

"I own your company," he said. "I own *you*." Oh, dammit all, why did those words make her…ache? "You never seem to show me the proper amount of fear."

"Real leaders don't rule with an iron fist," she hissed. "They understand that intimidation isn't the way to gain respect."

She shouldn't be talking back to him, but she could never control her tongue around him. They'd known each other for too long. Had spent too many years in the same household.

And she had spent too many years tearing strips off him when she'd felt like she had the upper hand. When she was the blood daughter of her father, the one who held a rightful place in their upstate mansion.

Things changed. Oh, how things changed.

"Says the woman who is no longer in a true position of leadership." He smiled. Showing his teeth.

She wouldn't scatter. She would not. She was not a wildebeest.

"Oh, but I am. As long as Matte is an independently operating entity beneath your large corporate umbrella, I am here to run it as best as I can. I am here to stand in the gap for my employees and give you the information black-and-white printouts can't."

"You're being ridiculous. Everything is electronic now. I'm not wasting resources on printouts."

He turned and started to walk out of the office. "You know what I mean. A flat, two-dimensional report reducing everything to statistics and cold numbers is hardly the be-all and end-all."

"That's where you're wrong," he said, taking long strides down the hall.

Elle had to take two steps to his one, her high heels clicking loudly on the marble floor as she hurried after him. "I am not wrong. It doesn't offer the whole picture. You can't possibly know how the company is really functioning. How each worker impacts the creative process. Matte isn't just a magazine. It's a line of cosmetics, a fashion brand. We have books and—"

"Yes," he said, stepping into an elevator, "thank you, I am very familiar with how my assets function."

"Then you should be aware of the fact that I have strategies in place that require all of the manpower I possess. Initiatives that take time to launch but will catapult this brand into worldwide recognition."

"Yes. So you said last time we met. And, unlike you, I don't drift off in meetings."

She growled and charged into the elevator after him. "I did not drift off."

He pushed the button to the lobby and the doors slid closed. Then he turned that dark, unsettling focus onto her. The air around them seemed to shrink, rendering the already crowded space impossibly tight. "No. I don't believe you did, Elle," he said, his voice as silken as his movements. "You were looking at me with a great deal of intensity. Too much to be on another planet entirely. What was it you were thinking about exactly?"

"Driving a pen through your chest," she said, smiling.

Because she would be damned if she'd say, *Tearing your clothes off and seeing if you're as good in reality as you are in my dreams.*

Even though she felt like that reality was written all over her face, across her skin in the red stain of a blush.

He offered her a wry smile. "You know I can't be killed like that. You have to cut my head off and bury it in a separate location to my body."

"I'll let the hit men know." She turned and smiled at him again, and he offered one in return.

The doors slid open, revealing the rather vacant bottom floor. Matte shared its offices with many other businesses, and with penthouses on the top floor. At this hour of the day not many people were coming and going.

"Where is it you're staying, Apollo?" she asked. "A crypt somewhere in Midtown?"

"The one just next to yours, Elle," he said, his tone light. "After you."

He extended his hand, waiting for her to step out of the elevator. She swept past him, moving through the lobby and going through the revolving doors. She stepped on to the busy Manhattan sidewalk, put her sunglasses on and stood there, tapping her foot.

Apollo emerged a moment later, straightening his suit jacket and standing across from her for a moment.

"Care to continue shouting at me while I walk?" he asked.

"I'm not shouting at you. I'm calmly explaining to you why you're wrong in your methods of handling my company."

He turned away from her, walking down the crowded street, his broad back filling her vision.

"Apollo!" Okay, she was shouting now. "We are not through with our meeting."

"I think we adjourned it."

"The general meeting," she said, upping her pace. "But *we* are not done."

"I'm just here," he said, gesturing to an old boutique hotel only two buildings down from the Matte offices. "Since I'm in town primarily to deal with Matte I thought I should stay close."

"Congratulations. How sensible."

"I have my moments. Judging by the fact that I'm a billionaire who successfully staged a takeover of your father's company, I've had several moments, actually."

"If you were as clever as you think you are you would listen to my plans for Matte. The answer isn't to reduce us down to nothing. You have to let me try and expand it, otherwise we really will die."

"You're assuming I'm trying to save you, dear Elle. Perhaps I just want to pull the plug."

"You… You…" She was sputtering now. She never sputtered. She blamed him.

"Villain. Scoundrel. I answer to any of those really."

"You have always been a competitive son of a bitch, but this is above and beyond."

"You're assuming this is a competition."

"What else could it be? You're ungrateful. For everything my father gave you. And for the fact that he didn't give you everything."

He chuckled, a dark, humorless sound. "Oh, you mean that he didn't give me his corporation, or Matte, in the first place? Why do you think he installed you, Elle? Your competence? No. He gave you the position to keep a foothold once I bought him out."

The words landed hard, hollowing out her midsection. Leaving nothing but a crater behind.

Like you didn't suspect that already.

She had. Of course she had. But the fact he knew it meant it was obvious. Possibly to everyone.

The doorman opened the golden door for them and Apollo paused to tip him before continuing on. Elle opened her purse and produced her own dollar, handing it to the man before going in after Apollo.

She was not allowing him to do her tipping for her.

"I am in the penthouse suite. It's very nice."

"Why am I not surprised that I just got out of a meeting where you were discussing tightening belts for my company, and yet you're staying in the penthouse suite."

He pushed the button for the elevator and the doors slid open. She followed in after, starting to feel slightly out of breath.

"I am not in need of money, *agape*, if that's why you thought I was mentioning cuts."

Agape. She hated that. He'd started using that on her

sometime when she was in high school. Just to make her angry. And some small part of her grabbed hold of it every time, holding it near. *Love.*

Oh, what a ridiculous, stupid…

She really hated her hormones.

"Why else would you mention cuts?" she asked, keeping her tone sweet.

The doors slid shut and she had the uncomfortable feeling of being trapped in a closed-in space again.

"Because *you* need the money. Matte needs the money. In a digital world your print publication is lagging and while you have certainly come up with innovative ways to compete, you haven't leveled out yet."

"But if you have enough—"

He chuckled. "I don't run a charity. I run a business. My corporation turns profits. That's what it does. I make money hand over fist, and I'm comfortable admitting that. I'm proud of it. But that won't continue if I don't refine my assets. Refining is a hot and painful process. It takes fire. And people being fired."

"Ha-ha. You're far too funny for your own good."

He frowned. "Was that funny? It wasn't meant to be."

The elevator stopped and the doors opened on a narrow hallway. Apollo stepped out and walked down a few doors, pausing to open it. "Come in," he said.

She very much had the feeling of being a small, vulnerable creature invited into the lair of a predator.

You are not a wildebeest. You are just as scary as he is. You are a lioness.

She stepped over the threshold and into the room. It was lovely, he was right. Ornate moldings and trim framing the space, the windows looking out over Central Park.

There was a large seating area with a bar, and off to

the left an open door that she could see led to a bedroom with a very large, dramatic bed.

She imagined, as tall as he was, he took up most of the mattress. That thought made her picture him—long, tanned limbs sprawled out on the bed. Would he look more relaxed in sleep? Would he seem less…lethal out of that custom-fit black suit that conformed to every line, every muscle in his body?

He closed the door behind her with a finality that made her jump.

"My team is the best there is," she said. "They have some of the most creative minds in this—or any—industry. You have to admit the fact that the Matte Guidebooks have been hugely successful. And the makeup guide actually helped to increase sales of the cosmetics. It was specific to the brand and that—"

"Again you are telling me things I already know. I didn't get to this position in life without paying attention. I understand that your team is important to you. But if I don't do what must be done, if I don't make the hard cuts, none of you will have a job."

"But I—"

"You seem to be under the impression that this is a democracy, Elle. Be assured, absolutely, that this is a dictatorship. I am not negotiating with you. And it is only by my good graces that your pretty ass remains in the CEO's office."

Heat and fury washed over Elle in a fiery baptism. "And here I thought it was because I'm good at my job."

"You are," he said, taking a step toward her. "But there are a great many people who would be good at your job. People who didn't get handed their position from their daddy."

"Oh, that's hilarious, Apollo. As if you didn't get a leg

up from my father, you Judas." She took a step toward him, rage propelling her now. "My father treated you like one of his own children. He put you through school."

"And I excelled on my own."

"Then you stabbed him in the back."

"I bought him out for much more than thirty pieces of silver, little girl. Perhaps what really hurts is the fact that you were betrayed by your father, not by me. He put you in this position knowing you would fail."

She gritted her teeth, doing her best to shake off his words. To not allow them to take hold. All of this reached down deep. To old wounds. To the way she'd felt she couldn't measure up to Apollo, the son her father had always wanted. To her own fears of being eternally inadequate. And he knew it.

She would not let him win so easily. "He trusted you. When you offered to help he didn't imagine you dismantling everything."

Apollo lifted one broad shoulder. "He made a mistake in trusting me."

"Clearly. You would betray not only the man who set you on the path to success, but your own mother."

"She's fine. Your father is hardly financially ruined. She continues to enjoy her status as his wife. And again, Elle, need I remind you your father sold Matte, and some of his other holdings, to me of his own free will."

"You had him in a position where he couldn't say no."

Apollo took another step toward her. He was so close now that she could see his eyes weren't completely black. She could see a faint ring of gold that faded to copper, then to deep brown. Could see the dark stubble beginning to grow in at his jawline.

Could smell the scent of his aftershave and skin.

"Interesting you put it like that. If dire financial straits take away choice you could argue my mother had little choice in marrying your father in the first place."

"That's ridiculous," Elle said. "She wanted to."

"Did she?"

"Of course."

"A cleaning lady offered the chance to live in luxury after years barely making it in the US? After years of homeless poverty in Greece?"

"That isn't… It has nothing to do with this."

"Maybe," he said. "Or maybe the point is that you can always say no, Elle." He leaned in. "Always."

She could barely breathe, her head swimming, her entire body on high alert. She was almost certain she had no blood in her veins, not anymore. It was molten lava now, heating her from her core.

She remembered so clearly feeling this way every time he brushed past her in the halls of the family estate. Every time she caught sight of him at the pool—his lean, muscular body so fascinating to the girl she'd been.

Only once had they ever come so close to each other. Only one other time had she ever thought he might feel the same forbidden desire that she'd felt from the moment she'd set eyes on him.

Apollo is going to be your new stepbrother.

Everything in her had rebelled at that, immediately. Because she had seen him and wanted him in a way she knew would be wrong once their parents were married. So she had distanced him. She had been…well, sometimes she'd been terrible. But it had been for her own survival.

It was even worse now. He was still her stepbrother. But now, any affection she'd ever felt for him had been twisted by his betrayal. She should have stopped obsessing about him a long time ago.

But she hadn't. She couldn't. She was a slave to this, to him. Always.

She hated it. She hated *him*.

And she had spent nine years resisting him. Embracing the anger, the annoyance and everything else she could possibly use as a barrier between her desire for him and her actions.

Giving in would be a failure. In terms of her self-control. In terms of her relationship with her father. What would he think if he knew she wanted Apollo? What sort of scandal would erupt if the media knew she was helplessly attracted to her stepbrother?

So she had denied it. Pushed it down deep. But she had been aware of it every time she saw him. Every glance. Every accidental brush of his hand against hers. Every time she went to bed at night, hot and aching for something she knew only he could give her.

But he had bought out her father's company. He was gunning for Matte. Her father had installed her as CEO to keep some connection to the company—just as Apollo had said. And she'd failed spectacularly.

She could feel everything slipping out of her grasp. The company. Her control. Everything.

And she'd never tasted him. Never had him. This man who was destroying her whole life. Who commanded her fantasies and called out the deepest, darkest desire from deep inside of her.

For what? For appearances. To triumph.

There would be no triumph here. She was losing. Utterly. Epically.

Why not have this? Why not have him?

It was all going to burn to the ground. She might as well go up in flames with it.

She could see his pulse throbbing at the base of his

throat. If only she had a pen in her hand. It would be so easy from this position to stab him clean through with it. But she didn't.

So instead, she reached up and grabbed hold of the knot in his tie, and wrenched it free.

CHAPTER TWO

APOLLO SAVAS DIDN'T entertain daydreams. He was a man of practicality and action. When he wanted something, he didn't sit around fantasizing about it, he took it.

That was the only reason he knew that it was no hallucination that Elle St. James, his stepsister and mortal enemy, was currently stripping his clothes off, her eyes bright, glittering with rage and desire.

He had resisted her, this, for years. Resisted her. Out of deference to the man he considered a father. Out of respect for all he'd been given.

But all of it had proven to be false, had proven to be a lie. And still he had roped Elle off. Had kept her separate—in many ways—from his plans for revenge.

And David St. James had known he would. Because whether she knew it or not, he had always protected Elle. She had always mattered.

But things had changed. And now she was tugging at his tie. And he was tired of restraint.

He reached out and wrapped his fingers around her wrist, holding her hands still. "What the hell are you doing?" he asked, his voice a growl.

She looked up at him, her green eyes round, those soft, sassy pink lips shaped into a perfect O. "I…" Color flooded her face.

"If you were thinking you were going to take my shirt off, either stop now and walk out that door, or keep going and understand that I will have you flat on your back and screaming my name in a very *different* way before you can protest."

Her color deepened, her eyes growing even wider. He thought she would run. Because Elle was a *good* girl, by the standards of her father. Though, she was stone-cold, aloof and fancied herself far above him.

It had made him want to destroy that facade from the first. He hadn't. Because he knew that she was innocent. Knew that she was nothing more than a cosseted rich girl who would be completely out of her depth with a man like him. A man who had grown up on the streets in Athens, who had learned the hard truths about life early on. About loss. About the true nature of people.

He had known that if he ever touched her it would violate the trust he had built with her father.

But if she was going to touch him now, if she was going to remove that barrier that had always loomed between them, then he wasn't going to put a stop to it.

Apollo Savas was a man who took what he wanted.

With one exception.

Elle.

He had wanted her from the moment she'd transformed from a girl to a woman. A haughty, rude woman who walked by him with her nose in the air half the time. Perversely, it had always made him want to have her even more.

She thought his hands were dirty. Thought he was beneath her. It made him want to put his filthy hands all over her. Made him want to pull her right down with him.

His biggest betrayal had never been buying St. James

Corp's most valuable assets and breaking them off piece by piece.

No, his biggest betrayal had started long before he'd discovered David St. James's true nature. It had begun long before he'd discovered the dark secrets surrounding just why he and his mother had been brought into the St. James home.

His first betrayal had been in the way he'd looked at Elle.

But everything was shot to hell now anyway. Every allegiance broken with his "family." Why not this, too? Why not slaughter the last sacred cow?

He had destroyed everything else. He might as well destroy this, too. And he would relish it.

Her hand was still frozen, holding on to his tie. Then, her eyes took on a determined glitter, her lips curling into a snarl as she yanked hard on the silken fabric, pulling it free from its knot.

He growled, grabbing ahold of that sleek high ponytail that had been taunting him from the moment he had walked into the boardroom today. He wrapped his fingers around her coppery hair and pulled hard, tilting her head backward. Her nostrils flared slightly, her lips parting.

They held their positions for a moment, staring at each other, clearly waiting to see what the next move was.

He had waited too long. He was not waiting another moment.

He would have her now. Strip away every prim and proper layer. Punish her with his kiss as he should have done that day she'd dared him at the pool. The only time the anger between them had given way and revealed the layer beneath.

Of course, she had acted as though nothing had happened after. And so had he.

But he would make sure this time she would not be able to act unscathed after he was through with her.

He wrapped his arm around her slender waist, drawing her up against his body as he backed them both toward the wall. It stopped their progress ruthlessly, her shoulder blades pressed firmly against the hard surface. He bent his head, kissing her neck, his teeth scraping her skin.

The sound that escaped her lips was raw and desperate, her hands clutching his shoulders, her fingernails digging into his skin through the fabric of his suit jacket. Then she slid her palms down flat, grabbing hold of the front of his shirt and tugging hard, sending buttons flying as she wrenched it open. She pushed his jacket from his shoulders, grabbing hold of his shirt and shoving it down, too. He unbuttoned the cuffs, helping her and her progress, and untucking it from his pants and throwing it down onto the floor.

She looked completely shocked, and wholly satisfied by her actions as she regarded his body. Then she pressed her palms to his chest and slid her fingers down to his stomach, her fingernails scraping him lightly as she did. She grabbed hold of his belt, making quick work of that, as well.

"Greedy," he said, taking hold of her wrists and drawing her arms up over her head, holding her there with one hand as he set to work on the buttons of her silk blouse with the other.

She fought against him, the color in her cheeks deepening, her breasts rising and falling with the shallow gasps of her breath. He chuckled when her shirt fell open, revealing an insubstantial red lace bra and he imagined she thought it made her seem daring.

She arched her back, thrusting her breasts into greater prominence. He tightened his hold on her, pressing her hands more firmly against the wall. "You don't get to set the terms," he said. "Not in the boardroom, not in the bedroom. I am in charge in *all* things."

"Always a competition with you, isn't it?" she asked.

"Oh, *agape*, it has never been a competition. How can it be when I always win?"

For the first time, he saw a slight flicker of doubt in her eyes. But it was quickly replaced by a challenge. "So insecure that you have to exert your dominance in such a cliché fashion? You are exactly the same here as you are in the office."

He leaned in, his lips a whisper away from hers. "You're going to pay for that."

"I hope this isn't an empty threat, Apollo," she said, the words throaty, enticing. "You seem to be full of those."

He closed the distance between them, closing his teeth around her bottom lip and biting her. She gasped and he pulled away. The flush in her cheeks had spread to her neck, had down to the full swell of her breasts. She might be angry, but she was aroused, too.

"One thing you need to learn, *agape*, is that my threats are never empty. It's simply that the consequences might be delayed in coming."

She looked down, then back up. "I do hope the coming isn't terribly delayed today."

Those words, coming from Elle's lips, seemed shocking. From any other woman it might have been commonplace dirty talk. Not even all that dirty when it came down to it. But from Elle? It had the desired effect.

He was so hard he thought he was going to burst through the zipper on his pants. His heart was raging, his hand shaking as he undid the last button on her blouse and pulled it from her shoulders.

He couldn't remember the last time a woman had affected him in such a way. If one ever had. But then, he had never been in a situation quite like this. His partner had never looked at him with lust and rage burning from her eyes all at the same time. She'd never looked quite like she wanted to strangle him and have her way with him in the same moment.

And, he had never been with Elle.

"I didn't realize you were a dirty talker, Elle." He scraped the edge of her ear with his teeth. "If you had been negotiating this way all along you might have been a lot more successful."

"You're a bastard," she bit out, turning her head and tracing the line of his jaw with the edge of her tongue. "A complete and utter—"

"And you want me," he said, releasing his hold on her and drawing his face back, pressing the tip of his nose against hers and meeting her fierce gaze. "So what does that say about you?"

"Oh, I know that all of this is the final nail in the coffin of my decency." She grabbed the end of his belt buckle and yanked it through the loops, then set about working on the closure of his slacks.

"Go out with style, I say." He slid his hands down her slender waist, to the full curve of her hip, and down farther, gripping the hem of her skirt and shoving it up roughly over her hips. No surprise, her panties were the same red lace as the bra.

Not that he was complaining.

"I took you for a white cotton kind of girl," he said. "Who knew that you had so many secrets?"

"You're never going to know my secrets, Apollo," she said.

"So venomous," he said, his lips touching hers now as he spoke the words. "And yet, you're dying to have me."

She put her hand between them, pressing her palm against his hardened arousal. "Same goes."

"I'm tired of talking."

And then, he crushed his mouth to hers, claiming the kiss he should have taken years ago.

Elle had no idea what she was thinking. She wasn't thinking. She was feeling. Feeling everything. Rage, need, arousal like she had never known existed.

She would like to be confused about this. About how this could happen. About how she could be doing this with a man she hated so very much. But lust and anger had always been twisted up together where Apollo was concerned. Well, maybe not always. But in the past few years. And that was when her desire for him had turned from a girlish crush into a woman's need.

She wasn't sixteen anymore. She knew what men and women did in the dark. She didn't need her own hands-on experience to be aware.

But somewhere, during all of that, Apollo had gone from being someone she trusted and admired—a member of the St. James family—to their bitterest enemy. And somewhere, as that change had taken place, her desire for him had changed, as well.

And now it was this strange, twisted thing that she couldn't begin to untangle. And there was no other man who made her feel anything near what he made her feel.

It didn't matter that it was sick. It didn't matter that it was wrong. What Apollo made her feel was pure adrenaline. Pure excitement. Even if it wasn't all good.

He made every other man she had ever gone out with seem like a bland, beige substitute.

That was why this was happening. Really, it was why it *needed* to happen. When this was over, she would finally be cleansed.

Her need for him would go down in one fiery ball of pleasure and rage. And when she looked at him she would feel...nothing.

Oh, she wanted that more than anything.

She kissed him back with all of that. All of the anger, all of the lust. His tongue swept against hers, his hold on her hips firm, blunt fingertips digging into her skin. Then he shifted his position, putting his hands between her thighs, stroking his fingers over the thin lace that concealed her desire for him.

She gasped, everything inside of her shaking. She had never been this intimate with a man before, and yet she wasn't afraid. She wasn't experiencing any virginal nerves. She was more than ready for this. It was the combination of years of fantasies. An explosion of... Well, of everything.

His fingers slipped beneath the fabric, gliding through her slick flesh. If he'd had any doubt about how much she wanted him, he couldn't doubt it now.

"Yes," he said, the word a growl.

The way he said that, the absolute, incontrovertible evidence of how much he wanted her in return radiated through her. Spurred her on. She grabbed hold of the waistband of his pants and underwear, tugging them down his lean hips. There was no place for tenderness here, no place for hesitation.

She reached between their bodies, wrapping her hand around his hardened length. It was her turn to shudder, her turn to growl. She had never touched a man like this. She had no idea he would be so very big. She was nearly weak with wanting him. This was why she felt hollow. This was what she needed to be filled.

He slipped one finger inside of her and her breath hissed through her teeth, the unfamiliar invasion shocking and immensely pleasurable.

She took hold of his arms, clinging onto his rock hard biceps as he continued to tease her with a preview of what she really wanted.

She looked up at him, her heart hammering in her chest. He was beautiful. There was no question. And she wanted him. She wanted him more than she'd ever wanted anything in her entire life. It was important that she know it was him. As if it could be anyone else. As if anyone else could ever make her feel this way. This exhilarating mixture of destructive anger and impossible need.

She kissed the corner of his mouth, tracing his lower lip with the tip of her tongue. He moved his hand from between her thighs, lifting it, grabbed hold of her bra and pulled it down, revealing her breasts to his gaze. He lowered his head, drawing one tightened nipple deep into his mouth.

Sensation shot through her like an arrow, hitting her low and deep. A low, harsh sound escaped her lips and she let her head fall back as she laced her fingers through his hair, tugging hard as he continued to pleasure her.

"Please," she whimpered, "please."

He moved away from her, then bent down grabbing ahold of his pants, pulling his wallet out of the pocket before producing a condom.

Her breath gathered up in her chest like a ball and held there, a heavy weight she couldn't move. She could only watch him. Look her fill at his beautiful, masculine form. He was even more beautiful than she had imagined.

He returned to her, his bare chest pressing against

hers as he flattened her against the wall. She looked at his face, his gorgeous, thoroughly despised, utterly beloved face.

She grabbed hold of him, bracketing his face with her hands and tugging him forward, kissing him hard and deep. He put his hand back between her thighs, this time pushing two fingers into her, stretching her gently. She was so ready for him. Beyond ready.

"Do it," she said against his lips.

He moved his hand, gripping hold of her hips, sliding one hand down her thigh and lifting her leg, opening her to him. He tested her slick entrance with the blunt head of his arousal. Then he thrust deep inside.

The pain was sharp, swift. Tears stung her eyes, and she shut them quickly because she didn't want him to see. She didn't want him to know. She had felt powerful a few moments ago, but this made her feel a lot more vulnerable. Vulnerable was not what she wanted. She wanted pleasure, she wanted her desire satisfied. She wanted to rid herself of this toxic, intense feeling she had for him once and for all.

But, she hadn't anticipated this. Not just the pain, but the feeling that she was breaking apart. The feeling that they were connected, closer than she had ever been with anyone.

Somehow, she had imagined the fact that she hated him might buffer against any other emotions.

But it didn't.

So she kept her eyes closed.

If Apollo noticed, he didn't comment. Instead, he fused his mouth to hers and flexed his hips, a flash of pleasure slowly overtaking the pain.

Slowly, all the discomfort began to recede. And she just wanted him. There was nothing else. There was no ugly history between them, there was no anger, no hatred. Nothing but an intense, burning need to be satisfied. She clung to him, to his shoulders, her lips pressed to his as he established a steady rhythm, pushing them both toward the brink.

He thrust hard and she let out a hoarse cry, raking her nails down his back. He growled, his rhythm faltering. And then, there was no more steadiness. There was nothing but a frantic race to the finish, his movements rough, intense. And she took it all. Every last bit.

He gripped her chin, tilting her face up, forcing her to meet his gaze. And she did. She didn't look away, unwilling to flinch in the face of his challenge. She shivered, tension growing more and more intense in the pit of her stomach, her internal muscles gripping him tight as her orgasm began to build.

He slowed his movement suddenly, withdrawing slowly before pushing back in hard. White light broke out behind her eyes, release exploding inside her like a bomb, a wild burst of aftershocks radiating through her, leaving her shaken, weak. And then he followed, his entire body going stiff as he shuddered out his own release.

He lowered his head, his teeth digging into her collarbone. She let her head fall back against the wall, a sigh escaping her lips.

They stood like that, for just a moment. And then slowly, reality started to creep in.

She had done it. She had given her virginity to Apollo Savas.

And suddenly, horrifically, all she wanted to do was curl into a ball and cry.

She pushed at his shoulders, and he withdrew. She began to look around at the ground, realizing that only her shirt had been entirely discarded. Everything else was simply askew. That was—frankly—slightly more embarrassing than the alternative. She hadn't even waited for him to undress her completely.

He would think she was completely desperate. He would think that she had been yearning after him for years.

It was the truth. Which was what made it particularly horrifying.

She straightened her clothes, tucking her skirt back into place, fixing her bra as she pulled her blouse back on. He said nothing. He simply watched her with those dark, unreadable eyes.

She smoothed her hand over her hair.

"Too little too late, *agape*," he said.

She froze, her hand still poised over her undoubtedly wrecked ponytail. "Excellent," she said, her voice so brittle she thought it might break.

"I am leaving in the morning."

"All right," she said, the words hollow, echoing in her head.

"I will not see you. I will not make any decisions about staffing changes until the next time we meet."

"I'm relieved to hear that."

"I'll be back in town on the twentieth. Make sure you keep your calendar clear."

With that, she could see she was dismissed. With no more fanfare than if they had simply finished a meeting.

And he was still naked. It was absurd. But she wasn't going to highlight the absurdity. Not when she simply wanted to get out of there as quickly as possible so she could have a complete and total meltdown.

"Then I'll see you on the twentieth."

She collected her purse, drawing the strap over her

shoulder and clinging tightly to it. To keep herself from…
Slapping him? Kissing him again? She wasn't certain.

"Excellent. Should I call you a cab?"

"No," she said, checking her watch. "It's… It's only
three o'clock. I have to go back to work."

She had to go back to work like this. With the impression of his hands still on her skin, her cheeks burning
from the brush of his whiskers against them.

"So it is."

"Goodbye," she said.

He tilted his head. "Goodbye, Elle."

CHAPTER THREE

ANTICIPATING THE TWENTIETH had become something of a reverse Christmas countdown. In that she hoped it would never come. It might have been nice to have an Apollo Advent calendar though. So that every time she thought about him arriving she could eat a piece of chocolate to try to deal with her stress.

When she arrived at the office that morning it was with an industrial-strength coffee, a bottle of ibuprofen and a very fake smile plastered to her lips.

Because Apollo was due to arrive—who knew when— to start handing down edicts from his high horse. And she was going to have to face him for the first time since they had... Since that day in his hotel room.

The very thought of that made humiliating color wash through her face. That day had been an aberration. Something that would never be repeated. She had, after all, gone the first twenty-six years of her life without sex. She should be able to happily get through another few weeks. Then, maybe when everything settled down, when Apollo stopped coming in and poking at her employees, reshuffling her business and in general upending her life, she would contend with the fact that she needed to find a relationship.

That was the problem. She had simply waited too long.

She had allowed Apollo and her desire for him to become so large in her mind that nothing else could compare.

Well, now she'd had sex. With Apollo, as it happened. So, question answered, tension diffused.

She was a modern woman. She wasn't going to allow him to make her feel ashamed about her actions. Even though, considering he was a relic of a man, he would attempt to make her feel ashamed. If for no other reason than he would be actively attempting to assert his dominance over her.

Well, no thank you. She was…indomitable.

She gritted her teeth, opening the door to her office and nearly dropping the coffee in her hand when she saw who was already sitting at *her* desk. "That's my seat," she said, the words coming out crisp and harsh.

"It's lovely to see you too, *agape*."

"Now, Apollo," she said, deciding that she was going to be the one to address the elephant in the room before he got a chance. It was there, she might as well be the one to name it. "Don't try to sweet-talk me just because we had sex."

"I wouldn't dream of it," he said, his lips tipping up into a smile.

"No, I suppose you wouldn't. That would require you to know how to sweet-talk."

"You rocked my world. I saw God. You have ruined me for all other women."

She gritted her teeth against the strange, ridiculous warmth that flooded her when he spoke. He was being a jerk, and she knew it. So his words shouldn't make her… anything. She took a fortifying breath.

"What you said," she said, waving her hand. "Sub- stitute 'men' for 'women', 'slightly disorganized' for 'rocked', and 'God' for… I don't know, maybe 'a really good cheesecake'? Not exactly divine, but adequate."

"You are in *typical* form today."

"I try for consistency, Apollo. It's part of my charm."

"I have rarely seen evidence of your charm. Your *charms* perhaps, but I'm not really speaking of your personality."

"Right, well, for some reason things have been especially difficult between us lately, haven't they? Though, I imagine not as difficult as things have been between you and my father. Have you spoken to him since you rammed that knife into his back?"

"Oh, yes. Of course we have."

"You're sick. How could you do that to your own—"

"He is not my own anything. I am not your blood, *agape*. And a good thing to or what happened between us would be off-limits. Both in the past and in the future."

She gritted her teeth, trying not to blush. She was definitely playing at being slightly more blasé and experienced than she was. But he hadn't called her on it yet. So she was going to carry on. "I would rather run my new Jimmy Choos through the shredder, thanks."

"Is that what the kids are calling it these days? I admit, that doesn't sound very sexy."

"It wasn't meant to be."

"Right. Tell me, Elle, how is my mother?" he asked.

Elle arched a brow. "How long has it been since you've spoken to Mariam?"

He shrugged. "Months? She doesn't approve of my betrayal any more than you or your father do."

"And yet you don't feel any guilt over it?"

"I have my reasons," he said, his tone so cold and hard it could cut glass.

"I'm sure you do, but none of them are compelling

enough for me or my family. I don't care what your reasons are. And your mother is well," she said. "I just talked to her last night."

It had been difficult to talk to her stepmother when memories of what had passed between her and Apollo had lingered so persistently. She had felt…guilty and completely transparent. Thankfully, Mariam had her own topics to discuss and hadn't seemed to notice Elle's general silence.

"Well," she said, clearing her throat, "as charming as this little detour has been, let's get down to business."

He reached up, touching the knot on his tie. "Oh, you meant *actual* business."

"You're a pig."

"I'm wounded. Now, I've been going over projections for the quarter. You have to either increase profits soon or you need to start cutting expenses. I can guarantee one, but I can't guarantee the other." He stood, placing his hands on the desk. *Her* desk.

She tried to cling to her anger. Anger that would hopefully be much more powerful than the attraction that was still surging through her. What was her problem? She was supposed to be cured. She was supposed to have inoculated herself to all future Apollo encounters. Cure yourself from a snakebite with snake venom, and all that. But she didn't feel cured. She did not feel at all inoculated. In fact, she felt a little bit dizzy.

"Of course you can't," she said, the words coming out harsh. "No one can guarantee a profit increase. But trust me, if we keep on going in this new direction—"

"This isn't about trust. It's about the bottom line. I have a great deal more experience in business than you do, Elle."

Those words rankled. In part because they were true.

In part because they dug beneath the suit of armor she had worked so hard to put into place today. It hit the wound beneath it that twinged every day. That she was her father's second choice through and through. When she failed at this, she would prove that she never should have been here in the first place. That if her father had had his way he would have put someone else in her position. That if Apollo weren't too important for it, if Apollo hadn't turned against them, it would likely have been him.

You decided failure be damned, remember?

Yes. She had. But it was difficult to feel committed to that now.

"But I care about this company."

"As do I. It's a part of my bottom line, and there is nothing I care about more than my bottom line."

"Well, Matte is only part of your bottom line because you set out to acquire it when you saw that it was floundering. You knew what you were getting."

"And without my influence this company would probably already be six feet under. Like the rest of the holdings I bought from your father."

"You fired the final shot into them."

"A mercy killing," he said, his tone hard. "Don't oppose me, Elle. I am not doing this for my own amusement. If I succeed, you will succeed along with me. I am not the enemy that you set me up to be."

She didn't know what to say to that. Except, it was a disagreement they were not going to settle. Not without blood anyway. "Yes, but you said you were standing there ready to pull the plug, so let's be honest. You aren't a savior, either."

"I never claimed to be."

"Well, don't stand there and pretend that you aren't the villain."

"Oh, did you think that's what I was doing? You're wrong there. I know full well that I'm the villain here, *agape*. If I had a mustache I would twirl it. Alas. You will have to settle for the assurance that I know full well where I stand in this little play. However, we do not have to oppose each other. I know that my presence is sinister. However, there is nothing you can do to fight it. But understand I will save Matte if it's at all possible."

"You're here to announce cuts today, aren't you?"

"Surprisingly, no. But I did come to discuss something with you."

"What?" she asked, feeling suspicious.

"I would like for you to come to my European headquarters. To get a little bit of an idea for how things run, to attend to some meetings there, and to attend a certain number of charity events."

"What?"

"What I would like to do is help revitalize the image of Matte. I would like to bring you into the public eye. Have you as the public face, so to speak. With a little bit of help you could provide a facelift all on your own. And then, maybe we would be able to avoid cuts."

She hadn't expected this. She was, in fact, struck dumb by the fact that he was extending a hand out. That he was offering her a chance to not only save the company, but to do it in such a public way.

She had been prepared to be the one left standing in the ashes. A phoenix who was not poised to rise. She had been prepared to go down in flames, with her hands on Apollo's naked body.

And now…now he was changing things. Again.

"You just expect me to pick up and go to Europe with you?"

"Yes. And I don't exactly expect you to have a major issue with being asked to spend some time in Greece with me."

"Your headquarters are in Greece still? Are you the last remaining corporation in the country?"

"I am successful. Worldwide. It would be a poor thanks to my homeland to remove the jobs and revenue I provide simply because there's been some unrest."

"Please, don't tell me you have a heart. Only a moment ago you were telling me that your decisions were based on the bottom line."

"I *don't* have a heart. I simply have a strong liking for dolmas and ouzo."

"That I can believe."

He smiled, and for a moment, she felt like she was looking back at the boy he had been. The boy she had known all those years ago. The one who had captivated her from the first moment she had laid eyes on him.

The boy she had proceeded to snipe at and torture with flippant remarks every chance she got. Reminding him that he wasn't really a St. James. Because she'd been nothing more than a little girl with a crush and she'd handled it like they were on the playground.

But though things had never been easy between Apollo and her, he'd been very close with her father. But as close as Apollo and her father had once been, they were just as distant now.

And she had been thrown into the middle of that divide. Tossed into a storm she could never hope to weather. Between two alpha males locking horns. One defending his turf, the other intent on destroying it.

So take control. Do this.

"Well, I'm not going to complain about a free vacation," she said, trying to keep her tone light. She wasn't going to show her hand. Not to him. Wasn't going to let him see that this mattered to her. That she was going to use this—whatever it was to him—to gain a handle on things again.

To redeem herself.

"Oh, this isn't going to be a vacation," he said, rounding the desk and making his way toward the door. "We will go to Greece and work. Additionally, there is a charity event in Athens that we will attend together."

"As business associates," she said, "I assume."

She couldn't even imagine her father's reaction. If he had any idea that she and Apollo— He would be furious. Disgusted.

The idea of disappointing him like that…of losing him altogether, was something she couldn't fathom.

Her mother had left when she'd been a child. She could barely remember her. But she remembered the hole left behind, because it was still there.

She couldn't go through that again.

Apollo gave her a dismissive glance. "What else would we be? The entire idea is to strengthen the brand. Should there be any suspicion that the two of us had—"

"There's no need to keep bringing it up."

"You're the one who seems to persist in bringing it up."

Elle crossed her arms, shaking her head, her ponytail swinging back and forth. His eyes followed the motion.

"You should wear your hair down," he said.

She abruptly stopped shaking her head. "I didn't ask you for fashion advice."

"And yet, I'm giving it. Because you desperately need it." He looked at her, his expression critical. "Yes, you need a slightly younger look. One that isn't quite so... ironed."

"Well, my clothes are ironed. Would you have them look rumpled?"

"I would have you look slightly less like a matron."

She frowned. "I do not look matronly. I have a very classic sense of style. It's chic."

"You certainly know how to flatter your figure." He didn't bother to hide that he was looking. "But you need more than that to be the kind of brand that people remember."

"I'm not a...brand," she sputtered, "I'm a woman. Where are you going?" He had walked past her, heading for the door.

"I thought I might go and speak to some of the staff."

"No," she said, hurrying after him. "I do not wish to unleash you on them. I don't want you talking about how their jobs may be in jeopardy when you make final decisions."

"Their jobs may well not be in jeopardy if you don't fight me every step of the way. People like a public face. You can provide that. You can be strongly associated with the brand, and in effect, become a brand yourself. A young, professional woman. Brilliant, fashionable. You can be that woman."

She rolled her eyes. "That does not sound like—"

"It isn't a negotiation. Either you comply with my plan, or you are subject to Plan B, which is making sweeping cuts and doing my best to lift profit margins that way."

She made an exasperated sound, following him down the hall. "I wish you wouldn't keep walking away from me."

"I have places to be. I want to take a look at the different departments. Get a body count. So to speak."

"We are *talking*." She scampered after him. "Of course I will agree to go."

He pushed the button for the elevator. "I'm glad to hear that. I get the feeling sometimes you're just opposing me for the sake of it."

"And I get the feeling that you're an ass to me just because you enjoy it."

He chuckled and she stepped in just as the doors began to close. "Well, you are possibly correct in that assessment. Anyway, you spent a great many years being an ass to me simply because *you* enjoyed it."

She let out a harsh breath and watched the numbers on the elevator as it moved. Suddenly, she was very aware of the fact that she and Apollo were alone again. She looked at him, just a quick glance out of the corner of her eye. She tried to ignore the restless feeling between her thighs. Tried to ignore the restless feeling in her body.

After what seemed like an eternity, the doors opened again, and they were on the floor that housed the marketing department. He stepped out of the elevator and began to sweep his way through the space like a destructive wind. As he whipped by, heads turned, expressions went from relaxed to terrified.

"See that? Your mere presence lowers morale. I hope you're happy."

"I don't care about morale." He paused by one of the desks. "Hello," he said, clearly attempting to be charming. "My name is Apollo Savas. I'm the owner of this company. What is it you do?"

The girl, a blonde who could barely be twenty-five, blinked rather owlishly. She seemed to be struck dumb by his presence. Either by the fact that he was the owner of the company, or by the fact that he was just so damn good-looking. Truly, it was a problem. Elle felt a moment of sympathy for her.

"I'm on the marketing team for the makeup line," she said, looking a little bit thunderstruck.

"Have you been satisfied with the performance of those products?"

"Well," she said, shuffling the papers on her desk around, "we have seen an increase in revenue this past quarter. And our relationships with vendors—"

"How do you plan to continue the increase? What do you think attracts consumers to this product? Why should they buy this instead of say…any other brand of lipstick? I am a man, I know, but I'm not certain why one sort of cosmetic might be more attractive than another."

"I… I…"

"Enough," Elle said. "You do not need to prod at my staff."

He turned toward her, an amused expression on his face, and suddenly she felt like they were the only two people in the room. That little blonde might as well have evaporated into thin air.

There was no question, she was not remotely as immune to Apollo and she would like to be.

Apollo would question the purity of his motives if his motives were—in fact—ever pure. They weren't, so he was certain there was something self-serving and wretched behind them now. Even if he didn't know precisely what.

He had wanted to impress upon Elle the importance of her complying with his plan. When he had left her after… After the appalling lack of control that had occurred in his hotel room, he had formulated a plan to try to improve things for her company. A foolish thing, perhaps. He didn't know why he should care about the fate of her magazine. Beyond the fact that it was a potential profit machine for him.

Perhaps it was the fact that she had become collateral damage in a war he'd never intended to bring her into. But David had placed her in direct line of the firing squad.

Apollo wasn't a kind man. At least, no one ever accused him of being so. And he had never made it a goal to be seen that way. He had cared about very few people growing up, and it had turned out those he had cared about most had betrayed him long ago.

And so he had stolen his stepfather's empire, started dismantling it. But he had left Elle at Matte. God knew why. He'd known in the end he would destroy it, destroy her.

Perhaps it was because he knew what it was to be caught in the consequences of the sins of the father. Hers and his. Perhaps because he knew that—whether or not Elle had been kind to him when they were younger—she was innocent here.

But now…now it was as though a veil had been stripped away from his eyes. He would have to use her. There was no other choice. There was no preserving her. That much had been made clear when he'd taken her against the wall.

It had been symbolic in many ways of that protection being destroyed. That desire to keep her safe from himself being completely and utterly ripped away.

He could no longer ignore Elle. Could no longer dance around the fact that he would have to destroy her along with her father.

He would use her. And he would discard her.

It had nothing to do with his desire to strip her naked again. To watch her pale skin flush with pleasure once more. It had nothing at all to do with that, because he was not going to allow himself the indulgence.

Indulgence was unacceptable. But revenge? That was sweet.

"Perhaps you would like to give me a tour of the rest of the department, Elle?" he asked, ruthlessly cutting off his train of thought.

"Of course."

They moved away from where they had been standing, and she continued on down the role of desks. "Just don't *talk* to anyone," she said, her voice hushed.

"Why is it that you think you can tell me what to do when I am in my own company?"

"Because I am the boss," she said, her tone sounding slightly petulant. "That has to count for something *somewhere*."

"Sadly for you, I am your boss. Being boss of a lot of other people doesn't give you extra clout. I am the final word. So let it be written, et cetera."

She swept through the little space quickly. "There you have it. And now, I expect you want to be going."

"No," he said, crossing his arms across his chest. "I'll head back up to your office floor and set up for a few hours, get a few things done. I do like to familiarize myself with my acquisitions."

Elle looked livid. Her jaw set, her lips in a flat line. "Can't you do that in your hotel room?"

The mention of his hotel room brought back illicit memories. "I could. But I want to get a greater sense for how things are running here. It is in your best interest to keep me around. I might grow attached. I might yet see the importance of this team you keep talking about."

She said nothing, but her expression took on a rather long-suffering edge. They walked back through the office space and toward the elevators again. She pushed the button, then pushed it again when the elevator didn't immediately appear.

"If I didn't know better I would say you were in a hurry to escape my presence."

"I *am*," she said, flashing a smile. One he very much wanted to kiss right off her pretty face. But he was still calculating. When. Where. What. He wouldn't touch her until he made those decisions.

If he touched her at all.

"I do admire your honesty," he said, instead of kissing her.

"What is taking so long?" She scowled, hitting the button again. Then suddenly, the doors slid open.

"Tenth time's the charm," he said, stepping inside.

She gave him a withering glance before moving inside after him.

The doors slid shut and he had the impression that all the air had been sucked out of the space.

The tension between them was unlike anything he had ever known before. Likely because she was the only woman he had ever bothered to resist. He could remember well the first time he had noticed her as a woman, rather than a girl. Sometime after her seventeenth birthday, when all of her snubs and cutting comments had begun to arouse even as they enraged.

When they'd given way to fantasies of him showing her how base and beneath her he truly was.

His attraction, swift, sudden and abhorrent to him, had hit him low and fast in the gut, so quickly he had not had the chance to guard against it. He had not expected to have to guard against an attraction to his chilly younger stepsister.

He had nearly acted on it back then.

He could well remember the time he'd come home from university to see her getting out of the pool. Sleek curves barely concealed by a hot pink bikini that should have clashed terribly with her red hair, but rather was all the more enticing for how incongruous it was.

And he'd gone over to her, and she'd said something snotty, as she usually did. Then he'd grabbed hold of her arm, and pulled her to him. Her green eyes had gone wide, those pink lips parting gently. Begging to be kissed.

But he hadn't. He'd watched the water drops roll over her bare skin, over her breasts, had imagined lowering his head and slicking up the slow-rolling water. But he hadn't done that, either.

He'd waited. Waited until her eyes had darkened with desire. Until he'd seen her breath speed up, the pulse in her neck beating at a rapid rate. He had held her arm until he'd been sure he'd turned her on. Until he'd been sure the little ice princess was hot all over.

Then he'd let her go, and turned away, hard as iron and fantasizing about what he might have had.

And now... Well, now he'd had her, hadn't he? He had answered the question he'd never meant to ask.

He looked at her now, at the sleek ponytail that begged for him to grab hold of it, to wrap it around his hand. Her long, elegant neck. The soft curve of her pale lips. His stomach tightened. Clearly, his lust for her was not so easily dealt with via one quick screw up against the wall.

"I wish you wouldn't do that," she said, pressing the button that would take them to the floor that housed her office.

"Do what?"

"I wish you wouldn't stare at me."

"I'm trying to unlock the mysteries of your mind," he said. "Or rather, I'm attempting to remember what you look like underneath your clothes." He knew that taunting her was the wrong decision. Knew that it would only push them back to the place he was so desperate to stay away from.

You don't want to stay away. You want her naked and panting in your arms again.

"Stop it," she said.

"You're so desperate to forget what happened between us."

"Nobody likes to remember rock bottom, Apollo. I consider having sex with you my own personal walk through the valley of the shadow of death."

"I'm honored, I'm sure."

"Honored isn't what you're supposed to be." She arched one finely groomed brow, her lips twisted into a sneer. She was so self-righteous when she was just as guilty as he was. So sure she was above this attraction that burned between them when she was just as enslaved.

He wanted her. The angrier he got with her, the more he wanted her. Whatever this thing was, the sick, twisted desire that was exploding between them, he couldn't measure it or assign a number to account for it. He couldn't parse it the way he could a business acquisition. It wasn't the simple desire he felt for the sort of woman he usually picked up to spend a few hours of fun with. It was much, much darker.

It was forbidden. Something he had told himself he couldn't have.

Perhaps that was why it was coming to bite him in the ass now. He didn't typically practice restraint. Maybe by creating forbidden fruit, by placing it in the middle of his personal garden and telling himself he could not eat it, neither could he touch it, he had created temptation.

That made the most sense. Since Elle looked like original sin. A brilliant, shining apple he wanted to bite into.

And why shouldn't he? His reasoning for resisting her didn't matter now. He didn't want to honor her father. And he still wanted to kiss that puckered expression off her face. So why the hell not?

"You don't like me," he said, that darkness compelling him now. "And yet, you do want me."

"Come now, Apollo, don't tell me you like every single one of your bed partners. We both know that sex isn't love," she said, tilting her chin upward, a faint blush spreading across her cheekbones, adding a kind of dissonance to her bold words.

Elle was certainly playing the part of experienced woman. She had gone up in flames in his arms, an equal participant in the conflagration. And yet, it didn't all ring true. Didn't quite piece together in a way that made sense.

He wasn't sure he cared to analyze it. It wouldn't change his actions either way.

"Perhaps. But sex and hate don't typically go together," he said. "And you claim to hate me."

"I do," she said, green eyes flashing. "I hate you for what you've done to my father. To me."

"Not enough to leave the company."

"That would be abandoning it altogether. What he built. What he's trying to keep hold of, in spite of you. I won't do that."

"I do admire your dedication. Your loyalty."

"Why do you admire my loyalty? You don't possess any of your own."

"We admire the things in others we struggle with ourselves, do we not?" he asked.

"I wouldn't know. I certainly don't admire anything in you."

He chuckled, turning to face her, closing some of the distance between them. Her eyes widened and she backed against the wall. It reminded him a little bit too much of what had happened the last time they had been alone in an enclosed space together.

"I think there are a few things you admire about me," he said, moving in a little bit closer. Her eyes widened, her pupils expanding, the green in her eyes reduced to a thin ring. Her mouth dropped open, soft and round, and begging to be kissed. To be explored. "You most certainly admire what I can do to your body. I think we both know that."

"I *do* possess some restraint," she said, her voice trembling.

"Do you?" he asked, his voice sounding rough, ragged even to his own ears. "Perhaps we should test it."

He reached out and hit the stop button on the elevator, his stomach tightening, feeling as though a fist had closed around it.

He reached out and took hold of her arm, mimicking that day out by the pool.

"You want me," he said. "Admit it."

"I will not," she said, reaching out, shoving him. But then her hand lingered on his chest, her breasts rising and falling with her rapid breathing. She looked up at him, her eyes wide, terrified.

"You want me even now," he said.

And it felt imperative he make her admit it.

She tapped against his chest with her fingertips before slowly curling her fingers around the material of his shirt.

Then she pulled him to her, kissing his lips hard, deep.

He tasted anger, and a hint of shame on her tongue. And he knew just how the two mixed together, because he felt it, too.

She groaned, pushing away from him suddenly, but he wrapped his arm around the back of her head, holding her steady, working his fingers through her thick, red hair. "You want me," he growled, "don't deny it."

"Wanting isn't the same as having."

With his other hand, he opened the top button on her blouse. "It's the same for us."

"It doesn't have to be," she said, sounding desperate.

"I think it does," he said, his voice rough. He didn't know himself. Not at all.

She reached between them, pressing her palm over his hard length, stroking gently through the fabric of his dress pants.

"I dreamed about you," she said, her voice hushed, her words rushed. "About this."

"So did I," he said, placing his hand over hers and increasing the pressure of her touch. "Every night."

"Have you had another woman since you had me?" she asked, her tone fierce.

"No." He suddenly thought of her touching some other man like this. "Have you had another man?"

She shook her head, curling her fingers around his arousal. "No."

He growled, pulling her into his arms and kissing her, rage and relief burning through him. The very idea of another man putting his hands on Elle made him angry. He wanted her. It had been too long. Nine years. Nine long years lusting after Elle St. James, even as he hated her family. Even when he was overtaken by the desire to see their destruction, he wanted her. It was unacceptable.

He would burn it out. He would burn it out and then it would be over. Afterward, he could discard her if he wished, but this would finally end.

He stripped her clothes from her body as quickly as

possible, nearly tearing the delicate fabric of her blouse in his haste. Definitely tearing her panties.

She didn't protest. Instead, she made a sweet little sound of pleasure as he wrenched the lace fabric away from her skin, as he stroked his fingers over her wet flesh, so slick, so perfect. She wanted him. There was no denying it, no faking it.

He could feel the evidence for himself.

He stripped all of her clothes from her body this time, leaving her completely bare to his gaze. He had spent so many years fantasizing about what she might look like. The size of her breasts, the color of her nipples. That beautiful thatch of curls at the apex of her thighs.

Yes, he had woken up from a deep sleep many times thanks to a dream about Elle's naked body. He had been— for so long— consumed with the curiosity of what lay beneath her prim clothes.

Now, he didn't have to wonder. Now he knew. But he had a feeling she would still haunt his dreams.

No. Because you will have her until you are finished with her.

Yes, he would. Even if burning it out meant reducing them both to ash.

He stripped his suit jacked off and cast it onto the floor, spreading it as wide as he could. Then he swept her into his arms, and lay her down on the fabric.

He didn't have time to worry about anything. He was too needy. Too desperate. Two more things to add to her list of sins, because ever since he had made his fortune, ever since he had pulled himself up from poverty he had ensured he was never needy or desperate.

He pressed a kiss to her inner thigh and she shuddered. Then he kissed her again, gratified to feel her tremble beneath his lips as he moved closer and closer to the heart of her desire.

"I am desperate to taste you," he said.

She bit her lip, closing her eyes and turning away as he flicked his tongue where she most wanted it. "Apollo," she said, "you don't have to…"

He planted his palms firmly on the soft globes of her ass, pulling her more firmly up against his mouth, tasting her deeply in response to her protest. She wiggled beneath him, and he wasn't certain if she was trying to get away, or if she was trying to move herself closer.

Either way, he didn't care. Either way, he was going to get what he wanted.

He brought his hands into play, stroking her with his fingers, thrusting one deep inside of her, reveling in how slick, how ready she was for him.

She was sweet, like dessert. A flavor he had never realized he craved until he had her on his tongue. And now, he knew that this was the thing he had been missing. This was what he had craved all this time.

He stroked her deeply, adding a second finger to the first. And she shattered beneath him, her internal muscles tight around him as she shuddered out her release.

"Oh, Apollo," she said, leaving no doubt that she knew exactly who she was with. Leaving no doubt that she wanted him. No one else but him.

"Are you ready for me, *agape*?"

She didn't speak, she only nodded.

He freed himself quickly from his slacks, not bothering to undo the buttons on his shirt, not bothering to move his hands any lower than his hips. And he thrust inside of her, the breath hissing through his teeth as she closed around him.

Yes, restraint was for other men. For better men.

He was going to conquer. Conquer his desire, his rage.

He would seize what he wanted. The only question was why he hadn't done it sooner.

He brought his hips against hers, his pelvis coming into contact with her clitoris every time he thrust deep inside of her warm, willing body. And he was lost, lost in this, in her. In Elle. And he didn't give a damn that they were in an elevator, he didn't care that he was using her. Nothing mattered but this.

He gave himself over to it completely, lost himself in the rhythm of her body, the slow, slick glide of their flesh, the soft, sweet sounds she made. The words that poured from her lips, hoarse whispers begging him to continue. To take her harder, faster, just please, *please.*

Inside, he was begging himself to hold off on finding his pleasure. He didn't want to go over the edge without taking her with him.

He wanted to do more than that. He wanted her screaming. He wanted her just as lost, just as obsessed as he was. Just as desperate to burn out the flame before it consumed his entire being. Utterly. Irrevocably.

He refused to be alone in this, in this destructive obsession. He would destroy her along with him.

That thought crystallized, clear and sudden in his mind as his release washed over him in an uncontrollable, endless wave. And then beneath him, she arched her back, crying out her own pleasure, her fingernails digging into his back, even through the fabric of his shirt. And he relished the slight bite of pain that came with the unending onslaught of pleasure. It was the only thing rooting him to the earth. The only thing keeping even part of himself under control.

And as she shuddered out her release beneath him, as

he skinned his hands over her bare skin, he realized exactly what he would do.

He would have her until he was through with her. Would build her up as the public face of the company. And when the time was right, he would drop the blade on the guillotine.

He would remove her from her position as CEO, and with that final move, remove the St. James family from his life. Close the chapter forever.

He would not simply burn out their desire, he would destroy her along with it.

He leaned forward, brushing his lips against hers. "Now there, *agape*, I'm not so bad, am I?"

CHAPTER FOUR

ELLE HAD OPTED to keep her mouth shut from the time she had slowly collected her clothing off the floor of the elevator. She stayed silent as Apollo's driver took them to her apartment and all while she packed her bags, with Apollo looming in the corner of her apartment, until they made their trek to the airport and boarded his private jet.

She attempted to keep the awestruck expression off her face as she gazed around the aircraft. She knew that he was rich. She just hadn't quite realized that he was *private jet* rich. She had been raised in very fortunate circumstances but, even so, her father didn't own his own plane.

Well, he certainly wouldn't *now* even if he had before. Because of Apollo. And it would do well for her to remember that.

The problem was she did remember. While they had made love or…whatever it was you called what the two of them had done, she was aware of who he was. How much he had done to destroy her family's legacy.

Still she wanted him.

She felt… She felt completely and totally frazzled. Somehow, she had ended up kissing Apollo again. And the moment they touched, it didn't stop there. It never stopped there. It *couldn't*.

Apparently.

"Do you approve?" he asked, sinking into the plush leather chair next to one of the windows that looked out on the tarmac. "Or am I to take that expression to mean you are terrified of your surroundings? It's very difficult to say."

"I like the plane. I'm a little bit afraid of being alone at thirty thousand feet with you."

"Afraid you'll join the mile high club?"

Dammit, *yes*. "I think we can both agree that whatever has been going on between us is not a good idea."

"It's a terrible idea. Take your seat so that we can ready for takeoff."

She looked around, elected to sit in the chair farthest from his. "For the record, I still hate you."

"Oh, I'm well aware," he said. "I think that was what you screamed in my ear only a few hours ago. Oh, no, I think what you actually screamed was 'more' and 'harder.'"

"It isn't like you weren't complicit."

"Complicit. *Explicit.*"

"What exactly is your goal here, Apollo?" she asked. She didn't trust him. Not one bit. She was not in a position to refuse his command that she fly with him to Greece. Neither did she entirely trust his explanation.

"That depends," he said, leaning back in his chair, his body all leashed power and tension. "Are you speaking of business—" his gaze raked over her body "—or pleasure?"

"I thought we both agreed that the pleasure angle is a poor one for the two of us to take."

"It is. It's a terrible idea, *agape*. We hate each other. As you have stated many times. Or, more to the point, *you* hate *me*. I have no such strong feelings about you."

"No," she said, her tone biting, "you don't feel anything for me or my father. You simply destroyed us for your own pleasure."

"Your father's company was hemorrhaging money long before I came by to deal with it."

"So why didn't you help him?"

"That's a complicated issue, Elle," he said, his words hard.

"I don't have any trouble understanding complexities. Go right ahead and explain."

"There is more between your father and I than you know."

"Enlighten me," she said, the words escaping through clenched teeth.

"Not now. But understand what I'm doing is for a bigger purpose."

"Your ego? Honestly, you're unbelievable. He gave you everything. He loved you best from the beginning," she said, voicing the words that she never had before. Words she had long believed. "And now you've betrayed him for money."

"Love," he spat. "What is love, Elle? Tell me that. Is it what your father feels for you? As he moves you around like a pawn, desperate to put you between me and his queen? Did he love me, or did he see me as another tool he could use? I don't put any stock in love. It has never done anything for me, so I will hardly defer to it now."

Her heart was pounding hard, her throat tight. And she knew what she wanted. She hated herself then, more than she had ever hated him. "What do you want from me?"

"In the short term? I intend to burn this thing out between us. A fire can't keep on forever, can it?"

"Are you suggesting we sleep together while we are away from New York?"

"I'm doing something much stronger than suggesting."

Rage turned to excitement, flickering at the center of her being and radiating outward. The idea of being with him again, of touching him again, made her hands shake. "I didn't realize you got off on coercing women into your bed."

"We both know I didn't have to coerce you into it at all. Also," he said, his tone pointed, "we have never made it to a bed."

The thought of being in bed with him seemed…luxurious. The chance to explore his body at her leisure, rather than finding herself at the mercy of the explosion that occurred between them every time they touched. The force of it propelled her, made it impossible for her to think, impossible for her to resist. What would it be like to make the *decision* to have him? To give herself all night to indulge in that long-held desire for him.

She had always wanted him. And she had hated him for it. She'd been so angry that he was so…untouched. So utterly uninterested. So she'd pushed at him, tried to make him angry if she couldn't make him want her. She'd taunted him. And finally, she'd decided to taunt him sexually.

She could remember very clearly choosing the smallest, brightest bikini she could possibly find—one that absolutely clashed with her red hair, but one she felt would get her the attention she desired—to try to catch Apollo's eye when he came home to the family estate over break.

He had approached her as she'd gotten out of the pool and she'd felt… Naked. Alive. Afraid. So she'd defaulted to her usual position.

She could remember turning to him, her lips curled. *They'll let anyone into the estate, won't they? How my family's standards have fallen over the years.*

His eyes had blazed then. With anger. And he'd grabbed hold of her arm. She hadn't been afraid, though. She'd been...electrified.

He had held her there, looked at her hard, and for one moment, one desperate moment, she had imagined that she had seen lust in his eyes. That she had seen interest. But then, he had released her and turned away, leaving her there as though nothing at all had happened.

But now, somehow, for some reason, he wanted her, too. *This is your chance. To put it behind you once and for all so that you can move on.*

"All right," she said, ignoring the thrill of excitement that shot through her. "I agree. We have to get back on proper footing so that we can deal with each other as business partners."

"You are not my partner."

"Whatever. Terminology aside I am agreeing to the idea of an affair. But it has to stay a secret. Can you imagine the scandal? Me. Dating my wicked stepbrother who stole my family legacy after he wormed his way into my father's good graces."

"Of course. I have no interest in parading my intimate association with you in front of the world. As I already said."

His words, his *tone*, rankled. "I find it funny that you speak of it as though you find it distasteful. Of course *I* do. Everyone who moves in business circles fears you. I can see why I would want to disassociate from you. But not why you would wish to disassociate from me."

He arched a brow. "I have a type, Elle. It is not buttoned-up redheads. As you know, gentlemen prefer blondes. Or, in my case, scoundrels prefer blondes, brunettes or redheads so long as they're willing to part their thighs. I like women who know how to smile. Who know how to have fun. I do not like little harpies who claw at me even as they tear my clothes off."

"You like it when I claw at you."

Heat flared in his dark eyes and she took that as a win. "I consider this a unique circumstance."

She wanted to ask him why he thought heat was exploding between them the way it was. She wanted to ask him if it was ever like this for him and the other women he had sex with. But that would betray her inexperience. And that was something she wasn't willing to do. She wanted to protect her vulnerable places. Wanted to shield everything she didn't know from him.

That was an old defense, and one that she employed daily. She hated asking for help. Hated appearing ignorant.

Her father was a hard man, and she had always had the impression that he was standing by waiting for her to disappoint him. So she never let him see when she was floundering. Never let him detect one bit of uncertainty in her. She had wrapped herself so tightly in her ironed-on exterior, so careful to never show a wrinkle. She had difficulty letting go of it under any circumstances.

And if she was determined to never let her father see her sweat that went even more for Apollo.

That meant she couldn't ask the questions that were gnawing a hole inside of her. They would just have to go unanswered. It didn't matter anyway. Nothing was going to come from her association with Apollo. Nothing except freedom from the bizarre hold he had over her—and her life.

She had spent far too long being preoccupied with him. She would just be glad to have it handled.

And if she was a little bit…giddy over the thought of some time to deal with the attraction…well, that was normal. People acted ridiculous when it came to sex. History was filled with examples. Wars were started over sexual desire. She could hardly expect herself to be above the kind of insanity that captured almost all of humanity.

She spent the rest of the plane ride musing about restraint and dozing on and off while Apollo continued to work. Every time she opened her eyes and looked at where he was sitting, he was maintaining the same position, his focus never broken from his laptop, or the spreadsheets in front of him.

It was strange, watching him from across the darkened cabin. He had changed so much in the past few years. The lines on his face becoming more pronounced, as though each year had left a mark behind, evidence of the living he'd done.

And as a teenager, he had never worn a suit. He had always kept his hair slightly longer back then, too. Now it was cropped ruthlessly short, as though he was trying to look like he had sprung out of the ground a very conservative billionaire.

She wanted to find that boy again. Strip off the layers and layers he'd put over the person he'd been. The one she had… Well, the one she had felt so many things for.

She let her eyes flutter closed again, and when she opened them, they had landed in Greece. Customs and passports and the like were handled in an efficient manner involving people coming to them and apologizing for any delays. After that, they were ushered into a limousine, all their bags packed quickly into the trunk as they departed straight from the plane to the highway.

Athens was an incredible sprawl she hadn't accurately pictured in her mind. The rolling hills were capped with white, not from snow, but from the stone houses packed tightly together, flowing along with the landscape.

The downtown wasn't anything like the glass-and-steel jungle of Manhattan. Ancient structures mixed with more modern buildings, the history and heritage of the nation evident in the intricate stonework, the massive pillars and marketplaces scattered throughout.

"Where are we going?"

"I have a villa just outside the city."

"Of course you do," she said. "But I thought we were going to your offices?"

"We will. At some point. But some adjustments have been made to accommodate some of our new goals."

"Meaning what?" she asked, tearing her eyes away from the scenery to look at him.

"I don't think it's that difficult to guess."

They drove out of the city, winding up the steep, packed hillsides. They escaped the sprawl, moving to an area where trees were more plentiful. Where houses were a little bit less common. Until they reached the top of a completely vacant hill that overlooked the sea. There, behind a secure set of wrought-iron gates was a white stone house that was even more imposing than the St. James family estate in upstate New York.

"Is this your primary residence now?"

He lifted his shoulder. "As much as any place, I suppose. It is my home, after all."

"I *do* know that. You were born here. You left here when you were eight."

His focus sharpened. "Have you been reading unauthorized biographies?"

"No," she said. "I just paid attention when you used to speak around the dinner table. I used to know you, Apollo, as difficult as it is to remember back that far."

An emotion she couldn't put a name to flashed through

his eyes. "I did not realize such memories were worth saving."

"Know your enemy, and all of that."

"I suppose so."

The limousine pulled closer to the house, and the driver put the car into Park. Elle opened up her own door, stepping out and looking up at the house. To her, it looked like a lot of cubes of varying sizes stacked on top of each other, large windows on all sides looking out at the hills behind them, and the ocean before them.

"It doesn't seem like you're afforded very much privacy," she said.

"Are you concerned that the village will see you naked? Because make no mistake, most of the time spent in this house will be spent without clothes."

The dark, sensual promise should have frightened her, offended her. Instead, it excited her.

"The thought crossed my mind," she said. No point in playing the prude now. Not when he knew full well she wasn't.

"Never fear. I can tint the windows at the flick of a switch, and we won't even have to sacrifice the view. But good to know you are on the same page as I am."

"I have great concern for my modesty." And her sanity.

"Well, I hope you don't concern yourself much with it in my presence." He walked ahead of her, moving to the front of the house. "Our things will be brought in momentarily. Come, let me show you around."

She followed him inside, her heart hammering, her mouth suddenly dry. She didn't know what might happen next. If he was going to strip her of her clothing immediately and press her up against a wall again. And if he did, what would she do? She would capitulate. She knew that from experience.

But he didn't make a move to touch her. Instead, he paused in the expansive entryway. "I think this is self-explanatory," he said, indicating the living area with the low-profile couch that was up against the wall, curving around to another. "Beyond that is the pool." He walked ahead, up the open staircase that led to the second floor. She followed him. "My office," he said. "The library, kitchen and dining area. I felt the second floor made for a slightly better view." He continued straight up the stairs, to the third floor and she quickened her pace to keep up. "That way is my room," he said, pointing down to the left. "And then here you will find yours." The opposite direction from his. He began to walk to her room, and she followed, feeling a little bit like a lost puppy afraid of losing sight of her master.

He pushed the door open and revealed a light and airy space. Everything was white. The bedspread, the gauzy curtains that hung around the bed frame. There were no curtains on the windows, just as with the rest of the house. The square, unobstructed glass pane afforded a brilliant view of the jewel-bright sea, and let in the pale, sun-washed light.

"There are several settings for the windows. One is a blackout setting. That way the sun won't disturb your sleep," he explained.

She nodded. "I'm not sure I understand," she said, looking around the room. "I thought we would be sharing a room."

He chuckled. "I don't sleep with my lovers, *agape*. I have sex with them. We don't need to share a bedroom for that."

Dammit. He managed to make her feel completely gauche and out of her depth even though she was doing her best to appear like all of this was commonplace for her. She'd been feeling like she was succeeding. Until this moment. She gritted her teeth. "Of course. How could I be so silly?"

"I imagine you typically date nice boys who like to spend the evening making love before they pull you close and cuddle you."

His mocking tone burned her down deep. She was starting to feel at a disadvantage again. She would not allow it. "Do I seem like the type of woman who enjoys cuddling?" she asked, arching a brow. "You cannot possibly guess at the sort of man I typically associate with. You don't even know me. Not even a little bit. You know what I've bothered to show you, and that's all."

"My mistake. If you will excuse me, I'm going to get ready for this evening. And I have a bit of work to catch up on."

"You worked the entire time we were on the plane."

"Impatient for me?"

She swallowed hard. She swallowed her honest answer, which was most definitely yes. "Just concerned you're going to fall over at the age of twenty-nine from high blood pressure or something."

"Your concern is touching. I will see you this evening for the charity gala."

He turned and walked out of the room, closing the door behind him.

She turned and looked out the window, gazing at the view. For some reason, this time, she had the feeling of being inside of a terrarium, but it didn't feel quite so open. Once that thought entered her mind she felt as if she were some kind of creature he was keeping in a cage until he was ready to take her out and play with her.

Somehow, back in New York this had all felt equal, like they were in the same space, wanting the same things. But not now. Silly, because he owned her company. She should not have felt equal with him in the workplace. Should not have felt like they were on the same footing at all. And yet, for some reason—her pride, her intense dedication to her business persona—she had felt like they were.

But not here. In his house, in this show of his incredible wealth, she felt vulnerable. Powerless. She was in his home country, a place where she didn't even speak the language, trapped in his house on the hill.

She wondered, for a moment, if this was what he had felt. Walking into her family home as a teenager, his mother engaged to a powerful man so far above her station. And he had been greeted by a stepsister so consumed with her own feelings, her own issues, that she'd been nothing but horrible. Had done nothing but try to make him feel completely unequal to the place.

She blinked, pushing back an unwanted wave of sympathy. That was in the past. What she'd done had been out of girlish fear of the strength of her feelings.

Apollo was not acting as a boy, reacting to fear. He wasn't reacting at all. He was a man on the warpath, and God help her if she got in his way.

CHAPTER FIVE

WHEN ELLE APPEARED at the top of the stairs that evening wearing the silk gown that he'd had sent up to the room earlier, Apollo wasn't sure he had the strength to attend the gala. No, most of him wanted to grab hold of her and drag her straight into her bedroom and strip it off her.

The emerald green silk gown seemed almost demure in the front. It had a high neckline, the delicate, shiny fabric skimming her curves. It rippled when she walked down the stairs, flowing over her body like water.

But it was the back he couldn't wait to see. He had selected the dress for that very reason. True to his word, he was intent on raising her profile in the company. All the better to make her family's humiliation more apparent. If no one knew who the St. James family were, if they were only aware of the companies, while the family itself remained faceless, his disgrace of them would not carry the impact he required.

In a few weeks he would cut ties completely. He would let her drown along with her father and the rest of the St. James family.

It was cruel. But what David St. James had done to Apollo's father, the way he had manipulated Apollo's mother...

He forced himself to smile at her. To practice some

form of charm. He did possess it, after all. Though he didn't often exercise it when dealing with Elle. He could have any woman he wanted, and had, even before he had become the man he was now.

The girls he had associated with from nearby all-girls institutes back when he had been a teenager had found him fascinating. None of them had ever intended on taking him home to meet their parents. But a great many of them had taken him to nearby gazebos, backseats of cars and vacant dorm rooms. He might not be the kind of man they could proudly claim, but they had certainly found him attractive enough for certain uses.

Of course, Elle had already proven she had no issues using him for her physical satisfaction while she despised him on a personal level. So, he supposed that there was no point in attempting to be charming now.

All thoughts of charm or anything else were completely emptied from his mind when he saw the side of the gown as she reached the bottom of the stairs. He could think of nothing more than the possibility of stripping it from her body now.

"Turn around," he said, his voice hard.

"Why?" she asked, turning to face him, her hands clasped in front of her, demure, as though she had no idea what she was doing to him.

"Turn around," he said, deciding that he would forgo charm completely.

A flash of color spread up her neck, into her cheeks. Clearly, even if it made her angry, she quite enjoyed it when he gave orders. She turned slowly, teasing him by taking her time. And when she revealed her back fully, his stomach tightened, his blood pooling in his groin.

The back of the dress was a deep V ending just above the curve of her rear, exposing her entire back, the edges glittering with delicate beadwork. The seams over the silken material served to enhance the round shape of her backside, creating an even more dramatic shape to her curves.

He wanted to take her back upstairs, not just so he could have his way with her, but so he could keep any other man from laying eyes on what he thought of as his.

"It does not matter how many men have come before me," he said, not realizing he was speaking the words out loud until they had already escaped his mouth. "You are mine now. You have always been mine, Elle." The words were more raw, more real than he'd intended.

But then, this feeling was more raw, more real than anything that had ever come before it.

He saw attachments for what they were. Saw clearly how easily feelings could be manipulated. But what he felt for Elle was beyond him. It could never be distilled into one neat emotion. Could hardly ever be defined.

He needed it gone. Needed to burn it out. So that in the end he could walk away from the St. James family and never look back.

Walk away from her.

She turned to face him, her signature red ponytail swinging along with the movement. "That's quite possessive," she said.

"I'm kind of a bastard. You have agreed to be my mistress until such time as we have burned out the attraction between us. That means you are mine. And mine alone."

"I hardly make a habit of overlapping lovers."

He took a step toward her, closing the distance between them. He wrapped his arm around her waist, planting his hand firmly at the center of her back and drawing her close to him. "I would not permit it."

"You might own my company, Apollo," she said, her voice low, sultry, "but you do not own me."

"That's where you're wrong, I think," he said, sliding his hand up the center of her back, cupping the back of her head. "Because for now those two things are the same. I own both the company and you."

"You're a caveman."

He wrapped his fingers around her ponytail, tugging hard. "Shall I drag you back to my lair?"

She gasped, the sound one of arousal, not fear.

"You can pretend to hate this thing between us all you want. You can pretend to hate my commands. But we both know that no matter how shocked and appalled you pretend to be, you want this. You want me."

She leaned in slightly, and he kept his hold tight on her hair. Then she pressed her lips gently against his before biting him hard. "I might want you," she said, "but it is not the way a woman *should* want a man."

"Take your hair down."

"I refuse to give in to your every command."

He shifted his hold on her, grabbing the bobby pin that was buried in the ponytail that wrapped one coppery strand around the rubber band that secured her hair, concealing it from view. Then he grabbed the rubber band itself, pulling it free.

Her red hair fell past her shoulders in soft waves, extra full because of the way it had been restrained.

She frowned, her brows locked together. "I can't go like this. My hair is a mess."

"It is perfect."

"I do not have to wear my hair to please you."

"Your hair pleases me however it is fixed," he said. "But this way, this way, all I can think about is burying my fingers in it. Pulling you toward me. Kissing you deeply. With it like this, I want nothing more than to take you straight back upstairs and make you scream my name. And so, I leave the final decision on how you wear it up to you."

She tilted her chin upward. "Well, it's already down."

He chuckled, the soundboard of satisfaction. "I thought you might come to that conclusion."

She narrowed her eyes. "I prefer you without a tie."

"It is a formal event."

"Without the black tie, with the first button on your shirt undone, so that I can just see your chest hair, all I can think of is you tearing the shirt open the rest of the way so that I can put my hands on your hard muscles. So that I can feel your heartbeat raging against my palms. I can think of nothing but leaning in, running my tongue over your skin. And so," she said, arching her brow before turning away from him. "It is up to you."

Apollo smiled and began to loosen his tie.

No matter that they were pretending to be merely business associates at the gala, Elle could not help but think the two of them looked like they had been engaged in sexual intimacy in the car on the way. Her hair was down, looking very much like he had already run his fingers through it. His shirt was undone, his tie long discarded.

And yet, they had not had the benefit of engaging in any kind of intimate activity.

When they had gotten in the limousine she had scooted as far away from him as possible, telling him she needed space, time to collect her thoughts. She did. She was exhausted, jet-lagged, and the nap she'd had earlier had only helped a little bit. Beyond that, she was still raw from their last encounter. And if they were supposed to appear in public together in a platonic fashion, she did not want the feeling of his touch lingering quite so strongly in the forefront of her mind.

Now though, she was regretting it. Now she sort of wished she had climbed onto his lap in the car and satisfied her desire for him. Anything to take the edge off the extreme arousal that was pounding through her even now.

The gala itself was beautifully appointed, held in one of the oldest and most sophisticated hotels in Athens. When she arrived, she was surprised to see that Apollo's name was on everything.

"You didn't tell me that it was *your* charity gala we were attending."

He shrugged his shoulder, taking a glass of Champagne off the tray of a passing waiter. "It did not seem important."

"I think it is rather important. I wasn't aware that you had founded the charity."

"It's very boring. Press junket stuff. The kind of thing that one says to improve their reputation with the media. It's a game I scarcely have the patience to play at the best of times. I did not see the point in trying to convince you that I was somehow a paragon of virtue simply because I donate money to impoverished families."

"You do?" In spite of everything she knew about him, in spite of her feelings about him, she could feel herself softening.

"Yes. Do not look at me like that. I am a businessman. Believe me when I tell you this benefits me in financial ways."

"Why are you so resistant to being seen as good in any fashion?"

"I do not like to raise people's expectations."

She blinked. "Why?"

"Because they will find themselves disappointed."

She looked around, taking in the beautifully appointed marble interior of the hotel, the impressive pillars, the glittering chandeliers. Couples dressed in the finest couture were already making their way out to the dance floor. She wished she could dance with Apollo. That he would take her into his strong arms and pull her up against his chest, hold her…just to hold her. So that she could relish his strength, his heat, if only for a moment.

She shook her head. That was extreme foolishness. She wanted nothing more from Apollo than for him to leave her alone and allow her to run their business as she saw fit. Well, that and sex for the sake of sex, until they had burned out the attraction between them.

She did not want him to hold her. She did not want to press her head up against his chest and listen to the sound of his heart. Did not want to spend an hour kissing him, just kissing him. *No*, she didn't want any of those things.

"I shall introduce you to some of my associates," Apollo said. "And to some of the members of the press who are in attendance."

"Oh, you're too kind," she said, keeping her tone light.

He pressed his hand lightly on her back, guiding her toward a group of people who were standing there conversing. He made introductions, and dropped his hand quickly back to his side, bringing a great deal of distance between the two of them as he shifted his position within the group.

One of the men was a businessman from Italy, another a Greek, who had his business in the United States. They started to make conversation about staying relevant in the age of the internet and online superstores, and she was so lost in the discussion that it took her a while to notice that

Apollo was no longer standing next to her. She frowned, searching the crowd quickly. And then she spotted him, out on the dance floor with a blonde woman wearing a dress with a hem that fell just beneath her butt cheeks. Rather nice butt cheeks too, Elle was loath to admit.

She fought to keep the scowl off her face. She knew that they were supposed to be playing the part of business associates but she felt this was taking it a bit far.

"I see Mr. Savas has abandoned you," the Greek man, Nikos Vardalos, said.

"Not at all," she said, taking a deep breath. "We are not here together. Mr. Savas is able to dance with whoever he chooses."

"Then I suppose you are free to dance with whoever you choose?"

She could always tell him she had a boyfriend. She often did that when confronted with men she wasn't attracted to in these kinds of situations. But Nikos was handsome enough, and Apollo was dancing with someone else. Really, it seemed rather silly for her to stay hidden away in a corner.

"Absolutely," she said. "I am always free to do whatever I want."

He laughed, treating her to a smile that she had no doubt often made women go weak in the knees. Sadly, not her. Not now.

But she pretended. She offered a smile in return.

"I like a woman who knows her mind. And does your mind tell you that you might want to dance with me?"

"I would be delighted."

He extended his hand, and she accepted it, wrapping her fingers around his. His touch was warm, but it did not light her on fire, not the way that Apollo's did. It was sort of comforting, to have a man touch her like this, and for her to feel so very little.

Every interaction with Apollo, every brush of his skin against hers, was so layered. Was so hot, so intense, she couldn't ignore it, or pretend it hadn't burned. It was never simple. It was always hate spread over lust, spread over a strange attachment that stemmed from all of the years they had known each other. And betrayal. The betrayal that was unique to what she felt for him because of how well they had known each other. Because of how she had felt about him for so long.

Because of the way she had trusted him.

And you betray your father by sleeping with this man. By wanting him.

Still, she couldn't help herself. Still, she could feel nothing as Nikos pulled her into his arms and swept her onto the dance floor. Still, she felt more when she looked across the crowded room and locked eyes with Apollo, who was glaring at her and her dance partner with dark rage.

Fine. He was welcome to be murderous. She didn't particularly care. They were here separately. He was dancing with another woman, and she would be damned if she would play the part of wallflower.

She shifted her hands lightly on her partner's shoulder, tightening her grip on his hand.

"I think Savas wants to kill me," Nikos said, his tone tinged with amusement.

"Oh, I don't suppose he wants to kill you," she said, her tone dry. "Anyway, he and I are associates, as I said before. And neither of us believes in mixing business with pleasure."

"Excellent. Then I shall never do business with you."

She laughed. "Well, that would be a shame. Since

you are in retail, I would very much like to do business with you."

"Perhaps it is crass of me to discuss this during a dance," he said, "but tell me more."

They spent the next two songs largely ignoring the music and discussing the various ways in which they could marry their two brands. She decided that she liked Nikos quite a bit even if he did not make her heart beat faster.

She only wished that he could.

He was Greek, he was wealthy, he had a hint of a gorgeous accent. Truly, if she had a type, this was it. If any other man was going to start a fire in her loins quite the way that Apollo did, this man would. But there was nothing. Absolutely nothing. It was an extreme disappointment.

Still, though she had not found a way to encourage desire toward another man, she had come away with a very promising business contact. They parted at the end of the song, and he did not try to make any sort of romantic overture. He must've sensed the lack of chemistry as profoundly as she did.

She was making her way toward a waiter to get herself a drink when she was all but accosted by Apollo. "Having fun?"

"It's a charming party," she said.

"Yes. I told you already that you would be with me and me alone while we work out the attraction between us, did I not?"

"I'm sorry, I was not aware that a waltz was on par with intercourse."

"You are playing with fire," he said.

"Then you are, too. Don't think I didn't notice your lovely blonde partner."

"It is expected of me."

"And you want my face in the paper. Therefore, I had better do something newsworthy. You put me in this dress that leaves me essentially naked, and now you're going to act as though my getting attention is not somehow essential to your *plan*?"

"All you have to do is simply walk into a room to gain attention, *agape*. Trust me on this."

"I find your assessment flattering, if slightly ambitious."

"I don't care whether or not you find it ambitious. It is the truth." He looked around them. "Even if you have not noticed, I have. Every male eye—and many of the female eyes—have been on you from the moment you walked in. You are absolutely the one to watch here."

"Is that so?"

"Yes. And when you make a large charitable donation in the name of the company, you will become even more of a conversation piece."

Her mouth opened, then snapped shut. "I did not know you were going to make use of my money."

"Of course I am. Anyway, it is a good cause, on that you can trust me. As I said, I provide housing and other necessities for families who have fallen below the poverty line. Surely you can find no fault with that."

"I suppose not."

"You sound so distressed. It must be terrible when I don't rise to the part of blackguard when it suits you."

"Sincerely awful. I can see why you prefer to pretend you're terrible. For consistency."

"I am nothing if not consistent."

She laughed. "If only that were true."

"What is that supposed to mean?"

"Exactly what it sounds like. You are not consistent,

I don't care how you frame it, I don't care what you say. You were a friend of my family, and then you betrayed us. There is nothing consistent about that."

His expression turned dark, fierce. He leaned in and her breath caught in her throat. She thought, for a moment, that he might kiss her. She hoped that he would. He did not. "From the moment I understood there was better than the circumstances I existed in I was determined to find better. When I went to a private school, knowing full well that I didn't belong there, I was determined to rise to the top of the class so that no one could question whether or not I had the ability to succeed in the realms of society into which I had been thrust. I have done nothing but hold myself up from the bottom with my brute strength from the moment I understood it could be done. If that's not consistency, I don't know what is."

"Yes, I know you pulled yourself up quite a bit. But it's quite convenient to forget that my father's money provided a ladder to help you out." She turned away from him and he grabbed hold of her arm, holding on tightly to her and pulling her back to him.

"I was willing to advance myself using any means necessary. Again, I claim consistency." He released his hold on her, straightening the cuffs on his shirt. "Go off and have fun. We will meet again at the end of the night. Do not forget to make your donation."

"Of course not."

"I imagine Luka would like to dance, as well."

"Are you off to find him?" she asked.

"No, but I suggest you should."

"Now you're encouraging me to dance with other men? There's that legendary consistency."

"No, I believe you're right. You should do what you

can to get your photograph in the news. And I shall do what I have to to get attention of my own. I will see you at the end of the evening."

walked out of the room."

CHAPTER SIX

BY THE TIME the car pulled back up to Apollo's house
later that evening he was in a violent temper. Elle had
done exactly as he had demanded and had danced with
every businessman within fifteen years of her age. And
she had charmed every single one of them. She had no
doubt delighted the media.

She had done exactly as he'd asked, and he was in-
censed. Spending the evening *not* touching her had been
akin to torture. But he was ready to move ahead with
their agreement. He was ready to claim her. To remind
her exactly why she was here, and who she was with.

They had not spoken in the car on the way back to his
villa. She was vibrating with indignation next to him,
but he didn't care.

When they got out of the car and walked into the
house he turned to her. "I want you to go to your room
and open up the top drawer of the bureau there. You will
find some other items that my staff has procured for you.
Make yourself ready for me."

He stormed off to his office then, pouring himself a
glass of scotch and downing it in one desperate gulp, relishing the burn as it slid down his throat.

He paced the length of the room, trying to figure out
exactly what happened to make him so agitated.

Jealousy.

He could not remember the last time he had ever felt jealous. If he ever had.

He closed his eyes, allowing an old memory to wash over him. Hell, the bikini. Yes, he had been jealous then in a strange way. Of the fact that she was young, with her entire life ahead of her. Of the fact that men had not yet discovered her, and he would not be a part of that discovery. He would have given everything to have been the first man to touch her. To have been the one to awaken her sensuality. Her every sigh, her every moan.

To have been the one who gave her that first climax.

Yes, he would have given anything to be that man at one time. He had been jealous then. Of a man who had not existed. And somehow tonight every man who had danced with her had become one of those nameless, faceless men who had come before him.

He hated them, even without knowing who they were.

He tossed his suit jacket onto the floor, stalking out of his office and going up the stairs toward her bedroom. She had better damn well be ready for him. Because he was not waiting another moment.

He threw open the bedroom door without knocking, and she turned to face him, still wearing the dress she had been wearing to the gala.

"I thought I gave you instructions to change," he said.

Her green eyes glittered with anger. "Yes," she said. "You did. But I have no desire to dress up like some strange interpretation of a fantasy that you have, brought about by your magnanimous staff."

"Expensive underthings offend you?"

"The idea that I might not want to choose my own? The idea that I might be interchangeable with any of the other women you consort with? That offends me."

"What do any of my other lovers have to do with this?"

"Everything. You are treating me exactly as you would any of them."

He clenched his hands into fists, his heart beating so fast it burned. "And you want to be special? Is that it?"

Her cheeks flamed. "I don't want to be the same. I don't want to be just one warm body of any of the ones you could have."

"Still you doubt my desire for you?" He undid another button on his shirt, then another, stripping it off as he walked toward her, feeling every inch a predatory animal. "What must I do to show you that I am your servant, *agape*? What must I do to show you that you own my body?"

The color heightened in her cheeks. "I own your body?"

"Do you think I want this? Do you think I want to be a slave to the desire I have for a St. James? If you think you hate me then just imagine how much I hate you. Your family. Your family name. Everything you stand for."

His words were coming out hard and fast. He was saying more than he had intended. He had never intended to bring this up with her at all. Had not intended to speak any of this to her until he was giving her her marching orders and ordering her to pack her things and vacate her office. He had not intended to reveal any of this until he'd unleashed his ultimate betrayal on to her.

But he couldn't stop it now. He could not stop himself. "If any woman at the party tonight had made me feel even a fraction of what I feel for you I would have taken her into the nearest hallway and pushed her skirt up. Sadly, I only respond to you. You have me on a leash, Elle. I hope you are happy with this revelation."

Her eyes were round, her lips parted slightly. "I don't

understand. You were part of our family. How can you possibly feel that way?"

"Easily. You don't understand what manner of man your father is, you don't understand what manner of man I am. When you were seventeen years old, parading around the family estate in your bikini, I would have liked nothing more than to put you flat on your back. I was a man of twenty, and I would have had you, sweet little virgin that you were. And even knowing how wrong that is, I hate every man who came before me. I regret not taking you then. Such wasted years, Elle. I could have rid myself of my hunger for you then. But I didn't. For what reason? To preserve some semblance of a conscience we both know I don't have? Pointless. But then, I still harbored illusions that I might be good."

"I... You wanted me then?"

"Did you not know? Of course not. You were blind. A little virgin."

"Stop saying that. I wasn't ignorant. It's just that you seemed angry...not..."

"As it always is with us."

"Either way, I'm not ignorant."

"Did I have the wrong end of it then? Please don't tell me you weren't already experienced or I truly will hang myself for being so foolish that I didn't have you."

"Why are you acting like this?"

He didn't know. He damn well had no clue. All he knew was that he was enraged. Over tonight. The other men who'd touched her. The orders she was refusing to obey. Over his behavior nine years ago. Over his behavior now. "Why are you refusing to wear the lingerie I provided for you?"

"Because I will not be one of your whores," she said. "Because I *was* a virgin when you had me at your hotel room. Your jealousy is misplaced while mine is certainly not."

Her words hit him like a punch to the gut. "A virgin?"

"Apparently it matters to you. Apparently you are quite proprietary and possessive, though you have not earned the right to be."

He growled, pulling her into his arms, grabbing hold of the sides of the delicate fabric of the dress and wrenching it down over her shoulders, tugging the bodice down low, revealing her breasts to his hungry gaze. "I am the only man to ever have you?"

"Yes," she said, her voice breathless.

"This pleases me much more than it should," he said, gripping her chin between his thumb and forefinger and tilting her face up to him. "All during the ride back to the villa I was contemplating the different ways I could kill each and every man who danced with you. In my mind, they had become your previous lovers. And I discovered that I felt rather violent about them. About the missed opportunity I'd had. You see, I wanted to be the one to teach you about pleasure."

She bit her lip, as though she were holding back a litany of words. Either curses, or the confirmation that he had indeed been the one to teach her about pleasure. He had a feeling she neither wanted to yell at him at this moment nor give him anything pleasant to latch onto.

"I did teach you about pleasure, didn't I? Against the wall in a hotel room. Dammit, Elle, you didn't tell me."

"Would it have made a difference?"

No. It made no difference at all. Not to anything. Not to what had gone before, and not to what he must do now. The fact that Elle had been a virgin changed nothing. She had been innocent of the wrongdoings of her father before he knew that, and she was innocent of them now. The fact he was her only lover might fill him with a sense of masculine pride, a sense of conquest, but it didn't change the fact that he would betray her in the end. That he would make an example of her and use her to wound her father.

The way her father had wounded his father. The way he had devastated his mother. The way he had devastated Apollo himself.

Whatever sins his father had committed, the rest of them had been nothing more than collateral damage. And so would Elle be. It was not fair. But none of this was fair.

It wasn't about fairness. It was about justice in the way that only he could obtain it.

"Yes," he lied. "It would have made a difference. I would have been much gentler with you." Except he knew he would not have. He would not take that fiery encounter in the hotel room back for anything. When Elle had unleashed all her rage on him. All of her desire. It had been the most singular experience of his life. He would trade it for nothing. It was a moment that belonged to him, one that could not be stolen no matter how low he sunk.

He was a villain, and now, he was embracing it fully.

He leaned in, kissing her, keeping it soft, keeping it light. She grabbed hold of his face, deepening the kiss.

He picked her up, carrying her to the bed and laying her down on the soft mattress, tugging the gown from her body. There would be no more talking tonight.

If he had his way, there would be no more talking until he was through with her. And if that meant spending the next two weeks in bed, then they would spend the next two weeks in bed.

CHAPTER SEVEN

THE PAST TWO weeks at Apollo's villa had gone surprisingly smoothly. It was strange to coexist with him and not fight. It actually reminded Elle of a different time. A simpler time. Back when they had actually liked each other. When she had looked up to him. When he had—apparently—had some sort of attraction to her that he had buried.

Of course, maybe they had coexisted so peacefully because their lives had been essentially separate. Unless they were making love. Which had not been confined to evenings, or to bed. She was certain that at this point, Apollo had taken her on every surface in the entire villa.

She was not complaining. It had been... Well, it had been the culmination of her most heated fantasies. It was strange. Like she was living a life borrowed, one that she could not possibly have in the long term, but one that was in many ways preferable to the one she had been living. She was still seeing to her responsibilities. Sometimes working in his office, sometimes from the office in his home while he was out.

She couldn't complain about the vacation. Of course, it was also difficult to justify the fact that she was sleeping with the enemy. Though, not literally, since they didn't sleep together. They had sex, and then he left.

"It's how I do things, *agape*," she said, amusing herself with her poor imitation of Apollo's voice as she paced the length of her bedroom.

A knock on her bedroom door startled her. She wondered if she had summoned him just by thinking about him. But he had just gone out to work a couple of hours ago, so she doubted he was back already.

She opened the door, to see one of his servants, Maria, standing there holding a package. "This is for you, miss," she said.

"Oh," she said, her whole body getting warm when she realized what it was. "Thank you."

After Maria left, she closed the door and opened the package hurriedly. Inside was a hot pink bikini. She had been planning this for the past few days. Maybe it was juvenile. But she wanted a chance to recapture the moment that both of them had missed. One that seemed to linger in both their minds.

She didn't waste any time getting into it, examining herself in the full-length mirror, watching as her cheeks flooded with color. She didn't make a habit out of wearing things that were so revealing. Though, honestly, after spending so much time naked with Apollo, she shouldn't feel self-conscious.

Still, she did.

That was different. That all happened during the heat of the moment. This was…premeditated. She had never staged anything quite like a seduction with him. And that's what this was. But she was aching for something, searching for something more. She couldn't deny that what she felt for him wasn't hatred at this point. It would be so much easier if it was.

She felt… Well, she felt a lot.

She took a deep breath, opening her bedroom door

and heading down the hall, down the stairs and outside to the pool. She was intent on being there when he got back. Intent on giving him the chance to make a different decision this time when he saw her in the bathing suit.

She slipped beneath the warm water, paddling over to the edge of the infinity pool, looking out over the view of the ocean. It was beautiful here. She hadn't thought it was possible to feel so at peace in Apollo's lair. Certainly not when she had first arrived.

She couldn't say they were growing closer, not exactly. But…it was more than it had been. For one thing, they could be in each other's presence for a full five minutes without screaming at each other. Sometimes they could go that long without tearing each other's clothes off, too. But only sometimes.

The thought made her smile, she lifted her face up to the sky, bathing herself in the warmth of the sun.

"What are you doing out here?"

"I finished work early," she said, turning, her heart slamming hard against her breastbone when she saw Apollo standing there, still dressed in the suit that he'd worn to work.

"Come here," he said, his jaw set, his dark eyes intent on her.

Elle draped her arms over the back of the infinity pool, arching her back slightly, thrusting her breasts up out of the water. "I'm enjoying the water."

"Elle," he said, his tone warning. "Do not make me come in there and get you."

"I think I would like for you to come in and get me. It's what you should have done nine years ago."

He smiled, a genuine smile. It wasn't one that was tinged with cynicism, neither was it mocking or laden with barely contained rage. It made her heart turn over in her chest, made it expand.

He began to remove his suit, starting with his jacket, then his tie, then slowly undoing the buttons on his shirt. There had been ample time over the past couple of weeks for her to become familiar with that gorgeous male physique, but familiarity hadn't made him seem commonplace. Not in the least.

He arched a brow, slowly placing his hands on his belt buckle, working the leather through the loop. Her mouth went dry and she fought to keep herself from moving closer to him. She was going to hang back. She was going to force him to come to her.

He undid the closure on his slacks, pulled the zipper down slowly, his eyes never leaving hers. He pushed his pants down his narrow hips, exposing himself to her. He was everything. Absolute perfection. Everything she had wanted a man to be and then some. No, there was no chance of him ever becoming commonplace in her eyes.

Slowly, he made his way to the pool, climbing down, the water rising up and concealing his body from her.

"You took my show," she said, just as he leaned forward, his sleek, athletic body slicing through the water effortlessly.

"I thought I would bring it to you," he said, approaching her, wrapping his arm around her waist and drawing her up against him.

"Oh," she said, "I guess I can appreciate that."

"I think you can more than appreciate that," he said, looking pointedly down at her breasts, at her tightened nipples, pushing up against the thin fabric of the bathing suit.

"I make it too easy for you," she said, not sounding even remotely regretful.

"I'm not complaining," he said, sliding his hand down her waist, resting his hand on her butt.

"Of course you're not. You're so certain of yourself, and all I have done is make you even more certain."

"I was named after a god. I came into the world with a rather inflated view of myself."

"Of course you did. How could I forget?" She lifted her hand, resting her palm on his chest. "I ordered this bathing suit for you."

Heat illuminated the darkness in his eyes. "I thought you might have."

"We have a chance to make a different decision." She traced the water droplets that were trailing down his chest, rolling into the grooves of his muscles. "I wish that I had done something differently then. Been a little bit bolder."

"You were young. You shouldn't have done anything. I shouldn't have done anything."

"I was young, but I knew what I wanted. And it hasn't changed." She looked up at him. "I still want you. I wanted you all this time, even when I was angry at you."

He wrapped his fingers around her wrist, lifting her hand to his lips, pressing a kiss to her palm. "Yes, I know you did. Believe me when I say the feeling is mutual."

Those words, those husky, delicious words, sent a little shock of pleasure through her. It wasn't strictly physical. It went deeper than that.

Unfortunately, all of this went much deeper than the physical. Much deeper than she wanted it to go.

"I do."

A smile curved his wicked mouth. "Listen to us. We have managed to converse for several minutes without fighting."

"A miracle."

"Perhaps. Though, I imagine we are skirting the edge of sacrilege assigning anything divine to the nature of things between us."

"Perhaps."

He had a point. What they shared was carnal, lustful.

No, not only that. Beautiful. Altering.

Impossible.

He was her stepbrother, he was her enemy. Truly, it was the enemy part that made it most impossible. The stepbrother issue would hardly mean anything. They hadn't been raised together. They shared no blood.

There's no affection, either. Not from him.

She squeezed her eyes shut, unable to look at him while she had thoughts like that. He closed the distance between them, pressing his lips against hers. And she just let it wash over her, warmer than the sun, more refreshing than the water they were standing in.

Desire assaulted her, her stomach tightening, a pulse beating low and hard at the apex of her thighs.

It had been just over a month since their first encounter in his hotel room in New York. Just over a month since she'd been with a man for the first time. It hadn't taken long for her to grow accustomed to it. For her to know exactly what she wanted. For her to learn his body, and to learn what hers desired of him.

He slipped his hand beneath her bikini bottoms, taking hold of her with his large palm. She loved his hands. Loved the feel of them on every inch of her. Loved looking at them. Spent a great deal of time fantasizing about them.

But then, it was like that with every single inch of him.

So many things did not live up to the promise. Did not live up to the hype. Apollo was not one of them. He took her every fantasy and superseded by leaps and bounds.

In comparison with the reality her fantasies of what sex with him would be like seemed childish. Simple.

She had known it would feel good, she had known she would find him attractive. She hadn't realized it would be so raw, so exposing. Hadn't realized it would strip her bare of everything, not just her clothes. She had thought it would just be physical.

That was such a simplistic thought. His body was the missing piece of hers. He was everything she ached for in the dead of night, the reason that she felt hollow sometimes. It was because she was desperate to have him inside of her. Only him.

She parted her lips for him, expecting him to conquer, expecting him to invade. Instead, he was gentle, his tongue sliding slowly against hers, the slick glide sending a sharp pang of need through her. So acute it was almost painful.

She forked her fingers through his hair, deepening the kiss, pressing her body as firmly against his as she could. She knew that if any of his staff members walked out now they would get a bit of a show. But honestly, her brain was too foggy with desire to really get a handle on that reality. She couldn't care. Not for her modesty, not for anyone's sensibilities. There was only this. Only him.

She lost all sense of propriety, all sense of loyalty, all sense of…everything when she was with him.

She became a new person. A different version of Elle.

She had to wonder what might have happened if she had taken the steps to close the distance between them nine years ago. If they would have forgotten about decency back then.

It didn't matter. They were doing this now. She tried to shove aside the thoughts of everything else that had happened in the ensuing years. The wedge that had been driven into the family.

Her father, his mother and her, all on one side of the gulf, with him on the other.

She didn't want to think about them. Not now. Didn't want to think about the father she could never be good enough for. The father who had preferred her stepbrother to her.

Probably still did, in truth. Even though Apollo had taken a chunk out of David St. James's empire, he probably privately celebrated his stepson's ruthlessness.

Apollo might have betrayed them. But Apollo never acted like he wished she were someone else. Apollo never made her feel like she wasn't good enough. He gloried in her body, in the attraction between them. It was more than she had ever had from…anyone.

The thought filled her with a sudden, intense swell of emotion. Whatever they had, whatever this was, it fed her soul in a way nothing else did. Because it was about her. It wasn't about the business. It wasn't about performing to his satisfaction. He cared about performing to hers. They were in this together. They wanted each other.

For once she wasn't striving for approval. Wasn't trying to live up to an expectation she simply never could.

Her father had seen Apollo as his hope. The son he never had. The heir she could never be.

Then he had trusted Apollo to bail him out, never speaking to her about anything. Never consulting her. He had always trusted Apollo above her.

And Apollo had betrayed him.

But that didn't stand in the way of her and Apollo. He didn't look at her and see the unfulfilled promises of someone else. He wanted her. In spite of everything.

It was balm for her soul.

He swept her into his arms, lifting her as though his arms were created to cradle her close. As though she was the perfect weight and size for him. As though this moment had been fated from the beginning.

He carried her up from the pool, striding right into the house, clearly just as unconcerned as she was about being seen. She had a feeling his staff was paid to look the other way when he was conducting affairs in his home. She shoved that thought to the side. She wasn't going to think about other times, other women.

Right now, she was the only one. That would have to be enough.

He started up the stairs, and she put her hand on his cheek, tracing the fine lines on his face. Additions to his features, new and fascinating. She remembered his face so clearly as a teenage boy. Smooth, pretty. Full perfect lips, amusement in his dark eyes, a kind of irreverent quirk to his brow.

He was no longer smooth. Dark stubble covered his jaw, his chin. Deep grooves bracketed his mouth, marred his forehead. The face that had once been pretty was now more rugged, more distinguished. The laughter in his eyes was gone, replaced with a kind of intensity that burned her from the inside out.

The irreverence was still there, though. It was one of her favorite parts of him. That dry, sardonic humor that would make her laugh in the strangest moments. That would take her from anger to entertainment in only a few moments. That would see her kissing him instead of screaming at him thanks to one well-timed comment.

He was one of the few men who had ever stood up to her. Who had gone toe to toe with her and made her feel like she just might lose.

Not for the first time she wondered at the ground

they had covered since then. Wondered about what had happened.

But she didn't have time to turn it over anymore, because they had reached the top of the stairs, and only a second later, her bedroom.

He set her down, water dripping down her body, pooling down around her feet. "I'm going to get the carpet wet."

"I can't say I am very concerned about that."

"Well, it's your carpet."

"Yes, it is," he said, one side of his mouth curving upward.

He regarded her for a moment before taking a step toward her, tracing the line down the edge of her bikini top, the tip of his finger only barely delving beneath. "This is the stuff of my darkest fantasies."

"A fluorescent bikini?"

He chuckled. "You. In this bikini. So much of that beautiful, pale skin on display. Your hair... It should look ridiculous with this color. Instead, you're simply everything bright. I wanted you then. I consider this my reward for good behavior." His smile turned wicked. "You know, I only wish I had known you were a virgin."

"Is that so?"

"Yes. Had I known you were a virgin I would have relished my prize all the more. I was obsessed with having you first. With teaching you about pleasure."

"You did," she said. She had held the words back from him two weeks ago. Because she had not been ready to share that with him. Had not been ready to confess just how much he had meant to her. What it had meant that he was her first lover.

Or why he was.

But there was no use in protecting herself now. She didn't want to.

"It was always you that I wanted," she said. "That was why even though I said I hated you, even though I was so angry at you the first time I kissed you, it went as far as it did. Because it was always you for me, Apollo. No matter how many years have passed, no matter what ugly words were spoken between us, it was always you."

Apollo knew he did not deserve the words that Elle had just spoken. He was using her. For these past two weeks he had been using her. To satisfy his need for her. Biding his time until he could get his revenge, filling the hours with the pleasures of her body knowing that in the end he would betray her.

There was nothing else to do. This thing between them could not last. And he could not deviate from his course of revenge against his stepfamily. Not now.

He had made up his mind. There would be wreckage. Collateral damage.

But he wouldn't think of it now. Instead, he would take that unearned compliment. Savor it. Hold it close. He would consider this the satisfaction of a desire born years ago. The revenge would be a satisfaction of a different desire, but it was a separate issue. In his mind, she wasn't a St. James. Not now. Now, she was his lover. As he had long fantasized.

When he was finished he would end his association with her and continue on, viewing her again as the daughter of his enemy, rather than his mistress.

He could barely tear his gaze away from her, away from her pale, delectable curves, so effortlessly displayed by the flimsy material of the bikini.

That she had done this for him... It was strange. It

created a shifting sensation at the center of his chest, made him feel as though the earth had tilted slightly. This shared memory that they had of this time when they had wanted the same things… It was strange to have it here in the present.

Just take it. It is a gift.

He would. Whether he deserved it or not. Because, as he had already told her, he was the villain here. Nothing would change that.

Slowly, ever so slowly, he untied the top of the bikini, peeling it away from her luscious breasts, baring them to his gaze. She was pale everywhere except for here. Here, she was pink. Pink and perfect and everything he desired. He leaned in, tracing the edge of her puckered nipple with his tongue before sucking her deep into his mouth.

"So sweet," he said, his voice rough and unrecognizable to his own ears. "Better than honey."

She shivered beneath him and he recognized his pleasure coursing through her body. He was learning to read her. Learning to understand what made her moan, what brought her close to the edge. Had learned how to tease her. How to hold her on the brink of climax without giving it to her completely.

He had never kept a lover for this length of time before. Always, he was finished with them after a couple of nights. A couple of weeks was unheard of. There was something…intoxicating about it. Something singular. To know one particular woman's body in such an intimate fashion. Of course, he was well-versed with the female body, but that was different. This was…

Well, this was Elle.

He imagined it would never be the same with another woman, no matter how long he was with her. Elle was a fiery, living fantasy come to life, everything he had ever imagined she might be and more.

It was a damn shame. He wished she was a disappointment. Wished that she was something he could despise. Wished that she could have done something, anything to confirm that he was right to carry out this revenge plot, and use her as he'd planned.

He wished he had left her as the brittle, buttoned-up woman she had seemed in his mind only a couple of weeks ago.

But now he knew her. Knew her body. Knew her soul.

That's ridiculous. You cannot know someone's soul. You haven't one of your own.

He pulled her close, taking hold of the tie on her swimsuit bottoms and tugging the thread roughly, then the other side, letting it fall to the ground. Trying to break the spell that she had cast over him with this bright, insubstantial piece of fabric. It was insane. And yet it was so...

He had advanced no further with her than where he had been nine years ago. He was still a slave to his desires. And now he was old enough to know that going out and getting any redhead at any bar would not suffice.

Now that he had had Elle, he knew that there was no substitute. Ever. There had never been another woman like her, and there never would be again.

He dropped to his knees in front of her, suddenly overwhelmed with his desire. He buried his face between her thighs, tasting her, deep and long, relishing the flavor of her desire as it spread over his tongue. He was insatiable for her. Desperate for her. He pushed one finger deep inside her slick channel, then another, loving the way that she bucked against his hand, the needy cries for pleasure that escaped her lips.

She was desperate. Like he was. She was in this with

him. He needed it proven. Needed to know for sure. He felt like he was losing his mind. He did not know himself now. Never in all his life had a woman made him shake. Never in all his life had a woman owned him in such a way. Never had a woman successfully erased visions of any other.

But she had.

He gripped her hips, holding her tightly against his mouth as he continued to pleasure her, until she shook just as violently as he did. Until she was on the verge. Until she was whimpering, crying out for release. Begging for it.

He loosened his hold on her, sliding the flat of his tongue over her as he rose upward, tracing a line to her belly button, up farther, until he was standing. Until he could capture her mouth with his. He pulled her up against him, let her feel the hard, insistent thrust of his arousal against her stomach. Kissed until he was dizzy. Until she was pleading with him to take her.

He rocked his hips against her, relishing the raw sounds she made, the feeling of her fingernails digging into his skin. It was always like this with her. Desire tinged with violence.

And he loved it.

He backed her up against the bed, and they fell onto it. He positioned himself between her thighs, pressing the head of himself to her slick entrance. He pushed into her easily, her arousal easing the way. She was so hot, so tight. She was made just for him.

As he seated himself fully inside her he had the strongest sensation that he was home. That he was complete for the first time in years.

A deep, strong emotion tugged at his chest, a sense of déjà vu that he didn't want to place. This was new and familiar all at the same time. And he rejected it. Didn't want it. But as his arousal built, as she flexed her hips beneath him, meeting his every thrust, he found he could not hold on to his control and keep the emotions at bay.

She wrapped her legs around his hips, and as she gave herself up to her own release, as his own climax crashed over him like a wave, those feelings crashed through him, as well.

And as he was tossed violently in the surf, he could think of one thing. Elle. That she was the port in the storm. That she was the constant. The North Star by which he had been guided for years. A star he had turned away from.

The realization left him feeling like his chest was full of broken glass. As though he had been wounded, invaded by sharp, shattered splinters he could never hope to remove.

He looked down at Elle, at her lips, flushed with desire, swollen from his kisses, her eyes, slumberous, satisfied. Looking at him as though he held answers.

He had no answers. At this moment, he had nothing but questions.

"Stay with me. Tonight," she said, "could you stay with me?"

And as terror tore at him like a rabid dog, he could do nothing but nod and pull her into his arms. But it did nothing to stop the hemorrhaging in his chest. Did nothing to stem the flow of pure, unmitigated fear pounding through him.

But Elle had asked him to stay. And so he did.

CHAPTER EIGHT

WHEN APOLLO WOKE, it was starting to turn gray outside. And Elle was curled up around him like a cat. He had no doubt, even for a moment, who he was lying in bed with. Who he had fallen asleep with.

He had never been close enough with a woman to even contemplate letting his guard down enough to fall asleep with her. In the past, the moment he finished making love with a woman, he left. There was no reason to linger. Sex, in his experience, could be perfectly impersonal. Sleeping with someone had seemed an intimacy he did not wish to contend with.

But he had fallen asleep with Elle, after she had asked him to stay. He had not imagined he would sleep. But it seemed natural. To hold her in his arms while they both drifted off. Bathing in the afterglow of the pleasure they had shared.

Suddenly, panic overtook him. He had a plan. A plan to make the St. James family pay for the sins they had committed against his family. To avenge the death of his father. The loss of his family fortune. The strange relationship Apollo's mother had been forced into by David St. James.

And every indignity he had suffered. Every moment he had been made to feel like he had not earned his position at the prestigious boarding school he went to. Every time he had to defend his placement in the boardroom because he had come from such humble beginnings.

She was weakening that plan. She was weakening his determination. And he could not let that stand.

He extricated himself from her hold, rolling out of bed. He forked his fingers through his hair, looking around, before remembering he had no clothes in her room. He wrenched open the door, walking down the hall completely naked. All of the staff would have gone home. Anyway, they knew better than to stare too long if they saw something shocking in his home.

Instead of going to his bedroom, he went into his office, taking a bottle of whiskey from the shelf to the left of his desk. He poured a healthy amount, and took a fortifying drink. Elle drove him to drink. This was the second time he'd turned to alcohol to deal with the effects she had on him.

Most women didn't affect him at all.

He had been determined to keep her with him until the attraction between them burned out, but he could see that something else was heating up between them, something he had no hope of burning out half so quickly.

Rage took him over. He didn't want to send her away. He could imagine it, telling her to leave. Never touching her again. Never spending another night with her. Anger overtook him, completely, dictating his next action. He took the half-full glass of whiskey and hurled it at the wall, watching the glass shatter, feeling no remorse at all.

The fact that the very thought of her leaving made him feel so helpless, so enraged was only more evidence that he had to send her away.

If he was going to take his revenge, he would have to take it now.

* * *

They had forgotten to tint the windows. That was Elle's first thought when she woke up the next morning. Her second thought was that she was alone. True to his word, Apollo had not spent the night with her. She shouldn't be surprised, but after she had confessed to him that he was her only lover, she supposed she had expected… something.

She supposed that she was foolish.

For wishing that things could be different. For wishing that something had changed between them. She didn't know what.

She sat up, clutching the blankets to her chest. And suddenly, Apollo came bursting through the door. "Good morning," he said, his mouth set into a grim line.

"Good morning," she said.

During all of the time she'd spent here, he had never come into her room unannounced. He had never come in unless it was to make love. He did not look like he had… that on his mind. Not in the least. He looked… He looked like he had come in with demons on his heels.

"I trust you slept well," he said.

"Yes," she said, a strange, uneasy feeling settling in the center of her chest. She didn't know why. She only knew that something wasn't right.

"I think it is time you left," he said, his words cold.

"But we… I don't understand," she said. "Yesterday we…"

"That was yesterday. And this is today."

She thought back to last night, to what had transpired between them. Had she done something wrong? Had he not liked her wearing the bikini and reminding him of that day? No. Yesterday he had enjoyed it. She knew he had.

"I'm not ready to leave," she said. "We agreed we needed to burn this out and I don't think it's burned out."

"A difference of opinion," he said, his tone hard. "For me, it is over."

"Apollo..."

"Also, effective immediately you have been terminated from your position as CEO of Matte."

"I... What?" She couldn't make sense of his words. She was naked, in bed, after having just spent the night making love with him, and he was firing her.

Two weeks. Two weeks she had spent with this man. In his arms. Kissing him, sharing her body with him... sharing everything.

"You heard me," he continued. His tone was flat. His eyes were flat. He was like a stranger. Only yesterday she had felt that she'd known him more intimately, more deeply than any other person on earth. And now she doubted it. She truly did. "I grow tired of the charade, Elle. Truth be told, I was planning on drawing this out longer. I was anticipating feeling a great sense of pleasure when I let you know that I was simply using you to hurt your father. I planned to set you up as the face of the company, to bring you into greater prominence so that when I made it very clear that I had taken all of your father's assets and left him ruined, the world would know exactly who he was, exactly what that meant. But frankly, I find it's just too tiring. So, I will have to be content in my revenge all on my own."

Her head was spinning. Revenge? She had been under no illusions that there was any affection between Apollo and her, but if anyone should want revenge, it was her. "You... You used me."

"Did you really think that I wanted you?"

She felt like he had driven a spike through her chest.

The cold, black words matching his cold, black eyes, making it impossible to pretend she had misheard. "Of course I did. As far as I know men can't fake..." She gestured toward the front of his pants. "They have to at least be attracted to a woman."

"It isn't just women who can lie back and think of England. What I really wanted, Elle, was to let your father know that I've taken everything from him. What would he think if he knew—?"

"Don't you dare, you bastard."

"Then I would have his company, and his daughter."

"You don't have me," she said, her throat tightening. "Two weeks, Apollo. Two weeks I gave you... I did..." She swallowed hard, panic taking over, tears threatening to fall. "I held nothing back from you! I trusted you with my body."

"A bad decision. I am untrustworthy. I have been from the beginning. You were convenient, darling, but let's be honest. Hardly more than a diversion, and one I cannot afford anymore."

"How can you say that?"

"It's true. Elle, be realistic. What could I possibly want with a near-virgin who's so cold she practically leaves icicles on my lips after a kiss?"

His words struck her like a physical blow. None of this made sense. She couldn't process it. But somewhere, in the middle of all the pain, all the anguish flooding through her like an unchecked tide, she found rage. The same rage that had propelled her into his arms in the first place.

And she clung it to it with everything she had. "How dare you?" she hissed, low and hard. "My father did everything for you. He paid for your education. He loved you—"

"No," he said. "He never loved me. He wanted to possess my mother, at any cost. And he did so. His very own Biblical fantasy where she was his Bathsheba and he sent her husband out to die."

"What?"

"Yes. My family was not always impoverished. Your father and mine were business partners, Elle. But they both fell for the same woman. My mother. She preferred my father. Your father bided his time, waited until he saw the opportunity, and then he used his sway with the board to vote my father out of the company. My father was ruined. Ultimately, he killed himself. My mother held out against your father's pleas for him to join her in the US. As his mistress. He was of course married to your mother then."

"I…"

"My mother agreed when I was eight, and we were starving. He established us in a home near his, and he came to visit often. From what I discovered later, he paid your mother off, then waited an appropriate amount of time before bringing my mother to the estate to be his wife."

"No… My father wouldn't… He didn't…"

"He did. He's a manipulative bastard who sees us all as nothing more than pawns. His actions caused my father to kill himself, it ruined my family. But I started to look into the history of my family. And when I found out why my father killed himself…why he was ruined…it all became clear." He paused. "It was your mother who contacted me."

Elle's mother who had long since abandoned the family. Whom Elle hadn't seen in fifteen years. "My mother?"

"Yes. She had seen me rising in business circles and

she…she found me one night at a bar. I didn't know who she was. Just another blonde who was after a night, I thought. But unlike most women, she didn't want sex. She wanted to talk. She wanted to tell me just what your father was."

"She came and found you? After all these years, not speaking to me for any of them, she came and found *you*? Are you that much more compelling to both of my parents?"

"In her case, I think she was compelled by revenge."

"Did she even ask about me?" Elle asked, despising the small sound of her own voice.

He said nothing, and it was his silence that spoke loudest. Of course she hadn't. She hadn't contacted her in years, why would she be concerned now? "I can't… I don't know what to think. I don't know how to process this."

His top lip curled. "Well, you will have plenty of time to process it while you stand in line filing paperwork to collect unemployment."

"Apollo… You can't do this."

His expression was granite. "I am doing this. It was my plan all along, and I am keeping to it. I am simply shortening the timeline."

Her stomach tightened, her entire body seizing up. She thought she was breaking apart from the inside out.

She had believed in him. Believed that he was the first person to see her for who she was. To want her for herself.

That was the worst betrayal of all. The fact that he'd used her. Not even because he hated her, not even because he wanted revenge on her, but because he wanted it on her *father*. Yet again, she was nothing. Nothing more than the most convenient chess piece on the board.

"Get out," she said, shaking now, trembling inside and out.

"It is my house."

"And it is my room. Leave me with what little dignity I have left." He turned away from her, heading toward the door. "I can't believe you. All the things you let me say. All the things you let me do. The bikini. As if I was… As if I mattered. But I never did. You're not any better than my father. Even if what you say is true, every word of it, you haven't risen above anything."

He turned back to her, his expression bleak. "I never wanted to rise above. I only ever wanted to drag you all into hell with me."

And with that, he walked out of the room, leaving her there, desolate and broken and certain she would never be whole again.

CHAPTER NINE

"IF YOU DON'T mind me saying, Mr. Savas, you've been impossible the past few weeks."

"I know *you* don't mind saying it, Alethea," he said, his tone hard as he looked at his computer screen, ignoring his assistant.

"It's true," she said, turning on her heel and walking out of the office. Apollo didn't look up until the door had been shut firmly behind her.

Damned woman. She was always speaking the truth. He should fire her and hire someone stupid, beautiful and biddable.

When he thought the word *beautiful*, only one face came to mind. Of course, that woman was neither stupid, nor biddable. And she was persistently in his head.

Particularly in his dreams. He had woken up hard and reaching for her and she wasn't there. Because he'd sent her away.

It had seemed necessary at the time. Like he needed to put distance between them. But the longer he spent without her, the more he questioned that decision.

After all, his issue had been his loss of control, but sending her away wasn't any more controlled.

He had removed temptation from his path, but he had

not successfully destroyed his lust for her. Because of that, he was suffering now.

There was no reason to do so, of course. She had nothing to do, nowhere to go. No job. He could have her back. Make her his.

The memory of her—the warm weight of her, her sweet scent, the way she sighed and said his name—haunted him. His days, his nights.

He was like an addict in desperate need of a fix. His hands shaking, sweat breaking out over his skin at the thought of tasting her lips. Feeling her softness beneath his palms.

She was his own personal designer drug. One taste had only sent him headlong into an addiction he couldn't shake.

So maybe that was the problem. Cutting himself off completely would never work. It would only leave him wondering what it would be like to have her one last time. To lose himself inside her. To feel her delicate fingertips skimming over his back.

Just the thought sent a rush of need through him, so hot, so swift it nearly sent him down to his knees.

He had never felt like this before. Had never felt the need to keep and possess quite so fiercely.

As her father felt for your mother?

No. This was different. But one thing he knew: he had spent too many years denying this desire. He would not continue on.

He had been forced into denial, into poverty as a boy because of her father.

He would not subject himself to denial of his needs again.

He would not go one more night without her in his bed.

* * *

Elle was certain she was dying. It had been four weeks since she had left Greece. Four weeks since she had left Apollo, jobless, broken and humiliated. At least none of it had made it out into the public.

All anyone knew was that she had been replaced in her position at Matte. No one knew about her relationship with Apollo, and that was about the only thing saving her from melting into a puddle and sliding down the nearest drain, disappearing forever.

As upset as her father was about the entire situation, at least he didn't blame her. Or, maybe she didn't care. She had no idea how she felt. In only a month her entire life had been completely upended. She was avoiding her father. Avoiding dealing with that situation entirely.

Everything Apollo had said, all of the things he had told her that her father was guilty of, had settled down deep inside of her, and created just enough doubt about… everything that she wasn't sure she could deal with right now.

And then, purely selfishly, there was the issue of her firing.

She stood up, the floor pitching beneath her as she rose from the couch for the first time in hours. Being unemployed was bad for her wardrobe choices. She had been wearing sweats for three days, because there was no one there to see her anyway. Yesterday she'd worn flannels with small foxes on them. Today, her pants had owls.

"Very sexy," she said, crossing the length of the apartment and heading toward her fridge. She opened it up, immediately swamped by the smell coming from the inside. She wrinkled her nose. Something did not smell right. But it wasn't like she kept that much food in the fridge.

She dry heaved, and slammed the door shut. She'd forced herself to eat when she'd first woken up, but nothing tasted like…anything. A broken heart did that to you, apparently. But any semblance of an appetite she might have was gone now.

She felt like she had licked the inside of the tennis shoe. Okay, that thought made her stomach feel even worse.

She heard a knock on her door, and she nearly jumped out of her skin. People didn't just gain admittance to the building, so it had to be someone who already lived here. Though, her neighbors didn't speak to her, so she had no idea who it was or what it could be about.

Taking a deep breath, she crossed the apartment and undid the dead bolt and the chain, jerking it open just as she realized she should have looked through the peephole first.

But it was too late. The door was open, and standing there was her worst nightmare.

Suddenly, the vague sense of nausea intensified and she ran from the room, losing her breakfast violently in the bathroom.

"Elle?" Apollo's voice was coming from behind her.

"Stay away," she said, shakily getting to her feet. "I'm…horrifying."

"You're sick," he said, his tone vaguely accusatory.

"I…wasn't." Except she had been—though not this sick—but off her game for the past few days.

"What are you doing here, anyway?" She wandered over to the sink and splashed cold water on her face. "Who buzzed you in?"

"Some young woman who lives down the hall. Nose ring. Pink hair. She thought I looked trustworthy."

Elle laughed. Bitter, hollow. "She thought you looked like you belonged in her bed. I would give her advanced warning, but I imagine she wouldn't really care either way."

"Sadly for her. I'm not on the market."

"Okay. If you aren't here to hook up with my down-the-hall neighbor, why are you here?"

"Would you believe that I came to check on you?"

"No."

"I want you back."

"No," she said, her tone incredulous. "You can't have me back. You were awful to me. You fired me."

"And now you don't have a job. I thought you might be interested in pursuing some sort of arrangement."

She laughed, flinging her arms wide. "And here I am, vomiting as you ask me to come be your mistress. Really, there are probably more romantic settings than the bathroom."

"You need money. You certainly need a way to occupy your time."

"You're despicable."

She swept past him, trying to hold her head high. Difficult to do when the man who had made love to you then humiliated you had just seen you puke.

"Maybe," he said, lingering in the door frame, bracing his hands against it. "But it doesn't change the facts."

"Oh," she said, the world tilting slightly. "I need to lie down."

He frowned. "How long have you been feeling sick?"

"I told you, I only just… That, in the bathroom."

"You've been otherwise feeling well?"

"Not really. But then, you humiliated me and fired

me. So I don't know how well you could possibly expect me to feel."

"I'm not talking about your emotions, I'm talking about physically."

"No. I have not been feeling very well. But your emotions inform things like that."

"Have you gotten your period?"

Her mouth dropped open. "What kind of question is that?"

"The only question that matters to me right now."

Ice shivered down her spine. "I haven't," she said. "But that doesn't… It doesn't mean anything."

"You're here vomiting and looking pale, you haven't had your period in the past month and you don't think that means anything."

"We…"

"Were not very careful."

No, they hadn't been. They hadn't used a condom in the elevator, and again during that last time at his home. So really… She hadn't had a period since the elevator. "No, I guess we weren't."

"And it didn't occur to you until just now that you might be pregnant?"

"No," she said, her hand flying to her mouth, her eyes wide. "No. I'm not… I'm not."

"You have no way of knowing that."

No. She didn't. Because she hadn't taken a test. And, while she had never been particularly regular, that hadn't exactly been a problem because she had been a virgin. Now…it was a bit suspicious.

"I mean, I would prefer to wait a few days…"

He had already pulled out a cell phone. "Yes, Alethea? Find a discreet women's doctor in Manhattan who can see a patient immediately. Text me the information once you have it. When I say immediately, I mean I'm about to get in the car and start driving. They had better be ready to see us."

He hung up, and she could only stare at him. "What are you doing?"

"We are going to answer this question once and for all, *agape*. And make no mistake, if you are carrying my child there is no question that you are coming back to Greece with me. Immediately."

He could do nothing but pace outside the office at the posh, private medical facility he had taken Elle to.

He had found himself back in Manhattan for business reasons, and then he had displayed a characteristic weakness and found himself at Elle's building.

He did not know what manner of witchcraft Elle possessed that she made it impossible for him to forget her. Forget how she made him feel. Whether it was four weeks in the past, or nine years— before he had ever even touched her. She was a woman who lingered in his mind in a way that none before her—or since—ever had.

He wondered now if she had been some sort of bad omen. If the fact that he had never been able to get her out of his mind had been a warning of some kind. If she were truly pregnant with his child, he could not discount that. He had never intended to have children. But the moment the idea that she might be pregnant had entered his mind he had known that he would take possession of his child.

After his own childhood, after the way he had lost his father, he knew he would never subject his own child to such a thing. To a life without the man who was meant to protect him.

He gritted his teeth. His own father's feelings had hardly been his fault. He had been pushed into ruin by

David St. James. The fault would always lie with St. James. Apollo however was standing on his own two feet. No one was pushing him anywhere.

The door opened, and Elle emerged, clutching a few pieces of paper, her face pale. He didn't need her to speak to know what the answer was.

He had never imagined being in this situation. He supposed that any man who was sexually active could potentially face it, but he had always been very careful. So it was never anything he had considered seriously. But he had not been careful with Elle. The theme in their relationship, and the consequences of that, were now coming home to roost.

There was no panic. There was not even any rage, though he had expected it. No, there was nothing but cold, clean determination. He knew exactly what he was going to do. What he would demand.

"I…"

"Yes, I think I can guess."

"I don't know what we're going to do."

"I know exactly what we are going to do."

Her eyes widened. "You do?"

"Yes. You will be coming back to Athens with me. And then, *agape*, you and I are going to marry."

Elle was dimly aware of the fact that she was sitting in Apollo's limo, essentially in a catatonic state. But she had just found out she was pregnant with the baby of a man who despised her and her family, a man who had left her jobless and broken when he had ended their affair.

She had never really thought about being a mother. Her own mother had abandoned her early on and not bothered to keep in touch at all. Her stepmother was a lovely woman, but often silent next to her husband.

And Elle's father was so…imposing. He didn't bend. He didn't show affection. It was like loving a rock.

She had never imagined trying to re-create that parent-child relationship with herself in the parenting hot seat. It seemed…completely unappealing. It also meant she was linked to Apollo. Forever.

As if you weren't before.

She gritted her teeth. She had no idea what to say. No idea what to do next. And as far as she knew she was being shanghaied and sent to Athens again.

That thought sent her into action. "I'm not going to marry you."

He chuckled, a dark, humorless sound. "Then prepare yourself for a custody battle that will drain you of your every resource."

She blinked. "Who said I would fight you for custody?"

The moment she said it, she realized that she would. Not because her parents had been wonderful, not because they had made her long for a parent-child relationship in her own life. But because they had demonstrated in a million small ways how unimportant she was. She would be damned if her own child would walk through life feeling like their mother couldn't be bothered with them.

Just the thought made her stomach clench in agony. Her own little one, believing that she didn't want them. She wanted to apologize to the little life inside her. As though it had somehow sensed her hesitance.

"If you don't feel strongly enough about our child to stand and fight for them, then I would gladly have you step aside."

"I won't," she said, her tone infused with conviction.

The numbness was starting to wear off. And even though she couldn't quite imagine what it would be like to have a child, even though she wasn't sure if she was devastated or happy, she knew that she wouldn't stand aside.

"You just said—"

"Yes, well, I am trying to figure out exactly where I stand. It might surprise you to know this but I didn't exactly fantasize about a life with a picket fence, a husband and children."

"It doesn't surprise me. A woman with as much white in her apartment as you have doesn't seem to be planning ahead for sticky fingers."

"I wasn't. You can be sure of that. But I'm also not one to walk away from my responsibilities. And I don't want any child of mine going through life imagining they aren't wanted."

"Then, marriage it will be."

Her mind was ticking over at a million miles a minute. "I would have a few conditions," she said.

She could not believe she had just said that. She knew that you weren't supposed to negotiate with terrorists or superalpha Greek billionaires who had far too high of an opinion of themselves. So, she didn't know why she was attempting it.

"Conditions, *agape*?" He sounded...angry. But interested.

"Yes. Conditions." Now she had to quickly think of her conditions. "New York is my home. I'm not leaving New York."

"I have a villa in Greece."

"I daresay you have homes all over the world. I know you don't have a permanent residence in New York, but I do."

"Your apartment is the size of a postage stamp."

"It's big enough."

"For you. There is no room for a child. No room for a husband."

She gritted her teeth. "I did not agree to taking a husband. Not yet. I have conditions, but I won't make my final decision until I'm certain that the situation is to my liking."

"I'm not certain you want to challenge my authority. I am a well-respected billionaire, after all, and you are unemployed. The daughter of a businessman on the verge of being washed-up. If your mother hasn't spent all of his payoff money by now, she's certainly close to it. What could you possibly give a child that I can't?"

"Love. Warmth. Human emotion?"

"I'm sure the court will be more impressed with my net worth."

"I don't think so. Everyone agrees that a child needs love above anything else."

"And you feel you are more qualified to give a child parental love that I am?"

She shifted in her seat. "Yes. I do."

"On what grounds? Prior to being unemployed you were a workaholic."

"I was not."

"Did you have a single friend who was not also a co-worker?"

She didn't even have to think about that. She knew the answer to the question. But whether or not they were from work Suki and Christine were real friends. Suki had brought cupcakes after Elle had been fired. *Friendship*.

Though the thought of cupcakes made her stomach turn right now.

"You're a workaholic, too," she said.

"I'm also a man and a billionaire. No one will judge

me for the amount of time I spend working. It is irrelevant. Not so for you."

"The point is, I am the child's mother and I don't think I'm going to have an issue retaining custody."

"I disagree."

"You will have to wait, Apollo," she said, her voice infused with iron, with a strength she wasn't sure she truly felt right now. "I'm not afraid of fighting you in court. To hear you tell it your mother was manipulated into a relationship with my father and now you want to do the same to me? How are you any better?"

"I'm not," he said, his expression bleak, cold. But only for a moment. Then his walls went back up.

"Name your conditions clearly."

"I want to stay in New York. I wish to have the child here. I wish to raise him here."

"The child will be Greek. He should be exposed to his homeland."

"Exposure is fine. But I want him raised here. I want to stay here. Because that leads me to my next requirement. I want my job back."

"The new CEO has only been there for a month. If I let him go I will seem capricious."

"There is a cost to everything. And that is the cost to having me without muss or fuss. Do you accept, or not?"

She wasn't certain if she wanted him to say yes, or if she wanted him to refuse. She wasn't sure what she wanted at all.

"I accept."

A strange mixture of relief and terror washed through her. "Excellent."

He pulled out his phone again. "Alethea," he said. "I require some real estate. A penthouse, Manhattan. Something large, but secure. No rooftop balconies or anything like that. Or, if there are balconies, they need to be secure. Childproof." He hung up.

"Is your assistant finding you a house?"

"No, *agape*," he said, smiling a smile that was not friendly at all. "My assistant is going to find us a home. Now do you agree to marry me?"

Elle took a deep breath and met that coal-black gaze. "If I find the conditions are met to my satisfaction. And if I feel you won't spend my whole life making me miserable. You said I was your revenge, Apollo. Until you see me as a woman—a whole woman, not your stepsister who you harbor rage against, not an instrument of vengeance to use against my father—you will not have me. Not in your life, not as your wife. That's a promise."

CHAPTER TEN

ALETHEA WAS NOTHING if not efficient, and by that afternoon he and Elle were standing in an empty penthouse at the top of the building in Midtown. It was spacious, though hardly the sun-drenched villa he chose to call home in Greece. But it would do.

"Do you find this satisfactory?"

"I have a… I have a house," she said.

"Oh, I have already taken care of listing it for you. Unless you wish to keep it as some sort of workspace, I figured it would be best to sell it."

"You're selling my house?"

"My men have been over there packing your things."

She whirled around, her hands clenched into fists. "Apollo! I can't believe you would do something like that."

He turned to her, arching a dark brow. "Really. You can't believe I would do something like that? And here I thought it was in keeping with my character."

She pressed her fists up against her eyes, as though she was trying to use them to hold back her rage. "Everything is changing too quickly."

"Things have been changing quickly for the past two months. First, we had sex. Then you went to Greece. Then we had more sex. You lost your job. Now you're having a baby and we're working at integrating our lives. It's a fast-moving train, life is."

In truth, his life had been stagnant for quite a few years. Yes, he had more money than he could possibly spend in a lifetime. His business had continued to grow. He had fixated on his revenge plan against the St. James family. But beyond that, nothing had moved significantly in years. His life was an endless array of beautiful women, meaningless events that required him to put on a suit and smile politely at those in attendance. This was…

This was the first time in a long time he had something new.

It wasn't the revenge he had planned when he'd come back to New York, but it was…interesting. He imagined Elle would take exception to him calling her accidental pregnancy interesting.

"Fine. It's very you. But you can't just come into my life and completely reorder it."

"Why not? You have done it to me."

She looked stunned for a moment. "Have I?"

"You are going to make me a father. If that is not upending my life, I don't know what is."

"I suppose it depends on how involved you intend to be."

He knew nothing about how to be a good father. He could scarcely remember his own. When the other man had been alive he had all but lived at the corporate headquarters for the business he shared with David St. James. And then, after that, after the disgrace, he had sunk into drugs and alcohol. Affairs. Only a few years later he was dead.

As far as David went…the man had been an attentive stepfather. He had been… Well, none of it mattered now. Because of what he had revealed himself to be.

"I am a busy man. A wealthy man. I plan to keep my involvement somewhat limited," he said.

"Then, I suppose your personal life doesn't have to change much. Oh," she said, her green gaze turning sharp. "Except you are required to remain faithful to me."

Her words hit him low and hard in the stomach. Punched the wound he had just been examining. He could not imagine wanting a woman other than Elle. He had not taken anyone else to his bed in the month since they had parted. Unusual for him.

In fact, from the moment he had taken over her father's company, from the moment he had first taken over the magazine and brought her back into his life on a semi-regular basis, he had not been with another woman. Because the moment Elle St. James had come back into his life his body had reignited its obsession for her. Still, he did not wish for her to know that. He did not want her issuing more edicts.

He had agreed to New York, because that was simple. He had agreed to giving her the position at Matte back because it was also simple. And quite apart from that, the fact that he was providing David St. James with his first grandchild was a whole new, delicious sort of revenge.

He no longer needed to throw her out of the company. No longer required to destroy St. James in that way. He had the man's daughter. She was having his baby. She would be his wife, Apollo was confident in that.

Yes, there was a great deal he could do with that. He was certain.

"I have no experience with fidelity," he said. "I will make no promises on that score."

"Then you will enjoy the single life. If you touch another woman, you certainly won't be touching me."

"I highly doubt that."

He and Elle could scarcely be in the same room together without tearing each other's clothes off. Today was an exception, brought about by the shock of her discovering she was pregnant and by the need to see to the logistics created by that circumstance. But he knew that very soon he would have her on her back begging for his possession.

Or she will have you on your back begging for hers.

He refused to consider that. Refused to think of things that way. She was a slave to the pleasure that ignited between them every time they touched, just as he was. He was not at a disadvantage. He was not alone in it.

"The perk of staying single is that I will be free to pursue other lovers," she said, shaking her head, her coppery mane shimmering in the sunlight filtering through the large windows that overlooked Central Park.

"I don't believe that," he said, rage a hot, living thing in his stomach. The thought of another man touching Elle was anathema. But she was bluffing, and he would call her on that.

"Why is that? I may have been a virgin before you and I met, Apollo, but now that you have shown me just how enjoyable sex can be I don't think you can possibly ask me to forgo the pleasure."

"I damn well can."

She laughed. "Careful. Your desperation is showing. You wouldn't want me to understand where my real power is in all of this."

She hit too close to the bone there, cut him far too deeply.

And suddenly, he did not care that today had been an emotional one for her. He did not care that she was in a fragile state. Only than only a couple of hours ago she had been sick in front of him, while wearing sweatpants. He always wanted Elle. Always. There was never a time when he didn't crave her touch. And this was no exception.

He crossed the vacant expanse of the living area, wrapping his arm around her waist and tugging her up against him, cupping her chin with his thumb and forefinger. "Do not push me, Elle. You will not like the result."

"Do not push *me*, Apollo."

"We push each other, *agape*, that's the honest truth. And look at where it has gotten us."

"Yes. I daresay it is not the most pleasant situation."

"I could make it much more pleasant if you weren't so stubborn."

She glared at him. "The same goes for you."

"You start again at Matte tomorrow. I will give your replacement a generous severance."

He released his hold on her.

"Excellent," she said, smoothing her clothing, her voice making it sound like she thought all of this was anything but excellent.

"I have arranged for all of our things to be moved into the penthouse by tonight."

She laughed. "That isn't possible."

He lifted his shoulder. "It is possible when you pay with cash."

She shook her head. "That's the problem with you, Apollo, you have never been denied anything that you wanted."

"I don't know, Elle, I felt fairly denied of my father after he put a bullet in his brain. And why did he do that? Oh, yes. Because his dear friend and business partner betrayed him. Yes, I know a little bit about deprivation. I refuse to apologize for enjoying luxury now."

She blinked. "I'm sorry. I didn't mean…"

He waved a hand. "I am not so sensitive. Anyway, this is par for the course between us, yes? We must tear strips off each other's hides. Because if we do not, we will tear each other's clothes off instead."

She sniffed. "Maybe once. But not anymore."

"You may cling to that illusion all you want. Either way, your things will be here by this evening. How you choose to spend your time between now and then is up to you."

The next day, when Elle walked into the fully furnished penthouse she felt dazed. Her life was changing so quickly. They were going to be sharing a space while he was in New York. Living together. And he wanted to marry her.

It made her stomach tight. Made her feel dizzy.

The terrifying thing was there was some small, delusional piece of her that felt...excited. As though this were some kind of fairy tale. As though the two of them were embarking on a real relationship. Possibly, a real marriage. As though he wanted her, because she was Elle, because of the heat and fire between them, not because she was carrying his baby.

He came back. He came back before he knew you were pregnant.

She held that close. Turned it over and examined it as though it was some kind of rare treasure that she wanted to keep shielded from the world. That she never wanted to look away from. He had returned to her before he found out about the baby. She didn't know what that meant. Yes, he had said he wanted her to return as his mistress. But she knew full well that a man like Apollo was more than capable of getting any woman he desired. He didn't need her. But he had still come for her.

And the moment he had found out about the baby he had taken charge, taken everything into hand and done everything he could to make their arrangement permanent.

It was perhaps foolish to assign any meaning to that, but she couldn't help it.

At the bottom of it all, at the end of everything, she just wanted someone who wanted to be with her. Maybe that was a sad admission. But she had been lonely for so long. For all of her life. And the way that Apollo looked at her, the way that he commanded her body, so fierce and intense, at the exclusion of all else, made her hopeful that there was more to his attentions than he was willing to admit.

Of course, he would not promise to be faithful to her.

She blinked, swallowing hard, continuing to examine the modern layout of the penthouse. "Which room will be mine?"

"Any one that you choose," he said. "Though the master bedroom already has your things in it."

"Not yours?"

He lifted his shoulder. "I have several other residences. I may not always be here as frequently as you are. My headquarters will remain in Greece. That means I will only spend a small amount of time here."

The idea of him being with other women flooded her mind again. Of course. He wasn't actually planning on living with her. Not really. Not all the time. He was taking possession of her, but he was holding her at arm's length. It shouldn't surprise her. But it did hurt.

And it did nothing to remove the traitorous beacon of hope that still burned down in the pit of her stomach. She should harbor no hope where he was concerned, and still that small part of her whispered: *But he came back before he knew about the baby.*

She wasn't going to let him see her hope.

"That's fine. It will be good for the child, I think, to have us in the same house sometimes. At least there is space. I think I might go lie down," she said, heading toward the stairs that led to the upper level of the penthouse and the bedrooms.

"You're welcome to. But we have a dinner reservation in four hours. I expect you to be ready by then."

She gritted her teeth. "Is this going to be nothing more than a series of edicts?"

"You keep challenging them, I keep trying."

"Well, thankfully a meal is not a marriage."

She continued on up the stairs. Then she walked down the hall and pushed open the door to her new bedroom. In her new house. Suddenly, her knees felt like they were going to buckle. Everything was so overwhelming. The decisions she suddenly had to make. She moved quickly to the bed and threw herself down on the soft surface. And then she did the thing she allowed so very rarely. She buried her face in the pillow and wept.

Elle was always beautiful. That was part of the problem with her. No matter that she was forbidden, either because she was his stepsister or the daughter of his enemy, she was too beautiful. But tonight, in a short cream lace dress, her skin looking as waxen as a doll's, her red hair falling softly around her shoulders, she was like a particularly terrified angel. Otherworldly. Ethereal.

And all he could think of was that he wanted to drag her into the pit with him. Make her fall, as he had done.

He had not lied when he had told her that all he had ever wanted was to bring her down to his level. To somehow make it acceptable for a man like him to touch a woman like her.

What does it matter what is acceptable?

He didn't even know what was acceptable anymore. So the question, he supposed, was moot.

He had not told her what the aim of the dinner was. She would be angry at him, but he could not see her resisting once she saw the ring.

He had gone to a jewelry store today and chosen the ring for her himself. A large square-cut champagne diamond that seemed to capture her particular brand of unique elegance better than a standard sort of engagement ring.

He had also chosen one of the most up-and-coming restaurants in Manhattan to perform the deed. Because there was guaranteed to be paparazzi lurking, even if they were hiding in the hedgerows, so to speak. And, beyond that, there would be people there with cameras ready to take pictures and post what they had seen to the internet. Getting the word out had never been so easy, and since discretion was the furthest thing from his mind, it suited him.

He took her hand, running his thumb over the smooth, silken skin. Some unknown, possessive, caveman part of him relished what was about to happen. The fact that soon he would put his ring on her finger, and the world would know that she belonged to him. He gloried in that. The fact that there would be a sign of his ownership of her.

That made him think of the baby. Of the fact that she would soon grow round with it, yet more evidence of the fact that he had bound her to him, irrevocably, intensely.

He did not know who he was just now. But then, with Elle, he never did.

She looked down at his hand as though it was a potentially dangerous snake. "I don't think you brought me here simply to treat me to a nice meal. Though, it was nice."

"And we have not yet gotten to dessert."

She drew her hand back slowly. "No, we haven't. And you have been perfectly pleasant bordering on solicitous through the entire meal. And so, I need to know what's happening."

"I had planned to wait until you were finished with your cake, *agape*, but if you are feeling impatient then I am more than happy to reveal the reason why I have brought you out tonight."

He reached into the interior pocket of his suit jacket and produced a small velvet box. Though he had not imagined it possible, more color drained from Elle's face. "Is that…"

He shifted from his position in the chair, moving forward, dropping down to one knee in front of where Elle sat. This was yet another thing he had not imagined doing in all of his life. Lowering himself like this. Getting on his knees before a woman. But if the charade was going to work then he had to commit to it. There could be no doing this halfway.

"Elle St. James, I would be very honored if you would accept the offer to become my wife."

He could feel the eyes of all the diners in the restaurant on them, could sense that everyone was watching. And then he heard the sound of shutters. And he knew that it was being documented, just as he had planned. Knew that it would be a headline in the business pages by tomorrow.

"I—I told you I couldn't answer this now," she said, her tone hushed.

If Elle hesitated, she would potentially cause trouble

for him. Perhaps, in his arrogance, he had overplayed his hand.

"I wish for you to become my wife," he said. "You are the only woman I have ever imagined spending my life with. Please, do me the honor of saying yes."

It was the truth, even if it was a misleading truth. In all honesty, he had never imagined taking another woman as his wife. But then, he had not begun thinking about taking Elle for a wife until this morning. So, he supposed there was room for interpretation with those words. But they were not a lie.

Yet her expression remained set.

"Would you like to see the ring?" he asked. If he was not enough enticement then perhaps the jewelry would be.

He opened the lid on the jewelry box, revealing his carefully chosen selection.

She looked at it, her face frozen. Unreadable. She lifted her hand, as though she was going to reach out and touch it, before drawing her hand back quickly, as if the ring was a snake that might bite her.

"No," she said.

"No?" he asked. He was on his knees, on the damn floor in the damn restaurant, and she had refused him.

He felt…at a loss, and that was completely foreign to him. And along with that hollow feeling came…pain. Deep. Stabbing.

She stood suddenly, stumbling around him. "I don't think I want dessert," she said, her voice strangled.

"Are you certain?"

"Yes. I told you I wasn't sure what I wanted and you—" she looked around the room "—you did your best to make this public so that I couldn't say no. You don't get to behave this way, Apollo. I'm not your pawn. I'm not anyone's pawn."

"We will speak more in the car," he said. "There is no point in discussing it here."

"Of course not," she said, "we would not wish for me to make a scene."

He did not have to worry about the check, as the restaurant already had his details, so he took hold of Elle's hand, and the two of them made their way from the restaurant, still with the watchful eyes of the other patrons on them. A quick push of a button on his phone, and his car was brought around to the front. He opened the door for her, then slid inside, and the two of them remained silent until his driver pulled away from the curb. After issuing instructions to take them home he raised the partition between the front seat and the back, shrouding them in privacy.

"Is everything a game to you?" she asked, once they were alone, her expression fierce.

"It is not a game," he said, his voice hard. "It is a strategy. I have spent the past several years planning my revenge against your family. I was finished with it. But now, here you are, and you are pregnant with my baby. I want what I want, Elle, and I intend on getting it."

"So what? You thought you could shock me into saying yes?"

"I thought the ring might do it." It had never occurred to him it might not. Had never truly occurred to him she might refuse.

"If I wanted a ring, I would buy my own. One that did not come with a husband attached."

"Marriage makes sense," he insisted.

"I don't care about sense!" she shouted, her voice filling up the space in the car. "None of this, not ever, not from the first time we touched, was ever about sense."

"Then why pretend it matters now? Why resist me when we both know you're going to give in?"

"Because you would say things like that. Because you think me giving in to you is an inevitability. Because you do not listen, damn you!"

"You're still behaving like you have a choice here," he said, hardening his voice.

"I'm a fool. I keep expecting to discover you feel *something* for me. Anything."

Her words were raw, honest, not the shotgun shells filled with anger her statements typically were. There was a vulnerability here. An honesty he had not anticipated. They scraped at him, tore strips from his hide.

"Of course I feel something for you," he said. "I want you." The words were much more raw, much more shattered than he wanted them to be. But he was rapidly losing control. Of this moment. Of himself.

It was always so with Elle. Always.

She shook her head. "That is not the same thing."

"And yet, it is all I have."

"Because you hate my family so much?"

"Touching you was a betrayal of my father. Of my mother. I had thought to take the thing between us and twist it into something I can use."

"You're that angry?"

"Everything that I built my life around was a lie," he said, his words escaping with a force that shocked him. "I thought your father simply cared about me. Instead, it was all a part of his twisted obsession with my mother. He allowed me to care for him, acted as though he cared for me, while the whole time he knew…he knew he was the reason my father killed himself. So you tell me, Elle, in my position would you not also crave revenge?"

"It solves nothing," she said. "You had your revenge in

hand. You had it for four weeks, you thought it was finished. You had ousted me from my position as CEO. You were done with me. Done with my family, and yet still you were back at my door. So tell me, Apollo, what has revenge solved for you? What has it fixed? Your father is still gone. And you still want me. You are in fact begging me to be your wife. Where is your power in revenge?"

He could not deny it, though he wished to. Though he wished he could tell her that he had been using her all along. He had shown his hand when he had returned to her apartment. When he had asked for her to be his mistress.

And it was not only to her he had shown his hand, but to himself.

"I want you," he said. "Quite apart from any plans for revenge."

"You think that would make a marriage work?"

"It would work because we would make it work. We are attracted to each other, is that not enough?"

"I don't know. I never gave serious thought to marriage. I don't know what I want out of one." She blinked. "Except I would like more than screaming at my husband. I would like more than wondering if he is away having an affair. I would like to be chosen. Just once. Not because of someone else. You know, I'm only the CEO of Matte because it was my father's last attempt to keep hold of his empire. And you... What you really want is to make me your wife so you can lord it over my father."

"I know you don't put stock in my desire for you, because it isn't emotional. I am not capable of the kind of emotion you are talking about. But I will tell you that had I been able to want any other woman, had I had dominion over my desire for you—I never would have given in."

"I'm supposed to rejoice because you didn't *want* to want me?"

"Yes," he said, simply.

"You truly are arrogant. And you don't understand women very well."

He chuckled. "I understand parts of a woman."

"I can't deny that. But I can also tell you that it leaves you cold after, no matter how hot you burn in the moment."

CHAPTER ELEVEN

ELLE FELT DEFLATED by the time they arrived back at the penthouse. She said nothing to him as they went inside, as she walked back to her bedroom and stripped off her jewelry. How had she ever thought she could handle this man? This man who was so twisted by his desire to injure her family that he was willing to consider anyone who stood in his way as collateral damage.

If he acted like a human man, with feelings and emotions and normal connections, then it would be a simple thing to make him understand. But he didn't. She had no idea how to appeal to this enigma. This immovable rock who looked like a man but didn't behave like one.

She remembered thinking only a few weeks ago that he was heartless. She hated that she was more and more convinced it was true.

She had known him for so many years, and yet didn't know him at all. She knew his body. Knew what made him shake, knew just how to taste him, how to touch him. And she had heard that dark edge that crept into his voice when he spoke about his past, that hinted at the pain he had been through. At how he felt about it all. About what it had done to him. But she could not for the life of her imagine him as a husband. As a father. She knew fragments of him. The boy he had been, the man he was now.

The ruthless and cruel businessman, and the solicitous lover. But those things did not mesh in her mind. She couldn't marry the details together.

She sat in her room for a moment longer, not bothering to change out of her dress, checking her emails and wasting time on the internet until an hour had passed since they'd come home. Then she stood, crossing the room before she had time to fully process what she was doing. Making her way through the penthouse toward his bedroom. She paused at the door, placing her palm on her chest, feeling the raging of her heartbeat beneath her palm. Then she pushed the door open. He was in bed, naked, his blankets pushed down low on his hips, his arm flung up above his head. He was not asleep. He opened his eyes when she opened the door, arching one dark brow. "Yes?"

She crossed the room, climbing onto the bed, staying on top of the covers, lying down next to him.

He shifted, leaning over as though he was going to kiss her. She held up her hand. "No," she said, "I want to talk."

"Well, *agape*, I do not talk in bed."

"You also don't get women pregnant, and you don't ask them to marry you. Given that I already had a couple of exceptions made for me, I would ask that you make one more."

"As you wish," he said, moving back into the position he'd been in when she had come in.

"I want to know you," she said.

He paused. "There is little to know."

"I only knew bits and pieces of your childhood. Whatever you told me. But I'm curious now about all of it. With what I know now, with what you know now, I am curious about everything."

Apollo sighed. "Okay. When I was born, I lived in a

beautiful home. But that did not last. My father worked all the time, and I rarely saw him. Then when I was very young, he lost his position in the company he owned with your father. What was done to him was ruthless, as you know. From there, we lost our home. We lost everything. We lived in…modest housing, to put it mildly."

She wanted to touch him. She had just decided touching was easier than talking, that kissing was easier than honesty. Their bodies were so much easier than anything else. But putting healthy distance between them, she didn't interrupt.

"My father did not take our descent into poverty well. He dealt with his issues by taking drugs, by drinking. Eventually, what little money we had was swallowed up by his addictions. We ended up on the streets. Shortly after that, when he saw what had become of us, when he saw what had become of the family, he killed himself. I will never know why. If he felt ashamed, if he thought we would be better off without him somehow. If he simply didn't want to try anymore. I can never know the answer. And in the end it doesn't matter. The decision was made. The years passed. But one thing I do know is that he would want recompense for what happened to him. For what happened to us."

"That he should have taken himself," she said, the words coming slowly, but with conviction. "If he cared that much he would've stuck around to get revenge himself."

"He couldn't. For whatever reason," he said. "Regardless, my mother and I found ourselves on the streets, then eventually in a horrible group home sort of place. That was when we were sent for. My mother gave very few details, but she said we were going to a new home. Starting over in America. There was a house. Small, I suppose, by some standards. But clean. We wanted for nothing. Suddenly my mother was able to be home with me, instead of desperately searching for work. I had a bed every night."

"I… I can't imagine what that would mean to you in those circumstances."

"I can barely remember. Though it's something I try to hold on to. So that I never forget what it means to be hungry. When you lose the memory of your hunger…you forget why you need success."

She nodded in the darkness. "I know what you mean." She was hungry, too. Not for food or shelter. But for approval she'd never gotten before.

"Your father had come to visit us many times. Sometimes a nanny would be sent to care for me and my mother would go away for a weekend. To be with him, though, I had a boy's understanding. Your father was always good to us. To me. And when he wished to marry my mother, when he spirited us both away to your estate, I thought… I thought we had everything. Suddenly, I gained the world that I had only ever seen glimpses of before."

"I remember you arriving. I was awful to you. Because you scared me. You were…the most beautiful thing I'd ever seen and I knew I shouldn't think that about my stepbrother…like that."

"I suppose not," he said. "You were smart to hold me at a distance, Elle."

"I don't know if *smart* is the word I would use. But it was definitely a defense that worked for a while."

He chuckled. "Yes, it did work for a bit." He paused. "I never asked you… I never asked what it was like to lose your mother like you did. I suppose…your father is as responsible for that as he is for the loss of my father."

The thought made her stomach sink. "I know my father isn't perfect but I have a hard time believing he was so manipulative. But then, I guess maybe I don't... He's a man who likes control, and a man who thinks nothing of pitting his children against each other. So why wouldn't he have always done this, with every person he could? He does it to his own flesh and blood." She moved closer to him, only a bit. "My mother mostly cared about parties and handbags. Lunches with her friends. She was a trophy wife. Her identity was in who my father was, and I suppose that's why I wanted so badly to find something else. To succeed at Matte. To make my own achievements. Except...they were my father's too, really. I was living out my father's plans in my need to please him, in my need to rebel against my mother. I did miss her," she continued. "I really did. Even though I was mostly cared for by nannies. She was my mother, and she smelled of Chanel and vanilla shampoo. And I loved her."

"Of course you did," he said. "My father was distant, a workaholic and an addict, and still I loved him."

"I was happy to have your mother. Mariam has always been good to me."

"But she is not your mother."

Elle's throat tightened. "No. She isn't."

"Nothing can replace what we've lost."

"I guess in a way both of our parents chose to leave us," she said. "Though...my mother could have chosen to come back."

"Or perhaps not. Perhaps she doesn't feel like she can. Not now."

"Maybe. When it became clear the takeover of the company was...hostile... When it became clear you weren't helping...my father put me in control of Matte. And I knew why. I knew it was to use me as a shield. But still, I accepted the position. He's…all I have, really, and I wanted to please him," she said. "I wanted so badly to be accepted. I just wanted him to be proud of me. And then you came in and bought everything out. I thought maybe if I could hold on to my position he would see that I have deserved it all along. But you fired me."

"Had I known your position as CEO was such a contentious one, I might have left you alone."

"I don't know that you would have, Apollo. It isn't in your nature."

"I don't suppose it is."

"I wonder what I would have done," she said, "if he had not selected for me. If I had not been so determined to prove to him that I could be everything that…that you weren't for him."

"You can try and find out, you know. You don't have to go back to work as you. You feel trapped there… There is no reason for you to be there."

"I feel like my team is counting on me. I poured endless hours into it. So much time and energy."

"But you do not have to be there. You are the mother of my child and whatever happens, I will support you financially. You can simply stay home with our child if you prefer. You can go back to school."

She laughed. "I feel like it's too late, really."

"I hope it's never too late to change what you are," he said. "In part because I have been many things in my life. A child of privilege, a gutter snipe, a charity case, wealthy again… We can always change what we are, as long as we stay on earth to breathe one more time."

His words settled heavily on her chest. His father had stopped breathing. And so he had ended his story. "I understand that," she said.

"So if you could do anything, what would you do?"

"I would like to advocate for people who can't do it for themselves. To use the fact that I enjoy challenging people to accomplish something good. A lawyer. But for children, maybe. For women who have been abused."

"That's a very worthy goal," he said.

She shrugged. "It's a fantasy. Anyway, I feel like I was making so much progress with the brand. Really bringing it into the modern era. I know profits aren't off the charts, but the books and cosmetics and the other tie-in products have really taken us to a new level. I want the chance to fight for my staff, for my team."

"Then that is what you will continue to do," he said.

"Why are you doing all this? Saying all this?"

"The baby," he said.

"Of course."

Her eyelids felt heavy now. It was on the tip of her tongue to say that it wasn't really what had brought them together, because he had come back for her before he knew about the child. So she had to wonder what exactly really had. But she was too tired, her brain sluggish, her body even worse.

They had never had a whole conversation without it ending in them yelling at each other or sex. She was almost entirely certain she had never felt comforted by his presence. But she did now. Just being near him. This man who had walked for so long, to gain everything he had.

Everything in her possession had been thrust onto her by her father, whether she wanted it or not. And yes, that came with its own burden. But he had been forced to make the choice to succeed. Yes, her father had paid for his schooling, but if he hadn't taken it seriously, nothing would have come from it.

Had she truly understood the sort of man Apollo was she would have been more terrified of him the first moment he had walked into her company. He was a man who set his sights on things with terrifying single-mindedness. With a kind of intensity unmatched by anyone else she had ever known. If she had realized when he had reappeared in her life that he wanted revenge and he wouldn't hesitate to use her, she would have been much more afraid. Would have behaved much differently with him.

Would you?

Or perhaps, they would be in the same place. In the same moment, in the same bed. Because as much as she wanted to believe she had a bit more common sense, the fact remained that when she fell for him it had nothing to do with common sense.

No, nothing at all. It was so much deeper.

She reached out, resting her palm on his chest, felt his heartbeat beneath her fingertips.

She had dreamed of this. Of simply holding him. Of listening to him breathe. Of sharing the sweet and simple intimacy that came from being near each other. Of touching just to touch.

It felt so good. To simply be with him. Not fighting. Not having sex. Just being.

For the first time in weeks, she felt some peace. She didn't want to sleep. She wanted to prolong this, for as long as possible. If she could choose one moment to stay in, it would be this one.

But sadly, time moved forward. And as it did, she drifted off to sleep.

When they woke in the morning Apollo was still there. Elle had half expected him to have gone off again, to awaken to him standing angrily at the foot of the bed and demanding that she leave. But that didn't happen. Instead, he was wrapped around her, his legs laced through hers. He wasn't wearing any clothes. She was still wearing the dress from last night.

He was awake, and he was looking at her, a strange expression on his face. "Good morning," she said, her voice coming out a little bit like a croak.

"Good morning."

"This is a strange morning after," she said, looking around the room.

"We didn't have sex."

"Yes, that's exactly what I mean."

"How are you feeling?"

"Oh, you mean after...all of that."

He let out a long, heavy breath. "Yes, after I behaved so poorly."

"Wait a second. Are you, Apollo Savas, actually acknowledging the fact that you behaved poorly?"

"Please, don't press the issue, or I will retreat back behind my rock wall of a heart."

"Sometimes I think maybe your secret is that you are not as heartless as you appear." After being convinced of the opposite last night, this was a refreshing feeling.

"We must all maintain our mysteries, must we not?"

"Maybe. I don't think I'm all that mysterious. I think that I reveal myself to you very easily."

"If only that were the case. I should like very much for you to be easier for me to read. And yet, I can't seem to decode you."

"Then you aren't paying attention. The fact that you thought I would crumble at the sight of an engagement ring says that you don't know me very well."

"You never let me."

She let his words take root inside her. They were not untrue. She knew that.

"I know. But after last night you know why. I was afraid. If I had let you touch me at seventeen then we would have been in this position back them. And as poorly as we're handling it now can you imagine how we would have handled it if we were still that young?"

"A nightmare," he said, laughing bitterly. "Yes, it would have been a nightmare."

"I was very afraid of you. Of what you made me feel. I've always been afraid of you." He had the power to devastate her. To tear her apart from the inside out. Apollo possessed so much more dominion over her than she wanted him to know about. Than she would like to admit, even to herself. But the fact of the matter was it had always been so.

"You must not be feeling particularly wonderful, considering you slept in your dress."

She scrubbed at her face. "I suppose I do feel a bit day-old."

"Stay right here." He released his hold on her and got out of bed, crossing the large expanse of the room and heading into the bathroom. She could hear the water start running. Her heart began to beat faster. He was doing something for her. Something thoughtful. Something kind. She wasn't sure how to handle it. So she just lay there, her heart putting a dull, unsteady rhythm in her chest. He returned a moment later, standing in the doorway, naked, and thoroughly unashamed. Of course, he had nothing to be ashamed about. His body was the stuff you could write poetry about.

But she had never been very good with poetry. She would rather lick his body instead. All over. From head to glorious toe, and every muscular inch in between.

Last night, and the no touching, had been… There had been something altering in it. The fact that they had been able to lie together and neither scream at each other nor tear each other's clothes off had been something of a revelation. But that didn't mean she was ready to give up touching him entirely.

Bad idea. You don't even know what kind of relationship the two of you have.

No, she didn't. But if she wanted to move it toward a real relationship, it might be best if she maintained a physical connection with him. At least, that was a handy justification for getting what she wanted. Which was to be back in his strong arms once again. To be brought to the peak of pleasure by his talented hands and mouth.

She shivered.

"If you are cold, *agape*, I have a warm bath for you in here."

For some reason, his tender words made tears prick the back of her eyes. "Okay," she said, standing up on wobbly legs and walking toward him. She paused in front of him and he gripped the hem of her dress, pulling it up over her head. He took over after that, dispensing with her underwear quickly. Then he lifted her up into his arms and set her gently in the deep tub. The water was perfection, as though he had somehow been able to reach down inside of her and figure out exactly what her perfect bath might be like. And then—further proof that he might be reading her mind—he got down into the tub with her, positioning himself behind her, having her press her back up against his broad chest.

"We have not gotten off to the best start. And when I say that, I mean going back more than a decade, we did not have the best start."

She nodded, not saying a word. He ran his hands over her damp skin and she shivered, her nipples tightening and hardened to points in spite of the warmth of the water.

It had nothing to do with temperature, and everything to do with arousal.

"But I think things can be better between us. I'm not… I am not angry at you, Elle. I was, I admit that. I was angry at you for making me want you. For creating a desire within me that I could not satisfy. That was… That was wrong of me."

"Are you apologizing to me?"

"Yes," he said. "I am apologizing to you, because you deserve my apology. I was cruel to you in ways that you did not deserve."

"But my father deserved it," she said, her voice hollow.

"Your father has nothing to do with this. Right now, he has nothing to do with you and me. We can forget that our parents are married. That I feel a sense of betrayal where your father is concerned. We can forget about all of it. Here, right now, we have to do that. Because if we are ever going to bond with one another, if we are ever going to come together and raise this child then there is history we must erase."

"What does that mean? What does it mean for my relationship with my father?"

He reached out and picked up a bottle of shampoo from the edge of the tub, squirting a little bit into his hands. "I don't know." He began to work the lather through her hair, and her heart contracted tightly in on itself. This was what she had wanted, what she had craved all along. This attention. This wonderful, luxurious attention.

He was focused on her now, wholly and completely. In a way that no one else ever had been. It made her want to cry. She would, if she wasn't so afraid of showing that weakness in front of him. Strange how even now, while he was being kind to her, she felt like she had to have her guard up. Like something was still missing.

That made her chest ache. Because she knew it didn't have to be that way. But she didn't know what else they could possibly have, either. They had spent so many years being unkind to each other. Those were the seeds they had planted for their connection, for their relationship. He was right. Maybe all that was left to do was start over. Maybe they had to forget their family. Maybe they had to forget their prior connection. Maybe there was nothing else but this. Maybe that was all there could be. Maybe it was the only way.

She suddenly felt desperate. For him. For his touch, for everything. Suddenly felt like the world would end completely if her mouth wasn't joined to his.

She turned slightly in the water, pressing her hand to his cheek and angling her head, kissing him, slowly, deeply. Trying to make it different from the other times they had kissed. She wanted this to be different. She wanted this to be the new beginning. To be the new start to something that wasn't toxic. To something that wasn't so deadly. Wasn't so dangerous. Maybe it would even be less all-consuming. Maybe it could be something easier. Something freer.

Maybe it would never be a normal relationship, but if he didn't want to use her, and she could trust him…then maybe it could be something.

He was motionless for a moment, as though he was deciding how to react. Then, he gripped her chin with his thumb and forefinger, holding her steady as he deepened the kiss. He kept it slow, too. Tasting her deeply, his pace leisurely as he swept his tongue over hers. As though he really did have all the time in the world. As though they might in fact have forever.

She turned completely, getting on her knees between his size, leaning in, tracing a line on his chest with her tongue, all the way up to his neck where she pressed an openmouthed kiss to his skin. She looked up at him, at the feral light in his eyes, signaling his very tenuous grasp on his control. She affected him. She really did. This had nothing to do with anger, nothing to do with revenge. It was Elle and Apollo, and nothing else in between.

Oh, how she craved that. That connection that was about the two of them and nothing else at all. She moved closer, straddling his lap, bringing the heart of her up against the uncompromising ridge of his arousal. She flexed her hips, rubbing against him, sending a sharp shock of pleasure through her body. He lowered his head, sucking one nipple deeply into his mouth, those two points of pleasure on her body joining up to create a sensation that threatened to overwhelm her completely. She grabbed hold of his face, held him steady, locked her eyes with his as she rose up slightly onto her knees, then lowered herself onto his arousal, taking him deep inside, sighing heavily as he filled her, satisfied her. Completed her.

Apollo Savas had been sex to her from the moment she first met him. From the moment she understood what transpired between a man and a woman in the dark. She had always acknowledged that. Had always known it to be true. But she had missed something. She had missed the most important part of the equation. He wasn't only sex. He was something more. Something deeper. Had it only ever been about sex she would never have been so afraid. But she had known that beneath that desire, beneath that base arousal, was something much darker, much deadlier, much more dangerous.

It had never simply been desire. It had never simply been anger. It was love. It was love then, it was love now.

She loved him. The thought sent a crack of lightning

through her, threatened to split her in two with the plea-sure that was building deep inside her. It created a tidal wave of emotion. Completion, satisfaction, despair. She'd never wanted to love him. She had always known that he could never love her back.

No one did. Why would he? Why should Apollo love her for who she was when her own father couldn't do that? When her own mother couldn't seem to manage it? Why should this man ever love her?

And only then could she acknowledge the fact that she had never hated him. Not really. She had loved him.

From the time she was a girl she had loved Apollo Savas. And when he had betrayed her family it had twisted into something new. Because she couldn't un-derstand how the man she cared for so much could do that to her family. When she had thrown herself at him in the hotel room it had been the last gasp of that love, desperate to be heard, desperate to be expressed. And when she had said she hated him it was only because hate was the other side of that coin. So close to love. So per-ilously close, she understood now. Because it was love twisted, turned into something ugly.

She realized then, as Apollo looked down at her with his dark eyes glittering, that he had loved her father. That he had loved her family, and that was why it had been twisted into this. That was why, in the beginning, he had gone so far to seek his revenge. To use her. To harm her.

Because of how love could get twisted up.

He gripped her hips hard, taking control of their move-ments, thrusting up inside her, chasing his release. And she was grateful, because she had gone weak. She could no longer take control of this, no longer claim control over this interaction. No, she was now at the mercy of it. At the mercy of him, at her desire for him.

He slid his hand around to cup her bottom, gripping her tightly, his fingertips brushing up against where they joined. That added bit of contact was enough to send her over the edge. Her mind went blank for one glorious moment, pleasure stealing over her, rocking her like a crack of thunder.

And when it was over, when it all settled, when she was still straddling him, their eyes on only each other, pleasure coursing through her like an endless wave, there was only one bright, brilliant thought in her mind.

She loved Apollo Savas. She always had, she had a suspicion she always would. And she knew, with just as much certainty, that he would never love her in return.

CHAPTER TWELVE

ELLE HAD BEEN quiet ever since they had woken up that morning. Or, more specifically, ever since he had given her a bath. He could feel her slipping out of his grasp. Even as they had reached the peak together, he had felt her pull away, and he didn't know what to do about that. He didn't even know what he thought about it. If it mattered. Except that for Elle, he had a feeling emotion mattered. That it was key.

He could take or leave it. He wanted nothing more than a connection based on honesty, on a contract. It was why he wanted marriage. He wanted to have a guarantee.

He didn't trust emotions. Not in the least. Not when his mother had led such a tangled existence based on the men who had professed to love her. Not when the man who had behaved most like a father to him had revealed himself to be the worst sort of liar. How could he even fathom putting stock in emotion under those conditions?

But Elle was most certainly a more emotional creature. If only he could figure out how to read her. If only he could figure out how to connect with her. He had tried talking, he had tried kindness. And then, she had initiated sex. Neither was the magic key. He wasn't sure there was a damn magic key. He found that disconcerting.

He walked around the expensive penthouse, learning the layout of his new home. Regardless of what he had said to her earlier about how much time he would spend with her and the child, he was anticipating trying to accomplish most of his work in the States, from now on. His own father had abandoned him through suicide. His stepfather had proven to be an imposter. He would not have his child living life with that sort of cloud over them. Money only solved certain things. He knew that for a fact. Coming out of poverty and into financial gain had shown him that there were still things that money couldn't buy.

If only Elle's undying affection was one of the things money could buy. It would make things much simpler. Instead, he was left trying to untie one of the great mysteries of the modern age, or any age. Feminine emotion.

As he was brooding on this, his phone buzzed in his pocket. He picked up quickly without bothering to look and see who it was. "Savas."

"What the hell are you doing with my daughter?"

It was the voice of his least favorite devil on the end of the line. "That depends on what you've heard."

"I have seen the headline in this morning's society pages. You proposed to her last night at a restaurant. By all accounts she refused you and stormed out."

"Then I fail to see why you're calling me. Obviously Elle is up to the challenge of handling herself."

"I am calling because I feel that I have the right to know exactly what led you to a place where you thought proposing to my daughter might end in a *yes*. Do not tell me you set yourself up for public humiliation on purpose, Apollo. I would not believe it."

"It's almost as though you know me," he said, his tone easy. "I had thought she might say yes."

"After all I have done for you—"

"Yes, after causing the suicide of my father, after blackmailing my mother into a relationship, how dare I not be more grateful?"

"I hardly orchestrated your father's death, Apollo, as you are well aware. Your father made his own choices. I was certainly ruthless in my desire to push him out of the company, but what happened after that was his choice, not mine."

"In my mind, you pulled the trigger. There is nothing on earth that will convince me otherwise."

"And so you're using Elle to get revenge?"

It was on the tip of his tongue to tell him that's exactly what he was doing. To let the older man know that Apollo had corrupted his only daughter. That he had gotten her with child. That he now held all the power. It all belonged to him. But then, she walked into the room, wearing soft, baggy pants, and a loose-fitting top. Looking soft and vulnerable, not the least bit hard and glamorous. And he realized that he could not say those things. He could not use her that way. She had asked him to see her as a woman, and he did. He had been the one to suggest they put it all behind them, to start new. And so, he would choose to do so. Now, he would choose to do it for her. For them.

"Whether you believe it or not, my association with your daughter has nothing to do with you."

Elle's head snapped in his direction, her eyes rounded.

"I don't believe it," David said.

"That is inconsequential. It is the truth. I intend to win her over, one way or another. I will obtain her hand in marriage."

"Why is it so important to you?"

"Because I want her."

"And you love her?"

The question hit its mark like an arrow striking a target. Nearly made him fall to his knees. He thought about love, what it meant to him. Certainly, his mother loved him, in her way. She was a fragile woman, not unsurprising considering all she had been through. And at times he wondered if she simply had no choice but to detach in order to protect herself from further pain. After the loss of her husband, after being blackmailed into marrying a man she had not chosen.

His father, his biological father, had been so consumed with the acquisition of material things, with his status, that he had preferred death over staying and protecting his wife and child. In that sense, Apollo could not deny David's words. Suicide had been his father's choice. And not anyone else's. Though he knew that there were many complicated factors that played into that. Depression, mental torments that he could not possibly understand.

It did not stop him from retaining a boy's perspective on it in many ways. He felt abandoned. He felt angry. Whether or not his father deserved more sympathy than that was irrelevant. Apollo could only feel what he felt.

And then there was David St. James. He had truly taken him in. Truly accepted him as part of the family.

He had been a father to him. More of a father than his own had ever been. He had raised him, taught him the value of hard work, paid for his education, taught him to take nothing for granted. Though he was a hard man, though he was distant at times, he was a solid, steady figure in Apollo's life. The man he had sought to pattern himself after. Discovering the depths he had sunk to in order to obtain Apollo's mother—as though she were an item to be acquired and not a human being, as though Apollo himself and his father were incidentals—that had shown him just how deep a lie could run.

The fact that his feelings for the older man had not been eradicated overnight—if ever—showed him just what a fickle and dishonest emotion love could be.

Worse still, all of that, every bit of it, was proof that his love twisted things. Changed them in permanent and ugly ways. He was like a lit match brought up against the edge of something fragile. Making the edges curl and darken, altered beyond recognition.

He couldn't do that to her. He wouldn't.

"No," he said. "No, I don't."

"Then you don't deserve her."

And with that, the line went dead. Those words echoed in his head as he turned to look at Elle, who was regarding him with a confused expression. "My father?"

"Yes. He is unamused with me."

"Did he see it in the paper? Was it in the paper?"

"Yes," he said. "Apparently your rejection of me has made headlines."

"Well, I would apologize but it really is your own doing."

"This is true."

"What did he ask you?"

"He asked if you were my revenge," Apollo said. "I told him you're not."

"Yes, I gathered as much. But what was the last question he asked you?"

His stomach tightened, dropped low in his midsection. "He asked me if I loved you."

She closed her eyes, her face going pale. "You said no."

Elle felt as though the ground was dropping out from beneath her feet. She had been shocked, thrilled, when Apollo had not taken the chance to eviscerate her father. When he had not used her as a weapon. Had not trotted out the baby, their affair, in a crass and unnecessary way. That when he had been asked directly if he was using her, he had said no. Even if it was a lie, even in part, he had stopped using her then. He had honored her request.

But then he had been asked if he loved her. And his answer had been no.

She realized then that it was nonnegotiable for her. She needed love. She needed for him to love her. There was nothing more important. Nothing at all.

She had dressed it up in all kinds of fancy descriptions. Had tried to convince herself that all she needed was respect. That they needed to find common ground. That she simply needed someone to want her as she was, and not as a weapon in some kind of scheme. But after their encounter in the bath, after that pleasure radiated through her, after she had felt the intensity of her own feelings for him, she knew that that wasn't the case. She needed more. She needed everything. And anything else would be doing herself a terrible disservice.

She wanted more for herself. More than simply heading up a company because she wanted to prove to her father that she could. More than marriage to a man for his convenience. In truth, as much as she wanted to give her child a home with both parents she knew that if they were living together under sufferance, if she made him miserable because he eventually bored of her, and he made her miserable because her love went unreturned, their child would know. He or she would sense the unhappiness, and for them to even suspect that their presence was the cause of that kind of relationship was something she could not place upon her child.

"I can't marry you," she said.

"What are you talking about? You showed me this morning just how irresistible you find me."

"That's sex, Apollo. We have had that through every-thing. When I was terrible to you, you still wanted me. When you took over my business, betrayed our family, I still wanted you. Even while I was thinking about stab-bing you through the chest with a pen, I wanted you. But that isn't enough for marriage. And right now? It isn't enough for me. I realized something this morning."

"That you are a contrary little thing who makes ab-solutely no sense?"

"That I love you. I love you with everything I have. It has always been that way. But I cannot, and will not, continue to accept this strange, leftover existence that I have cobbled together with the discarded pieces of yours and my father's manipulative plans. I'm the CFO at Matte because he wanted to play me against you, not because he thought I was suited to the position. I'm pregnant with your baby because you wanted to hurt him, and while I appreciate the fact that you didn't rub it in his face just now…that's our foundation. It's what we are."

"No," he said, his voice rough. "That is not our founda-tion. There was no calculation when I took you up against the wall in my hotel room, no ulterior motive when I had you in the elevator."

"How can I believe that?"

"Because it is the truth. I decided after I had you the second time that I would use what was between us to get revenge. Only because I was desperate to find some jus-tification for what you did to me. For wanting to indulge in this thing between us."

"And why'd you come back?"

"Because I wasn't finished with you!"

"But that's the thing," she said. "I am not a thing that you can pick up and put down at your convenience. Not a weapon that you can use at your discretion. I am a human being. I have feelings. I love you and I deserve to be loved in return." She shook her head. "If you cannot give me that then I will have to go out and find someone who can."

All of the anger drained from his face, his expression turning to stone. "You are correct. If that is what you want, then that is what you must find."

Her chest felt hollowed out, her heart thundering hard in the empty space. "That's it?"

"We are at an impasse, Elle. I cannot love, and you require it. I do not wish to hold you prisoner. I see no satisfaction in making you miserable. There was a time when I might have, but things have changed."

"Maybe that means you have feelings for me?"

"No," he said, his tone hard, definitive. "I cannot."

She felt like she'd been stabbed clean through, like she would bleed out on the floor, her pain, her love, everything for him to see. She wouldn't be able to hide anymore, as she had done for so many years.

She waited for something to come, for a cutting remark to rescue her, but it wasn't there. There was nothing to hide behind. Nothing but pain and love in equal measure.

And she wanted him to see it. Wanted him to know. She was done hiding. She'd done enough damage pushing him away so that she wouldn't be hurt.

She had hidden everything for years. Her pain, her desire, her love. And she was done. Pride be damned, she wouldn't hide herself anymore.

"Why?" she asked. "Why are you doing this? There is nothing stopping us, nothing stopping this except you, and I can't understand why."

"Everything I love turns to dust, Elle. I would not have you so diminished."

"I've been diminished already!" she shouted. "All of my life. To keep the peace, to try and do what my father wanted, to try and avoid…well, exactly this, with you." She swallowed hard, shaking, all of her repressed emotion, decades of it, pouring out now. "I'm done with that. I'm making demands now."

He stared at her for a moment, his dark eyes hollow. "I can't meet them."

"You won't."

"It amounts to the same thing."

And then he turned away from her, and walked out of the penthouse, closing the door softly behind him. She had a feeling that he would not be back.

She didn't want half a life, half a love. She didn't want a future with a man who wouldn't give her what she'd just realized she so desperately wanted.

So, she let him go. And she did her very best not to cry.

Elle approached her father's office with great trepidation. She was going to let him know that she was officially resigning from Matte. She was also going to tell him about the baby, and the fact that she would not be marrying Apollo. She took a deep breath, trying to ease the knot in her chest. Then, she raised her hand and knocked on the door.

"Come in."

She turned the knob and opened the door, stepping inside quickly. "Hello, Father," she said.

"Elle," he said, gesturing at the chair across from his desk, as though she were a business appointment he was keeping. "Have a seat."

She did. "I imagine you're wondering why I wanted to speak with you."

"Not particularly. I assume it has something to do with Apollo."

"Well," she said, "you aren't wrong."

"Have you decided to marry him?"

"On the contrary, I have decided that I cannot continue my association with him."

"I fail to understand why there was an association with him in the first place. He turned against me."

"Yes," she said.

"He fired you. Then, you got your job back, did you not?"

Her face got hot. "I know what you're implying, but it didn't happen that way. Anyway, I'm stepping down at Matte. I'm going to go back to school. I'm going to figure out what *I* want to do. Quite apart from your expectations, or his. I have been caught in the cross fire for too long. I just can't do it anymore. I have to find out what I am beyond this…desperate people pleaser. I have to find out if I can be more than your shield to block you from Apollo's wrath."

"Is that what you think?"

"Why would I think anything else?" she asked.

"And yet, you have never said anything."

"Yes, well, I wanted to keep the peace. I wanted to do the right thing, be the daughter you needed. But I'm over that now. I need to be the person I'm happy with, not the person you're happy with."

"Did I force you into the position at Matte?" he asked, his tone hard.

"You can't deny that you used me to try and stand between Apollo and the destruction of the company. It had nothing to do with me. You never intended to give any of it to me. You always wanted a son, and until he went rogue, Apollo was that son for you. I was never supposed to be the one in that position. You used me."

He lifted his shoulder, the lines on his face looking suddenly more pronounced. "Yes, I did use you. But how else could I defend my legacy? I knew you could do it, Elle. I had no concerns about that. I knew Apollo had… feelings for you. Feelings of some kind, and I thought that perhaps he would modify his actions if you were in the line of fire."

"And so you used me as a target."

"I knew you were strong enough. You might think it's because I don't respect or value you, but it is to the contrary. You're strong. I would not have shielded a son from such a thing, and I did not shield you."

"Am I supposed to be grateful?"

"I could see no other way," he said, his tone uncompromising.

"Is that why you ousted Apollo's father from your company all those years ago? Because you could think of no other way to be with Mariam?"

"Yes," he said, simply. Calmly. "It was the only way I could think of to win Mariam. And so I did what I could. But she stood by him. Had his child. And for all my sins, I never held that against Apollo. That he was the product of a union I despised."

"You don't get a medal for that, Dad," she said. "Not when you were so…horrible."

"I was horrible," he said, his tone hard, his eyes ice blue. "And I would do the same thing again. Make the same choices. I didn't intend for his father to kill himself, Elle. I am not a mind reader. I could not predict the outcome. I did, however, think that it was likely Mariam would leave him when he had nothing and I had everything. I was wrong."

"She loved him."

Her father nodded slowly. "Yes, she did. But she has learned to love me, I think."

"You think?"

"Yes. I do."

"Have you ever asked her?"

Her father's face went blank. "No. I haven't. But then, I'm not certain it matters. Not now."

Elle's heart crumpled. "I think it always matters. It doesn't matter when love comes, as long as you know it's there. Does she know you love her?"

"I destroyed her world to move her into mine. I cleared my world to make room for her. If that is not love then I do not know what is."

He didn't. Elle could see that. He truly and honestly knew nothing of love being two-sided. Of giving rather than taking.

He was an unbending man. Unyielding. All arrogance and a stiff neck. Unable to truly turn and look at anyone else.

"I think perhaps love isn't destroying worlds. Or moving people around like chess pieces," she said, her voice shaking. "I think maybe it's giving more than you take. Showing it, even when someone may never show it back. Being kind even when the other person is cruel. I think love isn't always balance, but if both are willing to give more than they take…it might be a beautiful, rare sort of treasure."

"I don't know about any of that, Elle," he said. "I do know that I have you, and I still have Mariam. In that I find some success, I think."

"Do you love *me*?" She might as well ask. She had already been rejected by Apollo, so there was really no reason to protect herself at this point. She had been flayed already. She might as well allow some salt to be rubbed into the wounds.

Her father only looked at her for a moment, his gaze unreadable. "Did you not know?" he asked.

"How would I?" she answered.

"I am your father, Elle."

"That doesn't make any guarantees."

"I am a man who has built my life on a foundation made of ruthless decisions. I did not become rich by following the rules. I did not obtain my wife by playing fair. I hurt Hector. I hurt your mother. I have never known quite how to handle the people in my life. But for all of that, I do love you."

It was still indirect. Still impersonal. But she felt it was very likely the best he could do.

She also saw, for a moment, herself in the old man's gaze. Waiting to be given what she wanted, all of her conditions met. No, she wasn't being unreasonable wanting love from Apollo. But she had to consider where he had come from. What he knew.

Apollo had been broken. Battered by life. People he had trusted had abandoned him. Betrayed him. He needed someone to show him something different. Needed someone to stand by him, no matter what. To take what he could give now, and trust there would be more in the future.

She would do that for him. For her. Just because he couldn't meet her here now didn't mean he never would.

She loved him. She would love him enough for them both.

"I love you," she said, because she thought she might as well practice saying it again, to another man who had difficulty hearing it, saying it. To continually practice this new start, where she didn't hide. Where she didn't try to make herself palatable. "In spite of everything."

"I haven't changed," he said. "I am the man you have always known. You just know a bit more of the story."

"Yes, well, the whole story is important. It doesn't mean I think you made good choices."

"I never asked anyone to sign off on my choices. I made my bed, and it has the woman I love in it. How can I have regrets?"

"Well," Elle said, "I'm going to go after the man I love now. Because he's pigheaded and stubborn and scared. And I'm okay with that. As long as I can be with him. Oh. I'm having his baby, also. That might be relevant, too."

That seemed to successfully shock her father. His gray eyebrows shot upward, his mouth dropping slightly open. "You didn't see fit to mention that sooner?"

"We got philosophical. I imagine this will be the only time. But… Apollo is the father of my child. You're married to his mother, you're both the grandparents of the baby." She frowned. "It's very complicated. And you're going to have to make some kind of peace with him."

"It may not be possible. As you said, the whole story changes things. And for him, I think it transformed me into a villain. One I cannot deny I have been in years past. I tried to make it up to him by giving him all I could. But as you have pointed out to me, my demonstrations are not always clear."

"You've both caused a lot of damage. Fighting, seeking vengeance, going after what you want with no care for others…it just has to stop. If it can't be anything more than a cease-fire then let it be that. But it has to stop. I can't be in the middle. I won't allow my child to be in the middle."

"And if you have to choose between me or him?"

"It would be him," she said, not even hesitating. "Assuming he felt the same way."

Her father nodded slowly, his lips curving into a smile. "Maybe you even understand my more ruthless decisions."

"Where Apollo is concerned I have no doubt I could be ruthless. Where my child is concerned... I would shed blood."

"I fear I was too selfish to make that choice," her father said. "And that I did not have the pride that you do."

"What do you mean?"

"I did not care if Mariam felt as strongly as I did. I only cared that I had her."

"Well, I lived too much of my life that way and I won't do it now."

Her father regarded her with...pride. For the first time she could honestly say she felt it. A strange moment because she didn't feel particularly triumphant. She only felt...broken. Sad. Pride was a poor salve for a broken heart.

"I need to be loved," she repeated, for herself as much as anyone. "And I need to be assured that my son or daughter will not be used as a pawn. Not for Apollo to hurt you, not for him to hurt me. I think you will find my love for my child the most ruthless of all."

"Then go," her father said. "Tell him. Go and be ruthless for love."

CHAPTER THIRTEEN

APOLLO WAS NO stranger to despair. While he had not been terribly conscious of the loss of wealth as a boy, the loss of his comfortable bedroom, his bed, had certainly been things he'd felt deeply. After that, the loss of his father. Then, the loss of the man he had come to think of as a father.

But he had never once experienced loss like this. A loss that was, in many ways, his own doing. There had been no control in his hands when they had lost their livelihood and their money, there had been no control when he had discovered the true nature of David St. James. But here... With Elle, he'd held the power. The power to tell her what she wanted to hear, to find a way to be the man she needed. And he had turned away.

"Coward," he said aloud to the empty space in his office. He paced in front of the window, looking out over the city below. He had gone back to Greece, because he had not known what else to do. Had not known where else to go. He felt helpless, and it had been a long time since he had felt helpless. He despised the feeling. More than anything. It was one of the many reasons he had turned so sharply, so hard, on David St. James.

Because when the revelation had struck him it'd been with the force of a killing blow. It had chopped his legs out from beneath him, left him gasping, shocked. He was not a man who took kindly to such a thing.

Wounded pride, Apollo? That is a very small reason to seek revenge. A very small reason to hold on to anger.

But what his father had been through… What his mother had been through…

He knew he should speak to his mother. But the simple fact was he was afraid to hear what she had to say. He had been from the moment three years ago when the revelations about David had become clear. He didn't want to hear what she had to say. For fear that she loved him. For fear that she was happy. For fear that she supported the decisions her new husband had made because it had resulted in the two of them being together.

But he knew now that he needed to ask her. He knew that he needed to find out why she had stayed.

He picked up the phone, dialing her number, dimly aware that it was very early in the morning in New York. "Hello?"

His mother's faintly accented voice came over the line. "Hello, Mother," he said.

They had barely spoken over the course of the past three years, and when they had, it had been very carefully. Because she had known that he was actively pursuing vengeance against her husband, and while she had kept her feelings to herself, he could always sense the fact that she didn't approve. Certainly, she didn't necessarily support him, as she had not demanded he take her with him, back to Greece. He was more than capable of supporting his mother now. She did not have to stay with David St. James. And yet, she did.

"Why?" he asked, with no preamble at all. He had not meant to launch straight into it like this, but he had been unable to help himself.

"Why what, Apollo?"

"Why do you stay with him? I don't understand. The truth about David St. James was hidden from me for all of my life. But it was not hidden from you. You knew exactly what manner of man he was. And yet, you remain with him. You could leave. I could take care of you until the end of time, and you would never want for anything."

There was silence on the other end. "Yes," she said softly. "I do know what manner of man he is. I have known David St. James since long before you were born. I knew him from the beginning. I met him when I met your father. I don't know why, but I have a tendency to love hard men. Though perhaps that is a good thing for you, I think."

Apollo chuckled. "I suppose it is."

"I did love your father. And I stayed with him even when we lost everything. Even when David ousted him from the company."

"Which David did to hurt him."

Mariam continued as if he hadn't spoken. "I do believe that at the time, your father already had a bit of an issue with drugs. Though they had not yet consumed him as they did later. He was working long hours, and he needed something to help him keep up. It was competitive. He didn't want to sleep. I rarely saw him. And I would be… I would be lying if I said we were perfectly happy. But I was never unfaithful to him. I knew that David had feelings for me. But I had chosen Hector. And so I remained with him. I remained with him until the end, when everything became so twisted, and so hard. By the time he died he was not the man I had first known."

"Because of David St. James."

"Yes, and no. Business is harsh and uncompromising.

It has always been so. Many men lose all their earthly possessions and come out the other side."

Apollo was having trouble processing what she was saying. "You're saying you harbor no anger against him over what he put us through?"

"I am sorry to tell you that I put much more of the blame at your father's door than I do at David's. Yes, he ousted him from the company, but had your father taken better care of our assets we would not have been destitute. Had he not completely given up, we could have come back from it. I had no skills. I was nothing more than a village girl who knew how to do little more than sew. And while that could support us in a very modest fashion it was never going to pull us out of poverty. When David contacted me... I am not proud of what happened after that, because for all of my sins, for all of my divided loyalty, the one thing that I truly regret was any part I might have played in the destruction of his marriage."

Apollo swallowed hard. It was difficult to hear such things. To take on the knowledge of his own mother's part in all of this. "Yes, well, you had a child to take care of."

"He did not force me into an affair," she said, her voice soft. "That was my choice. When he discovered how we were living he asked us to come, he offered to buy me a house, and to care for you. A relationship was not part of that. But I... I was lonely. And I recognized what I might have had. I regretted not choosing him, I think. Because he seemed stronger. That was my mistake, Apollo. His as well, but do not blame it all on him."

"Well, his ex-wife didn't care enough about her own child to stick around after she was deposed."

His mother sighed. "No, she did not. Again, it does not excuse my actions. But I do love Elle, almost as if she were my own."

"She knows that."

"I hope so. There was a time when I thought you knew that David loved you as a son, as well."

"I did believe that," Apollo said. "But when I found out the level he had stooped to to bring you to him, to get revenge because of his love being spurned, I could not simply stay in his home, stay as his son."

"It is done," she said. "It may have been wrong, but it is done."

"I loved him," Apollo said. "What kind of a son does that make me? I cannot love without it becoming something horribly twisted. You had to care for me, and that forced your hand. I loved my father, but it wasn't enough to make him stay... David..."

"None of this, none of the tangled web, is your fault. You should not place more consequences onto yourself. We were badly behaved adults, who got our children caught in the cross fire of terrible games. Neither of you deserved it. I wish very much your father had not killed himself. But he was not simply a victim, either. Your love didn't bring out the worst in us, Apollo. Your love was the best of us."

He swallowed hard, his throat suddenly tight. "None of it is simple," he said. "None of it. So I do not understand how I am supposed to sort through it all."

"I can't answer that question for you. I do know that it doesn't benefit anyone to hold on to anger. To hold on to the past. It twists you. That's what it did to Hector. It broke him completely. All of the anger that he felt toward David... I would hate for you to suffer the same fate."

"And so...you would simply forgive?"

"I cannot make the decision for you, Apollo. I should like, for the sake of our family, for you to find it in you to forgive. But it is your journey. Perhaps I was wrong to forgive. I do not know. I only know that I had choices before me and I took the one that made me happiest."

"We can never be a family as we were," he said, "in part because while you may love Elle as a daughter, I do not love her as a sister."

That declaration was met with silence. "I know," she said finally. "I have always known."

Those words nearly broke him. Shattered him entirely. She had always known, because his feelings had always been there. Every action, every cruelty, all the anger that had passed between them over the years had been there simply to disguise that fact.

From himself.

He had never managed to hide it from his mother.

"I do not know how I can be with her."

"We can only carry so much, Apollo. I have lived an imperfect life, and if I have learned anything it's that, at some point, we must put some of our burdens down so we can pick up things we would more gladly carry. These are decisions we make. We cannot wait for the pain to go away. We cannot simply expect the anger to fade, or the grief to stop biting. We must make choices. They are the hardest choices to make. But if you want to move on, then you must begin on your own."

"That simple?"

"No," she said. "That difficult."

"I know what I want," he said. "I just don't know if I can have it."

"You're angry at David, and that is understandable. You want revenge, and that I understand, as well. But I think you can see the way that revenge twists your own life. If you deny your love for Elle simply because you want to punish David St. James, then it isn't truly him you're hurting. Then the only person whose life you've destroyed is your own."

"You stayed because you love him?"

"God help me, but I do," she said. "Though I should not. Though he perhaps doesn't deserve it. There are many days when I don't deserve it, either. Though, in his way, I believe he loves me."

He could not say he envied his mother her relationship, her marriage. And yet, he could see that they had love for each other, even if it wasn't the sort he recognized. And what sort did he recognize? That, he supposed, was the question. Did he recognize it at all?

He had. With Elle, he had recognized it for the first time. And he had run, because it had been too much. Because, as his mother said, he was carrying too much anger to accept the love that she was asking for, that she was offering.

"I suppose I have a decision to make," he said.

But it was already made. There was no question. He loved Elle. And that meant whatever the risk, whether he was able to trust himself or not, whether he truly believed he knew how to love and how to accept love, he wanted to give her what he could. What he had. He wanted to give her everything. "I will have to get her back," he said finally.

"I hope that you do," his mother said. "I hope it isn't too late."

He hung up the phone and turned back to the sprawling city before him. He would need to get the first plane out. Or perhaps he should call her. But he didn't know if apologies such as this one should be done over the phone. He had hurt her, had said terrible things. Hurtful things. He did not deserve to ask forgiveness. But dam-

mit, if David St. James could earn the love of the woman
he wanted after all he had done, why couldn't Apollo?

He turned back to the door of his office just as it
opened. In strode Elle, looking red-faced, pursued by
his assistant Alethea.

"I'm sorry, Mr. Savas," Alethea said. "She insisted
that she had to see you."

"I do," Elle said, looking stubborn. He adored that
expression. That uncompromising, demanding expression. Elle was not an easy woman. She never would be.
But he didn't want easy. He wanted her. Always. Forever.

"It's okay, Alethea. I would like to see her."

Alethea shook her head. "Best you work out your problems, Mr. Savas. You have been mercurial of late, and I
find it irritating," she said, turning on her heel and storm-
ing out of his office.

"That is not the sort of assistant I expected you to
have," Elle said.

"Yes, well. At this point she knows where all the bodies are buried and I can't get rid of her. Sadly, she knows
that."

"I had to see you," she said.

"Why is that, *agape*?"

"Because I have something to tell you."

Suddenly, his stomach plummeted. "It isn't about the
baby, is it?"

"The baby is fine," she said.

"I'm relieved to hear it."

"It isn't about that. I mean, it is. But nothing is wrong."

"Well, before you launch into your speech, I must tell
you, I was on my way back to see you."

"You were?"

"Yes," he said, "I was. There is something I need to
tell you to. I spoke to my mother this morning."

"That's funny. I spoke to my father about… Well, I guess it must be fifteen hours ago or so. Since I am here now."

"I see. I needed to understand why she stayed with him. I needed to understand how she had managed to let go of everything that had gone on in the past. She helped clarify some things. For one, your father did not force her into a relationship. That is important for me to know. She admits they handled things poorly. But he did not force her."

Elle looked visibly relieved by the revelation. "I'm glad to hear that. That isn't something my father would willingly admit. He's such a stubborn old man. I think talking about his feelings is the thing he dislikes most in the world. But he did admit to me… He does love your mother. For all of his sins, he does."

"She loves him," Apollo said. "Somehow, she was able to let go of everything that had happened all those years ago. Somehow she fell in love with him."

"We don't have half of that baggage standing between us, and here we are unable to sort out our differences."

"There's a simple enough reason for that," he said. "I was a coward."

"You're not a coward, Apollo."

"Yes, I am. I was unable to admit my feelings for you nine years ago, and I found myself unable to admit them last week. Even to myself. But I love you, Elle. I always have."

Elle could only stand there, shocked, staring into Apollo's intense, dark gaze. He said that he loved her. He said that he always had, that he had simply been unable to admit it. That was not what she'd been expecting. She had flown to Athens, stormed into his office expecting a fight. Expecting to engage him in a knock-down, drag-out battle as she told him there would be no revenge. That they would be putting everything aside for love. Not theirs, but the love of their child. And yet, here he was…saying he loved her.

"I had a speech prepared," she said, her voice sounding hollow.

"Did you?" he asked, his eyebrows arched.

"Yes," she said. "I was… I was going to make sure you knew that our child was everything. That I would never use a child to get revenge on you, nor would I allow you to use our child to hurt me. And that under no circumstances would I allow our son or daughter to be caught in the crosshairs of your issues with my father."

"There is no danger of that."

"I… I see that. Because you… But I…" She suddenly felt a sharp pain in her chest. "I'm sorry."

"For?"

"You do love me. I knew you did. I really did. But I didn't trust it."

"Why should you take less than you deserve, Elle? Why should you take less than you deserve simply waiting around for me?"

"Because love isn't about what you deserve."

"Thankfully for me," he said.

"For all of us. We're about to have a child, and we're evidence of the fact that…parents make mistakes with their children. Even children they love."

"That is true."

"Love is…bigger than keeping score. It costs more than we could ever hope to earn. At least, it's supposed to. I need you to know, here and now, that I love you without reservations. That I believe you *do* love me. I understand what you've been through. I understand that you were used badly." She took a deep breath. "Your mother may have been able to easily forgive my father, or at least forgave him eventually, but she knew everything from the beginning. Your trust was betrayed in a way that hers wasn't."

Apollo shook his head. "The guilt that I felt over considering David a father figure to me was what truly enraged me."

"I recognized that. That what you felt was badly-used love. I did. Because I had experienced it with you. But even recognizing that, I was unbending."

"I want you to be unbending, my sweet, beautiful Elle," he said.

Her chest swelled, her heart feeling large and tender. "You do?"

"Yes. Because I want everything you are. Everything you will be. Because I want the woman you are, not simply the woman that makes my life easiest. I do not want you simply because you are the mother of my child. I do not want you because you are biddable, because you fit easily into the life I have created. I will rearrange it all for you," he said. "Somehow, I think I knew I would have to do that. And it frightened me. Again, you must understand that I am a coward."

She shook her head. "No," she said, the word coming out broken. "You are the bravest man I have ever known. Because you would open yourself up to love again even when your love had been so abused before."

"I hardly deserve a medal for accepting a gift so beautiful as your love," he said.

"Yours is beautiful too, you know."

His chest pitched sharply, his dark eyes glittering. "I was so convinced my love killed things. That it was toxic. How could I trust something that always turned into something so painful? So I denied it. What I felt for you. It was always there. I wrapped it up in anger, I wrapped it up in hate, because I wasn't ready to reach out and take it."

"I did the same," she said, her throat tight. "I told myself that I hated you, that I couldn't stand the sight of you, because in truth you were the most glorious, wonderful sight I had ever beheld. And I called my feelings something else, anything else, rather than accepting the fact that I might never have you. I pretended I didn't care rather than opening myself up and risking being humiliated. Rather than risking admitting what I might lose and how badly it might hurt. I hid my feelings, even from myself. See, I am more like my father than it seems on the surface."

"But you're here. You're here telling me now."

"If we can't learn from the mistakes of the people who came before us, then I fail to see the point of any of it."

"Yes." He shook his head. "You are very right about that. When I look at the mistakes my mother made, your father made, that my father made, in their pursuit of love, of money and success, I see nothing but a sad, tangled web. And in the end, I suppose what our parents have found is love, as best as they can have it."

"Yes," Elle said. "I think that's true."

"But I want more than that. I want deeper. None of the anger, none of the pride, none of those wasted years."

Elle laughed softly. "I suppose we already have a few wasted years."

"But no more. It is you for me, Elle. Only you. I want to make a life with you. With you and our child. I will get down on my knees and beg if I must, because my pride is nothing more than dirt if it keeps me from you."

"As enjoyable as I might find that, I don't need you to

beg. I love you already. I don't need you to do anything to gain that acceptance."

He crossed the space between them and her heart lurched, a thrill racing through her as he took her into his arms. This would never fade. It would never get old. Things had never been hotter, more intense between them because of the anger. The anger had simply covered the true intensity. It was only bigger now. Brighter, deeper. Now that she knew the racing of her heart, the intense surge of adrenaline that raced through her every time she saw him was not hate, but love after all.

"I love you," he said. "And I will lay down all of my anger, my need for revenge, my distrust and anything else that might hinder my ability to give you all that you deserve. Because if I am to be full, then I would have myself be full of nothing but my love for you."

"I was so hurt, Apollo, because I was afraid that you wanted me only for revenge. To hurt other people. And I never felt like my father loved me for *me*. I never felt like anyone in my life loved me simply because of who I am. But here you are, asking me to be difficult, asking me to be stubborn, asking for me to be myself. And I… I can hardly believe it."

"Then I will spend my every day, from this moment until the end, showing you just how much I love you, for all of the good, all of the bad and everything in between. I will do my very best to ensure that you never doubt that you are the one I love. You are the one I want. Whether you're a CEO, a lawyer, a cupcake maker, a police officer."

"I have never given any indication that I want to be a baker or a police officer."

"But you could be. You could be anything you wanted

to be, and you would still be Elle. And I would still love
you."

"There is a remarkable amount of freedom in that,"
she said, her chest swelling with emotion. "I don't think
you can possibly know what that means to me."

He pulled her closer, kissing her lips. "Then show me,
Elle. Show me."

EPILOGUE

SHE DID. AND she spent every day after that showing him, demonstrating her love for him. And he did the same for her.

It was one of Apollo's proudest moments when Elle graduated at the top of her law class. One of his happiest moments, sitting there, cheering her on as she walked onstage while he held their daughter in his lap, with their new baby in the crook of his other arm. He was so proud of what she had achieved, of what she had decided to go after. Of how she had decided to use her uncompromising nature and sharp tongue.

She was, in his opinion, the best lawyer in New York City, eternally advocating for women in difficult circumstances, and for children who had had injustice done against them.

If someone would have told him when he had first married Elle that he would only grow to love her more over the next decade, he would have told them they were insane. After all, how could anyone love more than he had on the day of his wedding? But he discovered just how deep, just how wide, love could grow. Each year, each child, each achievement and each failure added a texture and a richness to what he felt for her that stretched far beyond what he could have ever imagined.

On the night of their tenth anniversary, Elle came home from work, exhausted, frowning, possibly because the case she was working on was so intense.

He took her into his arms, not saying a word. And she wrapped her arms around him, leaning on his strength.

"I'm glad you made it," he said.

"Of course. This is the only place I want to be tonight." She looked up at him and smiled. "Are the kids taken care of?"

"I believe Alethea is reading them a bedtime story. But she is not a nanny, Elle. She made sure to tell me that as she went to perform the task. This was after hovering around them at dinner trying to get them to eat their vegetables."

Elle laughed. "Of course."

"And tomorrow David and my mother will be by to take the children for the weekend. They wish to contribute to our alone time."

"Very nice of them."

"Indeed." He brushed his thumb over her cheek. "Are you ready to go out tonight?" He examined the faint shadows under her eyes. "Or would you rather stay in?"

"I would love to go out. Because I want to go show off my wonderful husband."

"You cannot possibly wish to do that more than I want to show off my wonderful wife."

"We'll have to argue about it later." She let out a sigh, a long, contented sound. "We've been together for more than ten years. It's amazing how different this last decade has been from the one before it."

"The one where we both wanted each other, but wouldn't allow ourselves to have each other?"

"Yes. I have no clue what we were so afraid of. What we were waiting for."

"The more I think about it, the more I believe we were waiting for the right time. Where we could be brave enough, give enough, love each other in the right way. Had I kissed you for the first time when I was twenty years old, I would have only messed it up later. I would not have been a man who could have given you the support you needed through all of this."

She nodded slowly. "I don't think I would have been a woman who could have gone for her dreams."

"Do you want to know a secret, Elle?"

She nodded. "Of course."

"I like everything that we have. I treasure it. I enjoy my job. I am proud of yours. But you're my dream."

Elle smiled, all of her exhaustion fading, tears filling her eyes. "Oh, Apollo. You're my dream, too."

She drew up on her toes and kissed him, and it was like the first time. Every time with her was like the first time.

"Perhaps we won't make it out after all," he said.

She smiled, her expression a little bit wicked. "Yes, perhaps it would be best if we stayed in."

* * * * *

LET'S TALK
Romance

For exclusive extracts, competitions
and special offers, find us online:

f facebook.com/millsandboon
🐦 @MillsandBoon
📷 @MillsandBoonUK

Get in touch on 01413 063232

For all the latest titles coming soon, visit
millsandboon.co.uk/nextmonth